Reggie
In the Frame

First published in Great Britain in October 2014
by Wigmore Books Ltd.

Copyright © 2014 John Challis

The right of John Challis to be identified as the
author of the work has been asserted by him in
accordance with the Copyright, Designs and
Patents Act 1988

ISBN 9780-9569061-3-7

Wigmore Books Ltd
Wigmore Abbey
Leintwardine
SY7 0NB

Printed and bound by CPI Group (UK) Ltd, Croydon, CR0 4YY

Good Luck Brian!

Here's to you!

Reggie
In the Frame

A novel by John Challis

Challis

By the same author:

Being Boycie
Boycie & Beyond
Reggie - A Stag at Bay

Reggie - In the Frame is a novel.
The characters and situations in this book are entirely
imaginary and bear no relation to any real person
or actual happening.

Acknowledgements

I would like to thank the following people
for their support and encouragement:

Peter Burden, Joyce Brisbane,
Nina Burden, Ben Stone,
and my wife, Carol.

Chapter One

'*FLORENCE*!?' Rosita ffinch-Leigh's Colombian coffee eyes grew bigger and flared with suspicion. 'Why we are going to Florence?'

Reggie, her husband, didn't flinch; he knew when it was prudent to remain robust in his plans. But inside, he was hurt, for he loved his wife with a pure and unashamed passion. From the very first moment he'd seen her on stage at the Burlington Burlesque Club in Soho, which he'd owned at the time, he had considered her the acme of womanhood and the last word in feminine beauty.

Now, after ten years of marriage, and in his sixty-second year, his admiration for her was entirely undiminished. He looked across at her where she sat in a high-backed upholstered chair beside the baronial fireplace in their Victorian drawing room. 'Rosi, my little angel...' he growled tenderly. He leaned back to take a long draw on one of the cheap black Honduran cigars which had replaced his much loved Monte Cristos after recent financial meltdown had befallen him. 'Trust me,' he said, expelling a cloud of foul-smelling smoke across the room. '... trust me, trust my instincts and all I've learned about pictures in the last couple of months.'

Rosita curled a nostril at the acrid fumes. 'Reggie, what you are talkin' abou' you instinks?' Her thick Colombian accent had grown thicker with frustration. 'You know bollocks nothin' about pictures – jus' what a few slippy little fellows say to make you happy. Now you 'spec me to come on some wire goose chase with you across Italia, to finding pictures from some place you don't have a clue to look!'

Still Reggie didn't allow himself to wince, although he did turn his eyes from his wife's fiery orbs to the bucolic Shropshire landscape beyond the windows of the 19th century mansion in which he and Rosita lived.

Outside it was late August, and the gardens of Mortimer Towers continued to glow with warm colours and well-being. The sight of nature's rich beauty in the light of the setting sun above distant Welsh hills helped to keep Reggie calm and resolute; it helped to put into perspective his wife's doubts over his skill and judgement. 'My little sunflower,' he murmured in the gruff tones of the old market trader that he once was. 'I admit I don't know everything – not yet – but you know I'm a gabby sort of geezer and I'll soon blag my way to wherever those pictures were made – just you wait! I'll bring 'em back and the local geezers in the big 'ouses who know a bargain will snap 'em up.'

As far as most of the local geezers knew, Reggie ffinch-Leigh had arrived at Mortimer Towers to a haze of conjecture about his background, the source of his wealth, and the origins of his extraordinary Latin American wife. For the first few months of his living in Shropshire, as a former London street trader, he'd stood out from the farmers, rural tradesmen and rustic toffs who generally inhabited the hills of the Marches. But now, a few years on, he'd found a niche for himself among them, helped by his natural charm and quick understanding of how life worked out there.

Unlike a lot of incomers who had failed to integrate and fled back to the Cotswolds to be nearer London, he'd happily become more deeply embedded in his surroundings with each passing year, and he'd done it without even thinking about disguising his urban origins.

However, few of his friends and neighbours knew that in the last year there had been a major turnaround in Reggie's fortunes. He had lost almost everything he owned, as a result of dropping his guard and being seduced by a gang of silken-tongued, iron-hearted old Etonians into investing in an IT 'opportunity', which turned out to be a Ponzi scam of massive proportions, leaving him as belly-up and defenceless as a deceased blue whale.

Only his foresight in registering his home in his wife's name had prevented creditors from coming in and grabbing the house and all its contents. Rosita had fiercely resisted them like a lioness defending her cubs, and made Reggie swear he would never risk the house again. Mainly at her insistence, he hadn't let anyone know he was now broke and living off his wits in a way he hadn't had to for over thirty years.

Recently, in a previously undiscovered part of the rambling house, Reggie had stumbled on a cache of fine, apparently 18th century oil paintings of horses and English rustic scenes in big, handsome gilt frames. He took the view that as they'd come with the house, they were now his property, so, with an unquenchable urge to test the market, he had sold some of them for four, even five figure sums. When he'd been reliably informed by Jonty Cheney-Longville, great nephew of the house's former owner, who had stashed the pictures, that they were all high quality fakes conjured into existence some thirty years before in a workshop in or near the ancient and artistic city of Florence, Reggie had inevitably identified a business opportunity. And, due to the recent reversal in his own investment circumstances, he was in dire need of any business opportunities that came his way, however flimsy.

Reggie turned his gaze back to his wife. 'Listen, my beauty – OK, maybe I won't find where these actual pictures came from; maybe nobody makes 'em any more; maybe Jonty was talking bollocks when he said they were all Sexton Blakes – I mean, I sold 'em all right, didn't I? But it could be a great, bottomless pit of pictures to sell, and I'd have to kick myself if I didn't go and check it out for myself, wouldn't I? Anyway, you and me can have a lovely wander around the place, and you can ogle all those marble statues of geezers you're always on about.'

Rosita gazed back into Reggie's honest deep blue eyes, and felt herself melt into a warm goo. 'Oh Reggie, you such a lovely ottimist! At leas' we can have a good time, maybe some lushoose food and lotta romance.' Her eyes glazed happily at the thought. Reggie knew the crisis was past before the moment of reverie was noisily interrupted by a burst of Ravel's Bolero from Rosita's mobile phone. She picked it up from the table beside her, glanced at the caller's name and beamed with pleasure.

'Lara, darlin' – *Ola*!'

She listened, nodding with humour and pleasure for a few moments. 'OK, we come. *Ciao*, darlin'.' She put the phone down still grinning.

Lara Lydbury was Rosita's best friend – at least, here in England. She was chic, witty, clever and single, and lived in London, where she worked in the world of fashion and glossy magazines. She'd met Rosita at her hairdresser's several years before, and loved her because she was so eccentric, honest and funny, and because she'd turned out to be the most supportive friend she had. Since Rosita, to the amazement of all her friends in London, had moved out to live in the Marches with Reggie, Lara often came to Shropshire to stay with her father in the house in which his family had lived since around Domesday, and where she'd been born. On her way there, she would always stop off at Mortimer Towers, as she planned to that evening.

'Where are we going, then?' Reggie asked cautiously.

'To dinner, in Ludlow – at Le Pelican.'

'That'll be an arm an' a leg,' Reggie grunted morosely. He wasn't a mean man, but he'd only recently had to get used to being never much more than a few hundred quid away from boracic lint.

'Can't she come and eat here? You could give her some of your rabbit stew.'

'No,' Rosi dismissed the idea with a wave. 'She need us. Jason de Chateauneuf ask her for dinner, but she's no sure she want to handle him on her own.'

'Does he know we'll be there? I mean, he can't be that keen to see us after all the hassle and humiliation he thinks we caused him?'

'She is to meet him there, and she will come early, and say is coincidence to meet us, and tell Jason we must join them. She can do that; she is so funny!' Rosita shrieked happily.

'You're right,' Reggie chuckled. 'It'll be a laugh. And to tell the truth I do feel a bit sorry for ol' Jason. Still, if he wants to buy wines at some ridiculous price – that's his problem.'

Early that evening, the newest inhabitant of the village was walking leisurely towards the ancient oak door of the Fox & Ferret. This historic boozer was a long, squat stone building beside the old Roman highway that ran from south to north along the Welsh border. The newcomer opened the door and walked into a dark, low-ceilinged, stone-flagged bar which, in the early evening, was full of men clutching pints and wearing rustic khaki. They all fell silent at the sight of him for, though he'd never been seen in the village before, they all knew exactly who he was.

Jolyon Prestbury, now well into his seventies, held himself erect as he took in the gathering with bright, busy eyes set beneath a sweep of lustrous, snowy hair. He was well aware that he'd changed very little in the five years that had passed since his last appearance in Woolicombe, a rural TV soap set in Dorset, which had been running for decades.

Prestbury had always played his character, the despotic Col Miles Huffington, with only minor interference from make-up and costume, and thus for years had remained instantly recognisable to the millions of the show's viewers.

Foxy Warren, the village's leading wheeler-dealer, had been leaning casually against the bar when the actor walked in. Always alert to the scent of fresh meat, he'd clocked the famous face at once. In any case, his well-tuned antennae had already picked up that a celebrity actor had bought the large house on the edge of the village. He also knew from a few unauthorised research trips to the house that it would take plenty of furniture to fill it and would need a great deal of specialist labour to bring it up to the standards expected of a famous soap star.

A furtive, ferrety figure, Foxy detached himself from the bar and sidled up to the distinguished-looking actor, now standing just inside the door, from where he was scanning the cluster of locals like Nelson surveying the Spanish fleet before Cadiz.

'Hello, Huffers.' Foxy unctuously murmured the name by which Prestbury's character was familiarly known in the TV show. 'Welcome to the Fox & Ferret. Can I offer you a pint of excellent local ale?'

Jolyon winced at the 'Huffers', raising an eyebrow a fraction in protest, although he was constantly being accosted like this by members of the public; it was, in the end, all part of his old job. 'Why, thank you, kind sir,' he replied graciously, as if he were delivering a line from a restoration comedy. 'I'm told there's a fine local brew known as Floppidik. Do they serve that in this hostelry?'

'Bloody 'ell, squire,' Foxy spluttered, losing his cool for a moment. 'That's not ale; it's a kind of mega-potent cider there oughta be a law against.'

Prestbury dismissed the matter with a light wave of his hand. 'Then I'll have a pint of whatever you recommend.'

The other punters in the bar, emboldened by Foxy's approach, also started to cluster around the TV star.'

'Eh, 'Uffers, can I take a selfie with you?' one asked, brandishing his phone. 'It's not for me – it's for me Gran; she's still in love with you!'

'And still in possession of all her marbles?' Prestbury asked with a well-practised twinkle. These days he was seldom confronted with lines he hadn't heard before.

Once Foxy had acquired a drink for the famous visitor, he resumed his natural role as chairman of the welcoming committee. 'I 'ope you're settling in all right at the Witch's House."

'Witch's House?' Prestbury asked, fazed for a moment.

'That's what they call it. Usually when people comes to live there, they 'as the place properly exorcized after a couple of weeks, but the new lady vicar in the village don't hold with that.'

'Oh dear,' the actor muttered under his breath, wondering if he should be concerned.

'Dun' matter,' Foxy went on breezily. 'There's one of the travellers, Emmet Rafferty, he'll do it for not too much.'

'I see. Well, I didn't come in here looking for an exorcist. I just wanted to introduce myself and get to know who's who in the village.'

Foxy beamed. 'You leave that to me Mr Huffington.. Prestbury.....'

'Jolyon,' the retired actor interrupted smoothly, pronouncing his name "Joe-lee-ern". 'Please don't confuse me with some of the stuffy old characters I play.'

'Of course, Jolly-On,' Foxy gushed. 'Anyway this is Guffer Griffiths,' he went on, prodding a finger at the nearest local. ''E drives tractors on Perry Rokesay's land.'

Prestbury's ears pricked up at this apparent familiarity with a local grandee. 'Is that the Earl of Rokesay, of Rokesay Castle?'

'That's the one.'

'You call him Perry. D'you know him personally?' Prestbury asked.

'Well, I wouldn't call him that to his face, but 'e's a good enough bloke, and we all knows him – he pays the wages of half the men in this pub, them as works on the farm or in the quarry.'

'Oh, well... I must look out for him.'

'I expect you'll see him around – tall bloke, usually wears a sorta floppy hat,' Foxy explained. 'Now this is a man you needs to know,' he indicated a dishevelled, ginger-bearded character who'd just come through the door behind the bar. 'This is Crobin, the landlord of this crumblin' dump. He knows everything about anything as is going on in the village and the estate – ain't that right, Crobin?'

The landlord, in the eyes of his customers every bit as important as Lord Rokesay, gave a crooked nod of his head. 'So, you've met young Foxy Warren, have you? There's a surprise. And I has to know all what's goin' on; someone 'as to keep tabs on this lot,' he grunted.

'Are you a bettin' man, 'Uffers?' Guffer Griffiths asked excitedly.

Prestbury ignored the 'Huffers' this time. 'I've been known to have the occasional flutter,' he answered with good-humour.

'Crobin will allus take a bet – for anything you like – ain't that right Crobin?'

The landlord drew himself upright. 'I have been known, for the convenience of my regular clientele what I knows, to take the odd bet on behalf of the bookmaker in Ludlow.'

'I hope that I will soon come to be regarded as a member of your regular clientele. This ale...' he sniffed the pint of Three Tuns Bishop's Riddle that Crobin had just poured for him, '...has an excellent nose to it.'

Prestbury took a long swig of the local brew and smacked his lips appreciatively as he lowered his glass feeling, perhaps, that he might gain the trust of the people pressed around him. 'Now, one thing I was going to inquire was if anyone might have any good, big local

7

pictures to sell. My new dwelling seems to have come with several acres of blank wall. I do have a few of the area that I bought from an artist, years and years ago, when I was doing a season's rep at Llandudno. But I need about fifty more, so I'm looking for a decent discount for a bulk purchase. Do people around here sell pictures from time to time?'

'Hell, aye!' Foxy said eagerly. 'Course they do, but they usually puts them through Lennons the auctioneers. And of course, there's one feller who's been selling a few recently – nice stuff, big oil paintings of 'osses, big ol' fashioned cows 'n' stuff – that's Reggie ffinch-Leigh, up at Mortimer Towers. I can arrange a meet for you, if you want.'

'That would be very kind, young man. How about now?'

Foxy shook his head. He needed time to arrange an introduction fee for himself, otherwise, from his perspective, there'd be no point. In any case, it just wasn't possible. 'Nope,' he told Prestbury, 'he ain't there. My auntie Sue works up there, and I 'appens to know he's going into town to have a meal with his missus, her friend the lovely Lara, and Chatternerve from up at Panty-Hose, even after what Ol' Reggie done to 'im! But don't you worry, I'll have it fixed up in no time.'

'Chatternerve? From Panty-Hose?' Prestbury asked, happy that he was already on the scent of what sounded like prime local gossip. 'I think I'd like another pint of this fine brew. How about you, Mr Warren?'

'Hell, aye! But just call me Foxy – they all does.'

In a small dark restaurant in the middle of the medieval hill town of Ludlow, Reggie ffinch-Leigh's blue eyes shone around the room like beacons. He was standing by the table to which a haughty Polish waitress had ushered his small party. He was trying to tell his two female companions where to sit. At dinner on a Friday, Le Pelican was crowded with the first wave of visitors that seemed to descend every weekend on the small town to ogle its ancient buildings, wander around the fine antique shops, and above all, to eat in the famous restaurants. Few of them missed the appearance of the two women – both striking in very different ways – while they speculated on the identity of the tall, silver-haired man wearing elegant tweeds with the air of an old-fashioned, well-heeled country gent.

He seated himself between the two women – his wife, Rosita, curvaceous, Colombian former burlesque dancer, like a well-kept version of Nancy Del'Ollio, and her best friend, glamorous and thirty-something, whom the more savvy women in Le Pelican recognised as Lara Lydbury, writer and regular TV fashion pundit.

Once he'd settled, Reggie looked around critically at the other diners in the well-filled room. 'Bleedin' 'ell,' he murmured to Lara. 'Look at 'em all, sitting around like they're in church, hardly darin' to speak jus' cos this place has a bleedin' Michelin star.'

Lara grinned. 'I think it's rather sweet the way they take it all so seriously.'

Reggie chuckled. 'Not me. I like quality grub as much as the next man, but I'm not going to sit and eat it like a Trappist monk.'

Rosita chuckled. 'You don' do nothin' like a Trappy monk.'

Some of the other diners glanced at them nervously – perhaps because they thought that the chef might suddenly pounce from his kitchen and harangue them with foul language over their lack of reverence for his sublime offerings; others curled a nostril, as if they viewed Reggie's uncompromising London accent, like flatulence in church, an affront to the dignity of this temple to gastronomy.

'I hope you don't mind me roping you in for this,' Lara said, 'but I didn't think I could face a whole dinner here, on my own with Jason.'

Reggie shrugged indifferently. ''Course you can handle him, but who needs it? And if my Rosi says I gotta come and support you, I will. I'm impressed he's still trying – I mean – after the cold shoulder you've given him, he must be a bit of a glutton for punishment.'

Lara had been heavily pursued during the past summer by Jason de Chateauneuf, famous software entrepreneur from Newcastle, who'd made enough money to set himself up as Lord of the Manor in a large estate on the Welsh borders, not far from Reggie's own Victorian pile. She nodded. 'You could say I haven't encouraged him, and I can't think why he's still trying...'

'Si, course you know!' Rosita hooted in her Spanish-English. 'He fancies your pants off you. It don't matter how much you say him he is prize tosser, the more he want to conquer you!'

'Yeah,' Reggie agreed, 'these young, self-made billionaires are all the same – the more they can't have something, the more they want it.'

Lara shook her head in disgust. 'Yeah, sure. I mean, if he wakes up one morning feeling like a yacht or a Ferrari, he only has to pick up the phone. Unfortunately for him, he can't see that it's different with women.'

'Not with all women, it isn't,' Reggie observed gallantly.

Lara knew that Jason didn't know how to cope with Reggie's easy-going, languid irony, so when she'd agreed to have dinner with him, she'd made up her mind to ask Reggie and Rosi to come in to act as decoys. She didn't think Jason would walk out when he saw them there, but if it came to a showdown, she was prepared to stand her ground.

Reggie was looking forward to seeing Jason. He always enjoyed ribbing the young tycoon and winding him up, especially after Jason had suffered several hefty blows to his ego earlier in the summer. Reggie had been involved in some way with all these events. With a grin on his face, he caught Lara's eye and nodded towards the door. 'And here he comes now; he looks like a knackered bloodhound hanging on to a fading scent.'

Lara was grinning at Reggie's description when Jason de Chateauneuf spotted her. A slight, insignificant-looking man wearing pristine jeans and skimpy little cotton top from Dolce & Gabbana, he stood for a moment by the entrance, trying to guess if her smile meant she was either (a) pleased to see him or (b) just taking the piss.

When he walked over to the table, he ignored Reggie and Rosita as he leaned down to kiss Lara's cheek.

''Ello, Chatternerve.' Reggie greeted him with equanimity, deliberately using the locals' version of his name. 'How're you doin'?'

De Chateauneuf straightened his back and took a deep breath. 'All right, Reggie? What're you doing here?'

'We come in for a bit of nosebag – same as everyone else here.'

The punters nearest them shifted uncomfortably, trying to distance themselves from any talk of nosebags.

'Isn't that great?' Lara said brightly. 'When I saw them here, I said we'd join them. I knew you'd like that.'

De Chateauneuf choked back what he really thought, and managed to squeeze out a grin for them.

'Rosi, you OK, pet?'

'I no your pet,' Rosita tittered.

'Where I come from, that's a compliment,' Jason said, lowering himself into the chair opposite Reggie.

'Where you come from,' Rosita riposted, 'Reggie say they dip-fry Mars Bars.' 'You should try one, Rosi; you never know, you might like it.'

The young waitress who had appeared by their table frowned at this sacrilegious idea. She was clutching a sheaf of menus the size of broadsheet papers which she thrust at each of them. 'You like to order?' she asked in an accent from somewhere beyond the old Iron Curtain.

None of them even glanced at the tiny square of print in the middle of the large sheets, while Jason decided he might as well make the most of a *fait accompli* and take control of the party.

'What's the best champagne you've got?' he asked the waitress.

The girl looked at the list, and widened her eyes. '*Dom Perignon, 1966*,' she answered. 'Three hundred and fifty pounds.'

Jason nodded as if she'd said it was a tenner. 'I'll get a bottle of that.'

'Not for me, Chatternerve,' Reggie said. 'It makes me fart, and Rosi hates that.'

Lara laughed. 'Quite right.'

'Okay. We'll have a nice bottle of Chablis, too.' He dismissed the girl with a wave and turned to Reggie. 'So, Reggie, have you and your beautiful wife been away recently?'

'Not a lot; the social whirl of South Shropshire keeps us busy. But, as it 'appens, we are going to Italy in a couple of weeks.'

'Somewhere nice?' Jason asked in a way that suggested Reggie couldn't possibly know any nice places to go.

'I dunno,' Reggie said. 'We're going to Florence, and I've never been there before.'

'Bloody 'eck, man; it's stuffed full of American tourists with bloody great backpacks and arses like 'ippos.'

'On the Hippo Trail,' Reggie laughed. 'That's good. But we're going on a picture hunt.'

Jason seemed suddenly interested. 'Oh yeh? What sorta pitchers are you looking for?'

Reggie thought for a moment before divulging his plans. 'Old Bertie Cheney-Longville who used to own the Towers had got himself a few good copies of English sporting pictures. I found some he'd stashed away, and when I hung 'em in the house I sold a few pretty quick. His nephew, Jonty turned up at the house and told me Bertie had had 'em painted in a studio that mainlined in Sexton Blakes of English pictures, somewhere near Florence. I started thinking if I could get a few more, maybe I could make a bit of a turn on 'em.'

'To sell, like?'

'Yeah, like a sort of hobby. I miss a bit of wheelin' and dealin' and it'll give me something to do in Florence while Rosi's ogling Michelangelo's *David*.'

'My dream man!' Lara sighed wistfully. 'Cold and hard, with a bum like a nectarine.'

Jason couldn't stop a shudder of jealousy at the thought of Lara fancying a hunk of white marble more then she fancied him.

'But where d'you think you'll find these paintings?' Jason asked Reggie.

'I don't know yet, but you know, I'm still a trader at heart and I'll track 'em down.'

'I had a friend,' de Chateauneuf went on, 'who bought some pictures just like that, in a small alley, half way down the Old Bologna Road – I think he said,' he added casually.

'Don't you worry about it,' Reggie dismissed the advice. 'If they're there, I'll find 'em.' As he spoke, he made a mental note: 'Old Bologna Road – small alley'.

'Are you ready to order?' the waitress had brought the wine and was hovering now with pen and pad ready.

Later, when she and a waiter arrived with the main courses Jason's party had ordered, the Polish girl started a monotonous chant of all the ingredients and method of cooking for each of the four dishes.... 'line-caught hake tenderly poached in wheat-lager and loganberries....' She'd reached Rosita's, 'Slow roasted leg of an organically farm-reared duck, with breast pan-fried in Shropshire Cider Spirit and served with a coulis of pomegranate, kirsch, mace and gooseberry....' when Reggie raised a hand.

'Listen, darlin',' he said gently. 'The reason my wife ordered this quacker was because she read on the menu all what you're saying now. She doesn't want to hear a bleedin' litany about it; she wants to tuck it inside her gorgeous laughing gear before she dies of 'unger.'

The Polish waitress's jaw dropped; the pre-prandial chant was a key part of her duties, and she'd never been silenced mid-litany before. Rosita was nodding happily, picking up her knife and fork. De Chateauneuf chuckled with genuine mirth. 'Brilliant, Reggie! I've been meaning to tell 'em that every time I come here!'

'Why haven't you, then?' Lara asked.

The grin on de Chateauneuf's face faded. 'I just don't like upsetting people.' He shrugged his skimpily clad shoulders. 'Not like you, Reggie.'

'Me? Upset people?' Reggie looked puzzled. 'Anyone round here'll tell you I'm brimmin' over with milk of 'uman kindness.'

'Are you?' Jason came back quietly. 'Were you, when you deliberately stitched me up on that hunt race last spring? You cheated, took a short cut and forced me off the course, over that bloody great log. And you know if I hadn't of fallen off, I'd have won.'

'Jason!' Lara laughed. 'You're kidding! You're not still worrying about a trivial little event like that, are you?'

'It wasn't trivial to him,' Reggie laughed. 'I didn't have a clue what I was doin', but Jason had gone off and spent a bleedin' fortune having special lessons in race-riding, just so he'd beat me.' He turned back to Jason with a grin. 'Only trouble was, you didn't learn

13

how to jump.'

'It was meant to be a flat race. You wouldn't have jumped that tree,' Jason protested.

'I wasn't stupid enough to try. Anyway, it was just a crummy little hunt race, who cares?'

But Jason had the bit between his teeth now. 'And then you tried to make me look like an idiot when I was with all my friends at that hunt ball.'

'Was that lot friends of yours? I thought they were a bunch of Cosa Nostras up from the smoke and you wanted to impress them by playing the country squire.'

'I am the squire.' Jason spoke more sharply, in a distinctly un-squirelike manner. 'I own the house and the land for miles all round.... And then you talked that pompous old git into chucking horse shite all over my property.'

'Jason!' Lara gasped. 'Are you calling my father a pompous old git? And by the way, he didn't need any persuasion from Reggie.'

'Look Lara, I'm sorry but your dad looks down his nose at me like I'm some kind of a toe-rag – even though by the time I was twenty-one I'd already made more than all he ever inherited from his own dad.'

'But we won't enquire too closely where you made it,' Reggie grinned provocatively.

'From my software company, Jaysoft – I'm sure I've told you.' Jason answered, determined not to rise now.

Rosita smiled serenely. 'Now, Jason. Just to be calm; eat your hake in lager. We know you think Reggie made a fool of you last summer, but really, you jus' make a fool of yourself.'

Chapter Two

The next day, ten miles to the north-west, in Lydbury Manor, Sir Lancelot Lydbury, sauntered untroubled down the broad oak stairs towards his breakfast of egg, toast and *The Telegraph*. The Manor was a rambling, mossy-roofed dwelling of mellowed stone that could have starred in a hundred Christmas jigsaw puzzles, and had been in the Lydbury family for more than eight hundred years. He stopped halfway down the stairs at a 16th century stone mullioned window at the front of the house and gazed for a moment towards the nearby Welsh mountains. He nodded with happy satisfaction at their empty summits, where his land bordered Jason de Chateauneuf's ten thousand hilly acres.

A few months before, to show what he thought of the wind farm de Chateauneuf planned to construct along a four mile ridge, he had showered part of the site with a ton of well-rotted horse manure, using a trebuchet – a medieval engine of war like a giant catapult – which he'd painstakingly reconstructed.

Before the event, he'd asked his daughter if she could get a journalist from the *Brecon & Radnor Express* to come and witness it. Lara, while not discounting the power of the local newspaper, had also persuaded the regional TV newsdesk to send a reporter and cameraman. Video clips of the trebuchet releasing its stinking payload had immediately popped up on the web and Sir Lancelot, along with his outspoken views on wind turbines, had soon become a big YouTube hit.

He was to be seen with an avuncular smile, standing in front of the bucket of his trebuchet which was filled to the brim with steaming horse droppings. 'Do we really want to see our wonderful Welsh landscape buried beneath a layer of hideous technology?' he was saying, '.... when each of the monsters Mr de Chateauneuf proposes to put here won't produce enough power to light a small village – while on the fringes of North West Scotland lie dozens of barely inhabited islands which are subjected to almost continuous battering by gale-force winds?'

Clips had been shown on broadcast stations, and several reporters

15

had trekked out to the Marches in order to interview the bizarre backwoodsman who refused to come into any TV studios under any circumstances.

As Sir Lancelot stood on the half-landing of the great carved staircase, his eye was caught by a red sports car glinting in the morning sun as it sped up the drive between two rows of eighty-year-old hornbeams. He didn't know the car but he thought he recognised his daughter's driving as the gleaming Ferrari buzzed in like an angry wasp and slithered to a stop on the gravel in front of his house. In the silence that followed, Lara jumped out and walked with a jaunty stride across the forecourt towards the stone porch.

'Hiya, Dad!' Lara's voice, gentle but strong, echoed through the hall.

'My dear girl!' Her father greeted her as he reached the bottom of the stairs. 'What on earth are you doing here; and what are you doing in that beastly little car?'

'I told you I was coming.'

'Did you? When?'

'I sent you an email.'

'An email!?' Sir Lancelot exclaimed with disgust. 'Surely you know I know nothing about these things?'

'Yes, I know but doesn't Roly-Poly check them for you on the PC I went to so much trouble to set up for you?'

'I'm sorry to say that dear Mrs Rolson's been away for a few days. She's back this morning but I've been looking after myself.'

'What!?' Lara exclaimed. 'Boiling your own eggs? Doing up your own shoe-laces? Blowing your own nose?'

'I can assure you that has never been one of Mrs Rolson's duties.'

Mrs Rolson was Sir Lancelot's housekeeper, a woman of humble origins and high intelligence with a sophisticated sense of humour that appealed to her employer.

'Where has she been?' Lara asked.

'In London - staying with her niece in Chelsea.'

'Roly-poly? In Chelsea?' Lara opened her eyes wide in disbelief. 'Her niece lives in one of those tower blocks of council flats by

Battersea Bridge. She likes to be handy for the Royal Court, and a short bus ride from the V&A.

'I can't think how an old philistine like you ended up with such an erudite domestic.'

'Wha'ever – as you might say. She looks after me very well and deserves her time off. Anyway, why are you here?'

'I've been arranging with Rosi for my magazine to do a shoot at Mortimer Towers.'

Sir Lancelot shook his head in wonder. 'Why on earth would a glossy fashion magazine want to take pictures of a house that looks like a Victorian red brick wedding cake?'

'Because these days it's considered desirably kitsch and, besides, with a little help from me, Rosi's done an amazing job with the interior.

The long clock at the back of the hall made a noise like it was clearing its throat before it started to strike ten o'clock.

'My word, is it only ten? What time did you leave London?

'I stayed at the Towers last night – we had dinner at Le Pelican with Chatternerve.'

'Good God! Does he still speak to any of you?'

'Without wanting to brag, he wanted to have dinner with just me. But I didn't want to spend the evening alone with him, so I arranged for Rosi and Reggie to be there, and we'd just 'bump into' them. I didn't think I'd get away with adding you to the party.'

'I couldn't have sat for five minutes with the jumped up little crook,' Sir Lancelot sniffed.

'Crook? He may be a ridiculous and narcissistic little man, but I don't think he's a crook.'

'I don't know either, but I do know that his company, JaySoft, is based on smoke and mirrors. It seems people have heard of it because Jason is so obviously oofy – as he never stops telling everyone, and they assume that's where all the money comes from, given his parents were potless Geordies. But if you look at JaySoft's published records, its profits are much harder to establish. They all seem to have been ploughed back into new projects and developments.'

'How on earth do you know that, Pa?'

Sir Lancelot put a long finger to the side of his nose. 'Know thine enemy, as someone or other said in the Bible – or was it P G Wodehouse? When I decided I was going to fight this wind farm of his, I had everything about him researched, and I can tell you there are plenty of question marks.'

'But we still have our secret weapon,' Lara said.

Her father nodded. 'Of course, and I'll let you know when we should bring it into play. Is your friend Reggie still up for it?'

Lara grinned conspiratorially. 'Oh yes.'

'Good,' Sir Lancelot grinned. 'But you still haven't told me where you got that horrid little red car.'

'My old banger wouldn't start after dinner last night,' Lara shrugged at the vagaries of her own vintage DB5. 'So I left it in Ludlow, borrowed Jason's, dropped him at home before I went back to stay at Rosi's.'

Her father shook his head in wonder at the effect his daughter could have on what he would have thought were the most unsusceptible of men.

Rosita sat in the driver's seat of Reggie's beloved Bentley, a big handsome dark green model, which had emerged from the factory in Crewe in the late '50s. Unusually nervous that morning, she gripped the wheel like a child clutching the handrail of a fairground ride. She was gazing petrified at the winged "B" at the front of the car's long bonnet.

'My little flower, are you sure you want to do this?' Reggie asked quietly from the passenger side of the wide, green leather bench-seat.

'Yeah, yeah, I sure! If I go to be independen', I mus' learn – either drive... or ride the horse. All the women round here who ride the horse have behinds like hittopotamus – so, I learn the car.' Her eyes, Reggie acknowledged, were gleaming with unquenchable determination.

Reggie looked at her fondly, though doubt clouded his thinking. 'My little seraph, I'm not sure that driving's your sort of thing.'

'Jus' so long is automatic.'

Reggie shrugged with resignation, and looked ahead. 'OK then,' he said, 'Fire her up.'

His wife pressed the starter button set in the gleaming burr walnut fascia and the big old engine burbled into life. She moved the automatic gear stick into 'D' as Reggie had shown her, gingerly released the handbrake and applied her small right foot to the accelerator pedal.

The old Bentley moved off slowly, as if it needed little guidance from her. Gingerly, she turned the wheel towards the gap between the mighty brick piles on which a pair of elaborate wrought iron gates hung open. She snatched a glance at Reggie and grinned with excitement, before she turned her gaze forward to see a chunky silver Range Rover turn into the opening and head straight towards her.

'Aaagh!' she shrieked. 'Reggie, what I do?'

'Just take you foot off the accelerator,' Reggie said, trying to keep the panic from his voice, 'and put it on the brake.'

'OK,' Rosita gasped.

The big old car came to an abrupt halt; Reggie shoved the gear lever into neutral and climbed out to find they were a few inches away from the nose of the Range Rover. Relieved that they hadn't made contact, he looked to see who was in the visiting vehicle.

A handsome, older man with piercing eyes and a thick mop of white hair sat in the driving seat, looking back at him with interest and no obvious manifestation of road rage. He seemed somehow very familiar, though Reggie couldn't place him from among the ranks of the local upper crust he'd met, to which, judging by his fine rustic tweeds, this individual surely belonged.

'Turn off the car, Rosi,' Reggie said over his shoulder, aware that his wife might start to experiment with the controls if left unattended. As he spoke, the other driver climbed out of his car and walked towards the Bentley as Reggie climbed out. The man held out a hand in greeting. 'You must be Reggie Finchley,' he announced in a rich, resonant voice that reminded Reggie of the actor, Donald Sinden.

'ffinch-Leigh,' Reggie corrected, stressing the second syllable,

'...with two small 'f's.'

'How d'you do?' the other man said. 'I'm Jolyon Prestbury.'

It took Reggie a second or two to place the name, then he remembered: this man wasn't real – he was a character from a TV soap. 'No you're not; you're that bloke Huffers off Wassaname on the telly.'

Prestbury chuckled in a way that disguised any irritation. 'I'm not, you know. Huffers kicked his bucket five years ago but, luckily for me, I was unaffected, apart from a slight diminution in my annual income.'

'Yeah, 'course; you're a Max Factor, ain't you?' Reggie was now shaking the firm, unclammy hand that had been offered. 'Sorry, mate – it must be a pain in the doodah, 'aving everyone confuse you with a bloke who doesn't even exist anymore – and never did.'

Jolyon beamed and gave Reggie a look that suggested that, as a man of the world, Reggie would understand. 'It's a bit of a two-edged sword, actually,' he said. 'It's irritating, but I'd be very unhappy if everyone had already forgotten bloody old Huffington. And where did your name come from – with the two small 'f's?'

Reggie grinned. 'Yeah, you're right; it didn't come from my Dad; it was from out of the London telephone book, 'cos my first wife didn't want to be called Betty Bottoms – on account of that was the name I was born with.'

Jolyon nodded. 'Very wise of her. Anyway it's a pleasure to meet you. I was chatting to a splendid young man in the pub last night, a slightly soiled, entrepreneurial sort of individual who smelt strongly of horse-manure, called... Ratty, perhaps?'

'That sounds like Foxy Warren.'

'That's the fella! I knew it was something verminous. I told him I was looking for pictures to cover the internal walls of my new house and he said you were the man to talk to.'

Reggie chuckled. 'Only because I'm the only person he knows who sells a few bits and who might give him a backhander.'

'I assumed as much; but I'm quite grown up these days, and if I think you're asking too much in order to accommodate young Foxy, I can always say 'No'.'

'I'd heard someone famous had bought the old Witch's House but

I didn't know it was you. It's good to meet you. Welcome to the Wild West of the Welsh Marches or do you already know this patch?'

'I do a bit, actually. I've done a bit of time – what the criminal community might call 'stir' – in the repertory companies of the North Wales resorts and, years ago when I was a young shaver, I did a season as Romeo at the Ludlow Shakespeare Festival. I'd always loved the area and vowed that one day I would live here. My wife hated the idea, but now she's gone to that great Green Room in the sky, I can do as I please. I'm thrilled with the house.'

'It will take a bit of filling,' Reggie observed, 'especially if you haven't brought a lot of tack with you. I can probably help you with a few pictures... so, I suppose I'd better let you in.' He glanced at his car, where Rosita still sat, gazing curiously at Jolyon Prestbury. 'But I think I'll have to back the car first. I was just about to give my wife, Rosita, a driving lesson, and I can tell you, she hasn't quite got the hang of it yet.' Reggie walked round and opened the driver's door of his car. 'Rosi, my lovely flower, lesson's over for today. I'd like you to meet Mr Huffing..... Mr Prestbury; this is my wife, Rosita.'

Rosi slid her slender legs over the side of the seat, and stepped out. 'Course I know is Mister Pressbury. I am great fan.' She turned her chocolate eyes on the actor and switched them to main beam. He instinctively bowed.

'A great pleasure, Rosita,' he murmured huskily and, taking her hand, leaned down to kiss it.

With a glance up at the clear blue sky, Reggie climbed into the car and reversed it up to the wide sweep of thin gravel in front of the house. Rosita had gone into the house while Jolyon Prestbury had got back into his car and drove it up to park beside the Bentley.

Inside the house, holding a glass of red mulberry vodka, which Reggie himself had made the year before, the actor sat back in his chair in the high-ceilinged, high-Victorian room, savouring the irony of being shown 18th century English paintings of sporting horses by a man who had learned his sales technique behind a fruit'n veg barrow in London's Berwick Street Market.

They were on their third mulberry vodka when Rosita burst into the room.

'Here is Mrs Dove, come to speak with me about the village autumn show, and when I say to her you are here, Mr Pres'bury, she beg me to introduce her to you. I hope is all right?'

Prestbury lifted an eyebrow in a show of pleasure. 'Of course,' he murmured in the famous chocolatey voice, while rising to his feet, a little hampered by the mulberry vodka.

Looming behind Rosita was a tall, powerful-looking woman.

'This Diana Dove,' Rosita said, stepping aside to reveal a woman in her mid-fifties, dramatically good-looking and stylish in a maroon, calf length crepe rayon dress that might have come out of Biba in 1975.

Reggie had never met Mrs Dove, but he knew she was a well-known theatrical agent who had semi-retired from the business and recently decided to return to the Marches to live in her family home, Wicton Priory. Wicton comprised the rambling remnants of a former monastery, whose only occupant for the past year since her mother had died was, Diana said, her dotty Aunt Sylvia.

As someone who'd been in show business for nearly thirty years, it hadn't taken long for the local movers and shakers to press-gang her into producing the village's annual musical show. Reggie could only hope that she wouldn't scare away his famous new punter by trying to involve him in it.

'Mr Prestbury. What an honour to meet you!' she gushed. 'I had heard that a distinguished actor was coming to live in the vicinity, but I had no idea quite how distinguished.'

Reggie idly wondered if she meant it.

Jolyon, who knew Diana Dove by reputation, evidently decided to believe that she did. 'I deliberately didn't want to trumpet my arrival,' Jolyon said with plausible modesty. 'I didn't want anyone to make a fuss. I've come here to distance myself from my career. Of course, I still work – but only when I'm offered projects of sufficient quality,' he added significantly, perhaps aware of what Mrs Dove might have been working towards.

'Oh, of course, although I'm sure you'll want to accommodate those in the community you've chosen to live in.'

Jolyon Prestbury smiled enigmatically but said nothing.

Reggie tried to repair the awkward silence that followed. He held out a hand to the visitor. 'Pleased to meet yer, Mrs Dove,' he said in his unchanged London accent. 'I've heard you've moved back into the family drum up at Wicton Priory, and need a few bits of furniture. In case you're interested, I do a bit of antique dealing meself.'

Mrs Dove turned the full force of her blue-violet eyes on Reggie. 'How fascinating,' she said breathily. 'Is that some of your stock?' she asked, her attention being caught momentarily by the paintings, stacked against a table, which Reggie had been showing Jolyon.

Reggie nodded. 'Yeh, I do some nice pictures.'

But Diana Dove was reluctant to be distracted and turned her gaze full on the actor.

'This year Mr Prestbury, our production is going to be *Mamma Mia* – it'll be such fun!' She focused her large eyes on him, and challenged him to deny it. However, she'd evidently already worked out her strategy, and wasn't going to push her ideas now. 'But I'm intruding, so I won't tell you about it now. I'll give you a ring if I may, Mr Prestbury, and pop round to see you very soon?' she suggested, in a way that few men could have turned down.

He sighed, very lightly. 'I look forward to it, Mrs Dove.'

Chapter Three

A week after Jolyon Prestbury had called on them (and left with what he was happy to believe was an 'English School' painting of a Welsh mountain scene in the back of his Range Rover), Reggie and Rosita were sitting at a table in a bar beside the River Arno in Florence.

Reggie gazed happily at the fizzing Bellini cocktail in front of him. He grinned at his wife, who was also drinking a Bellini, and looked around, shaking his head in wonder at the thought of all the beautiful women who must have passed through this very bar over the past fifty years, and not one of them as lovely as his own Rosi.

He and Rosita had arrived in Florence the night before, and stayed in a small romantic hotel that had sent Rosi into ecstasies over its tastefully faded elegance. 'Look the wonderful ol' mirrors and lights,' she said excitedly. 'Is like you, Reggie, my darlin' – like they call shabby-chic – though you are more shabby.'

'Thank you, my rosebud. You love your tatty old antiques, don't you?'

'*That's* why I love you, innit? I so glad you brought me to this lovely place.'

Reggie was relieved that despite her original objections to the reasons behind this trip, she was evidently now prepared to enjoy it.

His main problem, though he hadn't admitted it to Rosita, was that he really had very little idea of where to begin his search for the source of the Sexton Blakes. Apart from Jonty Cheney-Longville, a cousin of the man who had lived at Mortimer Towers, telling him he thought the pictures had come out of an old castle up in the hills near Florence, he had nothing else to go on besides Jason Chatternerve's throwaway remark that a friend of his had found some good fakes in an alley somewhere off the Old Bologna Road.

While he was reluctantly considering whether he should take this seriously, his thoughts were interrupted by the arrival of man in a pale lilac suit.

Wearing a livid gardenia in his button-hole and carrying a slim, silver-tipped Malacca stick, the man had stopped in front of their table and was gazing at Reggie.

'Hello,' he said in very slightly accented English with a curiously contralto voice. 'Do I know you?'

Reggie shrugged. 'I'm Reggie ffinch-Leigh; this is my wife Rosita,' he said with a flourish.

The man's eyes didn't leave Reggie. 'I'm Harold Hampton. I live here in Florence, on the *Via Bologna*.'

'We live in Mortimer Towers,' Reggie replied, with a hint of pride, 'in the Shropshire Marches.'

Harold Hampton, Reggie judged, was in his eighties, but still spritely in his movements, and sharply observant.

The old man opened his eyes wide. 'Good heavens; you sound to me more like a Londoner, through and through. How long are you spending in Florence?

'Just a few days; we want to buy some pictures.'

Harold Hampton, still standing opposite them, nodded. 'It's funny how Englishmen have been coming here for centuries to buy pictures. I hope you find what you want.' After a moment's thought, he went on. 'Where are you dining tonight?'

'We haven't decided yet, have we, my lovely one?' Reggie glanced at his wife.

'Well, if you want somewhere unassuming but truly Florentine, can I recommend the Osteria Paolo? It's on the other side of the river, not far from the Ponte Vecchio.'

'Thanks, mate – Mr Howard – that's very kind of you. I appreciate that and we'll 'ave a butcher's.'

As the lilac apparition said a brief goodbye and wafted away with a lingering aroma of jasmine, Reggie gave Rosita a puzzled look. 'What did he want with us? We're not exactly his type.'

'I tell you, Reggie – he fancy you!'

'Nah!' Reggie laughed. 'I'm not that beautiful!' He looked out at the early evening sun beyond the windows. 'Tell you what; it's a bit cooler now; let's drink up and take a stroll along the river to the Ponte Vecchio and look for that restaurant Harold told us about.'

'What is Ponte Vecchio?'

'It's that wacky old bridge with all the 'ouses on it.'

They left the hotel and strolled hand in hand, marvelling at the beauty and antique patina of most of the buildings they passed and half-recognised statues they saw. They walked by several small workshops with public frontages selling versions of Florence's numerous sculptures. Reggie was struck by how old they looked, and stopped to examine some of them.

'I tell you what, my angel, these can't be really old – not at this price, but I reckon if we took a few of them home, left them outside to gather a bit of moss and bird poo, we could sell 'em and make a good turn on 'em.

Rosita nodded. 'They already look like they made 'undreds of years ago. As long as you don't say to the people they really old...?'

'Exactly. And when it comes down to it, they'd look great in any garden. I wouldn't mind some in our place.'

'If we got one, our Joan would be jealous, and maybe she feel hurt.'

'Joan', a genuinely antique bronze statue of a voluptuous Roman bathing beauty which Reggie had bought for his wife, had become her favourite possession. It stood clothed in little more than its own delightful patina in the rose garden at Mortimer Towers, fiercely admired and much coveted by some of the young travellers who lived on the edge of the village.

'Nah,' Reggie laughed. 'She wouldn't be hurt; she's got a heart of bronze. But if we buy a couple, we'll take 'em back, just to sell.'

With the noise and aroma of the rushing river keeping them company, they carried on until they turned onto a narrow street which ran between the small shops and restaurants crowded in on either side of the medieval bridge.

Rosita shrieked with delight. 'Oh My God, Reggie! Look these little boutiques; these jewellers; I don't know if I get to the end ....'

Reluctantly, and panting with restrained desire, Rosita did manage to emerge the other end without submitting to a serious attack of spontaneous shopping. Reggie was relieved; he hated having to tell his wife not to spend money; that'd be like putting her in a strait-jacket. 'Well done, my virtuous little *signora*. I never thought you'd make it across there without diving into your wallet.'

'There is so much lovely things here, Reggie, but I promise I wait.'

'For that, you deserve a nice bit of dinner.'

'I don't want much, Reggie; and I don't want to waste your money for buying pictures. Jus' a little thing – look there's the place the man, Harold say about. We go in there.'

Osteria Paolo was a small, honest-looking place, packed inside and out with students and less affluent locals.

'Looks down to earth, anyway,' Reggie remarked, pragmatically, 'like Harold said.'

They sat down inside at a small table covered with a checked cloth and Reggie picked up a menu. '*Frittata*, that's an omelette; that'll do.'

A spotless waiter soon appeared, oozing urbanity.

'Look at that,' Reggie remarked quietly to his wife. 'He looks like he'd be at home in the Savoy...'

'*Per favore*?' the man asked.

'Frittata,' Reggie said, trying a bit of Italian. '*Para* my wife, *frittata pomodoro*.' Rosie loved tomato omelette, he knew. He ran his finger down the rest of the omelettes listed on the menu. He couldn't speak much Italian and when he did, it turned out a kind of Latin hybrid, but a natural gift for communication allowed him to guess at the components of most of the menu. However, there was one which foxed him.

'I wonder what this one is Rosie – *frittata a piacere*? What's *a piacere*, when it's at home? Ah, he's in a rush. I've never had *a piacere*, so I'll try that.' He turned back to Rosita. 'When I'm in restaurants I always like to try things I never had before.'

'I know this, Reggie! Is why we had to eat some 'orrible tripe sausage when we go to Deauville last year.'

Reggie squeezed his face into a guilty wince. 'The *Andouillettes*? Yeah, well I'm sorry about that. I thought they were, like, bangers, not stuffed with cow's guts. 'Ow have the French got the cheek to moan about English food when they offer their punters something so disgusting!? It's not even as if they were just having a laugh; they say it's a favourite dish.'

The waiter coughed. If he knew what Reggie was saying, he gave no sign. '*Per favore, signor*?'

'Oh gawd; I forgot about chummy here. Now what am I going to have? Yeah,' Reggie looked up at the enigmatic waiter '*Frittata a piacere, por favor*.'

'*Si*,' the waiter shrugged. '*Questo*?'

'I just said – *a piacere*,' Reggie replied testily.

'*Si*?' the man replied, also becoming irritable.

'*A piacere*!' Reggie shouted

'*Si*! *Questo*?'

Reggie, incensed by the man's obtuseness, prodded the word on the menu with a stout forefinger. 'Are you havin' a laugh?' he demanded of the impatient waiter. 'This one – *a piacere*!'

A dishevelled young man at the next table, which almost touched theirs – probably an art student of some sort, Reggie thought – leaned over towards Reggie and spoke with a light Italian accent. '*A piacere* means: "of your choice"; you can choose to have several different things in your omelette.'

Reggie felt himself blush to the top of his head. He hated being rude, especially when he was in the wrong.

Rosita was shrieking with laughter. 'Reggie! Why you think you can speak Italian? You bloody fool!'

Everyone around them had begun to laugh too, while Reggie looked up sheepishly at the waiter. '*A pomodoro*,' he croaked, and looked away quickly.

'May I join you for a moment?' someone asked quietly, behind him.

He turned quickly and found himself looking up into the enigmatic pale eyes of Harold Hampton. If the man had just witnessed his embarrassing linguistic cock-up, he didn't show it.

A small frown crossed Rosita's dark features, but Reggie took the risk of ignoring her wishes. 'Yeah, why not' he said, moving a chair to make room. 'As you live in Florence, maybe you could mark our card on a couple of things.'

'I should be delighted to. Please excuse me one moment?' He moved off with short, bustling strides towards a nearby waiter to whom he whispered some instructions.

While he was away from the table, Rosita flashed her eyes at Reggie. 'Why you want this man to join us? He just fancy you, for Gossake!'

'So?' Reggie growled. 'Can you blame him?' He held up a hand to stem any come-back from Rosita. 'Listen, he obviously knows Florence, so maybe he can give us a steer. He says he lives on the Old Bologna Road...'

'If you think Chatternerve knows what the hell he is talkin' about,' Rosita shrugged her shoulders dismissively.

Before Reggie could answer, the lilac suit returned and drew out a chair on the far side of the table to Reggie. 'So what else brings you to Florence, Mr ffinch-Leigh?' he asked.

'My wife's in love with Michelangelo's *David*. And I want to see Botti-Wassaname's picture of Spring, in the U-fizzy.'

'Oh my dear!' A look of dismay had appeared on the other man's pasty visage. 'There really is much more to Firenze than those two. If I were you, I would visit the Bargello; the statues are much sexier there.'

'The Bargello?' Reggie repeated. 'We certainly will; my wife is very partial to sexy statues.'

The man dragged his eyes from Reggie and reluctantly acknowledged Rosita for the first time. It was clear that the length of her dark lashes, her shapely breasts and the fullness of her lips did not affect this man in the way they did most. 'Can I commend to you Michelangelo's statue of the *Young Bacchus*?'

'The Roman God of Booze – right?' Reggie offered.

Harold Hampton turned back to Reggie and nodded with a grin. 'You could say that. And look, right on cue, as you might say – a bottle of champagne I have ordered for you! I know how much my fellow Englishmen will only drink French spumante.'

The waiter placed an ice bucket containing a bottle of Pol Roger beside Reggie's chair, popped it open and filled three glasses.

Rosita ignored the one in front of her but Reggie took a sip and nodded his appreciation. 'Thanks, Harold; that's very good of you. But there is another thing we're looking for, that's a place where they reproduce sort of, like, famous English paintings.' Reggie faltered a little, suddenly conscious that perhaps their host wouldn't approve of a fake old-master production line. 'We need a few for a project in England. I heard there was a sort of workshop like that somewhere off the Bologna Road.'

The old man's face clouded once again. 'There is a place like that, but you really shouldn't get anything there. Those people are not what you might call entirely kosher.'

'Well, they wouldn't be, would they – churning out the Sextons, rippin' off the works of the great British masters, but that's what we need.'

He could see the other, apparently struggling with the notion that anyone should need such things. In the end he said, 'You'll find them at the Villa Antica. Tell them I sent you, and at least they won't rob you excessively.'

'That's very kind of you, Harold. I appreciate that.'

'Now, if you will excuse me, I won't interrupt your dinner any further. Enjoy your omelette.'

Once again Harold Hampton straightened himself and walked across the restaurant to leave.

Rosita watched him go. 'What he want?' she asked pensively.

'Just being friendly, that's all,' Reggie answered. 'Whatever, we might as well go and have squint at this Villa Antica he's told us about, and the young booze-god in the Bargello.'

When Reggie and Rosita had finished their tomato omelettes, the student who had earlier put Reggie right on the meaning of *a piacere* reappeared by the table. 'Did you enjoy your meal?' he asked.

'Yeh, thanks for your help. Why don't you sit down and have a drink with us?'

The student happily agreed. He accepted a large glass of red wine and told them his name was Alfonso. He kept glancing at Rosita, evidently smitten by her, and had warmed to Reggie and his cod-Italian. Once Reggie knew he was a native Florentine, he asked him if he knew Harold Hampton who had been with them earlier.

'Of course, everyone knows who is Harold Hampton. He is famous in England too, no? He is a great expert on art of the Renaissance. Also he is known to do some buying and selling of pictures.'

'He didn't look like a dealer to me,' Reggie remarked.

'Surely, the best ones don't?' Alfonso suggested.

'He told us a place to buy pictures.'

Alfonso shrugged. 'He would know.'

Reggie and Rosita left after a while, with Reggie's self-esteem restored by the young art student, as well as a glass of grappa given to him by the waiter whom he'd snapped at over the *frittata a piacere*.

As they ambled back to their hotel, arm in arm through the warm September evening, Reggie (and the grappa) thought his wife looked as magnificent as she ever had, and he concluded that he couldn't have been more content.

'Looks like that bloke Harold is kosher. I wasn't so sure, but if he's got such a big reputation round here, why would he talk rubbish?'

'I don' like him, but I guess he knows what he is saying,' Rosita nodded.

They were passing the locked open space where the fake-ancient statues were displayed. 'We definite must come back to get one of those,' she said.

'All right, my lovely Rose; once we got the pictures. I suppose you want one of the blokes.'

'That would make Joan happier.'

'If he was going to join her in the rose garden – which he ain't,' Reggie grunted.

The following morning, Reggie and Rosita walked out into the warm September sun to look for an artists' workshop in an alleyway off the Bologna Road. Progress was slow for, as they went, Rosita wanted to stop and look in every shop window; she wanted to follow a crocodile of American tourists disappearing into the Duomo. 'Reggie, we can preten' we are in their group, and get the guide for nothing.'

'Rosi, angel, it would be bloody depressing to trail around with a pack of gormless, big-bummed tourists who probably don't know where they are or what they're looking at. Let's do the business first, and then we can get back there.'

Rosita nodded her approval. She liked Reggie when he was on the scent and hard to distract. 'OK, how far we go?'

Reggie looked at his map of Florence and realised it was still a long way to walk. He flagged down a taxi which shuddered to a squealing halt beside them.

Reggie leaned down to the driver's window. 'We look for little street on *Via Bologna*,' he said loudly in English, reluctant to make a fool of himself again. 'There's a place that sells pictures there.'

The driver flicked a strand of long black hair from his face. 'Si, si.' He nodded at the back door; Reggie and Rosita climbed into to the small space in the back of the battered Fiat.

After the first few seconds of the journey, Rosita closed her eyes and kept them screwed up until Reggie assured her that they'd arrived. They were in a narrow cobbled street and had stopped outside a large flat fronted villa with a tiny, littered yard for a front garden, and a front door coated with peeling blue paint. Reggie knocked on it and a few flakes fell to the ground. 'Not too flash, then,' he nodded. 'That's a good sign.'

The front door opened and a small man with eyes that slid from side to side stood in front of them.

'*Si?*' he asked.

'Sorry, *no parli Italiano*.'

'I spik little *Inglesi*. What you want?'

'We were recommended to you by Harold Hampton. We're looking for 18th century English sporting pictures, and horses, and that.'

The man took a pace back and opened the door to let them in.

'*Signor, signora... benvenuti alla Villa Antica.*'

A tall, slender man of around forty-five, with neat black hair, walked forward to greet them lavishly.

He's a handsome devil – Reggie thought, and couldn't help himself from glancing at Rosita to see her reaction.

Rosita was grinning her appreciation. '*Gracias, Senor,*' she murmured in Spanish.

Reggie looked the man in the eye to let him know he wasn't someone to be messed around with. 'Harold Hampton sent us.....'

'I know,' said the young man, flicking a piece of fluff from his elegantly cut navy mohair suit. 'He has telephoned this morning to say you would come. You are Mr and Mrs Finchley, and you are very welcome. I am Franco Ficuzza.' He waved them with a slim hand towards a deep buttoned sofa, into which Rosita sank gratefully.

'Would you like coffee?' Ficuzza asked

Reggie nodded. 'Yeh, desperately.'

Once he and Rosita had large espressos in front of them, the Italian asked, 'What pictures you want to see?'

Reggie shrugged. 'Frankly, it doesn't much matter so long as they look like good 'school-ofs' any famous 18th century English painters and look like they've been around for a couple of hundred years.'

Ficuzza shrugged a shoulder. 'Our pictures won't fool the very top experts – unless it has been... arranged. You know that?'

'Yeh, not unless it suits them and or they don't have to put their name to it.'

'But many of our pictures have been through country salerooms in England without too much trouble.'

'I understand. What makes yours so good?'

'We go to a lot of trouble with the frames.' He reached behind him to pick up a picture about three feet by two. 'You see the gilding is quite rubbed, the backs well-covered with dirt, from dust that has come out of ancient places – cellars of medieval buildings. The canvas too has been impregnated with ancient dirt, and the oil paints are just as they were made at the time, while the surfaces of the paintings have also accumulated much soiling. But like I say, it is especially the frames that are good. This we make here, ourselves.'

Reggie was impressed. The paintings he was looking at and their frames were a lot more convincing than the pictures that Bertie Cheney-Longville had brought over from Italy thirty years before.

'I suppose it's all done more scientifically now, and you're right, these frames are magnificent, much bulkier than some I found at our house in England.'

Ficuzza shrugged. 'I know nothing about that. But if you buy from us on regular basis, we can give you very good service. How many you want to start with?'

'How much are they?'

'Two thousand euros – cash only.'

'OK; we'll take a dozen and see how they go.'

Ficuzza looked disappointed. 'You should take more.'

Reggie felt himself being manipulated and his defences went up. 'Maybe, but we'll just take twelve for now.'

'How are you going to ship them?'

Reggie shrugged. 'Airfreight?'

'No. You would have to apply for export licence, and then we get trouble.'

'What if I just drove them out in my car?'

'You came here by car?'

'No, but I can come back to pick them up.'

Ficuzza was nodding. 'That's the best. Is a big car?'

Reggie fished out his wallet from his jacket pocket and extracted a photograph of his old Bentley. 'Here,' he said handing it to Ficuzza. 'I can tuck plenty in that big boot.'

The Italian's eyes lit up. 'Perfetto! But you must not declare to Italian customs; we will not give you any receipt or papers or anything. Is entirely up to you. But listen, in a car like that you can take maybe 24 pictures. You pay for twelve, and the rest when you come back for more – okay?'

'That was a result!' Reggie grinned at Rosita as they watched Ficuzza drive away from their hotel where he'd just dropped them.

Rosita was less ebullient. 'You just to make sure they give you good pictures you can sell, not just put in old rubbish they can't get rid of theyselves.'

'Why would they do that, my angel?'

'Why he jus' give you twelve more without paying for them?'

'Simple – time and motion. He knows I'll shift 'em, so he knows I'll be back. And besides, he said we can go back the day after tomorrow to choose whichever we want.'

'Maybe,' Rosita agreed, prepared to be mollified. 'But we have to buy some statues, too, like we said. '

'All right, all right. Just 'cos you fancy these old roman gods.'

'Reggie, if the price is OK, we can make good profit; so long as you promise when we've sold some, we can keep one for the rose garden?'

That evening, Reggie and Rosita strolled through the streets to Harry's Bar, where they sat at the bar and ordered dry Martinis and chatted for a while with an English couple, Amanda and Jeremy Porter, dim, harmless Sloane Rangers, Reggie thought. He could see them struggling to work out where on earth the ffinch-Leighs fitted in back in England, especially when they learned that they lived in a large Victorian mansion in the Welsh Marches.

'Last time we were out here in the spring,' Jeremy said, 'we met a strange little tyke from your part of the world; he was throwing his money around, in this very bar – what was he called Di?'

'Something de Villeneuve?' his wife ventured.

Reggie guffawed out loud. 'Jason de Chateauneuf.... We know him. Lives up at a place called Pant-y-Groes , we call it Pantyhose.'

'I say, I hope he's not a great friend of yours?'

'No way!' Rosita giggled. 'Reggie *hate* him because he try to put up great willmills for electric.'

'You mean wind turbines? The Witherington-Smythes – I expect you know them – from Herefordshire – they had the same problem with their neighbour, one of those nasty agri-barons who just do what they want as long as it's going to make money.'

'I don't know about the Witherington-Smythes,' Reggie said, 'but I know the type of farmer who doesn't give a monkey's who they upset, if they can squeeze as much wonga as they can out of their property. And this little bugger, de Chateauneuf, he's like that; though he originally made his money in computer software.'

'That's funny,' Diana said. 'The chap we met said he was an art-dealer.'

Rosita shrugged. 'Mus' be a different fellow. This Jason knows nothing about paintings, even less than Reggie.'

'Oi, Rosi!' Reggie objected. 'But it is a strange coincidence, you meeting some one called de Villeneuve from up our way; never heard of him, though.'

With a day to use up before their follow up meeting at the Sexton Blake merchants', Reggie happily gave in to Rosita's enthusiasm for looking at statues and pictures. Before they headed off for the galleries, though, they went into the main local branch of a big Italian bank with a bag containing £20,000 in £50 notes which Rosita had taken from her account at the Nat West in Ludlow. After a brief interview during which it was accepted that Reggie wasn't laundering the money, they left with a much smaller bundle of 500 euro notes.

'That's handier,' Reggie remarked as he stashed it about his person.

Afterwards, at the Uffizi, they shuffled through the crowded galleries until, at the first sight of Botticelli's *Primavera*, Rosita almost swooned.

'Look, Reggie! Is just like our little orchard!' she gasped, gazing at the iconic pastoral scene of spring awakening in the form of an innocent, blonde teenage girl.

'Yeh, and that could be you in that see-through frock,' Reggie chortled in a way which upset the other English-speaking shufflers. 'I tell you what, let's get along to the Bargello, to have a look at those sexy statues Harold Hampton told us about.'

They left the Uffizi, crossed the piazza in front of the mighty marble *David*, and were soon sitting on a wooden bench in the first floor gallery of the ancient medieval palace, both gazing with fascination at a sculpture completed by Michelangelo in 1492. It was of the Young God *Bacchus* as a slight, debauched youth with tousled hair and toting a bunch of grapes while tripping along in a drunken haze, looking as if he were suffering a bout of hiccups.

'That's brilliant, isn't it, Rosi? I can remember feeling just like that, more than once, when I was his age.'

'But Reggie – look his willy!' Rosita shrieked in horror. 'Is broken – fallen off!'

Reggie dropped his eyes to *Bacchus*'s genitals and chuckled. There had undoubtedly been some traumatic episode in the life of the statue, perhaps in transit from one site to another. The stone member which, judging by what was left of it, had been clearly depicted in a state of rest, had been knocked from the pelvis and testicles of the unsteady youth. 'Poor bugger! Must have hurt. I wonder when that happened and who did it. Pity they couldn't find it and stick it back on, like they tried with that fella, Bobbit, d'you remember,' Reggie chuckled, 'whose wife chopped his off for fooling around?'

'Like I would to you if you fool around,' Rosita's eyes shone with sympathy for Mrs Bobbit.

'That's never going to happen, and I promise you, Rosi, you can have your own personal *Young Bacchus*.'

'Without his willy?' she snorted.

'Just for you, we'll get one made complete.'

The following morning, Reggie took Rosita with him to choose the twenty-four fake paintings he would take back to Shropshire.

Their reception at the Villa Antica was still polite, but less effusive than the first time. Reggie noted this, while pragmatically accepting the change in his relationship with Ficuzza, now that he was a committed punter, and would also be somewhat in hock to the Italian for half the stock he was going to take.

He and Rosita weren't offered coffee this time, but were led through the old house into a modern warehouse, apparently stuck on to the back. About fifty vaguely but not precisely recognisable oil paintings in elaborate gilt gesso frames were hung on three plain windowless walls in the otherwise empty space. Ficuzza excused himself and left the room with a nod of his impeccably coiffed head.

Reggie decided that his choice of pictures would be guided simply by whether or not he'd fancy them on the walls in Mortimer Towers. He walked around with Rosita, gazing at each of them several times, with his hands behind his back as he tried to imagine them in situ. 'I feel like one of those geezers who has to choose the pictures for the Royal Academy show each summer,' he murmured to his wife.

'Pooh,' she spluttered. 'These are much better than that!'

Reggie chuckled. 'I think I'll spread my bets and do a bit of pick-'n'mix – half a dozen gee-gees, half a dozen portraits of chinless aristos, a few romantic landscapes with ruins and some pictures of daily life among the rustics.' He nodded at a group of pictures, after Constable, of rural village activity.

After a while, Ficuzza returned, followed by the small shifty-eyed man carrying a tray of coffee, who put it on the table and filled four cups.

'You have chosen, *Signor* Finchley?' Ficuzza asked.

'I certainly have.' Reggie carefully indicated the twenty four he wanted and Ficuzza's little side-kick stuck a small yellow circle on each of them.

'They will all be carefully wrapped in plastic bubble,' Ficuzza explained, 'to protect the frames; they are a valuable part of the picture.'

'Fine by me,' Reggie said. 'D'you want the wonga now.'

'Wonga?'

'You know – moolah, spondulicks, bread.... the money,' he added.

'Oh yes. We want the money. Twenty-four thousand Euros, please.'

Reggie tugged small wads of notes from several different pockets and handed them over to Ficuzza, who stacked them carelessly on a table beside him.

'Achille,' he addressed his small gofer, who appeared to be the only other person on the premises. 'Please make sure *Signor* and *Signora Finchli* have all they need.' He turned and inclined his head at Reggie and Rosita.

'Forgive me, I have to go.'

'I'll see you next week, then,' Reggie shrugged. He been expecting at least a little more fawning on the part of his new supplier.

'Wait moment, Reggie – Mr Ficuzza ,' Rosita squealed before he could start walking away. 'There's other thing too - no?'

'What's that, my precious?' Reggie asked, a little apprehensively.

'The *Statue!*' his wife hissed.

'Oh yeh. Franco, before you go, can you tell us where we can get a copy made of the statue of *Young Bacchus*, like the one in the Bargello?'

Franco Ficuzza's stopped and tuned around. His eyes were lit up. 'Of course, we can get that for you.'

'That's alright Franco. I don't want to put you to no more trouble. Just tell us where to go – I mean, we've seen plenty of places doing most of the other well-known statues.'

Reggie sensed a quick hardening of Ficuzza's eyes. 'We will supply it, *Signor Finchli*. We will have it ready sooner than anyone else – in one week, when you come for the paintings – OK?'

'Hang on. How much will it be?'

'For you – a good customer, 2,000 euros, like the pictures. You can sell easily for £5,000, I think?'

'Only if it's really good – like really well-distressed.'

'It will be so distressed, it will be feeling suicidal,' Ficuzza chuckled in a rare display of humour.

'That's alright then,' Reggie said. Ficuzza was right, at that price there would be a good profit in it; and Reggie was delighted it had been so easy to sort out the statue. Ficuzza was turning to go again. '*Ciao*, then, Franco,' Reggie said with a big happy grin. 'I've enjoyed doing business with you. I'll see you in a week.'

'*Arrivederla.*' Ficuzza nodded and strode out of the room.

Achille, the gofer, sidled up to Reggie. 'I call taxi?'

'Nah. We'll walk. Come on Rosi.'

They left the old house and made their way up the narrow cobbled alley to the Bologna Road, where Reggie flagged down a taxi and hustled Rosita into it.

'Why you no take their cab?'

'You only want to take so many favours from people like that lot. They keep totting up a score, then ask you to settle it when they're good and ready.'

'Reggie, what you are talking about? You paranoy.'

'And why didn't he count the money I gave him? I'll tell you, cos he knows darn well nobody would dare to pay 'em short. You'd find horses' heads on your bed next morning otherwise. That's what we're dealing with here.'

'The Mafia?' Rosita laughed. 'Sellin' Sexton Blake pictures of English country? I don' think so Reggie!'

Reggie rented a car to drive to the airport next morning.

Rosita was impressed by the sights. 'How the Pizza Tower not fall over?' she asked Reggie, sitting snugly beside him on the plane.

He wondered what on earth she was talking about, shaking his head as they took off from Pisa to fly to Birmingham Airport where they'd left the Bentley.

'OK,' Rosita announced as they landed. 'I drive home.'

'No you don't, my eager little chauffeuse,' Reggie replied firmly.

'Reggie! Why you so chauvinist?'

'I'm not. It's just that it's all motorway until we get to Bromsgrove.'

'So?'

'You're a learner; you're not allowed.'

'OK then; at Bumsgrove, I drive.'

'If you want to,' Reggie sighed.

As Reggie steered the big green Bentley sedately along the motorway among the buzzing Birmingham rush-hour traffic, Rosita babbled excitedly about their trip.

'Reggie, you're lucky bugger to find those pictures so easy...' she shook her head in wonderment.

'I told you to trust me, didn't I?' Reggie said. 'And just you wait, I'll shift 'em in no time.'

'Where we sell them?'

'We've got a few choices. I could put them for auction at Lennons' Salerooms.' Lennons' were the local cattle and sheep auctioneers, who held a monthly 'fine art' sale of the better stuff from local houses. 'Or, maybe it'd be better to send then to one of the posher ones nearer London; or I could hang them on the walls at home, and invite people round to look at 'em. Or I could put 'em on e-Bay. Or maybe...' The thought had only just occurred to him. '...We could open a little gallery in Ludlow, and sell other pictures too. I reckon I've got a bit of an eye now, and that could be like a permanent thing. I've always liked a business with a Jack'n'Jill to dip into.'

'Reggie, you are carry away again. We don' want no shop – that's all hassles and money. Why don' you sell them in an open market? Look the price people pay for things in Portobello Road.'

'Now that, my clever Rosi, is not such a dumb idea!'

'There's good flea market in Ludlow; always I'm buying things there.'

'Yeah, I had noticed. But you may be right – that could work, so long as I let a few people know I've got these pictures. I could get Porky on the case. He could let slip, by mistake, like, there's some good pictures turning up on the market up here. He can be very subtle, ol' Porky can, and it could be enough to bring some up.'

'OK. Now is Bumsgrove,' Rosita announced. 'I take over.'

With some misgivings Reggie attached a pair of 'L' plates to the big chrome bumpers and went to sit in the passenger seat of the Bentley. Carefully, and unusually, he belted himself in, and tried to stay calm as his wife pulled out into the traffic of the small town. Luckily most of the other drivers made way for the venerable old car and its erratic progress, either out of deference or self-defence, and they reached the open country without touching any other vehicle.

Soon, though, they were crawling along behind a forty-ton lorry stuffed full of chubby lambs.

'Look the little sheeps!' Rosita exclaimed with a note of compassion in her voice. 'The Bastar's!'

'Who? The lambs?'

'No, the men who push them all in those 'orrible trucks! I going to go pass him and show him.' She started to pull the car over the central line, to see beyond the lumbering vehicle.

'Hang on Rosi, this isn't the place to start overtaking.'

'You can't see. I can, and I go to take over this bloody bastar'!' Rosi said grimly between clenched teeth.

'Just hang on Rosi. I know this road like the back of my doodah, and there's nowhere to pass for miles.'

'Jus' don't back-street drive, Reggie,' Rosita growled as she stamped her foot on the accelerator and the big four-litre engine surged a ton of metal passed the forty-foot lorry, around a long leafy bend.

Reggie's face turned eau de nil; he closed his eyes and clutched his seat belt so tightly his knuckles went white.

He looked up again to see another truck coming towards them, head on, at the far end of the bend. He heard Rosita snarl, 'Bastar',' as she looked over her shoulder at the lorry she had just carved up, shaking a small, bejewelled fist at the driver, as if oblivious of the oncoming lorry which had skidded onto the far-side verge to avoid smashing into the Bentley's imposing chromium grille.

Reggie closed his eyes, and thought of all the lambs cannoning into each other as their driver jumped on his brakes to avoid re-shaping the Bentley's elegant rear end.

Chapter Four

The following day, in the large, lavish kitchen which she'd bullied Reggie into having installed at Mortimer Towers, Rosita was drinking coffee with Diana Dove. When Diana had turned up unexpectedly, at the front door asking for Reggie, Rosita had told her he was out, but would be back soon. She'd also invited the visitor in. It would, she thought, give her a chance to assess what kind of threat the elegant and well preserved theatrical agent might pose. Once the coffee was made and poured, she'd carried on making a cake from a recipe in her well-worn copy of the *Jane Austen Book of Regency Fancies*.

Since Diana's first visit, before they'd gone to Italy, Rosita had been uneasy about the way she'd been eyeing up Reggie, even while she'd been focusing on Jolyon Prestbury. Jolyon, Rosita guessed, was being targeted for his thespian experience which he might be persuaded to bring to the village musical she was planning, but there'd been an acquisitive glow in Diana Dove's violet eyes as they rested on Reggie, and Rosita strongly suspected that she might have other plans for him.

Although Reggie himself seemed quite unaware of the attraction he held for a certain kind of strong-minded, adventurous woman, Rosita had noticed it often, and while she didn't doubt her husband's fidelity, she didn't see any point in testing it more than necessary.

She settled down to extract as much information as she could about the visitor on the grounds that knowledge was power. In several emotional conflicts over twenty-five years of busy love life, 'Know Thine Enemy,' had become a key strategy for her.

'Which kind of antique furniture you like most for your house?' Rosita asked.

Diana lifted a shapely shoulder draped in grey silk. 'I used to like nothing but the best Georgian mahogany; now that's all out of fashion, and I feel more comfortable with what they call Decorative Antiques.'

'Me too – tha's why I got Reggie!' Rosita chuckled to lighten the menace in her voice. 'How you get into the actor agency business?'

'My late husband, Johnny, left it to me. I took to it like a duck to water and for the last twenty years since Johnny died, I've had a ball.'

'You never want to get marry again?'

Diana made a small moue with a crooked smile as she flicked a grey-blonde tress from her forehead. 'Never found the need. I didn't particularly want a family – and now I'm passed the point of no return, anyway – and I didn't need the money.'

Rosita searched the other woman's unwrinkled, symmetrical features for signs of 'work', but was disappointed to detect none. 'What abou'... you know?'

Diana chuckled. 'You don't have to get married for that, and I love being a free agent in a world full of men.'

'Maybe in London is OK,' Rosita said, trying to sound unconcerned. 'But you won't find nothin' to play with up here.'

'Oh, I don't know,' Diana answered provocatively. 'Besides, I've still got my flat in Knightsbridge. But when my aunt Maggie left Wicton to me, I thought I'd try living there for a bit; I came up here a lot as a girl – in fact I had my first experience of love at the hunt ball at Rokesay Castle. So far, I'm loving it, and the showroom is beginning to bring in punters from all over the place. It's amazing how far people will come when you tell them there's somewhere to land their helicopter.'

Rosita felt she was beginning to make some headway in getting to know how Diana Dove operated when she heard Reggie come in through the back door. At first her eyes were fixed on Diana's, to judge her reaction, but when she turned to see her husband, she let out a scream so long and loud that Old Huggins the gardener, dozing in a chair outside the kitchen window, opened his mouth, causing the pipe he was smoking to fall to the ground with a loud clunk.

'My GOD!! Reggie, what have you done?' Rosita shrieked.

Reggie stood in the doorway, startled by her reception. 'Nothin',' he protested. 'But what's the matter with her?' he added, pointing to where Diana Dove had collapsed from her chair to the floor.

'How can I know!? You look like you murder someone – like *Jack the Gripper.* Why you are covered in blood, for Gossake!'

Reggie looked down at himself, and his white shirt and trousers heavily spattered with red stains. In each crimson stained hand, he held a large tub of freshly picked mulberries.

'It's these bleedin' mulberries – they're very squishy; you just got to touch 'em and they squirt juice all over the shop.'

'Oh my God! I thought was blood! Why can't you be more careful? Those stains will never go.'

'Relax, darlin'! It's not blood, is it? It's just mulberry juice; it'll wash out.'

As he was speaking, Diana Dove had opened her eyes and propped herself up on one elbow. Evidently she had heard the exchange between Rosita and her husband, and was already composing herself, rising to her feet with an elegant twist of her voluptuous behind. She held out a hand to Reggie. 'Forgive me, but you do make a pretty dramatic sight like that, though, of course, I completely understand. When I was younger and used to pick the mulberries at Wicton, I always did it just wearing my skimpiest bikini, then I'd have jolly good bath.'

Rosita flashed an angry look at her for daring to put such an image in her husband's head.

'Now that sounds like a good idea,' Reggie chortled. 'Rosi, remind me to wear my skimpiest bikini next time I go out picking.'

'Diana comes to see you, Reggie.'

Reggie, though never consciously flirtatious, couldn't stop himself from exerting a measure of his genuine charm when confronted with any woman, regardless of her attractions.

'That's very flattering. What on earth can an old duffer such as myself do for a sophisticated young lady like you?'

'I'll get straight to the point, Reggie. Before I came back to live at Wicton Priory last spring, I'd spent very little time up here since I was a teenager, and I decided to throw myself into whatever community projects I could if I thought I had something to offer. Knowing the theatre world as I do, I suppose it was inevitable I'd find myself doing the annual village musical, as you must have heard.'

Reggie nodded. 'Yes I've heard, all right. And I was here when you tried to manoeuvre old Huffers into it, which was a brave thing to to. It's been the lead topic of conversation in the Fox & Ferret for the last few weeks.'

'Then you may have heard that this year it's going to be a full-blown, sing-along version of *Mamma Mia*.'

'Yes, of course; they've all been talking about it. They say you've even talked our new local celebrity into taking a part.'

Diana assumed an enigmatic smile. 'Actually, I'm still working on Jolyon. Otherwise I've managed to cast most of the show so far, but as usual with these things, especially out here in the sticks, casting the adult male parts is proving a little sticky.'

'Often the way with adult male parts, but what on earth can an old buffer like me do for you?'

'You're not so old, Reggie – at least, you don't look it. What are you – about fifty? You look less.'

'Pwrrrrr,' Rosita spluttered. 'He don't look less than fifty!'

Reggie turned to her, looking hurt. 'My little fawn, why so cruel?'

'Because you sixty-three. OK, you don't look that, but to say you forty-something...' Rosita dismissed the proposition with a loud disgusted grunt.

'Oh, Rosita,' Diana said with soupy insouciance. 'How can you say that? There you are, married to a very well-preserved, attractive man, whom a lot of women would give their eye teeth for....'

'Now then, ladies,' Reggie protested awkwardly. 'Let's not get all technical. Diana what did you want to ask me?'

'Well. Not to beat about the bush...'

'You not beat any bush round here,' Rosita interjected indignantly.

Diana took a deep breath and went on. 'I wondered if you might appear in *Mamma Mia* as Harry?'

'Which one he,' Rosita jumped in. 'Is the gay one, no?'

'Well, yes.'

'Reggie – gay? You mus' be crazy! I never met a man who is so macho!'

'Of course, but he only has to act it; it just means he has to be a bit extra sensitive – maybe just a bit thoughtful, and I'm sure Reggie could do that.'

'Is ridicoolous,' Rosita grunted, chucking her wooden spoon back into the cake mix.

'Hang on, Rosi,' Reggie said, putting a gentle hand on her arm. 'It's only acting. And I always quite fancied myself as a....'

'As a gay?'

'No, no; I've never been in prison. I meant, as an actor.'

Diana was beaming. 'It would be incredible if you would play Harry.'

'But what part would old Jolyon play. He'd make a pretty good gay bloke.'

'I want him for Sam.'

Rosita gasped. 'The one play by Pierce Brosnan in the movie?'

'That's the one,' Diana nodded.

'But he much *older* than Pierce!' Rosita protested.

'He's a much better singer, though,' Diana said.

'That's not saying much,' Reggie chortled. 'I could sing better than Pierce Brosnan.'

'Frankly, Reggie, I could happily cast you as Sam, but Jolyon was once a bit of a star, and everyone knows his face.'

'Fair enough. You put me down for Harry, Mrs Dove. I don't want them saying in down the boozer that old Reggie ffinch-Leigh is too far up his own wotsit to join in the village frivolities.'

Diana Dove, stretched her neck to plant a big red 'O' on Reggie's cheek. 'Thank you, Reggie. With you in the bag, I'm sure I can reel in all the rest.'

As she stepped back, Rosita stood up decisively and inserted herself between Diana and Reggie, facing the woman. 'OK, if Reggie play, I play. I can dance. I can sing,' she shrugged. 'I professional for years. But for the village, I do it for nothing.'

Diana pretended to be surprised. 'Rosita, how fantastic!'

'What shall I play?'

'I haven't settled on anyone to do Rosie yet – so there's a coincidence!'

'Rosie? The crazy friend of Donna? Who Julie Water play in the film?'

'That's the one – a woman with loads of character and humour.'

47

'Hmm.' Rosita sounded unimpressed. Who is to play Donna?'

'I'm not sure yet,' Diana demurred. 'though I have someone in mind.'

'Can't I do her?'

'In many ways Rosie's a much more demanding role,' Diana said firmly, but gently. 'That's why I asked you to play her.'

'But I professional!' Rosita insisted, 'I should have leading role.'

Reggie observed that she was about to stamp her foot.

'Hang on Rosi, my little lovebug, don't get carried away. Just play the part Diana wants; it doesn't matter, it's not a bleedin' competition.'

Rosita took a deep breath, and relented. 'OK, I just play what you say,' she said, giving Diana's upper arm a gentle squeeze.

'Thanks so much, Rosie. I look forward to seeing you at rehearsals. I'll be emailing the schedule in the next few days. Then we don't have long to get it on.' She turned to Reggie and beamed her appreciation in a way that Rosita found excessive. 'Thanks so much too, Reggie and, by the way if you need some more mulberries for your lovely vodka I've heard so much about, do come along any time and pick mine.'

Diana swept from Rosita's kitchen trailing a wake of Nina Ricci, with the 'O' she had planted on Reggie still glowing red on his cheek. Rosita showed her to the front door. After Reggie heard it bang shut, Rosita was back in the kitchen where she leaped at Reggie wielding a sheet of damp kitchen roll which she started rubbing all over his face.

'Gawd, bloody hell, my little legume! What on earth are you doing?

'I removing Diana Dove's 'calling card',' she said, vigorously scrubbing his cheek.

Reggie laughed. 'She won't be the first or last woman to leave a ring of lipstick on my cheek.'

'Maybe no, but I don' want to see it.'

'It was brave of you to sign up for a part in this Mickey Mouse piece of theatricals.'

'You don't think I let her loose with you in a play without I keep a watch on her? She is after you, Reggie – you just see.'

'I'll just have to wait until I get back from Florence to find out. I've phoned Porky and he says he'll come with me, the day after tomorrow.'

'Why he going with you?'

'Because I'd get bored stupid driving all that way on my own, and you can't come because of this wedding at the house, so – I asked and he said "Yes". Anyway he's one of those blokes who's always useful in a crisis.'

'The only crisis you have with him will be if you both drink like fishes.'

'No, Rosi, this is business.'

Two days later, Reggie poked the nose of his Bentley out between the great brick gateposts at Mortimer Towers and drove though the quiet Shropshire lanes towards the motorway and the overcrowded South East. He was heading for Florence, via his cousin 'Porky' Bacon's house in Surrey, twenty-five miles from London.

Porky's mother had been born Muriel Bottoms, sister of Reggie's father, Sid, and his Uncle Arthur, both prominent costermongers in the Soho street trading community. Muriel had married Porky's father, Dennis Bacon, a feckless wheeler-dealer who operated on the outer fringes of the antique trade in Bermondsey and Portobello Road markets. Porky, more savvy and disciplined than his father, had done well in trading anything from cars to textiles and pork bellies. He was well-known and well-liked in the clubs and restaurants around Greek and Frith Streets, but had recently decided to move to what he called the 'sticks', in the heart of Surrey's stockbroker belt.

This was Reggie's first visit to Porky's sprawling new bungalow, known to the neighbours as 'South Pork' and set in a glade of silver birch and Corsican pine on the Surrey hills. When Reggie drew up outside the house on a large circle of golden gravel, Porky walked out of the front door to welcome him, opening a bottle of Pol Roger as he came. 'Reggie, my man! Let's drink to this new venture of yours with Winnie Churchill's favourite tipple, and hope by some miracle it makes a bleedin' profit.'

'I'll drink to that,' Reggie laughed. 'It better bloody work, or Rosi'll have my 'taters.'

'Come on into the 'umble abode,' Porky invited with a flourish towards a house that looked like a giant glass brick.

Reggie's cousin was well-filled and chubby-cheeked, with a large gold Octopus on a chunky chain dangling from his fleshy neck. He was wearing his customary Hawaiian shirt and knee-length pink shorts with Gucci sandals on his bare, perma-tanned feet. Coaxing his chubby legs into a bit of a swagger, he showed Reggie into the house and led him through a dwelling that was as modern and flashy as Mortimer Towers was Gothic and bogus.

Reggie blinked when they walked into a long living-room whose south facing wall was one huge pane of glass, revealing a spectacular view across to the North Downs. Porky waved Reggie to a white leather sofa twelve feet long, and put his favourite Barry White album onto a turntable.

'Bloody hell, Porky – you must have weighed out a lotta wedge to get this place built!'

Porky nodded smugly. 'It weren't cheap.'

'Where'd the wonga come from?'

'I told you when I was up at your gaff in the summer – some of my projects are going well, and my rag trade enterprise with the Cypriot boys is doing very nicely.'

'Is that the company you told me about – Bubble &Chic?'

'That's the one. We're selling to all the high street chains now. And remember those moleskins I got from you?'

'How could I forget?' Reggie moaned, thinking of all he'd been through to find and ship 200 live moles to Ireland, only to discover that they'd been ordered by a gang of insane terrorists. They were going to use the moles to blackmail the Irish Government by threatening to release the animals simultaneously on all the nations' finest golf courses, when not a single mole lived in Ireland, north or south. 'When all the little buggers croaked from those poisoned worms, I thought I'd had it.'

''Till I come to the rescue and took 'em off your hands,' Porky chortled. 'We turned 'em into little kind of weskit things they call jillays. We marked 'em up about a thousand percent, and they've flown out. Come to think of it... could you get us a couple of thousand more?'

Reggie groaned. 'Not at the price you paid!'

'Maybe we can up it a bit; we'll see. But what's the story now, Reggie? What exactly are we going to pick up in Florence?' Porky asked, topping up Reggie's glass.

'Twenty-four beautiful Sexton Blakes of 18th century English oil paintings – landscapes, portraits, 'orses that sort of thing – all distressed just right, looking old, and genuine, but like they've just had a bit of a clean up. And all in bloody great gilt frames. You'll love 'em!'

'Never mind what I think. I mean – look at my pictures!'

Reggie turned around to see hung on the back wall several large paintings of naked women in broadly suggestive poses, and a well-known semi-erotic picture of a man and woman misbehaving in a hotel corridor. Porky waved at it proudly. 'That's a real Jack Vettriano – not a bleedin' print, yer actual original!'

'Yeh, well, never mind,' Reggie said. 'You're right, though. We obviously don't have the same taste.'

Porky shrugged a chubby shoulder. 'S'long as you know you can sell what you're gettin'.'

'No problem,' Reggie said, not admitting to any doubts he might have felt. 'They're top quality fakes. All right, they wouldn't fool a big-shot expert, but they're more'n good enough for 99% of punters who don't mind spending five or six grand if they think it'll fool their mates into believing there's a few hundred grand's worth of picture on the wall. What worries me is that I got 'em so cheap, and they're letting me take double the number I've paid for, on tick.'

''Aven't you paid 'em nothing yet?'

''Course I have –twenty grand!'

'Reggie, mate, if you've already laid out twenty grand, they know you're serious. Do you know these geezers who sold you the pictures will even be there when you turn up to collect 'em?

''Ere, Porky – stop tryin' to wind me up. Of course, they'll be there.' Reggie took a quick breath as he contemplated the scenario

Porky had suggested. 'Nah,' he said, 'people like I've been dealing with wouldn't be pissing about running a con like that; they're too big for that.'

'Are they Reggie? Are you sure? I mean, the whole art of the con-man is all about his ability to act, very well, and wiv extreme sub-tlety.'

'I know that, Porky,' Reggie said, beginning to feel irritated.

'Maybe you did once, but you've been out of play – buried in the sticks for a while now. You don't come across a proper old-fash-ioned conman out there, do yer?'

'Don't you believe it! There are tons of geezers out in the back-woods, just waiting to pull one over you if they think you'll take your eye off the ball. There's plenty of 'em know about conning. I was tucked up by a bloke who sold me a piece of furniture I'd al-ready sold him for less than half the price.'

Porky chortled. 'I 'eard, Reggie. You must of felt a right todger.'

'Who told you?'

'The lovely Lara; she said you sold a bloke a table, he put it in the auction, you thought it was the pair to the first one, which would make it worth three times as much, so bid for it like a drunken farmer at a cattle sale.'

'Yes,' Reggie admitted ruefully, 'that's about it. That's what I'm saying – they're not so stupid as you think.'

'But Reggie, how did the bloke know you were going to come in and bid for it?'

'I reckon he made sure they put a picture of it on the front of the catalogue and he reckoned I'd spot it.'

'But I 'eard you came out of it well ahead, you jammy bugger.'

Reggie grinned. 'I was a bit lucky when I got it home, and this other bloke turns up saying he had the other half of the pair. 'Course, it turns out he was a relation of the old boy who used to own my gaff and left a pile of stuff mouldering in the stables.'

'We all need a bit of luck, Reggie, but I'd say you get more than your fair share.' He raised his glass. 'And long may it continue.'

'I'll drink to that.'

'And I'll drink to the lovely Lara.'

'Porky, you can't be serious. She's not like some footballers' WAG who'll yield her all for a sniff of chardonnay. What d'you think a beautiful, sophisticated classy girl like her would see in you?'

Porky chuckled enigmatically. 'You'd have to ask her.'

'Porky, you want to be careful; she's a very independent girl. Jason de Chateauneuf – you know, the geezer that lives near us who made a ton of wedge on computer software – he's been lusting after her all summer, she's strung him along and made a real arse of him.'

'Yeah, but he's a fake; I'm real, and the ladies know the difference.'

With Barry White still groaning about '*Lerve*' from the speakers behind him, Reggie sighed. However similar in stature Porky may have been to the American singer, he was deluding himself if he thought he'd get anywhere with Lara. 'What the hell,' Reggie said. 'Here's to the lovely Lara, *and*... the even lovelier Rosita!'

In the morning, Porky stumbled bleary-eyed up to the Bentley and climbed in beside Reggie. 'Cor! You and your bleedin' apple-jack.....'

'Porky, you didn't have to finish the bottle.'

'But like you said – it's a bit moreish.'

'Like Othello?'

'What?' Porky shook his head, puzzled, and winced at the pain it caused.

'Never mind,' Reggie chuckled as he pressed the starter button. 'Let's get on the road.'

As they pulled out of the drive, Porky turned to Reggie. 'How are we getting over the Munch, then?' he asked.

'The Munch?'

'It's what the Frogs call the English channel.'

'We're not going over, we're going under,' Reggie replied.

'Under!? Through that effing tunnel? We're not! I can't do that – not in my state. I get terrible claws-trophobia and I'll just throw up all over your lovely green leather.'

'Bloody hell, Porky, you're a grown man aren't you?'

'Not when it comes to twenty five miles of tunnel.'

Reggie was philosophical about Porky's affliction. 'What the hell! I'm not going to risk you discolouring my upholstery. We'll take the old batto.'

The big green Bentley rolled sedately off the ferry at Calais and purred across the northern French plains, around Paris and onto the big motorway south. As they were cruising between the small rounded hills of Burgundy, Porky, who had been snoring beside Reggie for an hour or more, suddenly grunted loudly, jarred out of his slumbers by his mobile phone bleeping with a message. He looked at the screen, glanced at the next road sign on the auto-route and sat up in a panic.

'What's up, cousin?' Reggie asked.

'We've got to come off at the next junction. I didn't say because I didn't know until I got that text, but we can stay near here for the night.'

'If you say so,' Reggie shrugged. Porky always seemed to know someone wherever he went. 'You'd better tell me where to go.'

Porky directed Reggie off the main road and along some small lanes winding through thousands of acres of vineyards, where great bunches of dark grapes looked as if they were nearing their peak.

'They'll be picking this lot soon,' Porky observed, 'and then jumping up and down on them with their great hairy plates of meat.'

'Is that what they do?' Reggie asked.

'Course not, you dopey pillock, not any more, not in the big Chatters. I came here for the vendage a long time ago when I was wandering down through France to meet a bird in the Rivi-erra. Then a few years ago, I came back.'

'I never knew that,' Reggie said.

'There's a lot about me you don't know,' Porky chuckled. 'Anyway, turn into this gate.' He nodded at a grand pair of gates they were approaching, marked by a small stone lodge. Reggie steered the Bentley through and onto a long avenue which curved up a gentle slope to where, framed by a stand of huge oaks and cedars, stood a 16th century pale stone chateau with a tiled roof of lozenge patterns and round pointed turrets on each corner.

'Bloody hell!' Reggie gasped, 'that's like something out of a fairy-tale book. Is this where we're staying? Do they do B&B?'

'They do, for us – at no charge.'

'Good God, Porky! How come?'

'It so happens that last year when I was driving back from a bit of falling down the snowy slopes of the Alps, I thought I'd drop in and see the place where I'd worked all them years before. Besides, my wine cellar needed a bit of topping up and I knew they used to do a bit of what they call 'disgustation' – that's like tasting – and flog a bit from the old cellars. I didn't come up here, but round the back where the cellars are and to my amazement, the female who came to show me round was the grown up version of a lovely little chick I'd frolicked with a bit when I came to pick here thirty year ago. It turned out she'd only gone and married the boss; he was getting on a bit, then he's croaked, and the whole gaff's hers now.' Porky grinned. 'She seemed well pleased to see me, and we got talkin' and talkin'; we found we had what they call a good bit of rappor, and the next thing I know I'm staying in the old chatter for a couple of nights.'

Reggie stopped the Bentley on a large circle of gravel in front of the great house, whose pair of sweeping stone steps led up to the front entrance. As he switched off the motor and Porky climbed out, one of the double doors opened and a slender, elegant woman in her late forties came out and leaned over the stone balustrade.

'My big fat Porky! Hurrah!' she trilled in excitement and a soft French accent. 'And in a beautiful Bentley!' She came tripping down the stairs and ran across to Porky to fling her arms around him.

Reggie couldn't miss the warmth in their embrace. When they un-clenched, Porky turned and took Reggie's arm. 'This is my cousin, Reggie ffinch-Leigh. Reggie, this is the lovely Justine, Madame de Harcort – I call her Mrs Hard Core, 'cos she's tough as old army boots.'

Madame de Harcort's green eyes sparkled above her soft, lightly tanned cheeks. 'Porky, you are so kind! I've missed you! Mr Finch-ley, welcome to Chateau Harcort – is a pleasure to meet a cousin of Mr Bacon.'

Later, in a large room overlooking the park, Reggie savoured a glass of the Chateau's latest vintage, while he marvelled at its owner's charm and sophistication, and wondered how on earth she and Porky had developed their 'rappor'. Later, when Porky had gone off to have a bath and, he said, a bit of a nap before the evening got going, Justine stood up and took Reggie by the hand. 'Come with me, Reggie. I know you are a businessman, because Porky has told me. And I think I have something you might like very much to buy – something which people in England go crazy for.'

She led him to a room at the back of the house, evidently some kind of office with many different bottles on display. 'See, I have this very old Chateau Harcort, 1949. It was said to be perfect, but no-one has tasted it for fifteen years; so the people here won't risk it.' She made a little gesture of disgust at this pusillanimous attitude. 'I have about twenty cases, and because you are a friend of Porky's, I offer it to you for two and a half thousand Euros for the lot, plus shipping and UK taxes.'

Reggie felt himself grow warm at the prospect. He could instantly think of half a dozen Shropshire land owners who would jump at the chance to get some seriously old wine which no-one else would have.

'I'll have them,' he said without hesitation. 'I'll pick 'em up on our way back from Florence.'

'Will Porky be with you?'

'Yeh, of course. I booked him for the whole trip to keep me company.'

'Parfait!' Madame de Harcort declared with a happy grin.

Porky and Reggie were careful not to overdo the chateau's product at the dinner Madame de Harcort had prepared for them and were able to set off early the following morning for the rest of their journey.

'I hope you were comfy in that bloody great bed Justine gave you?' Porky asked as they headed south.

'I certainly was – slept like a hedgehog on Mogadon in winter.

How was yours?'

'I don't know,' Porky said with a smug grin. 'I never went near it.'

'Oh dear!' Reggie groaned. 'Such a beautiful, elegant, intelligent woman, too.'

Porky chuckled. 'But most of all, a woman.'

Chapter Five

After travelling the 450 miles from Chateau Harcort, Reggie's un-ruffled Bentley purred into Florence and pulled up outside the small hotel where he and Rosita had stayed a fortnight previously.

When Reggie came down from having a wash in his room, Porky was already perched on a stool at the small bar, talking convincing cod-Italian to the man behind it. He turned and grinned at Reggie, bright-eyed after a few hours sleep in the car. 'Nosh,' he announced. 'That's what we need – and plenty of it!'

'No wonder you're beginning to look like Billy Bunter on steroids,' Reggie said. 'As it happens, I know a place not far from here, Osteria Paolo, just the other side of the river. They'll do a mas-sive plateful of omelette and chips.'

'Lead on, Reggie!'

In the restaurant, they were shown to a table near the one Reggie and Rosita had occupied two weeks before. They had just sat down when the waiter who'd served Reggie the last time glided over to welcome them and to take their order.

'Frittata a piacere, signor?' he grinned at Reggie.

'I tell you what, *signor*, you choose this time,' Reggie smiled back. *'Y tu fratello?'*

''Ere,' Reggie protested, guessing that 'fratello' meant brother. 'He's only my cousin, and I don't look like him – I mean look at the size of him!'

'Never mind, eh Reggie?' Porky commiserated before turning to the waiter. *'Con funghi, pomodoro y jamon,'* he went on in what sounded to Reggie like fluent Italian. *'Y due.'*

They ordered a bottle of local Chianti while Porky looked around with approval. 'It's good it's not all poncey food here. How did you and Rosi come across this place, then?'

'We were aimed at it by a strange geezer we met in Harry's Bar. He was the bloke who told us where to find good Sextons, too.'

'That was a bit handy wasn't it? Why did he hook up with you?'

Reggie chuckled. 'Rosi reckoned it was because he fancied me, for gawd's sake!'

'No,' Porky agreed. 'That don't sound very likely.'

'I think maybe he's one of those ex-pats who misses home some-times and likes talking to Brits when they come here.'

'What did he look like?'

'Not too tall, neat silver hair, floppy sort of mouth, in his seven-ties, wearing a purple suit with a pink flower in his button hole.'

Later, when Porky had demolished his double order of enormous omelettes with a mountain of chips and sunk a second bottle with Reggie, he sat back and looked around.

'Bloody hell – is that your bloke?' he asked.

'Where?'

'Behind you,' Porky said. 'Him, there! The bloke in the turquoise suit? No, don't turn and eyeball him! He's seen you now anyway. He's coming over.'

Reggie pre-empted Harold Hampton by getting to his feet and holding out a hand in greeting. 'Hello, Harold. What are you doing here?'

Harold pursed his lips in a flash of irritation, but quickly reverted to a thin smile. 'This is my default dining room,' he said with a shrug. 'But of course I'm delighted to see you. What brings you back?'

'We never had the chance to tell you last time. We went round to see your friends off the *Via Bologna*...' Reggie faltered a moment in response to a curt, unspoken sign from Harold to keep his voice down.

'Yes, yes, quite,' Harold hissed testily. 'Good. Actually, I had heard.'

'You did? Oh well, I suppose it's a small place. We went to look at the statues in the Bargello, like you said. Matter of fact,' Reggie went on with a grin, 'we're having Michelangelo's *Young Bacchus* copied – to see if we can sell statues like that in England.'

'Well I never,' Harold murmured. 'Anyway, it's a pleasure to see you. Do be sure you let me know when you come again, won't you?'

Reggie detected a hint of menace in the old man's delivery, and made a mental note of it for future reference. 'Yes, of course, and this is my cousin, Porky Bacon.'

Harold's interest perked up for a moment. 'Really? Any relation of the fabulous Francis?'

'Yeh, sort of,' Porky said with less than his usual conviction.

'I see,' Harold said. 'Never mind.'

'Oh dear!' Porky sighed as Harold walked away. 'He's left a bit of a pong in his wake.'

'It's lavender water, that's all.'

'I think maybe Rosi was right about him fancying you – maybe he likes a bit of rough.'

'Hang on, Porky – if it was rough he was after, he'd have been all over you like a rash.'

Porky chuckled. 'Just 'cause you're wearing your best Savile Row tweeds.... You think he can't see through that?'

'There's nothing to see through. I've never pretended to be anything I ain't. I'm a London costermonger, born'n'bred, and I don't care who knows it. But that doesn't stop me from wearing, good old classic English gent's suitings, does it?'

'No,' Porky chuckled. 'Course it don't. And no one knows better'n me just how genuine you are. But it is interesting that chummy there – whassisname?'

'Harold Hampton'.

'Seems to know what you've been up to.'

'He put me on to the geezer with the Sextons. He's probably been down to sort out his bit of a backhander.'

'I reckon,' Porky nodded.

'And tomorrow you'll meet the geezer.'

Reggie sensed as soon as they walked into Franco Ficuzza's empty echoing parlour, that the Italian didn't like the look of Porky. He was used to his cousin having this effect on people when they first met him, partly because of the uncompromising girth of his stomach, but more perhaps for his unmistakable air of supercilious confidence.

The Italian's greeting was noticeably less warm than at their first encounter. 'I'm glad you came back when you said you would. Everything is ready and we want it out of the studio. There are the twenty-four paintings you selected, and we have your *Young Bac-*

chus finished.'

'Fantastico! Fabuloso!' Reggie chuckled, surprised to find that he was more excited about the idea of the sculpture than of the paintings. 'But how big is the statue? The Bentley may be the size of a truck but there might not be room for it with all the pictures.'

'Is OK. It's not a big sculpture, we scale him down just a little and is separate from his plinth.'

'But does he look right?' Reggie asked, concerned that if they'd scaled it down too much, he wouldn't be able to get the right money for it.'

'Franco smiled thinly. 'Don't worry. You have no trouble to sell the statue, I can assure you, maybe for three times what you pay me. If you don't, just bring him back when you come for more paintings.'

'That's a deal, then. Let's get it all loaded.'

The pictures all fitted snugly inside the old car's capacious boot, but although *Young Bacchus* turned out to be only five feet, four inches tall, the only way they could fit him into the Bentley was lying on his back at an angle across the shiny green leather of the back seat. It was only then that Reggie remembered with a jolt that he'd promised Rosita he would have the *Bacchus* reproduced with set of complete and undamaged genitalia.

'Hang on, Franco,' he spluttered. 'I thought I told you, we wanted him with his willy back on.'

Franco Ficuzza's face froze. 'Mr Finchley, here we are dealing in the best possible forgeries; we do not adapt them to our customers' personal tastes. If you don't want him, by all means leave him here; we will have no problem selling him elsewhere.'

Reggie didn't argue; he agreed with Ficuzza; Rosi just didn't understand the value of authenticity, even if it was in a fake.

'Bloody 'ell, Porky,' Reggie said with a laugh as he drove the car out of town to pick up the Pisa autostrada. 'I can hardly believe I've got all this fantastic tack in the back of my motor.'

Porky nodded. 'All saleable for a good turn, and *all legal*! Those pictures look very kosher, I'll give you that. The only thing worries me is Young Chummy without his todger looks a bit too new for my liking. Won't the punters want him with a bit more age than he's showing?'

'Yeah, you're right. I'll have to spray him with slurry and stick him outside in the weather for a while to give him a bit of patina.'

Porky nodded. 'So what's the story now?' he asked. 'Straight back to Calais and the ferry?'

'Not quite.'

'Why, what else are we doing?'

'We've got to stop off and pick up a bit of wine from your friend Madame Hardcore.'

'Oh no! She's never flogged you some of her old stuff, has she?'

Reggie glanced across at his cousin who was sprawled across the passenger seat like a medicine ball with arms and legs. 'Yes, and why not?'

'She tried it on me the first time I went back and I reckon she has a go at any sucker that comes along. I'm surprised you fell for it.'

'Porky, what are you talking about? I thought she was a friend of yours?'

''Course she is; and a lovely woman, but she ain't got what you might call a load of scruples, Reggie – she never had. Why do you think she and me get on so well?'

'Well, I had a good look at what she's sold me, and I reckon it's OK. Besides, I never like to go back on a deal, once I've shaken on it.'

Porky heaved up his fleshy shoulders in a gesture of indifference. 'That's all right, Reggie boy, if you wanna waste your money. You said you wanted to get straight back after we'd loaded up the Sextons, but I ain't complainin'; I get to spend another night with Madame Hardcore. '

Reggie was struck how Justine de Harcort lit up when she saw Porky again. He'd always been surprised and, if he was honest, impressed by the way his cousin often seemed to charm the most unlikely, beautiful women. At the same time, he wasn't going to be persuaded by Porky to back out of the deal he'd struck with her. It occurred to him that Porky didn't want him to do a deal with her out of simple jealousy; he wanted to keep her all to himself.

Justine, on the other hand, was delighted that Reggie had returned to complete their deal. He wondered if she'd been expecting Porky to talk him out of it. Now they were there, she insisted that they stay the night and she backed up her invitation with a delicious meal made from animal body parts whose origins Reggie was reluctant to enquire about. After dinner and a few glasses of Madame de Harcort's finest Cognac, he tottered up the wide sweeping staircase to his bedroom, while their hostess whisked Porky away.Reggie came down to breakfast in the chateau next morning to find his cousin and their hostess already out on a warm, sunny terrace in front of the house, drinking champagne. Justine stood and kissed him. 'Bonjour Reggie; you 'ave sleep well?'

'Like a baby.'

'Good. You pay me for the wine now?'

Reggie blinked. 'Yes, of course, if you want. I'll write you a cheque.'

For just a moment, Madame de Harcort's eyes narrowed into icy green slits before she put a smile back on her face. 'OK, Reggie.' She leaned into him, and gripped his forearm with strong slender fingers. She gave him a soft smile and murmured under her breath. 'If it ricochets, I come over and cut off your *couilles*.'

Reggie managed to hide his astonishment and recovered fast enough to reply, also sotto voce, 'Now I can see what you and Porky have in common.'

Justine stepped back and grinned. 'I get my man to help you load the wine.'

In front of the house, Reggie opened the rear doors of the Bentley.

'My God!' Justine shrieked. 'Who is that in the back?'

'That's *Young Bacchus*; we picked him up in Florence.'

'But what has happened with his little – how you say?

'His willy? It got broken off about three or four hundred years ago.'

'Quel dommage – when he is so sexy! But you won't get twenty cases in here, what about the back?'

'Full of pictures. I'll take what I can of the wine, and either collect the rest next time, or you send 'em by freight.'

'If you come again, be sure to bring Porky with you, please?' Madame de Harcort asked with unexpected meekness, before having a sudden thought. 'Where do you live, Reggie?'

He always liked being asked this. Despite his house's abject ungainliness, he loved Mortimer Towers and, like a proud father, he was quick to tug a photograph of the beloved place from an inside pocket. 'Here you are,' he said, holding it out for her to see. 'My lovely gaff, in deepest Shropshire, close to Wales.'

Justine de Harcort blinked her bright green eyes and winced at the sight of it; although brought up a simple village girl, she had an instinctive, French sense of style which she had nurtured vigorously since becoming the lady of the chateau. 'Oh,' she said, struggling for something complimentary to say about the house. 'It's very big.'

Reggie chuckled. 'It's what English estate agents call "imposing", which really means it's a big ugly lump that would make a good loony bin. But me and my missus, Rosita – we love it like an ugly kid. And these days, it's what the glossy house mags call kitsch. And Rosi's made it fantastic inside – you should come over and have a look some time.'

'I was thinking, I feel like a trip to England. I haven't been there since my 'usband die. Maybe I bring the rest of the wine with me.'

'You'd be very welcome, Madame de Harcort. I think I can get ten cases in here. Would you be able to bring the other ten?'

'For sure, I will be 'appy to.'

Reggie had driven happily across France and it was only as they entered the port of Calais that he started to feel nervous. Reggie didn't often feel anxious, but when he did, he would whistle snatches of random tunes while drumming his fingers on the big walnut steering wheel.

'For gawd's sake,' Porky rebuked him. 'Stop that effin' whistlin' of yours. There's nothing to be worried about – you haven't got any dodgy cargo, have you?'

'Of course not, but just the thought of those nosy bleedin' Customs the other end always makes me windy.'

As he drove off the ferry at Dover, Reggie tried not to grimace when a British customs officer waved him into a search bay. A tight-lipped man in a cap strolled across to the Bentley and leaned through the driver's window. 'Good morning sir. Nice vehicle you have here and.... Oh my God!' He reeled back. 'What is that in the back?'

'It's a statue of a Roman god,' Reggie explained with studied calmness. 'The *Young Bacchus* to be precise.'

'What's happened to him?'

Reggie explained that it was an accurate copy of the original which had suffered the loss of the organ many centuries before.

'What a terrible thing to happen to a bloke.' The customs officer shook his head as he stood back and waved them through.

Although he wasn't importing anything he shouldn't have been, Reggie's habitual guilt made him heave a big gasp of relief as he and Porky drove out of the dock and into the town.

Once they were clear of the port, Reggie chuckled. 'I s'pose he thought if we were daft enough to bring in a knackered Roman god just like that, we wouldn't have anything else to hide.'

'Gawd knows what was going through his tiny bonce. All I know is – I get very grouchy when geezers in uniforms start rummaging through my kit.' He glanced at Reggie. 'Maybe he just liked the look of your honest boat race.'

'He was a good judge of character then, wasn't he?'

Porky grinned. 'Yeh, Reggie you was always too honest for your own good. Too honest and trusting.'

Two hours later, perched on the huge sofa in Porky's living room in front of the panorama of the Surrey Hills visible through the picture window, Reggie wasn't feeling too honest; he and his cousin were trying to think of the best way to sell the first ten cases of Chateau Harcort '49.

They started by Reggie opening one of the musty old bottles he'd bought from Madame de Harcort.

'Bloody hell!' Reggie groaned as he pulled the cork and inspected it. 'Look at the state of that cork! It looks like Gozilla's chewed it up and spat it out.' The cork had perished completely and was sodden with wine. 'And see all this gunge at the bottom?'

There were a good couple of fingers of sediment in the base of the bottle. Reggie poured the wine gingerly, so as not to disturb the murky sediment, filling a glass for each of them.

Porky picked his up and was the first to take a swig.

'Aaaagh!' he spluttered, banging his glass down on the glass coffee table in front of him. 'Blistering bollocks!! I wouldn't put that on me fish'n'chips!'

'That bad, eh?' Reggie murmured and took a sip. 'Oops!' he gasped as the wine hit his taste buds. 'You're right – real dragon's pee. I wonder if they're all like this?'

''You betcha,' Porky said. 'Madame Hardcore wouldn't have sold them to some gullible Brit if she'd thought they were okay in parts.'

'I can't sell this to any of my local toffs, even if their palates have been shot to shreds by guzzling Tesco dregs. They trust me, believe it or not; some of them even like me, but that could change very sharpish if they thought I'd tried to palm them off with some dodgy old wine. I'll have to sell it to Jason de bloody Chateauneuf. But how the hell am I going to convince him to take it?'

'Simple,' Porky chuckled. 'Chuck away what's left in that bottle. Hang on to the empty and give it a good rinse. Then you'll have to invest in a fresh bottle of good old burgundy that should still be drinkable. That'll cost you a few quid, but a sprat to catch a mackerel.'

'I can't stand mackerel,' Reggie muttered.

'That's got nuffin' to do with it, Reggie. Just get your mate Chatternerve round to see you about something or other. While he's there, invite him to have a drink of this amazing old burgundy you've bought from the chateau. Tell him how rare it is, and expensive, otherwise he won't get interested in it – £100 a bottle, say.'

'A ton a bottle!?' Reggie choked. 'That's a bit strong, even for Chatternerve. And I only paid a tenner.'

'Reggie, that's what your serious wine boozers pay – they say the geezers from the big Irish racing studs come over and pay a grand a bottle for the right stuff. You get something pretty good as a ringer, tell him it's a ton a pop, he'll have a slurp, he'll like it, and he'll like it even more when you tell him you've bought the last bottles they had, and he can't get any. Then he'll try to buy it off you. Play hard to get for a while, then say you'll let him have ten cases – half of what you've got, and it'll cost him twelve grand.'

Reggie was nodding. 'That's definitely the right psychology for a bloke like him. And it wouldn't be dishonest doing it to him; it'd be more like teaching him a valuable lesson, wouldn't it?'

'Of course it would, Saint Reggie,' Porky said with a grin as he stood up to slide back the window to let a little breeze into the room. 'I tell you what, I wouldn't mind a look at a couple of them pictures you got from the Mafia bloke.'

'He's not Mafia,' Reggie said dismissively. 'But I'll get a couple from the car and we'll have closer gander.'

Reggie and Porky went out and pulled two of the paintings from the boot of the Bentley and carried them inside. Porky gazed at one of them, depicting some kind of rustic gathering – a village wedding – which might have been painted by Constable, but for one detail he spotted.

''Ere, Reggie – take a butcher's at this; these little geezers in the background, they look like that gang of cockle-pickers that got caught by the tide up in Morecambe a few years back.'

Reggie went to look at the picture over Porky's shoulder. 'Bloody hell! You're right. They look Chinese!'

'The people up front don't, only the ones at the back. Maybe they got different people doing different bits.'

'Could be. I hope there's not too many like that.'

'You'll have to check,' Porky advised.

'Course I will, but at least, if anyone tries to tell me I'm selling them as the real thing, I can say – hang on, these have obviously been painted by Chinese artists. How would I be selling them as right?'

'Will that help you,' Porky asked doubtfully.

'Yeh, 'cause I reckon most of the punters who buy these will know they're not kosher, but they'll have their own reasons for wanting to buy them.'

'Reggie, me old mate, you're kidding yourself.

Reggie sighed. 'Maybe I am. But I can't do much about it now, so I may as well look on the bright side. Anyway, maybe there aren't any others with the same little oriental folk in the background.'

'Let's hope, for your sake,' Porky said soberly. 'You and your bloody optimism – it'll be the undoing of you.'

When he arrived home next day, Reggie was still cursing himself for his carelessness in not checking over the merchandise more carefully when he'd picked it up from Franco Ficuzza's place. He was thinking it must be about lunchtime as he turned the big steering wheel of the Bentley to aim his car between the gateposts of Mortimer Towers, and was confronted with the sight of a van, an old Shogun and a police vehicle drawn up haphazardly in front of the house. 'Oh Gawd, what now?' he muttered and carried on driving around to the back where he tucked the Bentley under a bamboo shelter out of the sun. He walked through the stable yard and let himself in the back door of the big brick mansion.

He could hear some kind of row going on towards the front of the house, dominated by the powerful, unstoppable contralto tones of his own dear wife.

He followed the noise and found a cluster of people in the hall, including two young men of unruly demeanour who both had blood trickling from their nostrils.

Reggie recognised one of them as Mickey Rafferty, nephew of Reggie's friend, Emmet Rafferty. Emmet was the senior member of a sprawling traveller family who had inhabited the area for the last thirty years.

PC Paul Lank, the young policeman who was responsible for the village, and a policewoman who was fingering her side handle truncheon in a manner that was threatening but faintly erotic, were in the process of handcuffing both youths.

Rosita carried on shrieking at Mickey as he was being led away.

'Rosi, what's going on?' Reggie bellowed to be heard over her.

'Is bloody Mickey; he has pinch our lovely statue – I know is him, but he deny it.'

'What – Joan? Why? Where's she gone?'

'He won't tell us. That's why I so furious.'

'How do you know it was him?'

'Who else could it be?' Rosita asked him as if he were simple. 'He was at the wedding, to be a guest, and when the wedding was over, Young Huggins come rushing to tell me the statue is gone.'

'But it could have been any of the guests, couldn't it? They were a pretty dodgy gang, by the sound of it. They must have been if they invited Mickey as a guest.'

'Reggie, I foun' him – with this other boy, hanging around by the plinth this morning. What is he doing there? He knows about it for sure – I can tell from my instinks – jus' from his eyes.'

'That's not enough, Rosi. And who was the other young geezer? Reggie asked, knowing that there was no point arguing with his wife once one of her supernatural instincts had come into play. 'Think about it Rosi, Joan is very recognisable; there's only one of her, and we'll get the police to show her on telly. Whoever's got her will have a helluva job shifting her,' he added hoping to mollify his wife a little.

'But that won't bring her back!' Rosita wailed.

'You never know,' Reggie said. 'But in the meantime, it so happens we've got a replacement.'

Rosita looked up sharply. 'What we got – the *Young Bacchus*?'

Reggie nodded. 'Porky reckons he looks a bit too clean and needs a bit of aging. I was going to have him sprayed with cow dung and stood around for a few months to grow a bit of moss and patina.'

'You said when we were in Florence, if he look good at home, we can keep him!' Rosita clapped her hands with excitement.

'Now don't get your hopes up, Rosi. You know I'll have to sell him in the end. But at least we've got something to put on Joan's plinth until we get her back.'

The young policeman, known locally as PC Plank for his slow, clumsy manner, having loaded his two suspects into the back of the police car, had come back in to talk to Rosita.

'Now, then Mrs Finchley, I'll need few more details. When did you first notice the statue was missing?'

'This morning, when I go to cut some roses for the house. I go in the wall garden and find those two 'ooligans hanging about, and no Joan.'

'What were they doing?'

'They were sitting down leaning against the stone rock thing she stand on; they were just smoking wha' they call spliffs.'

Reggie couldn't stop himself from butting in. 'Rosi, my little hybrid tea, if they'd just nicked the statue, they wouldn't be sitting there smoking weed.'

'That's why we nicked 'em,' PC Lank said. 'We want to find out where they got the stuff – and for resisting arrest.'

Rosi was incensed. 'But, you take them for stealing the statue, no?'

PC Lank heaved a chunky shoulder. 'Maybe – if we can find it. When did you last see the aforementioned artefact?'

'Yesterday morning, before the wedding start.'

'So there was a twenty-four hour window?'

'Window?' Rosita demanded. 'What you talk about window – they just chuck her over the wall and pick her up the other side.'

'Which,' Reggie said, 'makes it even less likely Mickey and his mate took her.'

'Perhaps,' PC Lank said, pulling out a small black notebook and short, much gnawed pencil, as if coming to an important decision, 'you'd better describe the item for me, please?'

'She was so delicate, so beautiful..!' Rosita started huskily.

Reggie held up a hand. 'Rosi, darlin' – he doesn't want an art review from the bleedin' *Guardian*. I'll tell him.' He turned his bright blue eyes on the young copper. 'She was a bit of a short-arse – only about five feet two, perfect scotch eggs, mostly naked but with a sorta sheet draped over 'er – brilliant work – like you could see through it, and she had breasts like a pair of mangoes and a bum the shape of a ripe nectarine. She was bloody heavy, too!' Reggie sighed. 'We called her Joan; we liked her very much and we'll miss her.'

PC Lank took a few minutes to write Reggie's description in his notebook. 'Thank you very much, Mr Finchley. She sounds lovely. We'll do our best to find your friend – your artefact. Mrs Finchley.' He nodded cautiously in Rosita's direction before turning and clumping out of the room to take his prisoners back to the police station in Ludlow.

When the sound of the police car had faded down the drive, Reggie took his wife by the hand and led her into the drawing room. He sat her in a high-back wing chair with a large balloon of applejack.

'Now then, my little cauliflower, we've done all we can about Joan for the time being, so tell me how the wedding went,' Reggie asked as he sank back in a chair opposite

Rosita's eyes lit up. 'It was fantastic, Reggie! Really horrible – I never see such crazy big dresses – all the brizemays look like pink meringues, the men all wearing same 'orrible shiny silver suits. The mother was so drunk she fell on the wedding cake – after they have cut it, thank God! But they pay everything we agree in cash – ten thousan'! And they break nothing.' Abruptly she became morose and angry again. 'Of course, I don' let them in the house, but they take Joan from the garden!'

'Now, my little angel, don't go gettin' in a six'n'eight. You done brilliantly – an' stop worryin' about Joan – it'll make you feel ill, and it won't bring her back. Now you can do me a favour – you can ask your mate, Lara, to come and stay – as soon as you can – and get Chatternerve round for a meal. I need to get him in the house so I can flog him a bit of wine I bought in France.'

'Wine!? Reggie, what the hell you do? Is bad enough you do the antiques and the pictures, and the horses when you know nothin' about them, but now you buying wine – and you always say you know bugger all about wine.'

'I know I always say that, but it's just to stop people asking my views and me putting my foot in it by being too honest. I've drunk enough wine in the last fifty years to learn a thing or two. I always know when it's really good, and I know when it's over the hill and about as drinkable as camel's pee – which this stuff happens to be.'

Rosita chuckled. 'Oh Reggie – you can't do it to him again.'

'I've got to, Rosi. Once a deal's been started, you have to go through with it, whatever way you can, so at least, if you can't make a good turn on it, it'll wash it's own face. You know that's the way it works.'

Rosita sighed. 'All right, I fix the dinner, but also I feel sorry for Chatternerve because he keep getting his hope up over Lara – he is crazy about her.'

'That's the least of my worries.'

'OK, but I give you something else to worry about. This morning, Diana Dove telephone to say there is a meeting for everyone who is being involved in *Mamma Mia* at the Village Hall tonight.'

'Oh for gawd's sake! I've just driven all the way back from Florence and I'm not sure I'm up to treadin' the boards, even if it's only the village show.'

'We mus' go, Reggie. I not have Diana Dove say to all people in the village that Reggie ffinch-Leigh is no reliable.'

'All right, my Rosi,' Reggie murmured, resigning himself to the inevitable, and got to his feet. 'But now I'm going to find the HugHugginses to help me unload my haul from Florence. D'you know if they're around?'

Harry and Albert Huggins, father and son, were the Mortimer Towers gardeners, but since Reggie had stubbed his financial toe so heavily, in order to justify paying their wages, he used them for any other tasks which his wheeling and dealing might throw up.

'Harry is in the wall garden, clearing up where Mickey an' his frien' put Joan over the wall. They trample all over the flower borders.'

Reggie was glad of the opportunity to get away and think about what might have happened. He walked outside and across to the small wooden gate that opened into a garden that had supplied fruit and vegetables for the large family and a dozen servants living in the Towers at the time of Queen Victoria. Now it consisted of some formal rose beds and borders around the edges, which gave Rosita all the flowers she wanted, and at the centre of it, a large rocky plinth, conspicuously lacking its statue.

Harry Huggins straightened himself as Reggie approached. ''Lo, Mr Finchley – how was Italy?'

'Came back with a good carload. Can you and your dad give me a hand to unload the stuff?'

'Dad's gone off to get the dogs ready for tonight's rat hunt up at Mr Prestbury's.'

'Bloody Hell, 'as anyone warned old Huffers what goes on?'

'I don't know.'

'I might have to go up and see that,' Reggie said. 'But what do you think's happened here?'

Harry shrugged. 'It looks like someone drove a tractor up t'other side of the wall and lifted the statue out on a rope, attached to a front bucket.'

'Using it like a crane?'

'I reckon.'

'But how did they get Joan over here from the plinth?'

'It looks like they just knocked her off her pedestal, like, and rolled her across the garden to here.'

'They say you should never put a woman on a pedestal – too late now. Is there any talk in the village?'

'Not yet. But I'll keep me ears open, and you can be sure Ol' Crobin at the pub will know before anyone else.'

Diana Dove stood with her usual poise on the scuffed and worn floor of the low stage in the Village Hall, where her kitten heels kept catching in gaps between the boards. She wore a pair of half moon specs on the end of her elegant nose and a simple jersey dress. Rosita guessed it must have cost plenty; she nudged Reggie who was already trying to nod off beside her on one of the metal tube and canvas chairs. 'She is so skinny,' she whispered, not very quietly. 'But is the fashion, I suppose, to look like twig insect, so clothes sort of dangle off the pointy bits.'

Reggie looked up and grunted. 'I much prefer curves like yours, my juicy little peach.'

Diana Dove tapped her pen on the music stand she was using as a lectern. 'Good evening, everyone – thank you for coming. If we want this village to be proud of its show, then we have to start working on it right away. We've got precisely one month before we give our first performance. You've all had copies of the script, I hope.'

'No M'am ,' a young male voice echoed from the back of the hall. Everyone turned to find that it was Mickey Rafferty's.

Rosita drew in a sharp breath. 'Why is he want to be in it? He will be in jail for stealing our statue,' she hissed at Reggie and everyone else within a few yards.

'Shut up Rosi; he didn't do it.'

'How you so sure?'

'Emmet told me,' Reggie said simply.

Emmet Rafferty, Mickey's uncle, was a man Reggie respected above almost everyone else in the village because, despite the disadvantage of being born and reared in an Irish travelling family, and having to make a living out of buying and selling objects and artefacts on the fringes of the antiques trade, he had shown himself to be one of the straightest men Reggie had ever met. 'And if he says he didn't – he didn't.'

'Sshhh.....' people around murmured.

And Diana Dove went on. 'First I'd like to introduce a very familiar face, whose owner has agreed, for absolutely no consideration, to take one of the leading roles in our musical, that of Sam, one of the possible dads – and the sexiest one – in this wonderful plot.' She turned and looked into the shallow wings of the stage. 'Ladies and gentlemen,' she announced, relishing the moment, 'our star, and mentor in this production, Mr Jolyon Prestbury!'

Jolyon stepped out with the broad smile of a time-hardened professional and gave a small, almost regal wave to the enthusiastic reception he had from everyone else in the hall.

'How did she get him?' Rosita whispered angrily.

Reggie shrugged both shoulders. 'I dunno, but she's pretty tasty; I should think she seduced him.'

Rosita stabbed her husband in the fleshy side of his midriff. 'She no tasty! She too curvy!

'Thank you all so much for that kind welcome,' Jolyon was saying. 'And thank you for inviting me into your community with such generosity. I have to tell you, for years as I was planning my exit from the great Metropolis, I vowed I would restrict any further outings on the stage to highly paid, much-hyped productions destined for London's West End – not am-drams in village halls in remote corners of Shropshire. But I have to tell you that your producer,' Jolyon turned and bowed graciously at Diana Dove, 'is as persuasive as any hardened old Shaftesbury Avenue operator.'

'Thank you, Jolyon, and I know that you know what immense prestige you will bring to our show, and we are all hugely grateful.'

She started clapping until everyone in the hall, anyway bowled over by the announcement, joined in vigorously. None of them doubted what a coup it was to have Jolyon Prestbury in the show.

Reggie leaned in to Rosita's ear. 'Gawd knows what she must have done to him to get him on side. She's an operator, all right.'

'You call it operator; I call it somethin' else...'

'Thank you all,' Jolyon boomed from the stage and stepped down to sit on a seat in the front row.

'So, here's what you've all been waiting for..... the cast list.'

Diana, comfortably in her stride, went on. 'The part of Sophie – the girl who is to be married – will be played by Linda Swift...'

Rosi whispered to Reggie, 'Is Library Linda, no? Who rode into the lake on her Viking charger at the fete?'

Reggie nodded. Linda was an alluring but bashful twenty year old known to everyone as Library Linda, on account of her job travelling around with the County Mobile Library, doling out Mills & Boon romances.

'Donna's friend from New York, Tanya, will be played by Belinda Buckton.'

This announcement was met with noisy approval, to which she responded by standing up, turning to face the audience with a serene smile and taking a bow.

'Donna's English friend, Rosie, will be played by Rosita ffinch-Leigh.'

Once again the hall echoed with laughter and whistles of approval – evidence that Rosi's sometimes incomprehensible English wasn't seen as a serious obstacle.

'Harry, the English banker who is one of Sophie's possible dads, will be played by Reggie ffinch-Leigh....'

'Cor!' said some. 'Bloody hell!' gasped others, and 'There's not much gay about Reggie,' joined by a lot of tittering.

'Bill, the Danish sailor will be played by Terry Cotter; Sky, Sophie's young groom, by Mickey Rafferty.'

This was greeted with cheers, as well as incredulous laughter. Mickey was known in the village as a rogue and was always the first suspect when anything went missing, but most took the view that though a rogue, he was, at least, a loveable one – partly due to his engaging charm, partly to his wicked black eyes.

Mickey yelled cheerily from the back of the hall. 'OK, but who's gonna be Donna?'

Diana waited while the hubbub, and vociferous speculation quietened down.

'The role of Donna – as played in the film by Meryl Streep – will be played in our production by...' she strung out the moment as if she were naming the winner of a TV Bake-Off. '...Me!'

There was a stunned intake of breath. It hadn't occurred to anyone that Diana, who was directing the show would also play a part in it. She wasn't an obvious performer.

The silence that followed was broken from the front row by the sound of Jolyon clapping vigorously, which inevitably prompted everyone else to join in.

Reggie turned to Rosi. 'Looks like they think it's a good idea, and I reckon they're right.'

'Poohh,' Rosi muttered, unconvinced. 'She will look offal in doongarries!'

The following morning, Reggie asked the Huggins, Old and Young, to help him unload the Bentley.

Rosita watched with excitement as they carried the paintings into the house and propped them around the walls of the main entrance hall and the drawing room, where they looked magnificent against the neo-Gothic, dark oak linen-fold panelling.

'There are brilliant, fantastico!' she cooed with approval. 'But because the frames, they all looking the same.'

Reggie shrugged. 'The paintings are all very different. Maybe it would have been better if they varied the frames a bit, but I've got a sneaky feeling that some of these paintings may have been done in China – or somewhere in the far east, and they only have the frames made locally in Florence – and, you know, same as any other business, they need to keep costs down, and I suppose it's cheaper if they make up all the frames in bulk.'

As he spoke, he toured round the two rooms, looking minutely at each picture. To his intense relief, there were no more that depicted small oriental people in the background; it looked as if the 'Constable' village wedding was the only one. 'Anyway, I'll mix up these ones up with the other stuff I'm going to buy – and, maybe, if it looks like a problem, I'll swap some new frames for old.'

Rosita was still staring at one of the pictures propped in the hall, it was the 'Constable' village scene. 'Reggie, you crazy bloody fool! This picture got all Chinese peoples in it. Why you don't look before you take it?'

'Rosi, my little nectarine, don't get all aereated. I know about that one, and, yes I should have checked, but I'll unload it all right, and I've just had a good look – it's the only one.'

'Is this why you say they made in China?'

'Yes, and 'cos a few other people have told me that's where they come from these days. But what the hell? I don't reckon we've paid much over the odds, and we wouldn't have had that lovely trip to Florence, would we? And I couldn't have driven in my Bentley to Shanghai, or wherever, to pick them up. And, by the way, I wouldn't have got the *Young Bacchus*, either.'

Rosita's eyes lit up. 'Can I see him?'

'I've asked the Huggins to put him up in the stable yard. They should have done it by now.'

He led his wife through the back door, and beneath the stable yard arch. 'There he is!'

The statue, placed on a temporary plinth of a three foot slice through the bole of a recently felled Wellingtonia, was a faithful replica of the twenty-two year old Michelangelo's extraordinary depiction of the debauched, charming young god, tripping along, happily inebriated with a bunch of grapes hitched to his shoulders to show the source of his merriment.

'Reggie!' Rosita shrieked. 'Where is his – you know?'

' Rosi, don't make a fuss. Franco said they would only reproduce honest authentic-looking works of art, not alter them to please personal preferences – and of course he's quite right.'

'Like Chinese at English wedding?' Rosita sighed and prodded the truncated organ. 'It is so sad to see that, when he is such handsome boy. Reggie you must tell me that you didn't ask Mickey Rafferty to steal Joan.'

'Of course I didn't – and he didn't either. There's no way he'd have nicked it and then come back and hung about by her empty plinth, smoking weed.'

'You didn't ask anyone else to take it, so you can sell it?'

'Of course I didn't, I know how much she means to you, and to me. But we'll definitely put *Young Bacchus* in her place until we find out what's happened to her

The next time Diana Dove came to Mortimer Towers, after Reggie suggested that she drop the scripts round, Rosita was watching from her tall, stone-mullioned kitchen window. When she arrived, the elegant antiques dealer stepped out of her small sports Mercedes, which she'd parked at a provocative angle on the gravelled forecourt, and strolled across to the house in the most non-utilitarian dungarees Rosi had ever seen.

'Oh my god... Reggie! Come look at Diana in doongarries! Is fantastic.'

'I don't know about fantastic,' murmured Reggie over her shoulder, knowing he had to choose his words carefully.

Rosita scuttled off to greet Diana beneath the ornate porte cochere which, in a fit of vanity, the 19th century owner of the Towers had stuck onto the front of the house.

'Diana, you look amazing!' She planted a big red 'O' on Diana's pale cheek. 'Come in. Do you have the scrips?'

'Thank you, Rosita. Yes, I have. It's pretty much taken from the film, frankly, though I've improved on it at a few points.'

'Is Harry – the one Reggie must play – is he still gay?'

Diana was surprised by the question. 'Obviously I couldn't change that; it's a sort of key element.'

'It is?' Rosita asked, doubtfully.

'But, Rosi, darling, you mustn't worry about it. It's just a bit of fun, and Reggie will be terrific... simply because he's so jolly macho.'

Rosita stopped for a moment as she was leading Diana across the hall to the drawing room (having decided that someone like Diana wasn't used to being entertained in kitchens). 'You think my husband is so jolly macho?'

'Of course,' Diana trilled, with a sudden hint of nervousness.

'But just don' forget he's mine,' Rosita said huskily, as she resumed progress across the hall.

Reggie heard the exchange and thought he should join them to make sure they kept the peace. He appeared from the kitchen door. 'Ullo, Diana. What can I get you to drink? Champagne, applejack, Martini?'

'Oh, that would be lovely, with just a gnat's bladderful of vermouth.'

Reggie grinned. 'Can't guarantee that. I'm not sure how big a gnat's bladder is. Do gnat's even have bladders?'

Rosita, who didn't like it when she lost track of a conversation, and was somewhat in awe of Diana, interjected. 'No matter about gnats, Reggie, please to get the drinks.'

When Reggie had mixed, shaken and filled three cocktail glasses, using his approximation of a gnat's bladderful of Martini, he, Rosita and Diana sat in the drawing room where the evening sun shot beams across the room and turned the walls to gold.

After her first sip, Rosita couldn't hold back her curiosity. 'Diana.....! How did you ask Jolyon Pretsbury to be in your show?'

'It was rather a coup, wasn't it? But I was determined to get him; let's face it – with him on the posters, we'll fill the place for all five shows. And it'll make everyone else up their game.'

'Yes, but how di' you persuade him?'

Diana didn't answer at once; she smiled enigmatically for a few moments. 'My late husband used to love trout fishing, and he always used to say if the fly you were using wasn't working, then try another, then another until you find one which does.'

Rosita shook her head impatiently. Where she came from, fishing with flies represented the slowest way of feeding your family. When people wanted fish from the river, they threw a stick of dynamite into it. 'What fly you use?' she demanded.

'*Dove's Seduction*, you could call it,' Diana said with a grin, and Reggie rumbled with laughter.

'What is this *Dove Suction?*' Rosita was sure they were laughing at her, though she'd a good idea of what Diana had done to land her big fish. 'You use often, no?'

Since Reggie had arrived back at Mortimer Towers with his twenty four high-quality fake pictures, he'd spent a week or so considering all the possible places in which to sell his new stock of '18th century' sporting pictures and portraits. He could open a gallery, with all the razzmatazz and expense that would involve, or he could send them to auction, but he'd decided that might be unpredictable, especially if the auction houses decided not to get behind them. He rejected eBay as an outlet and after a week of weighing up the options with Rosita, he'd come round to her idea that the least risky, and most cost-effective way of doing it would be through a street market.

Rosita had raised a problem, though. 'Reggie, only trouble is it means it look like you going back to be being street trader, when our friends here think you are retired tycoon.'

'So? If I tell them it's my hobby, they'll believe me. They know I love a bit of wheeling and dealing; they won't think it's peculiar or anything. Anyway, street trading's what I know about and, as you say, my thrifty little helpmeet, it'll cost next to nothing to set up and operate. It'll take a little while before the punters notice, but they will, trust me. After all it was your idea to do the market and, my clever little canary, I reckon you were right. I'll keep a low profile, and just wait for word to get around among the trade. And, I'll ring Porky to plant a few pointers among some of the punters down south. But first, we must go out and do a bit of buying, and that'll give us a chance to give you some driving practice in the Bentley – God knows you need it.'

Over the fortnight that followed, Rosita drove the Bentley thousands of miles to auction sales – some small and scruffy in village halls; some large and snooty in purpose built sale rooms, all offering a variety of oil paintings, water colours and prints in every kind of frame and condition. Reggie found Rosita's sentimental gut reaction useful in identifying pictures that would be easy to sell on a market stall, provided they were cheap enough. He had a bit of an idea himself of the kind of thing that he might sell a few notches up the market from £200 to £1,000, with which he could supplement his stock, so his high quality fakes wouldn't stand out too obviously, especially at prices that would be a lot higher then the average in the Castle flea market in Ludlow where he was hoping to shift them.

When Reggie rang Porky to urge him to get out and about and tell anyone who might be interested about his good quality 'school-ofs', although sounding a little doubtful, his cousin promised to have a word with the dealers he knew around London who might be interested enough to flog all the way out to Shropshire to see what was there.

'Don't you worry, Reggie,' he said. 'I won't push it too hard; I'll let it slip out, before I stop myself, like I want to keep it to myself – that'll whet their appetite.'

Reggie whose initial confidence in the scheme was beginning to falter, now that he was about to put his toe in to test the water properly, clung on hard to this offer of Porky's, as he prepared himself for the first session of raw market trading he'd undertaken for a very long time.

Chapter Six

Early in the morning on the following Sunday, Reggie's Bentley purred into the square in front of Ludlow Castle. The time-mellowed stone of the ancient fortress glowed in the sunshine and, beneath two rows of bright red and white awnings, the square was already full of traders filling their stands. Chirpy, canny, optimistic, world-weary, shifty, eager or anxious, they were all busily preparing to sell their bizarre array of random antiques, or brocante as some of them called it.

'*Crappalata*, more like,' Reggie muttered to himself as he glanced at the stuff being pulled out of battered old vans around the edge of the market.

Among the rustic furniture dealers exchanging cheery banter from their stalls, women huddling in vintage coats were perched alongside rails crammed with musty fur coats and fifties cocktail dresses, alongside moth-chewed tweed jackets, collarless shirts or battered brogues with half-inch soles – tangible residue of dead men's lives. Wispy ladies sold bits of old kitchen tack, household pottery and clusters of Staffordshire figures as knocked about as the hooligans hanging around the Hereford A&E department on a Saturday night.

Punters out to catch whatever early worms were on offer before the sharp-eyed dealers spotted them were already pacing between the half-filled stalls, clocking the merchandise at each with a rapid sweep of the eye.

Some of the locals noticed the Bentley arrive, knowing whose it was, and wondered what had brought Reggie so early to the market.

Behind one of the stalls, already set out with old woodworking tools, bits of assorted rusty hardware and unclean pictures in battered frames, stood Emmet Rafferty, eagle-eyed totter and leading member of the local traveller community. He, too, spotted Reggie's car, and watched as it approached and pulled up behind his stall.

The driver's window slid down and Reggie's healthily tanned face appeared, with a good-natured beam. 'Morning, Emmet. Is that my pitch?' he asked, nodding at the vacant tabletop beside Emmet's.

'Aye,' Emmet nodded. 'D'you want a hand setting up?' he asked in an accent that hovered between Donegal and the Welsh Marches.

'Nah,' Reggie laughed. 'I was pitching stalls before you were born.

In order to dilute the impact of his top quality Italian Sexton Blakes, Reggie had done well with his planned raids on the local salerooms with Rosita over the past fortnight. His determination to buy every cheap old picture that came up had yielded a few dozen 18th and 19th century paintings in oil or watercolour, all cheap, some crude, others good – for the most part, indifferent examples of provincial art of the period.

He parked the car behind his stand and stepped down from the gleaming old Bentley. To anyone who didn't know him, he could have been an old lord of the shires, dressed in slightly rumpled oat-meal linen jacket, a pink & white windowpane check shirt, with a yellow silk scarf around his neck and faded red cotton trousers, while his thick white hair was swept back from his forehead in a single uniform wave. On his feet he wore a pair of burnished chest-nut Chelsea boots. He went to the back of the car, lifted the lid of the capacious boot and started pulling out his stock. He carried the pic-tures over to the stand he was renting from the town market and stacked them against the irontube frame.

Reggie had arranged to pitch next to Emmet, while on his other side was a stall manned by a short, ferret-faced individual who sold taxidermy of assorted fauna and anything connected with the killing of it – fishing kit, hunting paraphernalia and shotgun-related things. The ground around his stand was covered in deceased animals, stuffed and mounted in unlikely poses. At the front was a pair of foxes with scarlet paint dripping from fangs clamped respectively around a moth-eaten pheasant and a flaccid hare, along with a rare pine marten of an implausible ginger hue, crouching on a beech log.

Emmet strolled over to have a look with Reggie. 'That's not right, to be selling a protected animal like a pine marten – they just made it illegal,' he observed provocatively.

The shifty-looking trader shook his head vigorously. 'Thass' not a pine marten – s' rock marten – from Poland.'

Emmet and Reggie laughed out loud, and turned back to Reggie's stand.

'Cor, you bin busy Reggie,' Emmet said, looking appreciatively at Reggie's stock.

'I've been enjoying myself. There's a few lovely pieces I came by...'

'When you was in Italy?' Emmet prompted smartly.

'Did I tell you that?' Reggie asked, startled he'd been so indiscreet, even with Emmet.

'No, but I can see there's some there you wouldn't have got out of Lennons or Queensland.' Emmet was talking about the two local auction rooms; Lennons was respectable and middle of the road; Queensland provided a last chance for quantities of domestic utensils and decorative items discarded by humbler households – the bottom rung on the downward recycling process leading, if no buyer was found, to final consignment to the woodburner or the county landfill; it was also a source of a few surprising bargains. 'And I guessed you must have gone to Italy to buy something – specially when you went back again so soon.'

Reggie was a little dismayed to have his Italian purchases identified so swiftly, but Emmet was exceptionally sharp – tactful too, though, if asked.

'Don't bother to mention Italy to anyone, Emmet, will you?'

'Course not, Reggie, not after all we've been through together.'

Reggie nodded his appreciation and touched the side of his nose. 'Ta, mate, and you never know, some of the stuff I've bought in to mix among these lovely 18th century pictures might sell for more then you'd think, now they're in better company.'

As Reggie arranged them before putting up a wire screen on which to hang them, Emmet was crouching down to have a better look at one of the Florentine fakes. 'This could be a kosher Stubbs; if you sell it too cheap, you could be in trouble. And this,' he added, picking up a small canvas that had been part of a job lot at Lennons, 'looks like a Cox senior – could fetch a bit.'

Reggie leaned over Emmet's shoulder to look at the painting. He knew Emmet was well clued up on local painters, and had picked up a few himself from house-clearances he'd done over the years.

David Cox, Reggie gathered, was popular among local collectors.

'You think that's a Cox then?' Reggie asked with a sudden tingle.

'Nah – I said it looks like a Cox.'

Reggie let himself down gently. 'Don't do that Emmet; you know how naive I am.' He started to hang the paintings he had for sale, making sure that he mixed up the clean-looking Sextons with his tattier local purchases. He began to feel his pulse quicken again at the imminent prospect of some good, old fashioned market trading. Already the bargain hunters and professional dealers were stopping to look at what he had for sale, with some who recognised the quality of a number of the pictures on show not disguising their surprise at seeing them in a market like this.

When he'd got his stall looking as he wanted it, he'd put up seven of the pictures from Florence, including the Village Wedding that might have been painted in William Constable's studio, interspersed with around twenty of the purchases he'd made on his two week buying spree with Rosita. He stood back and surveyed his wares.

'Wotcha think, Emmet?' he asked his neighbour.

'Very tidy,' the tinker observed, with a nod and a hint of envy. 'You should do well.'

Reggie made his first sale shortly after eight o'clock; it was of a good little oil painting of a Hereford bull (always popular close to the origins of the world famous breed), along with another of a saddle-backed pig of implausible dimensions. They went for two hundred pounds each. He'd bought them both for a hundred at a weekly junk sale in the village hall where Diana Dove's *Mamma Mia* was to be performed.

Emmet who was watching chuckled with approval. 'You're a lucky bugger.'

'It's not luck, it's skill,' said Reggie, then, with a grimace, 'I haven't had a bite on any of the good ones.'

'Yeh, but you're looking for five grand apiece for them, and that's a helluva lot for this market.'

'We'll see,' Reggie murmured, hanging onto the hope that Porky had done something to stir up a bit of interest among the London dealers he knew. His thoughts were interrupted by the arrival of his wife with Jolyon Prestbury, who had offered to drive her into town a couple of hours after Reggie had set out.

Rosita kissed her husband and, as practical as she was flamboyant, pulled a large thermos flask of coffee from her raffia shopping bag and was soon filling a trio of large Gaudy Welsh china mugs with strong Colombian coffee.

'How you gettin' on?' she asked.

'Sold a couple of little 'uns,' Reggie said, sipping his first shot of coffee. He nearly lost the mug when his wife nudged his shoulder.

'Look,' she whispered noisily, 'there is Lord Rokesay with his wife.'

Reggie looked across the square to where Lady Rokesay was cruising serenely among the stalls, quietly taking in a lot more than she was letting on, stopping every so often to pick up something and ask its price.

'Why she buy stuff here?' Rosita wondered.

'Because, my little bunch of purple heather, it's the thing to do – look how many pieces of tatty old rustic furniture and kitchen crappalata you see in those glossy interior magazines you and Lara are always looking at.'

'Reggie!!' Peregrine, 20th Earl of Rokesay, had spotted Reggie and was weaving his way between the other traders towards his pitch. Tall and lanky with a complexion a few shades paler than his favourite burgundy, he was wearing a loose tweed jacket and a soft felt hat. 'Blow me down if it isn't the Berwick Street Barker himself behind a market stall!' Perry Rokesay declared. 'How very appropriate!'

'Morning, Perry,' Reggie responded to the new moniker with which the affable earl had recently dubbed him. 'You're up bright and early.'

'The memsahib demanded it, and as I'd heard you were doing a bit of wheeling and dealing up here, I thought I'd come and take a look.' As he spoke, Perry's quick and practised eye was assessing Reggie's wares. 'My word – I spy a bit of quality here! Is that a school of Reynolds?' The lanky peer leaned across Reggie's table to take a

Flea Market

closer look at a portrait of an 18th century lady with big, blue-grey hair and a fastidious mouth. Against a background of a classical stone mansion, a whippet with heavily protruding ribs was sidling around the edge of the woman's voluminous dress. Reggie had attached a price tag of £4,800. 'This could be useful,' Lord Rokesay murmured. 'I'll ask Lydia to come and have a look, once she's accumulated all the domestic rubbish she's threatening to stuff in our new London house. Good heavens!' he exclaimed, indicating the whippet in the picture, 'that dog's either very malnourished or seriously anorexic; perhaps its mistress starved it as a way of vicarious slimming.'

As he straightened himself, Lord Rokesay appeared to notice Jolyon for the first time. He hadn't met him before. 'Ah! You must be Huffers, our new resident soap star. I'd heard you'd bought the Witch's House.'

'The estate agent didn't call it that when I bought it,' Jolyon said pragmatically.

'He wouldn't, would he? Was he a little bald fella?'

'That's the one,' Jolyon confirmed. 'But we haven't been introduced....?'

Reggie stepped in. 'This is Perry, our local big-cheese aristo – also known as the Earl of Rokesay.' He turned to Jolyon, 'And this is Jolyon Prestbury, well-known Max Factor off the telly.'

The two men shook hands warmly, each recognising the other's public persona.

Perry also turned to Rosita. 'Senora Finchley, good morning to you too.' But characteristically, his attention was soon caught elsewhere and without warning, he drifted off with a small wave of his hand. 'I'll tell Lady Rokesay about the woman with the dog,' he said as he went.

Reggie watched him until he was out of earshot. 'Let's hope his missus likes the picture,' he observed. 'It would be good to send one up to Rokesay Castle.'

'He seems very charming, your local aristo,' Jolyon observed

'He's a genuine bloke,' Reggie agreed, 'though a bit short on attention span.'

They were watching Perry drift between the stalls, nodding this way and that to all the people he knew, when Reggie became aware that his stock was being scrutinised by an olive-skinned man of about forty and medium height, wearing clean Levis, an old American flying jacket and aviator sunglasses.

He turned away to drink his coffee and speak to Jolyon. 'I hope you're happy with those paintings you got from me?'

'I certainly am! The pair of horses and the Longhorn bull look magnificent in my main hall. You must come and see them. In fact, if you come next Wednesday, Emmet will be there to exorcize the place, and banish this blasted ghost everyone tells me about and I've never seen.'

Reggie had been wondering how Emmet had managed to establish himself as the local exorcist. Mainly, he guessed, it was because the local vicars were unconvinced of the existence of anything like a ghost, which had risen from the dead and weren't prepared to compromise their lack of belief.

Emmet heard what Jolyon was saying, but he was dealing with a small, rough customer who wanted to buy a well-used but still functional mole trap. As soon as he'd finished the transaction, he joined the group behind Reggie's stall. 'Don't you worry, Huffers – by the time I've finished with that bloody ghost, you'll never hear from her again.'

'But that's the point I'm making,' the actor protested. 'I haven't heard from her at all yet, and I've been rather looking forward to meeting her, before you send her packing.'

Reggie had asked himself if, in fact, the ghost at the Witch's House, and those in several other houses in the area bought by people from 'away', were no more than a means of extracting paid employment from the new occupants.

'Excuse me, mate,' the man in the flying jacket had moved in closer, keeping his eye on the portrait of the woman Perry had been looking at. 'Can I have closer butcher's at her?'

Reggie noticed the strong London accent, and wondered if this was one of Porky's customers. 'Yeh, sure,' he replied, and stepped aside to allow the man closer.

The punter had a good look at the painting, turned it round to inspect the back and checked the frame for any blemishes. Evidently satisfied, he grunted at Reggie. 'Take four grand for it?'

Reggie shook his head with a friendly grin. 'I think I've already got a punter for it at that price.' He nodded at the £4,800 tag.

'Four and a half?'

Reggie knew the man must have seen Perry showing interest in the picture. He shook his head again, as nonchalantly as he could. 'Sorry, mate.'

'Hmm.' The man grunted, groped in the front pocket of his jeans for a moment and pulled out a wad of used notes.

Reggie found it hard to contain his excitement at this first sale of one of his Florence purchases, but he managed to keep calm as the man counted the notes into his open palm.

'There you are; four grand, eight hundred.'

Reggie trousered the wad, picked up the picture and passed it to the man. 'There you are – one painting, school of Joshua Reynolds entitled – *Tight-arsed Georgian Lady, with Skinny Dog.*'

The punter nodded without offering any display of emotion at his purchase. 'If you ever have more like this one, let me know.' He pulled a small notebook and a Bic biro from his hip pocket, tore out a sheet and scribbled a number on it. 'I mean that, seriously,' he added with an edge of menace to his voice.

Reggie casually took the bit of paper and stuffed it in his breast pocket as he watched the first of his Italian Sextons get swallowed up in the growing number of people milling around the market. Once he was out of sight, he turned to Rosita with a big happy grin. 'There you are, my golden delicious, first sale, and not the last, I'd say. And I doubled my money.'

'Makes the pictures I got from you look good value,' Jolyon murmured with approval.

'Come on, Jolyon, I wouldn't tuck up a local, would I?

'Not unless it was Jason Chatternerve,' Emmet chuckled.

'Now Reggie...' Jolyon Prestbury drew himself up into his *Jane Austen Regency Buck* stance. 'Will you permit me to take your wife off and acquire for her a real cup of proper Italian style cappuccino at the Tippling Toad?'

'Why do you want to give your trade to that moody old Spaggho-phile?'

'Because, my dear Reggie, he's the best – and you know it.'

Reggie did know it. Since the Toad had been opened halfway down High Town by former TV chef and famous grouch, Muffin Magee, it had become his favourite watering hole, usurping even the venerable Castle Inn in his favour. 'All right, take her,' he said with exaggerated brusqueness, 'as long as you bring me back a large frothy and one of those little pastry things.'

Half an hour later, Jolyon still hadn't reappeared with Reggie's cappuccino; Emmet had got tied up in a long disputatious dialogue with one of his many unruly relations, and Reggie had sold another of his local purchases for three times what he'd paid for it at Lennons. He settled down on an old wood and canvas director's chair with 'The Godfather' printed across the back and was deep into the latest edition of the Antiques Trade Gazette, when he was in-terrupted by a quiet female voice.

'Excuse me.'

Reggie lowered his reading matter, and glanced up from the trade gazette to find a small woman with a thin, furry face like Mrs Tit-tlemouse squinting closely at one of a pair of equestrian paintings. They were both uncannily close to the style of the younger Herring, a famous 19th century horse painter, which Reggie had priced at £5,200 each, or £10 thousand the pair. These price tags had already provoked a few gasps from passing punters who'd never seen a pic-ture selling for more than a few hundred pounds at the Sunday Flea Market.

'How much is it without the frame?'

'Why do you want it without the frame, madam?' Reggie man-aged to sound both unctuous and supercilious at the same time.

'Because the frame looks newer than the picture and I've got one at home that'll match the age of the painting. I can't think why you haven't put it in an old frame yourself.'

'Because,' Reggie said slowly, getting to his feet and towering over the potential punter, 'I think it's a very handsome frame that shows all the signs of having been made in the 18th century, though I'll admit it has been cleaned a bit. However, if you really want me to sell you the picture without it, I'll knock a tenner off.'

The woman filled her small chest and stood up straight to deal with what she clearly perceived as a crooked old market trader.

'I may not like the frame,' she said, 'but I know it's worth a good deal more than ten pounds.'

Reggie had learned long ago as a trader that if one is going to capitulate in a negotiation, it's worth doing it with good grace. 'You're a very perceptive lady,' he grinned knowingly, leaning forward and lowering his head closer to hers. 'I'll knock off a ton.'

'A ton?'

'A hundred,' Reggie clarified.

'I'll give you four and a half thousand for it,' his buyer said, before clamming her small, lightly moustachioed lips together in a way that convinced Reggie no better offer would follow.

'Done,' he said. 'Do you want to take it now?'

'Not yet,' the small woman said firmly. 'I'll give you five hundred pounds now – with a receipt – so you don't try and get a better price from someone else, and I'll bring the balance when I pick it up without that frame.'

Reggie took her money and watched her bustle away. He was fascinated by the way people often didn't conform to first impressions. He ruefully acknowledged to himself that with her initial timid appearance, she had managed to put him off his guard and, as a result, had just done a very good deal for herself.

'What the hell,' he told himself, 'the frame's worth a few hundred on its own – to the right punter.' And he'd still cleared a profit of at least two grand on the picture.

Reggie had just finished removing the carefully aged and distressed canvas from its carefully aged and distressed frame, when his cousin Porky Bacon loomed into view in front of his stand.

'Porky, my boy!' Reggie exclaimed. 'You never said you were coming.'

'No. It was like a bit spur of the whassaname. When you told me on the dog and bone you had young Chatternerve coming round this evening so you can sell him the wine, I couldn't resist being in at the kill.'

Reggie chuckled. 'I thought maybe you came to see which of your punters had turned up?'

Porky grimaced, looking embarrassed. 'No. I don't think any of them have. To be honest, I didn't get that much of a reaction out of any of them.'

'Really?' Reggie asked. 'Well, one of them's been. I sold him a good School of Gainsborough. He hasn't been gone that long. In fact... ' Reggie had just spotted the man in the leather flying jacket driving a convertible vintage Jaguar out of the top car park, not more than twenty feet away, with the *Tight-arsed Georgian Lady and Skinny Dog* protruding from the back seat where it had been strapped in '...there he is now.'

Porky squinted at the driver, who'd had to stop his car to let by several others coming the other way. 'That's not one of my punters,' Porky said, shaking his head. 'Never seen him before in my puff. He doesn't even look like a picture dealer.' He pulled his phone from his pocket, flicked it into camera mode and held it up to take a shot of the man before he drove out of the square.

Reggie shrugged. 'Oh well, what the hell, he paid full price for the thing.'

'How'd he pay?' Porky asked sharply.

'In readies, of course!' Reggie pulled his wedge from his pocket for Porky to see. 'Maybe they're just good pictures,' he added. 'And I sold another to a little old lady – that one there – she didn't want the frame for some reason.'

Porky leaned down, with some discomfort, to inspect the frame, propped behind the canvas. 'They are a bit heavy these frames.'

'I don't mind – I'll get rid of it to someone, but I think I'll put it away for the time being,' Reggie said, picking it up and putting it in the boot of the Bentley which was still parked where he'd unloaded it.

Coming back, he grinned at Porky. 'I don't blame you wanting to see Chatternerve – should be a good show. I had to get him to come tonight 'cos he's off to some gaff on a cape in the south of France tomorrow for a few weeks. Anyway, you'll be very welcome, and you'll be glad to hear Miss Lydbury's coming too.'

'Yea, she told me.'

'Ah,' Reggie said, as it dawned on him. 'That's why you've come up!'

'It's only one of the reasons, Reggie. Which reminds me, I heard from Madame de Harcort. She says she wants to come to England to see me and, while she's over, she'll come up here and drop off the other ten cases of Chateau Harcort you're waiting for.'

'That'd be good,' Reggie said. 'Maybe I can sell 'em and get 'em delivered to Chatternerve before he gets back from France.'

'So long as he bites tonight and buys the first lot,' Porky qualified. 'Look, I'll see you later; I'm off for a grappa and a hunk of salami from your mate, Muffin Whassaname.'

'You should find my missus there, with Jolyon Prestbury.'

'What? You mean old 'Uffers off *Woolicombe* – your new mate you were telling me about?'

Reggie nodded. 'More like Rosi's new mate; he's always hanging around at the Towers now. Still, I did manage to flog him a couple of the pictures I found stashed in the cellars – I reckon he'll be back for more.'

'Best of luck then.'

Reggie watched him go with a twinge of envy. Reggie, too, had enjoyed the time when he could do whatever he felt like – when there were no calls on his time other than to entertain himself.

But – on the other hand – he put his fist in his pocket and squeezed the wedge of used notes nestling there. He had sold over ten grand's worth of pictures already and it wasn't ten thirty yet – and he had an endless supply to replace them!

With this thought in his head, he noticed an old man in a shapeless tweed coat of ancient vintage approaching his stand with a determined look in his eye. He smiled happily and prepared himself for some sales pitching. This was a punter who'd spent half an hour looking through the cheaper stock earlier in the morning and Reggie didn't have to work hard to sell him a small watercolour of a flock of sheep drinking on a bend in the River Wye while their youthful shepherd dallied amid the long grass on the bank with a young female who might have been a maiden, but didn't look as if she would be for much longer.

'I bet that was you when you were a young shaver, eh?' Reggie grinned as he took £150 off the old fellow, who chortled happily at the memory of riverside frolics as he walked away with his picture.

But Reggie's merriment was abruptly interrupted by a harsh growling and barking from the direction of the ferret-faced man's stand beside him. He swung round and saw a well-fed Staffordshire bull terrier gazing with frustrated fury at the pine marten, which remained just out of the dog's reach, immobile and rigidly perched on its beech log. The dog let out another blast of canine invective, heaving furiously against the chest harness to which his lead was attached.

At the other end of the lead, Reggie wasn't surprised to spot Lady Wynyates, wife of Sir Compton Wynyates, Her Majesty's former plenipotentiary to the Republic of Uruguay. Reggie knew the dog's owner, and he was always pleased to see her.

'Cecilia,' he bellowed over another tirade of barking.

Lady Wynyates looked to see who was greeting her. 'Reggie!' she bellowed back cheerily and, distracted for a moment, slackened her grip on the dog's lead just as it was mounting another lunge at the unresponsive pine marten.

In less than a second the Staffy, Boris by name, had his strong jaws firmly locked around the stuffed rodent's torso, wantonly detaching it from its long-time resting place on the log, before shaking it like a bull with a matador's cape, producing a flurry of wadding, shredded fur, unhinged limbs and moth-eaten head. The stall holder had turned puce at the sight, making him look not unlike the ginger pine marten which the dog was destroying, while he wailed in despair at the demise of the star item of his stock.

'You little BAStard!' he yelled, grabbing the first thing he could put his hands on – a mounted pair of twelve-point stag antlers – with which he tried clumsily to beat off the terrier. In view of Lady Wynyates' attachment to the unruly dog, it was lucky for him that he failed to make much contact, although that didn't stop her from retaliating on the dog's behalf. She snatched a long hunting crop from his stand and lashed out at him, with far more accuracy than he. 'How dare you strike my dog, you little runt!' she bellowed.

The ferret-faced dealer ducked and cowered under the onslaught, while Boris the Staffy, abruptly losing interest in the lifeless, scent-less ex-animal, backed off, stood still and looked up, calmly quizzi-cal, at his sometimes incomprehensible mistress.

Reggie watched the whole show with glee. He thought Cecilia Wynyates one of the most magnificent women he had ever met, and was delighted that she seemed to like him too. Now she'd noticed that Boris had quietened down and her opponent was out of range, inspecting the damage she had inflicted on his person, she dropped the crop and looked around. There was little left of the pine marten, although the stall holder, feeling safer now, crept round to pick up odd scraps of fur and feet. 'Someone's going to have to pay for this,' he murmured defiantly but under his breath.

Reggie laughed. 'I don't think so. It was illegal merchandise.'

'It wasn't! Wuss a beech marten from Germany.'

'Bollocks!' Emmet joined in. 'It was a rock marten from Poland a coupl'a hours ago.'

'My God!' Lady Wynyates took her cue. 'Are you trying to fob off taxidermy of endangered species? Do you have no concept of mankind's custodial duties in conserving nature's more fragile fauna?'

'Wha..?' the ferret face gaped.

'Come on! Hand it over,' Lady Wynyates demanded. 'I'll need it as evidence.'

'No way!' the trader gasped and sidling round to grab all the rem-nants of the stuffed beast, he gathered them into a discarded Tesco bag and ran off towards the car park that opened onto the square.

Reggie, Lady Wynyates, Emmet and the small crowd that had gathered to watch the conflict were all bellowing with laughter.

'Teach the little bugger right,' Emmet chortled to general agree-ment.

'Well done, Boris!' Lady Wynyates boomed. Boris wagged his tail as he turned his attention to the fox with a hare between its jaws. 'No you don't!' his owner roared and, tugging him back by his lead, dragged him away to safety in front of Reggie's stall.

'So, you're a stallholder today,' Lady Wynyates declared. 'I thought you were a gentleman of leisure.'

'This is leisure – to me. Some people play bridge, other dreary old duffers play golf. Me – I like a bit of wheeling and dealing; and I feel at home on a market pitch.'

'Maybe, but you look like a bloody duke in your red trousers! And the Bentley behind you does rather make it look as if you don't need the money. Still, let's see what you're selling.

She leaned in to have a closer look.

'Good God, Reggie! There are a few damn fine pictures here!' She was nodding appreciatively.

Reggie wasn't sure he wanted her to buy one of his Sextons, although the price he was asking ought clearly to have conveyed that there was something not right about them.

But she was already warming to a deal. 'At least you won't want to put up too much resistance to any offer I make – not after that rotten little dog-cart you sold me for the pageant.'

'Cecilia,' Reggie protested. 'I already apologised for that, and I offered to give back all your wonga.'

'I appreciate that, of course, Reggie, but nevertheless – I'd like you to tell me what you'll take for that very nice picture.' She was pointing at the second of the pair of 'Herrings'. It depicted a dappled grey thoroughbred, wearing only a highly polished headcollar and being held by a liveried groom. 'It looks just like the hunter I had when I was a gal – Spotty Dick, he was called.'

'That's a nice name,' Reggie reverted instinctively to market banter before he could stop himself. He really didn't want to spout sales tripe at Cecilia, and he certainly didn't want to stitch her up. 'But listen, Cecilia,' he said through the side of his mouth, moving up close to her. 'It's a Sexton!'

'Sexton?'

'Blake – fake!'

'Of course it is!' Lady Wynyates declared. 'You think I can't see that? It'd hardly be the real thing at that price. But it's awfully well done! If I hang it on my wall, somebody will have it off me before the year's out – and for twice what I'm going to give you for it.'

Reggie gurgled with relief. 'Cecilia, you naughty old hustler!'

'Less of the 'old' if you don't mind. And someone has to make a living in our household. Compton spends all his pension publishing his memoirs and smutty novels. I see you're asking £5,200, so I imagine there'll still be something in it for you at £2,000.'

'Cecilia!' Reggie tried to look hurt. 'Do I look as if I'd be loading it that much?

'Yes, but what will you take?'

'Four and a half.'

Lady Wynyates came straight back at him. 'Two and a half!'

Reggie winced. 'Four.'

'Three – and that's my final offer.'

Reggie sighed. 'All right – three and a half.'

'Done!' Lady Wynyates declared. She grabbed Reggie's hand and squeezed it like a lemon. 'I'll be back with the money and someone to carry it for me. Don't you dare sell it to anyone else in the meantime.'

She strode off with Boris the Staffy, now docile and trotting behind her. As she passed the stand next to Reggie's, she shot a final withering glance at the ferret-faced dealer who cowered behind his stall, still nursing a nasty bruise on his forearm.

Reggie watched her go with great satisfaction, feeling that this was exactly the kind of sale he'd wanted to make – where the punter was aware of the shortcomings in the pictures' history, but didn't mind because they thought they could use them either to sell on and make a turn, or to hang them in their drawing rooms, just to impress their less knowledgeable friends.

As he watched Lady Wynyates disappear among the crowd of punters, he calculated that provided the deals were completed, he'd sold over £12,000 of his Florence pictures, which was as much as he'd optimistically hoped to shift in a day – and it was still only eleven o'clock.

'Reggie?' a soft, female voice wafted from the front of Reggie's stand. 'Perry wanted me to look at a picture you have for sale.'

Lydia, Lord Rokesay's wife, was a gentle, arty-looking woman with a taste for picturesque cottage artefacts from the preceding centuries, entirely unsuitable for use in Rokesay Castle, and even less so for the Rokesay London residence in Belgravia, where most of it ended up.

'Morning, Lydia. Yes, he said he wanted you to have a look at a portrait of a stout bird with big hair and a skinny dog, in the style of Thos Gainsborough, but a London dealer turned up and offered me the asking price, and he's already driven off with it.

'I told Perry if he liked it he should have bought it, and it sounded nice, but never mind. Oh look, here comes your lovely wife.' She smiled at Rosita who, still escorted with marked gallantry by Jolyon Prestbury, had walked in from behind Reggie's stall. To Jolyon she said, 'Are you Huffers? Peregrine's been telling me about you; he's very excited about having a television person nearby.'

'Hello, Lady Rokesay; I'm Jolyon Prestbury,' the actor insisted.

'Yes, of course,' Lydia conceded graciously. 'You must come up to the castle and do a turn for us some time.'

'A turn, Lady Rokesay?' Jolyon asked, sounding, Rosita thought, just like Colonel Brandon in Jane Austen's *Sense & Sensibility*. 'What do you mean by a turn?'

'Just some nice little piece of drama?' Lydia said vaguely, aware that she had committed some kind of gaffe. 'But I'd better go now.'

Jolyon, pretending not to be hurt, inclined his head. 'A pleasure to have met you.' He turned back to Reggie. 'May I return your lovely wife to you? She has been suitably fed and watered. '

'You make her sound like the horse in that picture,' Reggie said, indicating the 'Herring' painting that Lady Wynyates had said she would return to pick up.

'A very fine picture, Reggie,' said Jolyon with an assumed authority. 'How much is it?'

'Sorry to disappoint you but it's not for sale. Lady Wynyates has bought it.'

'She has excellent taste.'

'If you say so, Jolyon.'

Jolyon chuckled. 'In the meantime, Reggie, as promised, I bring you sustenance,' he proclaimed. 'Tuscan wine, smoked mussels, olives, Parma ham and delicious bread.' He pulled the bottle and the food from a wicker basket he'd carried up from the Tippling Toad and spread them on one side of Reggie's table. 'And I just bought these rather nice Georgian glasses from the charming fella over there,' he added, placing a pair of fine twist-stemmed Regency glasses on the same surface, alongside the bottle of Chianti.

Reggie was impressed by this largesse. 'Thank you, Jolyon, but have you got something to open this bottle?'

'I do indeed.' From a pocket of his navy linen jacket he whipped a large piece of Irish bog oak root attached to a corkscrew, and plunged it into the top of the cork.

A small crowd, attracted by Jolyon's famous face, had gathered around the stall, and it was clear that he was performing to his public as much as to his friends as he filled the two antique glasses.

Reggie picked one up and winked at Rosita. 'Down the 'atch!' he said, and drained it in one.

Rosita laughed with the onlookers; she knew he'd done it to annoy Jolyon.

As Reggie lowered his glass he spotted Cecilia Wynyates approaching with her husband. 'Ah, here comes Lady W to collect her picture – and pay for it, I hope,' he added, by way of a greeting to her and Sir Compton.

'My dear fellow, of course.' Compton pulled a cheque book from an inside pocket and flourished it, evidently designated paymaster. 'Cecilia tells me it reminds her of her old Spotty Dick.'

The punters, several deep around the stall now, laughed with abandon while Sir Compton looked around bemused, as he took out a fat fountain pen and unscrewed the cap.

Reggie tucked a cheque for three thousand five hundred pounds, made out to Mrs Rosita ffinch-Leigh, into his wallet as he watched Sir Compton stride off on his short legs with the picture secured under one arm.

'Reggie!' Rosita whispered with unusual discreetness so that Jolyon, who was still hanging about talking to Emmet, wouldn't hear. 'That is fantastic that you have sell three of your new pictures. I knew it would be good here.'

'Yes my little Colombian cabbage, but they had to be the right pictures, too, and don't forget, I've sold three of the cheap pictures I bought at the sales.'

Rosi patted his cheek. 'Yes, Reggie, you are very clever man!'

'Mind you, Mrs Tittlemouse still has to pick up her picture; she left a monkey on it, but she's got four grand to pay.'

Emmet had been explaining to Jolyon, not for the first time, about the process involved in exorcising the ghost of the infamous witch from his property.

'But I don't understand,' Jolyon asked. 'If you've exorcised this spirit already, why do you have to do it again?'

'Because,' Emmet said, as if he were explaining a simple idea to a child, 'every time an owner dies, she can re-enter the domain.'

'How come?' Jolyon demanded impatiently.

'How should I know?' Emmet protested. 'I'm not the Almighty, am I?'

Reggie guffawed. 'You can't argue with that, Huffers. Emmet is not the Almighty, that's for sure.

He was still laughing when the small whiskery woman re-appeared with a shifty youth by her side.

'I've come to get my picture,' she said in her quiet voice.

'I've got it here, ready for you, without that handsome frame.' Reggie leaned down and picked up the canvas, which had a good accumulation of grime and dust around its edges.

'Good,' the woman said. 'Herbie will carry it.' She nodded at the vacant-looking young man, who stepped forward and took it from Reggie. She handed Reggie a cheque, folded in half. Reggie was about to tuck it into his breast pocket when he stopped to unfold it.

He glanced at it and winced. 'This is for three eight,' he said. 'There was a balance of four grand to pay.'

'I know, but I know and you know that you didn't allow me enough for the frame, especially if it is, as you said, the same age as the painting.'

Reggie engaged in a quick internal tussle between his principles and his inherent need to do deals. It was two hundred pounds light, but it was still showing him a profit of eighteen hundred quid, plus whatever he got for the frame. He gave his customer a wry smile, sighed and with a shake of his head, glanced at the cheque again, folded it and tucked it in his pocket.

'Thank you, Miss Wheeler-Smith,' he muttered through tight lips.

She gave him a quick, uncommunicative glance and walked away, with Herbie following her, carrying the painting.

When Reggie was sure she was beyond hearing, he turned to Emmet, looking injured. 'Bloody hell! She turned me over there; she knew I'd never give her the cheque back for the sake of two hundred quid – but still, two hundred's two hundred.'

'She's known for it,' Emmet said. 'You've to add a bit on when you see her coming.'

'Who is she then?'

'Susan Wheeler-Smith, aunt of Rosanna, the county councillor. She owns half the town, and a load of empty farmhouses up in the hills. She's as mean as a starving cat, though. She's obviously got a frame at home going spare and she doesn't want to waste it, so she just found something to complain of in yours, and pinned you against the ropes.'

Reggie was shaking his head. 'And Londoners think people out here in the sticks aren't sharp.'

'Never mind, Reggie,' Rosita said, using her talent for restoring a husband's battered ego. 'You done really good! Now, I get Huffers to take me home, and I ask him to come for the dinner tonight with Chatternerve. Also Lara and Porky coming too, no?'

'That's it, Rosi.' He gave her a kiss on her cheeks and lips, and watched with pride as she walked off briskly across the square, trailing Jolyon in her wake.

Her instincts were spot on, Reggie thought –Huffers at the table would put extra pressure on Chatternerve to show off and splash his cash by pushing hard to get Justine de Harcort's dodgy wine.

By two o'clock, Reggie had had enough.

'Listen Emmet, I'm packing up. Nobody's going to come and buy one of the big pictures now.'

'Three's not bad,' Emmet said.

'And five of the cheapos.'

'Listen, Reg, there's dealers here would a' been 'appy just to sell them five – so you done all right.'

'Maybe. Anyway, I'm off, but I wanted a quick natter with you. We've got Chatternerve coming round for a meal tonight; I've got some wine I think he'll buy, and Rosi's invited Huffers, too.'

'He's a bit eager, in'ee? Runnin' round here and there like her bloody slave – you wants to watch him.'

'My Rosi knows what she's doing,' Reggie grinned. 'She likes to put geezers who are a bit up themselves in their place. But can we meet up at the Fox & Ferret later for a pint, about six?'

'OK, Reggie – and I'll give you a hand putting this stuff in the Bentley.'

Chapter Seven

In the Fox & Ferret, amid an atmosphere still rank and smoky from a lock-in the night before – when no-smoking laws were always abandoned – Reggie insisted on buying the first round.

'I haven't had a session on the market like that for years,' he admitted to his traveller friend. 'And I got a real buzz out of it.'

'I could see,' Emmet nodded. 'Once a trader, always a trader.'

'But the best bit was selling those Sexton Blakes from Florence. I always had the idea – ever since Jonty told me old Bertie Cheney-Longville had got those paintings from Italy years ago. 'Course, I was lucky to find somewhere that still does 'em.'

'I 'eard them fakes mostly come from China these days – they got factories doin' it; that's what I thought when I saw them funny little fellas in the picture of the wedding party in the village.'

'Hmm,' Reggie grunted guardedly. 'But that's what you've got to do in life, isn't it – look out for the chances and leap on them when they come up like a rat on a pork chop?'

'Who told you about the place that turns 'em out where you went?' Emmet asked shrewdly.

Reggie thought for a moment. He didn't want to give too much away to Emmet, who was just as much a chancer as himself. He sighed, resigning himself to telling a little truth. 'It was a strange little gay geezer we met in the bar at our hotel. But, listen, me old mate, I wanted to ask you about Joan, our statue that's gone AWOL. It hasn't turned up anywhere yet. You told me when I saw you just after it happened that it wasn't your lippy nephew Mickey who nicked her. But are you still sure it wasn't?'

'I'm sure. It was that other young bloke as was at the wedding. Carson, he's called – a sort of cousin like, from Gloucester way and a right chancer. Mickey admits to me he was already a bit plastered, and he told Carson about the statue, showing off like, and took him into the walled garden to see it. After that Mick was so knocked out by some wacky baccy the bloke gave him, he can't remember a bloody thing until he woke in the field aside the garden wall next morning, and saw him again. And he talked him into going back into the walled garden and smoking more spliff, sitting on the stand where the statue was.'

'Didn't he notice then that the thing was missing?'

''Course Mick could see the thing had gone, but he didn't really think about it, and then your Rosi comes into the walled garden and finds 'em, with Mickey pretty much out of it again. She goes berserk, he says, rings the rozzers and PC Plank turns up.'

'Yeh, but didn't Mickey ask Carson what had happened to Joan?'

'Carson told him it must have been nicked by someone else from the wedding, and Mickey reckoned they wouldn't be sitting there smoking weed on her plinth if Carson had anything to do with it. O' course, when the rozzers turn up, they nick 'em both for theft, but they couldn't make nothin' stick, and they didn't even bother to do 'em for the weed.'

'And you reckon this Carson bloke set it up like that?'

'Course 'e did, and some of his mates – or his cousins, more like, would have had the statue away in a pick-up long afore morning.'

'Rosi's had it put up on all the lists of stolen tack on the interweb, even done one of those tweeter things about it with a photo, and she says it's gone virile or something so whoever took it won't ever sell it – they'll only ever get the scrap money.'

'That'll be a tidy bit for bronze.'

Reggie nodded. 'I s'pose the insurance'll pay us out, but I'll miss Joan, and so will Rosi. Luckily, I've got something to put in her place in the meantime.'

'What's that then?' Emmet asked.

'A lovely stone statue, a real good copy of one we saw and liked when we were in Florence. It's by Michelangelo – the *Young Bacchus*...'

'God of booze,' Emmet got in sharply.

Reggie grinned. 'You know some surprising things.'

'For a traveller, you mean?' Emmet added.

'I suppose I do,' Reggie admitted. 'Like, how the hell do you know anything about exorcism, or whatever it is you're doing at Huffers' place on Tuesday?'

'I don't know much, but I've come across plenty of real haunting in my time. I just make up a few rituals and incantations, and the punters seem to like it. You should come; your Sue Price will be there, helping me out and we'll try and make it special for Huffers; he's paying a monkey for it.'

'No wonder he's a bit leery about it,' Reggie chuckled.

'Jus' as long as he don't go round complainin' to the Ol' Bill; you know what they're like with us travellers – nick us first; ask questions a couple of days later. Mind, I've got a bit of insurance out on PC Bloody Plank.'

'What's that?'

'Mickey and me was down by the river. I was going to teach him how tickle a few trout, down at that pool in the bend by Yaffle Wood. No one can see you there – not until they're right on top of you. I reckon that's why PC Plank was there, on the bank. I allus go cautious, so he never heard me coming. Any case, Library Linda was with him and makin' such a racket, he wouldn't have heard any way.'

'Library Linda? What was she doing; why was she making a racket?' Reggie asked.

Emmet gave him a quizzical look. 'What d'you think? It was what you might call passion.'

'Good God!' Reggie laughed. 'Her and PC Plank?'

'That's right – and Mickey was well sore about it. He was hot for Linda before – but to see her with a rozzer..... He whips 'is phone out and takes five or six pictures of 'em.'

'What, *in flagrante delicto?*'

'Whatever the 'ell that is.'

'Well... you know. Having... you know.'

Emmet nodded with a grin.

'Who'd a thought it?' Reggie mused. 'What did you do?'

'Nothin', o'course. Backed off and crept away. Never got any trout mind. Funny thing is, I seen a few others down there over the years, doin' the same sorta thing. Must be well known for it.'

'Why, who else did you see?' Reggie asked, feeling a twinge of guilt about wanting to know.

'Terry Cotter, the demon Potter, with his little skin boat tied up to a sally tree. Reckon he was planning for him and her to leave differently. People are very nosy round these parts.'

'People are very nosy round every part – that's why the Sun news-paper sells so much. Did they see you?'

'No. They was so busy I untied Terry's boat and it was ten yards down the river afore they noticed it gone,' Emmet chuckled.

'Who was he with?'

'I ain't sure but I reckon it was Jones the Beef's missus, Daisy.'

Reggie was shocked. Jones the Beef was a local butcher and en-trepreneur who had recently opened MeatWorld – a large foodstore and farmshop. 'Bloody hell!' he said. 'What a den of iniquity! It sounds like they're more lively here than my punters at the Burling-ton Burlesque club in Soho.'

'And I've seen others.'

Reggie suppressed the urge to ask who. 'Maybe you could make a few quid selling your stories to the Advertiser?' he suggested.

Emmet bridled. 'That would be a bit tacky.'

'What about PC Plank?'

'I still wouldn't tell the papers. Anyway that paper never says noth-ing nasty about anyone, till they've acherly been banged up.'

Reggie drove the Bentley back to Mortimer Towers in a thought-ful mood. He'd had a great day at the Flea Market and, always glad to glean a little inside knowledge, he'd enjoyed his chinwag with Emmet. He was also looking forward to offloading his dodgy wine on to Chatternerve, as much for the sport of it as for the financial ne-cessity.

At the Towers, Rosita and Lara were preparing dinner with the help of Rosi's cleaner from the village, Sue Price. 'Saucy' Sue was Foxy Warren's aunt, a focal figure in village life and a handy two-way source of local gossip. Reggie and Rosi knew this and made use of it sometimes by holding sotto voce conversations, just loud enough for her to hear, when they wanted to leak an idea to the vil-lage.

Reggie saw her and nodded with a friendly grin. 'I hear you've got a leading role in the exorcism this Tuesday.'

'Oh yes. I often do. Emmet likes to feel his customers get their money's worth.'

'But do you reckon it'll work?'

'Allus I know is them spirits never come back after he's done it,' Sue said simply.

Rosi shrieked with laughter. 'Maybe because they were never there at all!'

'Oh, but they come back when new people moves in.'

Reggie chuckled. 'I bet they do!'

'Are you going along to watch?' Lara asked Rosi.

'Huffers has asked me to, but I don't think so.'

'I bet he's bloody asked you!' Reggie said; he was going to expand but stopped himself when he remembered Sue was there.

Later, Reggie, Rosi and Lara made sure that Sue couldn't overhear them by sitting down to chat near the edge of the broad stone terrace that overlooked the lake on the south side of the house. On a wicker coffee table between them stood a bottle of vintage Pol Roger which Reggie had opened to mark the successful sales launch of his Florence Sextons.

Lara, who had arrived in Shropshire only an hour before, was impressed by how well he'd done. 'Frankly Reggie, when I first saw them, I thought you'd have a bit of trouble getting more than a few hundred quid for them. Of course, you sold two to private punters, who are always easier to convince, but you say you sold one to a London dealer, and that proves me wrong.'

Rosita, chuffed about her husband's success, pressed Lara. 'But do you know about this type picture?'

'Quite a bit; before I knew you, I worked at the Courtauld, and the Wallace Collection. I used to do a lot of repair and restoration then – I loved it, actually, and rather miss it but, as I wasn't prepared to take up shoplifting like some of my friends, I needed a bigger salary to pay for the kind of clothes I like.' She shrugged. 'So I became a well paid-hack and a talking head on telly. But the point I want to make about your Sextons is that, even with the most convincing of fakes, even if they're not of specific originals, there's always some little thing that gives them away – in the paint, or the canvas, or a detail in the picture. Look at that wedding scene in that bogus 'Constable' of yours – there's something very dodgy about the people in it. Or sometimes it can be some crass anachronism – a fashion or a hairstyle that's wrong, or a Regency fop using a mobile phone.'

Reggie tilted a bushy eyebrow. 'Lara, I can't really argue with you; you know loads more than me about it all, but the fact is, what I reckoned was not whether they looked spot on, but whether or not they looked right enough for punters to buy them for their various different reasons, even knowing they are quite right – like Cecilia Wynyates. She seemed to spot her 'Herring' was a wrong 'un right away, but she didn't mind; she knows she'll sell it on, sooner or later.'

Lara laughed. 'You're right, of course, Reggie. I know about art, but you know about punters, and there are always punters for crap art – look at Jack Vettriano's prints, or Jeffrey Archer's novels, or Katherine Jenkins' singing.'

Rosi was giggling happily; she loved hearing her friend put the boot in on Jo Public's rotten taste. 'But I *love* Jack Vettriano's pictures, and Katherine Jenkins is so beautiful.'

Reggie shook his head in wonder at the depths of his wife's taste, and topped up their three glasses. 'Anyway, I'm happy,' he said. 'I reckon if I can turn over three or four of these highly desirable fakes each week, I could net two or three hundred grand a year, and that would keep my extravagant little missus well coiffed and blinged.'

'Reggie!' Rosita protested loudly. 'I don' care if you never give me no more Tom Foolery. I love you for your mind and your body.'

'I'll drink to that,' Reggie crowed. 'But,' he went on more seriously, 'tonight we've got two tasks with Mr de Chateauneuf. First of all, we've got to get him to buy the plonk that Porky's French *paramour* tucked me up with, and then we've got do what we can about making him back off this 'orrible plan to scatter bloody wind turbines all along that beautiful ridge.' He waved a hand toward the rising hills in the west which marked the boundary between the Welsh and Saxon nations.

Lara was shocked. 'What are you talking about? I thought he had withdrawn his planning application back in August.'

'You're right; he did, but your father rang me earlier today. He's

been monitoring all applications that come in, and he says Chatternerve has just resubmitted his, with a couple of minor alterations,
leaving out those turbines that would be sited nearest to your dad's
land.'

'Bloody hell!' Lara exploded. 'The two-faced little shit!'

'Look, don't have a go at him this evening; we need you to stay on
good terms with him while we get this deal done. After that, as far
as the wind turbines are concerned, we've still got our secret
weapon.'

'You mean the letter I photocopied up at his house after he lured
me up Caradoc Mount and tried to seduce me?'

'Yes, that one,' Reggie said. 'I've got the copy you gave me, here
in this envelope.' From the manila envelope he pulled out a single
sheet of paper and unfolded it. 'Here, I'll read it.....

Memorandum:

To J d C

From G O

*To confirm that GO has a valid option to purchase from J d C an
area of land of 5 acres at Pant-y-Groes known as Dunkerton Moor
and outlined on the attached map. The purchase price will be at current, unimproved valuation, and this option will remain valid until
Dec 31st 2020.*

Please sign and return.

We haven't got the map, but it's pretty clear anyway, and at the
bottom there's some unreadable signature – which I guess belongs
to G O, whoever he is – but it has no other signature for J d C, which
is obviously Jason de Chateauneuf.'

'So, what is this? Rosi asked.

'Basically, it's an agreement giving an option to this G O person
to buy five acres at the north end of the Pant-y-Groes ridge; I should
think at least a couple of the sixty wind turbines would be plonked
there. Without permission for the wind turbines, the land's worth
diddly-squat; with permission, it's got to be worth tens of thousands
from the potential turbine income. As a legally binding document,
I reckon it's a bit iffy, especially as we haven't got a copy signed by
Chatternerve. But as evidence of nefarious shenanigans over what's

being proposed up there on that ridge, it could be dynamite.' He looked at Lara. 'It depends who G O is.'

'I hope you're right,' Lara said. 'Dad said it must be Gareth Owen, the planning officer for the local authority. And in these cases, apparently, the committee doesn't generally vote against the advice of their officers, unless there is some overriding external pressure, like from local Freemasons.'

'OK, I think we need to sit on this bit of paper. To get the most out of it we'll have to produce it at a public hearing, so it can't just be brushed into a corner somewhere. But whatever you do, don't get shirty with Chatternerve this evening; I don't want him walking out before he's bought the plonk.'

'You could sell to him a lovely picture, too?' Rosita suggested.

'I think one thing at a time as far as flogging him stuff goes.'

'Shh,' Rosita hissed. 'Here comes Sue.'

Sue Price was moving swiftly across the terrace towards them with a phone in her hand which she proffered to Reggie. 'Mr Finchley, it's Mr Porky.'

Reggie took the phone. 'What happened to you, cuz? You went off to the Tippling Toad and never came back.'

'I did come back, but you'd gone home early,' Porky's chubby tones resonated from the phone. 'I got caught up at the Toad with a friend of yours – a lovely creature called Diana Dove – and I asked her to come with me to dinner at your place tonight. 'Ave you got enough scoff for a skinny bird? I told her you wouldn't mind.'

'Bloody hell, Porky! You're a quick worker. I suppose we can squeeze her in somehow.'

'All right, Reggie – see you later. Cheers mate,' Porky said and hung up before Reggie could change his mind.

Rosita was glaring at him. 'Who we are going to squeeze in? Some woman Porky have pick up?'

'Sort of, but it's OK; it's Diana Dove.'

Rosi was relieved. 'Thas' good, maybe with Porky here, she keep her hands off you.'

'Why would someone like Diana Dove be interested in an old geezer like me?' Reggie laughed.

'She is interested in *all* geezers,' Rosi said simply.

'She must be, I suppose, if she's coming with Porky.'

Lara smiled at the rivalry she sensed between the two London cousins. 'But I bet she fancies Reggie more.'

Rosita shrieked. 'Noooo!'

'Don't worry, my little Spanish gardenia, I'll fight her off. But first, I've got to go and prepare my ringers.'

Reggie rose from his chair and walked back up to the house. From his study he collected an unopened bottle of the ancient Chateau Harcort, and the empty one whose contents he and Porky had spat out vigorously at Porky's place after they'd arrived back in England. He opened the full one and poured the wine down the drain.

Earlier in the week, as Porky had suggested, he'd driven up to the good wine merchants in Shrewsbury where he'd invested in four of the best bottles of burgundy they could offer, of renowned quality, but not nearly as old as the Harcort. He now opened two of these and transferred their contents to the empty bottles, which he took back into the house and placed on the sideboard in the dining room.

Rosita had asked her guests to come at half past seven, and as the chimes on the eight foot clock in the Gothic hall at Mortimer Towers struck the half hour, the bell hanging outside the front door jangled with it.

Sue loved her weekly dose of the implausible goings on at *Downton Abbey*, and was very proud of the little black dress and white frilly apron that Rosita asked her to wear for certain occasions. She bustled eagerly from the kitchen to admit the first of the dinner guests.

'Evenin' Mister Chatternerve,' she said, holding the door open for him and bobbing a small curtsy, as Reggie had instructed her to do for him.

Gratified, Jason strode through the hall and into the drawing room with the long stride of a short man. He was in a dark Hugo Boss suit, with a plain white shirt and no tie.

Lara threw Rosita a glance with a quick curl of her lip, just before Jason leaned down to kiss her on both cheeks.

'How're you doin', pet?' he asked in the strong Geordie accent he still used as a mark of his own authenticity, despite his pretensions to the local squirearchy.

'I'm good, thanks, Jason. And I'm sorry – I never thanked you for dinner at Le Pelican last month. Time seems to have raced by since.'

'That's all right.' Jason straightened himself and addressed Reggie who was offering him a glass of champagne. 'That seems like yesterday, but I hear Reggie's been to Italy twice since then, and become an art dealer.'

Reggie nodded. 'Yeh, Rosi and me flew out for our Florence trip, found the pictures we wanted, then I had to go back to pick 'em up.'

Before Jason took the glass from Reggie, he turned to kiss Rosi, who was standing beside her husband to greet him.

'Hello, Chatternerve,' she said. 'I so pleased you come to dinner before you go to south of France.'

'It's a pleasure to see you too, Rosi. How did you like Florence?'

'I love it!' Rosi gushed. 'I saw so many beautiful things. A little man we met – call Harol' Ham-ton – he tell us to see the statues in the Bargello because they are sexier, and we find a fantastic one there call *Young Bacchus* – is a beautiful young fellow, very drunk, who is God of Wine, and we have copy made of him. Unfortunately, his willy fall off; is going in the wall garden because we have Joan pinched.'

'Sounds great!' Jason said, wondering what she was talking about, and finally put his hand around the glass Reggie was holding out to him. He took a hurried swig and turned back to Reggie. 'I saw Lady Wynyates at the garage and she said you were selling pictures in the flea market this morning and she bought one off you.'

'She did – a nice school of Herring – said it reminded her of the horse she used to hunt when she was a kid – Spotty Dick.'

Jason laughed. 'She told me. Did you shift any more?'

Reggie wondered why Jason cared, and guessed he was just prying out of sheer nosiness. 'A few local pictures I've bought around the place.'

'What about the fakes from Florence?' Jason asked bluntly

'Miss Wheeler-Smith bought one.'

'That woman who owns half the town?'

'Does she? I don't know,' Reggie shrugged, resenting Chattern-erve's interrogation.

'Any others?'

'I sold a 'Gainsborough' to a dealer from London.'

'That must be good, then – if the dealers are takin' them.'

'Yeh, I hope to shift a few more next Sunday.'

'Is that the only place you're selling 'em?' Jason asked, as if it mattered.

'Unless someone turns up here at the house. In fact, Huffers is coming tonight; he might want one.'

Before Jason had time to react to that, there was a clanging from outside the front door. 'Ah, that's probably him,' Reggie announced and went out to the hall. 'Sue,' he called, 'can you let Mr Prestbury in, please.'

A few moments later, Jolyon Prestbury made his entrance, his smile perfectly tuned to register his pleasure at seeing his host and hostess, as well as their pleasure at seeing him. He managed to in-clude the other two guests, whom he hadn't met before, with a small interrogative lift of one eyebrow. Having shaken hands with Reggie, and planted three kisses on Rosi's cheeks, he turned to smoulder at Lara.

Lara stood up and Rosi took her hand. 'This my very good fren', Lara Lydbury.' 'Of course,' Jolyon cooed. 'I've seen you many times on the box, speaking so lucidly about the Paris fashions. What a de-light to meet you... in the flesh, as it were.' His eyes dropped to Lara's understated cleavage, before settling with full wattage di-rectly on her eyes. He gathered up the fingers of her spare hand and lifted them to caress them with his lips.

Lara couldn't suppress a titter. 'Gosh!' she said, with a little Mar-ilyn Monroe gasp, 'you did that awfully well; you must have had many years of practice.'

Jolyon knew when he was being made fun of, and lowered her hand gently. 'Very many years,' he smiled equably.

While this exchange was taking place, Reggie was aware of Jason lurking sulkily behind the actor. 'Jolyon, this is Jason de

Chateauneuf.'

Jolyon, perfectly aware of the other guest's presence, swung round and held out his hand, which Jason took coolly.

'Mr de Chateauneuf,' Jolyon gushed. 'What a pleasure. I've heard all about you, and your magnificent estate. I gather you've done great things to it.'

Jason was immediately mollified. 'It had been pretty neglected for a long time; I'm lucky enough to have made a few quid, and I thought it was my duty to tidy it up a bit.'

'That's admirable,' Jolyon said. 'If only there were more landowners like you.'

Jason looked like he'd just won a cup at the County Show.

Inwardly, Reggie cheered. Jolyon subjecting the young tycoon to a blast of his high-impact charm would go a long way to softening him up and making him want to impress the famous old actor. But Rosita was beginning to look twitchy.

'Where is your cousin, Porky, and Diana Dove?'

'Relax, my little sunflower – I can see them now, coming up the drive in Diana's rag-top Merc.'

Porky Bacon and Diana Dove, unlikely as that seemed to Reggie, had evidently spent a few hours together at the Tippling Toad. He wondered what it was about the loud, chubby Londoner that attracted sophisticated women like Diana and Justine. But he also observed with some trepidation the iciness that seemed to hover between the elegant, hard-nosed theatrical agent, and his own highly assertive wife.

'Diana,' he boomed, 'Come and tell me how the play's going? I've learned my lines already.'

'I bet you haven't!' Diana expostulated, and came to sit near Reggie. She seemed glad of the chance to talk about her production of *Mamma Mia* that was to take place in the village hall in two week's time.

'Frankly,' she said, 'I wish to hell I'd never stuck my neck out and agreed to do it. Bloody Jolyon's already backed out.'

'Why?'

Sales Pitch

'I told him I was going to let everyone act with a crib sheet, and if they didn't want to sing to the Karaoke tracks I've got, they could just mime to the original. I was just being realistic but he turned white and flounced off.'

'Well, you can see how he might find that a bit beneath his dignity. I mean, he was quite a big star. Though I gotta say, I didn't see how you were ever going to get all your cast to learn their parts and re-hearse the singing in time – assuming any of them can bloody sing!'

'I took the view that the whole show would be easier for the cast and probably for the audience if we did it that way. At least we won't be held up with drying and prompts. The idea was to produce an en-tertainment for the ordinary people of the parish, not a bloody entry in the National Drama Festival.'

'If you think you'll get away with it, you're braver than I am,' Reg-gie shook his head doubtfully. 'I'm glad I haven't got a song. Who's going to play Sam, now Huffers has backed out?'

Diana grinned. 'Compton Wynyates – he's got a lovely tenor voice and he'll be singing his part.'

'You don't think the audience – even in this village – won't notice that he's about forty years too old for the part?'

'Of course they'll notice – and they'll love it. Sir Compton is very popular round here.'

'Let's hope so. And, by the way, Rosi's put you next to Huffers at dinner – you won't scrap with him after he's let you down, will you?'

'Don't you worry Reggie; I've already made it up with him.' Her blue-violet eyes sparkled lasciviously.

For the second time that day, Reggie was surprised by the shenani-gans going on in the district and he found himself looking round to check that Rosita hadn't somehow overheard. She was looking straight back at him with narrow eyes and tight lips.

'Right,' Reggie said loudly. 'It's nosebag time. Let's go through to the dining room.' He waved his party towards the door.

When they were all sitting around Reggie's heavy oak Gothic table in the Victorian chamber that was the dining room at Mortimer Tow-ers, Sue Price served the first course while Rosita, at the head of the table between Chatternerve and Jolyon, wanted to bring Diana Dove into the conversation.

'Diana is making a big village show,' she told Jason, 'in jus' a few weeks. She is crazy; she make Huffers do a part,' Rosi cackled happily. 'Top TV star in our village musical – fantastic!'

Jolyon lowered his head humbly. 'I fear I have had to withdraw my services, much as I wanted to contribute to this vibrant little community. I hope I shall get another chance, though.' He shot a warm smile at Diana.'

Diana smiled back serenely. 'I'm sure you will.'

'What musical are you doing?' Jason asked, half interested.

'*Mamma Mia*!' Rosi shrieked. 'Isn't it great? I am Rose, the loco friend of the bride's mother, Donna, who is, of course, Diana.'

Jason was shaking his head, trying not to laugh. 'That's amazing. Don't tell me Reggie's in it, too.'

'Of course! He's the Colin Firth part –Harry!'

'The gay guy?' Jason tittered.

'I think,' Jolyon pronounced, 'Reggie will do it wonderfully; he's a natural.'

''Ere,' Reggie bellowed from the other end of the table. 'I 'eard that!'

'I suppose old Lydbury's in it too. I should think he's pretty theatrical.' Jason said sourly, with a quick glance at Lara.

Lara's father, Sir Lancelot Lydbury, was Jason's neighbour and his main protagonist in the battle of Pant-y-Groes Wind Farm.

Rosita sensed that Jason, on good behaviour so far, might be about to turn awkward and mess up the ground for Reggie's sales pitch. 'No, of course he isn't; he's real, old-type English gentleman.'

Relieved to see that Lara hadn't heard Jason, she skilfully steered the conversation away by bringing Jolyon back in and provoking him into telling a few tales of famous actresses he'd worked with. She was sure that Jason was as susceptible as anyone to celebrity tittle-tattle, and she could guess how much he might admire and envy a man like Jolyon Prestbury his household name, easy sophistication and legendary charisma, and how eager he would be to impress the actor.

Sales Pitch

After Reggie had carved the leg of lamb they were having for their main course, he picked up the two bottles bearing the label of Chateau Harcort's 1966 vintage from the sideboard.

'I always think,' he said, as Sue started handing round the slices of pink meat, 'that with these lambs that've spent the summer on the Welsh hills, eating heather and juicy wimberries, the best thing to drink is a strong old burgundy.'

Jolyon nodded sagely. Absolutely!'

'Luckily for me,' Reggie went on, '...and you lot, I was able to buy twenty cases of this direct from the chateau, from Madame de Harcort, who owns it.' He walked around the table and filled everyone's glasses, leaving the remains of a bottle at each end.

Jason picked up the one nearest him and looked at it. 'When did you get it?'

'When Porky and me were on our way back from Florence with my pictures. Justine de Harcort is a friend of Porky's, so we'd stopped the night there on the way down. Justine offered me some of this very special vintage and I arranged to pick it up on the way back.'

'It's bloody old, Reggie,' Jason remarked, inspecting the label closely. 'How do you know it's even drinkable?'

Jolyon had already taken a sip from his glass. 'It's absolutely delicious,' he declared, with as much emphasis as if Reggie had written a script for him.

Diana Dove, up until now subdued at the table and perhaps a tad embarrassed at having turned up with Porky, had also had a drink of it and joined in. 'It is. Reggie, you clever man; this is a really exceptional wine.'

From the corner of his eye, Reggie saw Porky grin and wince.

'Glad you like it,' Reggie said graciously. 'Of course, I tasted it first,' he went on. 'I wasn't just going to take a punt on it – not at £50 a bottle.'

Jason took a tentative sip.

Reggie, who had drunk, as he often claimed, the product of many acres of vineyards in his lifetime, still didn't really know what he was looking for in a wine, but he had found that the ones he liked best tended to be the most sought after and had learned to trust his instinctive palate. But he had no idea how much Jason knew.

'It's good,' Jason was saying, after another sip. 'In fact, it's gre-ate! Though I thought it would be mustier, somehow, being so old, and in the bottle for so long. Do you think your Madame de Harcort would sell me some of this?'

Jason was holding his glass up to a candle on the table, giving Reggie the chance to exchange a quick glance with Porky.

'No way, mate,' Porky answered Jason's question. 'Reggie got the last of it. I was pretty pissed off, I can tell you, but she wouldn't renege on her deal with him, not even at twice the price. She's sort of old fashioned like that, even when I did offer to pay double.'

Reggie was pleased at the effect this was having on Jason, though worried that Porky might bullshit his way into a corner. But Jason, now oblivious to anything else going on around the table, carefully refilled his glass from the bottle in front of him, and took a hefty draft. Already a little woozy, he leaned across Diana Dove who was sitting between him and Reggie.

'Listen, Reggie. If this lover of Porky's won't sell me any, would you sell me what you've got?'

Reggie wouldn't allow his excitement to show on his face, and he hoped Jason couldn't see the flush that tinged his skin. 'Jason, I'd love to help you out, of course, but I only got the last twenty cases.'

'Listen Reggie, I know how you like a deal, man, so why don't I give you for ten cases what you paid for twenty, like? Then you'd have got your ten for nowt. How good a deal is that?'

'Bloody temptin' – I won't deny it. But let me think about it.'

'Don't leave it too long.'

'I'll let you know before you leave tonight, OK?'

As Reggie had hoped, Jason had quickly been taken over by his obsessive acquisitive persona and wasn't going to let go. 'You'd be crazy not to,' he pressed, 'not if you call yourself a dealer.'

Reggie could hardly believe that Jason had swallowed the bait so comprehensively and with so little help from himself. He stood up. 'I'll think about it, Jason,' he said lightly, 'but right now I've got to look after a couple of things.' He picked up one of the Chateau Harcort empties and strolled from the dining room. Quickening his pace, he crossed the hall swiftly to his study where he had a case of the original Chateau Harcort, and the second magnum of good burgundy he'd bought in town. It was clear from the way Chatternerve was guzzling the wine that Reggie would have to produce another bottle – probably two if Huffers' thirst was up as well, while he and Porky would have to look as if they were joining in, too.

He took the empty bottle, another unopened one and the magnum out into a corner of the stable yard, uncorked the magnum and quickly filled up the empty bottle. He was about to pour the contents of the fresh bottle down the drain when he changed his mind, hurried inside and brought back a decanter which he filled with the original Chateau Harcort. He'd been gone only a few minutes when he walked back into the dining room carrying two more opened 'Chateau Harcort' bottles, which he placed at each end of the table.

'There you are,' he said carelessly. 'Help yourselves but don't slosh it about too much; there's a bit of gunge in the bottom.'

'You mean sediment,' Jason observed critically. 'You should have decanted them to get rid of it.'

Reggie noticed with a tingle of pleasure that Jason's arrogance was beginning to get up Diana Dove's nose, now wrinkling like a lioness's at the scent of blood as she turned to him.

'So, Jason – it is Jason isn't it?' She didn't wait for an answer. 'Are you something of a connoisseur?' Her manner made it clear that she didn't think that likely.

'I know a bit about wine,' he answered guardedly.

'People like you make sure you know a bit about everything, and a lot about nothing.'

Jason bridled. 'What are you on about?

By now, the other conversations around the table had petered out, while everyone tried to latch on to what was happening between the supremely self-confident female theatrical agent and the self-made, aggressive, chronically insecure multi-millionaire.

Reggie and Rosita exchanged wary glances. Jolyon raised an eyebrow; he secretly relished local arguments like this.

Diana had turned to face Jason full on and pinned him with both eyes. 'You come up here, to this magical, mythical part of the world, and buy up property in country where you have no roots, and which you clearly don't begin to understand, and think you can throw your weight around, playing with the landscape and the balance of nature, and expect to ride roughshod over the wishes of the people whose forebears have lived here for centuries – like Lara's family, and like mine, as well as a host of yeoman farmers and their workers who are actually part of the landscape and have inherent rights to it which you will never have, however much land you buy.'

Jason had turned white, and a vein in his temple was throbbing visibly. 'Joost what are you accusing me of!'

'Your plan to stick a string of hideous and completely useless wind turbines the whole way along the ridge you own – out there.' Diana waved an imperious hand towards the window, in the direction of Chatternerve's estate. 'Upsetting everyone, even those who wouldn't normally give a damn!'

Jason looked around the table, sensing the lack of sympathy with his own position. If he thought about fighting his corner, he decided against it.

'Look,' he said calmly, 'I just want to do my bit in saving the planet.'

'That's not why he's doing it,' Diana Dove said, with no intention of relinquishing her grip on the debate and turning back to face Jason. 'You're just doing it for the money, aren't you? You've bought this bloody great estate, and then you've found it doesn't make any money, so you're trying to extract whatever you can from what's just a bit of government propaganda – not helping Mother Earth one jot!'

Jason glowered at her. 'If you must know,' he paused dramatically. 'I withdrew my application last month!'

Lara laughed and was about to tell him that they already knew he had reinstated the application when Rosita raised her hand slightly to discourage her from pursuing the issue. Lara understood this wasn't the moment to wind up Chatternerve. 'Yes,' she said. 'You told me. That was very noble of you.'

Jason looked uncomfortable.

Diana looked at Lara in surprise. 'Has he withdrawn his application, really?'

Lara nodded. 'He did; he told me last month and I checked.'

'In which case,' Diana said graciously to Jason, 'I apologise.'

Chatternerve gave her a feeble smile. 'That's OK,' he said and, to Reggie's immense relief, the row had blown over for the time being.

When they got up from the table after dinner, the four bottles of burgundy had been drunk, and Reggie insisted that the men switch to the 1948 Malmsey he'd found hidden away in the cellar of the house when he'd first arrived. He was down to his last case but reckoned it better to sacrifice that, than blow the Burgundy deal, now that he didn't have any more satisfactory substitute.

Jolyon and Jason were both seeing the world through the rosy glow of the large quantity of wine they'd drunk, enhanced by the knowledge that it was nearly fifty years old. They happily accepted a glass of the even older Malmsey but, feeling drunk and extravagant, both insisted on being shown all the pictures Reggie had brought back from Florence.

Reggie, feeling the effects of the wine and a little like the staggering *Young Bacchus* himself, was past caring about selling pictures, but he led everyone through to a sitting room at the back of the house. He'd been thinking it might make a useful gallery, and he'd put all the pictures in there, on the floor, leaning against three walls.

There were still twenty-one left, which Huffers and Chatternerve descended on like buzzards on a dead rabbit. Diana Dove looked at them one by one, less intently and more circumspectly, with lips fastidiously pursed.

'Reggie, these aren't real pictures; they're pieces of decoration.'

Lara, beside her, instinctively came to Reggie's defence. 'Diana, that's a bit harsh. I know you've been buying this kind of thing for years... and years, and I agree they're not a hundred percent, but Reggie's not offering them as authentic originals.'

Diana sniffed. 'They'd be fine in the corridors of the Lanesborough or Brown's Hotel, but no real collector would want them.'

Jolyon stood up from examining a pair of mountain landscapes with highland cattle and figures. 'Luckily for me, I'm not a real collector, and I really like these. I also have acres of wall to cover. Reggie, what'll you take for the pair?'

'To you, Jolyon, national treasure and long-term punter...' Reggie slurred '...ten grand the pair.'

Jolyon had not accumulated the wealth he had by being an easy touch. 'Come on, Reggie! I'll give you six.'

Chatternerve, as if suddenly awakened from a reverie, cleared his throat and spoke quietly. 'I'll give you ten for 'em, Reggie.'

Confused, Reggie did a sharp double-take. He was fairly certain Jason knew what they really were. 'Are you sure?'

'Sure I'm sure. Wrap 'em now and I'll take 'em with me. Cash all right?'

Reggie guessed that Jason was just trying to show Huffers who was the Alpha male in the room, but his crass display of spending power had put a dampener on the gathering. Jolyon looked miffed at being so soundly gazumped, and no one wanted to look at pictures any more.

Reggie and Porky helped Jason load his ten cases of Chateau Harcort 1966, minus the four bottles that had been 'opened', into the back of the Porsche Cayenne in which he'd arrived. His two newly acquired Highland landscapes in their big ornate frames they slid in over the top of the wine.

Before he climbed into his car, Jason made an unexpected attempt to persuade Lara to come back with him to Pant-y-Groes, for a 'nightcap'.

'That's very sweet of you Jason,' she said firmly, 'but I've had all the drink I want, and I'm going to stay here tonight.'

Jason went, with Diana and Jolyon leaving soon after in their separate cars, while Reggie, Rosita, Porky and Lara stood on the step inside the porte cochere watching them go.

Porky stretched himself to put an arm around his taller cousin's shoulder.

'Reggie, mate, that was a result!'

Rosi was grinning too. 'I tol' you he would buy a picture – and he took two!'

Reggie shook his head. 'Yeh, but I don't understand why. He must know he could get them himself cheaper in Florence; I mean, indirectly it was him who told me about Ficuzza's place.'

Porky was surprised. 'Did he? You never said that.'

'He didn't tell me in so many words. In the end, it was Harold Hampton who actually aimed us at their doorstep.'

'Maybe he just fancied those pictures, and couldn't be bothered to get 'em hisself. I mean, he's got a very big pile of wonga to play with... and,' Porky added, 'he had the chance to outbid old Huffers. I reckon that's why he's done it.'

'Si, si!' Rosita exclaimed. 'It was almos' like he just didn't want Huffers to have them at all.'

'And talkin' of wonga,' Porky went on, 'he's given you ten grand for the Sexton Blakes and just under twelve for the plonk, and he's produced it all in readies – he must have had it stashed in the car somewhere. What's all that about?'

Reggie shrugged his broad shoulders. 'Search me, mate. He might have his reasons for carrying that much around with him. Speaking personally, I'm bloody glad he had it. I wouldn't have wanted to wait around for three weeks till he gets back from Cap Wassaname to get my dough, and also he might have tried to drink some of the plonk by then – and then I'd never have got it!'

Lara laughed. 'Poor Jason! I almost feel sorry for him, opening up the first bottle and discovering he's bought ten cases of vinegar! Or was it really that bad?'

'Phoar!' Porky snorted. 'Too right it was! Real rough old vinegar – mixed with camel's pee!'

Reggie nodded. 'It was 'orrible! I nearly threw up when I tasted it – though mostly because I realised I'd been taken to the cleaners by Porky's French floozy.'

''Ere, she ain't no floozy, and you know it.'

'All right, all right, though how she ever allowed you near her is a bloody mystery. But listen, Lara if you want to know what it tastes like, I put the wine from the last bottle I opened into a decanter; it's in my study. We can go in and try it if you like.'

'Oh Reggie,' Rosita wailed. 'Why we gotta do that?'

'You don't have to, my little vine leaf. But Lara would like to, wouldn't you?'

Lara nodded. 'You know my warped sense of humour – I'd really like to taste what Chatternerve just paid a hundred quid a bottle for.'

They sat on soft chairs in the drawing room when Reggie ceremoniously carried in a tray, containing the decanter and four glasses, and a champagne bucket. He filled each glass half way, and put the bucket on the floor in the middle of the room. 'That's where to put it if you can't swallow it.'

He sat down with the others and they all looked at the wine first, turning their glasses and holding them up to the bulbs in the vast crystal chandelier that hung from the centre of the ceiling.

'It's surprisingly clear,' Lara said. 'I thought you said the one you drank was full of gunge.'

'I left most of the sediment in the bottle,' Reggie said. 'Go on, then, who's going first?'

Rosita shook her head. 'Not me!'

'Orright,' Porky sighed. 'It's not going to kill me.' He took a deep breath to prepare himself, and a second as he put his nose over the top of the glass and sniffed. 'Smells all right,' he said, and took a sip.

Several emotions in swift succession registered on his rubbery features – surprise, pleasure, confusion, frustration – before he put the glass on the table beside him and looked at it in bemusement.

'Are you sure that came from one of the bottles you got from Justine?'

'Yeh,' Reggie said, with horrible misgivings. 'Why?'

'Because,' Porky said slowly, 'it's bloody beautiful! I've never drunk anything so lovely in my whole puff!'

Rosita shrieked and stared at her husband. 'Reggie! What the hell you have done?'

'Hang on, Rosi.' Reggie carefully picked up his glass and, like Porky, sniffed it, raising his eyebrows as he did so. As he lifted the glass to his lips a dozen questions crossed his mind, all crammed into a second or so.

Did Porky have a clue about what he was drinking?

Or was he having a laugh – a bloody cruel laugh?.

Or had he, Reggie, muddled up the wines somehow and this was from the magnum, which he certainly knew had been pretty superior stuff – if at only £40 a bottle?

Tentatively he tilted the glass until the first drops of wine seeped between his lips and met his tongue, then tipped it enough to swill the liquid around inside his cheeks.

Stunned, he swallowed, and took another, larger mouthful, let it wash over his tongue and drain slowly down his throat, sensing the exquisite texture and subtle balance between the sweetness of the original grape and the bitterness of its fermentation, along with a host of other overtones and flavours that brought instant, powerful memories of autumn woodland, summer berries, the spicy scent of ox-eye daisies and the soft aroma of damp moss after a summer shower.

Slowly, he put the glass down on the table in front of him, and closed his eyes. For a brief moment, he wanted to weep.

'Why do I do these things?' he asked himself, audibly but quietly.

Rosita was anxious. 'Reggie,' she asked gently, 'what have you done?'

He looked back at her bleakly. 'As usual, I've rushed in, not done my homework, not double-checked. One sip from that first bottle, I just thought they were all gonna be like that; but really – it was bloody obvious, that first one was corked; it must have been letting in air for the last fifty years. No wonder it had gone.' He shook his head. 'I've often heard that between about five and ten percent of bottles are corked – unless of course they're the cheapo stuff with a screw top, which never lets in air!'

Porky, now on his third or fourth gulp was sitting back on his chair with a happy smile on his face.

'Reggie, cuz, don't beat yourself up. You've just made a massive profit on it, and only because you had to sell it to Chatternerve, and that meant upping the price because he's such a prat.'

Lara, also drinking the wine with glee, nodded vigorously. 'That's true, isn't it Reggie? If you hadn't thought it was horrible, you'd have sold it to people like my dad for twenty quid a bottle.'

'That's the point. I'd have liked to have sold something really good like this to my mates for a very fair price.'

'Reggie, for Gossake!' Rosita burst out, 'You done a fantastic deal! Bloody good!'

'Rosi, don't you understand? That's what's upsetting me most – it was only a fantastic deal because I cocked it up!'

Chapter Eight

In the morning, Rosita and Reggie were in the kitchen, drinking their first cups of coffee and reading the newspapers which had just been hurled through the back door when Porky came in. He was bleary-eyed and moving slowly after finishing most of the decanter of Chateau Harcort '66 on his own the night before.

'Cor, I need a fag,' he groaned and pulled a pack of Camels from the pocket of his rumpled jacket.

Rosita leaped to her feet. 'No, no! Not in here!'

Reggie threw him a sympathetic glance. 'Sorry, mate. Even I can't smoke in here – specially not my new Costa Rican smokes – and I'm meant to be the master of the house. I'll come outside with you.'

Reggie led Porky through the French doors from the kitchen and out on to the terrace, where a September sun shone weakly. From there they strolled across the broad lawns that swept down the slope between the house and the lake, over which blue cedars spread their reflected boughs.

'It was lush, that wine, but I sort of know how you feel about that cock-up over it,' Porky was saying between long pulls on his fag and bouts of coughing. 'But I can't say I've ever felt guilty about making a bloody great profit. Of course, my old man was a twister, weren't he; never told the truth 'cause he could never see the point. But you, you really don't like to twist the facts, do you?'

'I'd say I've had to duck and dive most of my life, and that often means mucking around with the *actualité*, as the geezer said. I just felt bad, thinking I was stitching Chatternerve up – even if he deserves it really – and all the time, I wasn't – so I felt all that guilt for nothing. And now he's got ten cases of the best wine I've ever tasted.'

'Yeh, but lucky you!' Porky said, grabbing his cousin's forearm and squeezing it hard. 'You've got another ten cases coming, and even when you've paid for 'em you'll still have a big fat profit out of it.'

'But also, Porky, I'm pretty pissed off that Chatternerve is going to have that lovely wine to show off to all his mates, with them all thinking how clever he is!'

'In all fairness to him, he's a good punter – went straight for the deal, even if he didn't know he was drinking the wrong stuff, because he recognised it ought to be a good deal; and it's turned out right for him.'

Reggie nodded ruefully. 'Yeh, I suppose, but it's a real pain in the arse having to deal with my conscience every time I do a deal that's a bit iffy.'

'You've done enough of 'em!'

'Because that's all I'm good for,' Reggie groaned. 'I'm just not up to doing a good, straightforward deal and making an honest turn on it.'

'Reggie, Reggie... for gawd's sake. Stop goin' all soppy on me! You're all right! You're a geezer, and you've never done nothing that'd get your collar felt.'

Reggie sighed. 'To be honest, that's mostly because the idea of doing a bit of stir scares the hell out of me. I don't want to be molested in the showers by some perverted old murderer.'

'What makes you think they'd want to molest you?' Porky laughed.

'Yeh, you're right,' Reggie perked up. 'Not now, they wouldn't. But listen Porky, there's one last thing I gotta ask you. When you next see Justine, whatever you do, don't tell her how incredible that wine was, will you?'

'Look, Reg, if she doesn't know, that's her look out. I guess she must have done the same as you – opened one dud bottle and thought the rest were the same. 'Course I won't tell her, and I'll tell yer when she's coming so you can arrange to get your ten cases.'

They had reached the lake when they heard a female voice floating down from the house. They turned around to see Lara walking barefoot across the grass towards them.

'Reggie,' she said, 'Rosi says you've had a new statue put up to replace Joan. I thought I'd have a look.'

'Porky hasn't seen it either,' Reggie answered. 'We'll come with you.'

They walked up the side of the house, beneath a wall of glowing wisteria to the Gothic wooden gate set in the brick wall of the old kitchen garden.

Although the gardener, Huggins and his son still kept up a good supply of vegetables from the space, Rosi had insisted on turning most of it into a rose garden, and having Joan placed on a stone pedestal in the centre. Since Joan had gone AWOL, her place had been taken by the *Young Bacchus* only the day before.

The stone god, like Michelangelo's original sculpted in 1495, appeared to totter on the plinth as if he would trip over his muddled feet at any moment.'

'He's amazing,' Lara whispered in awe. 'You can almost smell his wine-soaked breath. And yet, he's really handsome, and so sexy!'

'Cor, you girls and your statues!' said Porky. 'How can you call him handsome? He looks like that young mate of Reggie's – what's he called – tall, young skinny bloke with a lovely estate up the dale, floppy hair and not much going on in the chin department.'

Lara couldn't help laughing. 'You mean Archie Pemberton? *Bacchus* does look a bit like him – rather weak in the jaw line. But Archie's quite attractive too, as long as you don't press him for an intelligent view on anything.'

'Lara, you're harsh,' Reggie remarked drily. 'But you're not wrong.'

'On the other hand, as far as I know, Archie isn't quite so lacking in the genital department.'

Porky chuckled. 'Yeh, let's hope not for his sake. Reggie, where's this bloke's todger gone?'

'According to Ficuzza, this is a dead copy of the original, and they say the willy fell off that about three hundred years ago. And, of course, nobody knows quite what it looked like before, so no-one's ever tried to replace it.'

'Quite right,' Porky chuckled. 'You wouldn't want to be sued by some ancient god for misrepresentation.'

Porky and Lara left together in Lara's drop-head DB5; she was going to drop him at Ludlow station before driving on to stay with her father at Lydbury Manor.

Reggie and Rosita watched them go, but as they walked back to the house, a gentle crunch of gravel announced the arrival of a big black BMW.

They waited while the car came to a halt and a large man, wearing tight cord trousers and a navy blazer buttoned up and straining over his torso clambered out.

'Is this Mortimer Tarrs?' he asked in a hard East London accent.

'S'right, mate,' Reggie replied in similar argot.

'I'm lookin' for a geezer called Reg Finchley.'

'I'm Reginald ffinch-Leigh,' Reggie answered warily. 'What do you want?'

'I 'eard you 'ad some nice pictures for sale.'

'I've got a few good 18th century portraits and landscapes.'

'What about some good sportin' pictures – horse racing and that.'

'Are you a dealer?'

'Sort of.'

'A collector, then?'

'Nah, not really, but I like to buy that kind of stuff.'

'You'd better come in then. This is my wife, Rosita.' He gestured towards Rosi, who gave the man a faintly disapproving smile.

They walked up the stairs from the porte cochere and through the front door.

'This way,' Reggie said unceremoniously, leading his prospective punter across the hall to the back sitting room.

'You want coffee?' Rosi asked.

'Nah, I'm not stoppin' long.'

Reggie made a face which the man behind him couldn't see. This person wasn't behaving like any punter he'd come across. He opened the door to his temporary gallery and held it open for his visitor.

The man didn't hang back; he walked straight up to the nearest stack of pictures against the wall and started flipping through them. He went through the other two stacks in the same way, before he turned to Reggie.

'There's a couple here I want,' he said. 'But my mate said you had a nice... I think he said Herring? But it was of an 'orse. Does that sound right?'

'Yeh,' Reggie said, becoming increasingly puzzled by the man's obvious ignorance. 'I did have a nice one – a dappled grey racehorse being held by a groom in livery. But I sold it to a local, funnily enough, Lady Wynyates of Teme Manor in the village.'

'Right,' the punter said. 'But didn't you have two of them?'

Reggie was careful not to let his doubts about the man's bona fides show, but he couldn't think of any reason not to tell him about his sale to Miss Susan Wheeler-Smith.

'Where does she live,' the man asked.

'In Ludlow somewhere, as far as I know,' Reggie replied. 'She bought it from me at Ludlow flea market, paid for it and took it away with her.'

The man nodded slowly. 'OK, then,' he went on decisively, pulling forward a pair of rustic landscapes. 'I'll have these two.'

Reggie did a swift double-take. 'Don't you want to know how much they are?'

'My mate said they was about five grand each.' He lifted an eyebrow. 'Take eight for the two?'

All Reggie's instincts suggested he should play him a little, like a salmon on the line, and wind him up on the price; on the other hand, a deal was a deal and, maybe, for whatever reason, the man would come again if he treated him all right.

Reggie's instincts won.

'Sorry mate, I can get five apiece for 'em all day long.'

'Orright, then, two for nine.'

Reggie shrugged a shoulder. He was happy with nine. 'Cash?'

''Course.' The punter was already fishing a roll of fifties from an inside pocket of his badly fitting navy blazer. A grimy comb fell out with the wedge and fell on the floor. He didn't bother to pick it up, and started counting out a hundred and eighty grubby notes.

Reggie counted them mentally with him, and took them when his customer handed them over, putting them straight into his own pocket. 'That's fine. Want a hand out to your car?'

'Yeh, orright.'

Carrying them out to the car, he felt he owed the man at least a little small talk. 'So, you're a friend of Porky's, then?'

The punter opened the boot of the cars and put the first picture in. 'Porky?'

'My cousin, Porky Bacon?'

'Nah,' he shook his head. 'Never 'eard of 'im.'

Reggie watched in amazement as the BMW crept off down the drive. Rosita had come out too. He looked at her and shook his head.

'Never in my whole puff have I done a deal like that. He didn't seem to give a monkey's which pictures he took. Any dealer I've ever met would have taken a load more interest and a collector even more.' He heaved a shoulder. 'What the hell! I bought the pictures to sell 'em, why should I care why they buy them?'

'Who tol' him abou' them?'

'I didn't even ask. He'd never heard of Porky, so it must have been the bloke with the greasy hair and leather jacket who bought the 'Gainsborough'.' He scratched the quote marks in the air with his index fingers.

At ten the following morning, Emmet rattled up the drive to Mortimer Towers in his battered Toyota pick-up to take Reggie over to the Witch's House – where Jolyon Prestbury had recently moved.

'All set, then?' Reggie asked, removing a grimy rat trap from the passenger seat as he climbed in.

'Oh yes. Mickey's on standby, so's Saucy Sue. Crobin should already be in the

cellars – he knows the old tunnel that runs from the ruins of the priory.'

'Wouldn't Huffers know about that?'

'Shouldn't think so, it's been walled off for years. That's how we done most of the hauntin' there.'

'But he was round at our place on Sunday for dinner and said he'd never heard anything.'

'Yeh, that's cos I was bit dozy about gettin' it done, but he has now.'

The former TV soap star was showing a marked caginess, Reggie observed when he arrived at the rambling mansion that was to have its ghosts expelled – a building that represented five centuries of bodged construction, ending with an addition of late Victorian Gothic fantasy on the front elevation.

Huffers, normally notable for his relaxed and debonair disposition, stood in front of an oak Gothic throne beneath a long bannistered gallery that ran round three sides of the space. He appeared nervous and suspicious as a small gathering of twenty or so collected inside the dark panelled Gothic hall of the house. On a carved pew against one wall sat Sir Compton & Lady Wynyates, legs crossed, arms folded as if they were waiting for the curtain up at the RSC.

They had all, like Reggie, come to watch Emmet perform his exorcism.

Reggie made his way over to stand beside Jolyon. 'You look like you could use a drink,' he murmured in his ear. 'Have you seen the ghosts yet?'

'Good God, no!' The actor forced a chuckle. 'This is a complete pantomime, really; I just thought it would tactful to go along with it.'

Reggie enjoyed a little harmless mischief. 'I wouldn't be so sure,' he grunted and before Huffers could respond he moved away to a stand a couple of steps up the broad timber staircase, where he would have a good view over the heads of all the other spectators.

Five minutes passed as four more spectators arrived, until Emmet stepped up onto a small dais. 'Keep quiet, dead quiet, everyone,' he ordered huskily, and silence fell at once, interrupted only by the shuffling of feet and noisy breathing in anticipation of what was to come. 'First we must close all the shutters and curtains. Foxy, you see to it.'

Foxy Warren, village rat-catcher and jack-of-all trades noisily closed and barred the shutters on all the windows in the hall and the front part of the ground floor, before pulling their heavy damask curtains across. When he was finished the only light was from the bulbs on a cast iron chandelier in the centre of the hall, with an added glow through the doorways from lights in the four adjoining rooms.

While Foxy was doing this, Emmet clad himself in a white hooded garment he'd brought with him in an Aldi bag – a cross between a monk's habit and a Klansman's robe.

They all waited in the gloom for a few more minutes, in total silence now, until with a mighty boom from the bare oak boards of the floor, the lights went out in the hall and all the rooms around it.

Even Reggie felt himself start.

In a low murmur, Emmet began chanting in a language that was completely incomprehensible to the gathered witnesses, except Reggie, to whom it was faintly familiar.

The exorcist allowed his voice to rise and fall, rise and fall again, dwindling into a dramatic silence, followed by another thunderous boom further away in the house, still from below.

From the dining room, in the 16th century part of the building, a scurrying sound could be heard, getting nearer and nearer, until abruptly the lights came back on and most of the women in the room screamed as a dozen large, healthy brown rats raced across the floor of the hall, brushing over the feet of some of the spectators.

'Begone, servants of Satan,' Emmet bellowed in English as the last of them scuttled out of the hall.

The bulbs in the chandelier flickered and dimmed, leaving just enough light to see an amorphous white entity glide slowly around the gallery, pause and return much more rapidly, partially disappearing at the end, straight through a wall. From where Reggie stood, on the third step of the staircase, it appeared to collapse and float out of sight above Huffers.

Reggie, lowering his gaze to Huffers, managed to snatch a glimpse of him before the lights went out again. The actor's face was pale silver, as if lit by a summer moon and in the few seconds Reggie could see him, he looked genuinely petrified.

Reggie, shaking a little himself, was fascinated and deeply impressed by Emmet's production.

Emmet himself carried on chanting in the unknown tongue for another minute, before he allowed his final phrases to fade away into a deep silence. After a few more seconds another loud boom from even further away in the house, reached them with some palpable vibrations.

Emmet didn't speak for a while longer, until the silence was broken again, this time by the deep throbbing of a massive caterpillar tractor ploughing a nearby field, reaching a headland, roaring and turning away.

The lights in the hall came back on and slowly grew in intensity, until they were brighter than they had been at the start of the ritual. Sir Compton Wynyates was looking disappointed, but his wife seemed thrilled by the whole thing.

Reggie wanted to clap. He could almost believe that Emmet's mumbo jumbo and special effects had rid the house of some unwanted spirit. One glance at Huffers, grinning nervously, showed that the actor did believe it.

Reggie, anxious to clear up his own uncertainty over what had happened, turned and walked quickly up the stairs to the gallery above. He looked down into the hall, relieved to see that no one had followed him. He walked briskly round to the point where the white apparition had disappeared through the linenfold panelling and found, caught on a splinter in the board floor, a piece of white material.

Checking once more that no one was watching he leaned down and picked it up discreetly. It was a plain sheet, bearing the label: "BHS 100% Bri-Nylon, non-iron". Bundling it up, he carried on and slipped through the door at the end of the corridor. This led into a small space, with a couple of doors off it, one slightly ajar. Reggie pushed it open and stepped in, to see a female body of generous proportions sitting on an iron bed, clothed entirely in a black body stocking, pulling a full-face, black cotton balaclava over her head.

Once it was off, she looked up and grinned. It was Saucy Sue. 'Hello, Mr Finchley.' 'Hello, Sue. You dropped your frock in the gallery.'

'I knew it must'a caught on summat; it damn near strangled me, it was allus I could do not to start coughing and choking.'

'I think I was the only one who saw.'

Sue looked relieved. 'I hope so, else Emmet'll be pretty pissed off.'

'I won't tell him,' Reggie promised.

In the Fox & Ferret afterwards, Jolyon Prestbury bought drinks all round.

'God, I enjoyed that!' he told Reggie as they leaned on the thick, well-worn elm board that was the bar.

'You looked scared stiff,' Reggie said bluntly.

'Good God, no! I realise it's just a kind of initiation process the villagers like to put the incomers through to see what they're made of.'

'And to take a monkey off 'em.'

'Frankly, I was thinking of throwing a cocktail party up at the house, for the whole village. At least I don't have to do that now and that would have cost a bloody sight more than five hundred quid!'

'OK, Huffers – I'll believe you!' Reggie grinned. 'And, you've had a few rats moved on from your property, as well as what you might call your traditional ghosts.'

'Actually, between you and me,' the actor said quietly, 'those rodents were a bit scary.'

'Yeh, I wonder where they came from?' Reggie said, making a mental note to ask Crobin later.

Sir Compton, Her Majesty's former plenipotentiary to the government of the Republic of Uruguay, had walked up to the bar and was standing beside them. 'Well done, Jolyon; you must be feeling very relieved.'

Jolyon couldn't judge whether the ex-diplomat was being serious. 'So long as you enjoyed it,' he said, lightly, and sidestepped around Sir Compton to move further along the bar where some awestruck fans, still not used to having a real-live celebrity in their midst, were waiting to talk to him.

'Once an actor, always an actor, I suppose,' Sir Compton muttered disdainfully. 'That 'exorcism' was a ridiculous charade; not that I'm blaming your friend, Mr Rafferty; in these days of deep recession, a man has to make a living however he can, as long as he doesn't break the law.'

Reggie grimaced. 'Ain't there a law against releasing vermin into another man's abode?'

'Oddly enough, no. Anyway, in my view, that actor deserves it, letting people down like that over the village show. Still, at least I can sing my part, which is more than he could.'

'Oh yes; you're playing Sam now, aren't you. Congratulations. I'm sure you'll be very convincing.'

After a couple more drinks, Sir Compton was harried away by his wife, who nudged Reggie on her way out. 'Love my Spotty Dick,' she confessed in a loud whisper to Reggie.

'You can't beat a nice Herring,' Reggie grinned

The onlookers, hearing their conversation, drew back uneasily at this incomprehensible exchange. Reggie allowed himself a discreet smile as Sir Compton and his wife battled their way through the crowd to the front door of the pub. Before they had reached it, the door swung open, and the unexpected figure of Peregrine, 20th Earl of Rokesay strode in, removing his floppy trilby as he did, and the hum of conversation in the bar faded.

'Ahh!' Lord Rokesay, unaware of any reaction to his entrance, boomed affably at Sir Compton. 'Our man in Montevideo.' He pronounced it Monty Video. 'I thought Montevideo was a TV documentary about growing citrus fruit – until I discovered Pol Roger '66,' he intoned, aping the '70s TV advertisement for Vodka, and laughing with pleasure at the joke.

Sir Compton took the baton without a pause. 'And I thought Saint Tropez was a Trappist Monk.'

Perry Rokesay chuckled back appreciatively. 'Very good to see you, Compton. Why is there such a crowd in here?'

'We've just been witnessing the exorcism of Mr Prestbury's house.'

Perry Rokesay looked blank for a moment. Glancing around the bar he spotted Jolyon. 'Huffers!' he bellowed. 'Good God, were you possessed by the devil, or something?'

Jolyon bridled slightly, but managed a polite smile. 'I cast out most of my demons before I hit fifty,' he said with awkward self-depre-cation.

'Oh, good,' Perry said and turned back to Sir Compton, whom he asked more quietly. 'What's he talking about?'

Sir Compton gave his shoulders an extravagant shrug. 'Goodness knows. He's an actor – all codpiece and no bollocks, as Chaucer might have put it.'

'Ye..es,' Perry said slowly. 'I see what you mean.'

'But I enjoyed it, nonetheless,' Sir Compton went on. 'Emmet Rafferty has a natural gift for the theatrical – his Irish genes, no doubt. The extraordinary thing is that the ceremony, such as it was, reminded me of a similar one I witnessed among the indigenous people of Paraguay.'

'That reminds me,' Perry broke in before Sir Compton expanded. 'There was something I've been meaning to ask you.'

The former ambassador adopted a quizzical manner.

'Yes, why is it that all these Uruguayan footer players keep biting their opponents? Is there a history of cannibalism in that country?'

'I think we need to tread carefully here,' Sir Compton replied. 'First, it doesn't happen very frequently, and I believe there are also European players who occasionally attack with their teeth. Secondly, when it does happen, I think it's normally about aggression, rather than nourishment.'

Reggie couldn't help a chuckle as he enjoyed this exchange at arm's length, but he had to leave before he could join in. Emmet was driving him back to the Towers, and Emmet wanted to go.

'Well done,' Reggie said, once more perched on Emmet's passenger seat. 'That was a great show. Maybe you should go into theatricals like Diana Dove.'

'What? Do all that for nothing? No thanks. Mr Prestbury was dead chuffed with it all; he's sure the ghosts are gone and gave me an extra hundred.

'You must have to lay out something for your team.'

Emmet laughed. 'Not a lot. They're in it for the craic.'

'How much did Crobin charge you for the rats?'

'I caught them rats. Crobin just let 'em out through a loose floorboard in the dining room and they raced after a scent trail Mickey put down earlier. They ran well, didn't they?' Emmet grinned.

'And Mickey was stationed down by the fuse box, with a resistor?'

'Yeh – not too shabby, eh?'

'By the way, do you know what ritual you were chanting?'

'No, it was something I heard an old fella I knew practising for some kind a ceremony. I thought it sounded pretty good, so I asked him to teach me; I always knew it would come in handy.'

'I know what it was; I've had plenty of Jewish mates, back in the Burlington club days, and I've been to a few bar mitzvahs in my time.'

Emmet laughed. 'Let's hope old Huffers hasn't.'

On the way back to Mortimer Towers, Reggie took the opportunity to ask Emmet if he could find him a dog. 'Rosita's keen to have a nice-natured terrier,' he said, 'to get me out walking, and to deal with the rodent population in the barns.'

'That'd be no trouble at all. It so happens there's a litter waiting to be gone. I'll bring you up a nice little bitch.'

Reggie also persuaded Emmet to give him a hand the following Sunday, when he was having his second session at the Ludlow flea market. They agreed that they would share a stall, to dilute the effort needed and the impact of Reggie's high-priced, high-quality pictures. Reggie thought they would look more plausible and more of a bargain surrounded by a wider selection of old rustic paraphernalia.

'OK, then,' Emmet said as he dropped Reggie outside the front door of Mortimer Towers, 'I'll pick you up Sunday, about half six, and we'll go to the market together.'

Chapter Nine

The morning after the exorcism at Huffer's house Reggie woke up to the aroma of freshly brewed coffee, wafting up, through the hall, up the stairs to the vast square bedroom where he and Rosita slept.

Thinking kindly of his wife, he sat up in the faux Empire bed which Rosita had insisted on buying when they'd moved in, took in the fine morning sun that was lancing its autumn beam across the room, splashing over the hand painted wall-paper which had been ordered by a Cheney-Longville and applied before the First World War. He wrapped his scarlet silk dressing gown around him, and shuffled across to a tall sash window that overlooked the lawns and the lake which shimmered in the sun's oblique rays.

Happily sniffing the coffee trail, he followed it, like a bloodhound after a Dartmoor escapee, down the stairs until he came into the kitchen. There his heart warmed to see the tanned and raven-haired vision that was his wife, staring at the screen of her laptop with her features twisted into puzzled indignation.

'Look – Reggie! What the....? Is this *crazy?*'

'What's the problem, my little bunch of purple sprouting? What are you getting so aereated about on a fine autumnal mornin'?'

'I look the news on the site of the *South Shropshire Heral'*. There have been two burglaries in one night, near to here.'

Reggie shrugged. 'OK, I'll check the insurance; make sure the alarms are all right.'

'That's no why I so angry. One is Sir Wynyates and Cecilia; the other is Miss Wheeler-Smith.' She turned to look at Reggie to allow the significance to sink in.

Reggie flopped hard into the nearest chair – a rickety Georgian oak construction whose joints immediately protested. He'd spotted at once the connection between the two crime scenes – at least to the extent to which it impinged on his life.

'That is very weird... that it should be two people who bought pictures off me – but I can't see why there should be any reason for it.'

'No.... no,' Rosita was reading to the end of such details as were given. 'From Miss Wheeler-Smith, the house was definite broken into, but it say that nothing was taken. From Teme Manor – where Sir Wynyates live was taken..... a small quantity of silver... and a "painting of a horse in the manner of John Herring, Senior"! Thass the one, isn't it?'

Reggie nodded. 'That's the one, all right, but why the hell wasn't Miss Doodah-Smith's taken too – it was the same style and vintage.'

'Obviously, Reggie – it wasn't the same burglars.'

Reggie considered this. 'Maybe it wasn't. It's not as if these people are next door to each other. The two pictures could just be a bizarre coincidence. But why didn't the second bunch of thieves reckon it was not worth nicking Miss Wheeler-Smith's? It's no worse than Spotty Dick.'

'Reggie, for Gossake – is coincidence!'

'I don't know. Who else besides us knew who bought the pictures from me?'

'Why is matter?'

'I need to check out every possible connection, to be sure it wasn't about the pictures.'

'So...' Rosita folded her arms and leaned back in her chair, deliberately taking her eyes off the screen '...Who know who you sol' them to?'

'Emmet – I guess – but whatever else he does – he doesn't do burglary; he's not such a fool. And, anyway, like I say, he's basically straight – I'm certain of it. The only other person I can think of is the geezer who turned up here Monday, and bought those two without really looking at them.' Reggie closed his eyes and scratched his head. 'I told him where the others had gone because I couldn't see any real reason not to. Any case, he didn't even seem to care which ones he took.'

'I phone to Cecilia, make sure she is all right.'

'Good idea,' Reggie nodded, then changed his mind. 'No, let's go round and see them. Hang on while I get a bit of kit on.'

Reggie sat in the passenger seat, tying his shoelaces while Rosita drove the Bentley haphazardly the mile or so into the village to call on the Wynyates at Teme Manor.

Once she had laboriously parked the elegant old car diagonally across the middle of the forecourt, she glanced at Reggie. 'Oh my God! You have designing stubble!'

'What?' Reggie blinked; his wife's way of saying things could still catch him out.

'You haven't shave.'

'They won't give a monkey's. They'll probably think it's designing stubble, like you said.'

They were stepping down from the car when Cecilia walked into view, carrying a trug laden with courgettes.

'Rosita, Reggie! How lovely to see you. Would you like some cog-its?'

Reggie leaned down to plant a kiss on each of Lady Wynyates' cheeks. 'You seem very calm and collected for someone who's just been burgled.'

'You've heard then? The fact is I can't see any point in getting in a state over these things. What's rather bizarre is they only took a few spoons and Spotty Dick – isn't that extraordinary?'

'But you're not too worried about it?' Reggie observed, genuinely puzzled.

'Luckily, I got Compton to insure it first thing yesterday morning – at twice what I gave you for it.'

'But won't they detect a bit of rodent odour?'

Cecilia lightly lifted one shoulder. 'There isn't a rat to smell. We told the insurers we wanted to insure it for the sum we did because we reckoned we'd bought it well and that's what it's worth. We've had our stuff covered by the same underwriters for years, without ever making a claim. They won't quibble.' She waved then towards the house. 'As you're here now, why don't you come in and have a cup of coffee.'

Rosita was still baffled by what had happened and Cecilia's reaction, but seeing her perfectly relaxed about it, she was pleased for her.

Inside, in a room cluttered with furniture from the Jacobean to the 1960s, they sat on musty old sofas and drank coffee. Sir Compton joined them shortly, also quite relaxed about what had happened.

'I'd have been livid if they'd taken any of my collection of South American native erotica, because that's irreplaceable. But it seemed all they were after was Spotty Dick.' He shook his head in amazement, 'I mean Reggie, I don't want to seem rude, but it wasn't that important, let's face it.'

'And I never told anyone it was,' Reggie agreed mildly. 'But did you know that the other person who was burgled last night in Ludlow also bought a picture from me on Sunday?'

Sir Compton did a quick double-take. 'I did not. Maybe they wanted the pair.'

'They can't have done, because they never took the other one – at least the bit on the *Herald's* website said they left empty-handed.'

'Why?' Sir Compton asked. 'Were they disturbed?'

'It didn't say,' Rosi observed.

'Maybe they couldn't find it?' Cecilia suggested.

'We'll have to ask the Old Bill,' Reggie said.

'Who's old Bill,' Cecilia asked.

'Never mind all that, dear. No doubt all will be revealed in due course,' Sir Compton said, as if he were bored of the whole topic already. 'Now I want to ask Reggie about his part in this blasted musical I've let myself in for.'

'Let yourself in for?' his wife asked. 'Fell over yourself to get it, you mean.' She turned to Rosita. 'Ever since he first had to rig himself out in his ambassadorial knee breeches and knickerbockers, he's been potty about dressing up.'

'Only as an outlet for my repressed thespian tendencies,' Sir Compton protested. 'Besides, I'm playing Sam. He's a New York banker. Not much dressing up involved there.'

'But you're about thirty years older than your character.'

Sir Compton nodded enthusiastically. 'Diana is quite keen for me to age down a little.'

'Is she?' Cecilia asked. 'I wouldn't have suggested you went for it if I'd known she had the hots for you. I thought it was Huffers she was after.'

'Diana Dove is after Reggie,' Rosita said emphatically. 'I can tell by the way she strip him with her eyes.'

'Rosi,' Reggie laughed, 'you've got Jolyon Prestbury panting after you like an old stag at rut – do you see me complaining?'

'I think we're all mad,' Sir Compton said. 'But then a little madness is very good for offsetting dementia – it takes some of the tension from your consciousness. And Reggie, I understand your character dances at the wrong end of the ballroom?'

Reggie laughed. 'I'll manage – it's called acting.'

Emmet drove in through the gates of Mortimer Towers at half past six on Sunday morning and stopped his pick-up in front of the grand porch, where Reggie stood waiting. It was so dented and coated in mud that there was no way of knowing what colour it might have been when it rolled off a Japanese production line twenty-five years before. When he'd first arrived in the area, Reggie had noticed the vehicle pottering around, then got to know Emmet, who always seemed busy in it, picking up stuff he'd bought and dropping things off when he'd sold them – incessantly involved in myriad deals.

Reggie had envied Emmet and the non-stop trade in which he seemed to be engaged. But since he'd found himself in a position where, simply in order to survive, he'd had to revert to the kind of dealing he'd done in his earlier years, Emmet had seemed like his most obvious ally. Reggie also savoured the irony that, although he lived and looked like a country gent (even if he still sounded like a Soho costermonger) and drove around in a vintage Bentley, he was more or less boracic lint, while Emmet in his shapeless old Harris Tweed jacket and moleskin trousers, driving around in his Japanese rust bucket, had accumulated and stashed away a small fortune.

'Mornin',' Reggie shouted and waved an arm to indicate that Emmet should drive around to the stable yard at the back. Here he had stacked all his pictures – the Florence fakes and the local saleroom purchases – ready to load onto the back of the pick-up.

Emmet climbed out, carrying a small wicker shopping basket. 'I got somethin' for your lovely missus.'

'What the hell's that?'

Emmet put a hand in the basket and lifted out a skewbald terrier pup with bright brown eyes and a glossy coat. 'Is this the sort of thing she wanted?'

A big grin spread over Reggie's face. 'That is exactly, one hundred percent what she was after. I'll go and get her.'

'But it's only half six!'

'She won't mind! Not when she sees that!'

Reggie was right. Rosita came down in a fluffy dressing gown and her eyes lit up like lights when she saw the puppy.'

'Oh, Emmet, she is so beautiful!' She took the animal from him and held it to her bosom, chirruping loudly in the universal language of dog lovers. 'Thank you so much....... I go to call her Teresa – Teresa the Terrier, no?'

She stayed outside cuddling the dog while Reggie and Emmet strapped the pictures on top of Emmet's trading stock in the covered back of the truck.

When they had finished, Reggie kissed Rosita farewell and climbed onto the passenger seat, pushing another terrier, a small wire-haired individual called Charlie into the well, and disposing of a pair of mole traps behind the seat.

'You been catching oonts, then?' he asked, using the local word for the small velvety beasts.

'Just for my mum,' Emmet answered.

Reggie remembered what Porky had said. 'We could have an order for a load more.'

'What – live oonts?'

'No, no. Just the skins. Cousin Porky's done really well with the last lot.'

'If you don't want 'em live there's no need to get 'em from Owen the Oont, then. You tell us what you can pay, and I'll tell the family.' Emmet's 'family' consisted of around thirty individual families, some static, most roaming the back roads of Gloucestershire and the Marches, this time of year working in the region's orchards and hop yards, where opportunities for mole catching were prime.

Reggie was tempted. When Porky had mentioned that he might take more, the memories of the last disastrous mole deal had put him off, but there was something that appealed to him about gathering up hundreds of moleksins from a tribe of travellers, and sending them to London to be converted into high fashion, which would feature in the pages of the ultra-glossies, like the one Lara wrote for.

Reggie felt a happy anticipation of the day's trade that lay ahead as they set off through the empty Sunday morning lanes for Ludlow.

From a small khaki webbing bag, he pulled a thermos flask. 'Rosi was determined to get up with me at sparrow-fart to make us a decent drop of coffee, so we'll have some before Muffin opens the Tippling Toad at eleven.'

He half filled two plastic mugs and stuck one in a circular holder in front of Emmet. 'So,' he went on, 'what have you got for the punters today?'

As they often did, they soon found themselves wrapped up in lively conversation about many things, from whether or not Emmet should buy from a dead farmer's widow a 1948 Alvis he'd found in a barn, buried beneath a tarpaulin and five tons of ancient hay, to when Reggie might have to head back to Florence for another batch of Sextons. But after ten minutes, Emmet had to slow down and stop when their way was blocked by a small police patrol car and, standing in front of it, holding up a quivering hand, was PC Paul Lank.

Once Emmet had turned off the engine and wound down the window, PC Lank walked up to the driver's side.

'Oh,' he said. 'It's you!'

'You always was pretty quick on the uptake,' Emmet agreed.

'We had a call that a suspicious vehicle was seen heading in this direction.'

'Suspicious? What way suspicious?'

PC Lank grimaced. 'Well, you know, out and about early, and very old, like, probably no tax or insurance.'

Emmet raised both eyebrows. 'Sounds like you're harassing me without cause, PC Plank.'

'No, I'm not. And where's your tax disc?'

Emmet turned to Reggie. 'Here, have a rummage in the glove box.'

Reggie opened the drop door in front of him and rummaged. Among the old petrol receipts, catalogues and failed betting slips he found a tax disc for the car. He passed it to Emmet who handed it out of the window to PC Plank.

The young policemen scrutinised it, took his cap off, scratched his head and sighed. 'It's up to date,' he said. 'But it should be where I can see it.'

'It is – it's in yer 'ands,' Emmet said.

PC Lank handed it back. 'Put it on the windscreen where it can be seen, or you'll get done.'

'Why should I, if I've paid for it?'

'Because.... because that's the law,' PC Lank tried to say firmly. 'And let me have a look at your licence.'

From his jacket, Emmet pulled out a grubby wallet – overstuffed with cards and chitties, from which he plucked a large folded sheet of paper and handed it to the policeman.

PC Lank opened the paper and read it. 'This is your gun licence.'

'Yeh, you said you wants to see my licence.'

'I meant your driving licence.'

Emmet shook his head. 'You can't see that.'

'Why not?' PC Plank asked, straightening his back to show his indignation.

'Because Charlie's ate it.'

'Where's Charlie, then?' PC Lank leaned down again to look through the window, where his eyes met Reggie's. Reggie was grinning broadly. 'That's Mr Finchley, not Charlie,' PC Lank said.

'No, but that is.' Emmet pointed a firm forefinger at the terrier trembling with frustration beneath Reggie's legs.

PC Lank acknowledged the dog, and stood up straight once more. Emmet continued to look at him without flinching, until the young copper turned and walked around the pick-up, pretending to do something useful while he tried to work out what he should do next. He stopped to rattle a light here and there, bent down to examine the tyres. Once he'd circumnavigated the vehicle, he stopped by Emmet's window again.

'Looks like Charlie's been busy; looks like he's chewed the tread off your rear offside tyre, too, and I'm going to have to book you for that, as well as your missing driver's licence.'

'You're supposed to give me time to bring any documents into the local nick.'

'I can fine you for the tyre, right here and now.'

'Before you do,' Emmet said, pulling his phone from his jacket, 'take a look at the snaps I've been takin' down by the river.' Holding on firmly to the phone, he selected a shot and held it so PC Lank could see it. 'I don't go in for this Tweeter business much, but my nephew, young Mickey – you know him – he's dead keen, and good at it, with loads of followers in the village.'

As PC Lank stared at the image, the blood drained from his face.

Emmet waited a good half a minute before he removed the instrument from the policeman's gaze, turned on the ignition, put the vehicle into gear and slowly moved off.

Emmet turned to Reggie with a quiet smile on his face. 'That'll keep him off my back for a while.'

Reggie was glad that turning up at the market in Emmet's pick-up was a much less flamboyant business than arriving in the Bentley had been. Together, they unloaded all Reggie's pictures and then began to stack Emmet's collection of ancient garden tools, woodworking implements and old agricultural machinery around their stall, mixed in with the paintings. When they'd finished they stood back to admire their pitch.

'That's much better,' Reggie said. 'It somehow makes the Sextons look more real, sitting amongst all that junk of yours.'

'You can call it junk, but there's plenty of punters for it – not just old blokes on nostalgia trips, but a lot of women who like the shabby look – they loves to put those things around on window sills and mantle shelves. I've sold pig troughs and old chaff cutters and wood hay rakes and all sorts to put inside the house.'

The church bell had not long struck half seven when Emmet started selling. Reggie was impressed. He asked Emmet what he had paid for some of things he'd sold.

'Nothin', mostly, or next to nothing.'

'Where does it come from, then?'

Emmet shrugged. 'All over. Often I finds it in outbuildings, and barns on farms where they've rung me to come and do their rats or moles, or to buy their coppice wood.'

'Do you buy from them?'

'Not much. They usually doesn't have the eye, or the knowledge and can't see no value in the old stuff – they think they'm useless objects which'll cost 'em to dump. They gives it to me, stead of a tip. That's why I go out and do the jobs – there's no one else would ever get to find it.'

Reggie nodded his approval. 'It's good, isn't it, and eco-whassit – all this stuff gettin' recycled, and finding new homes.'

'Yeh, and prob'ly it'll get handed down to the next generation who'll think it's worth summat because their mum and dad did. It's like stuff caught in the net by the Queensland salerooms; otherwise that goes off to fuel the woodburners, or piles up in the county landfills – and there ain't so many of those left now. They're desperate lookin' for holes to fill. If you ever finds yourself with a nice big hole, Reggie, to rent it to the council. I got one – a worked out ol' quarry, all overgrown, no one wanted. I bought it, and now I earns more for fillin' it with rubbish than they ever got for the stone!'

Reggie laughed. He loved the way Emmet sniffed out his deals, and pounced on them before the opposition even saw them.

Reggie was pouring himself a fresh cup of coffee from the still warm thermos flask, mentally thanking Rosi for her thoughtfulness and thinking what a lucky man he was to be wed to such a lovely, caring creature when he spotted two men making their way across the market in his direction. He wondered if they were coming to look at his pictures or Emmet's stuff. When they stopped in front of the pitch, their demeanour was determined and uncompromising. Experience had taught him that hardened dealers tended to use strong body language from the earliest stages of negotiation; he thought it likely that this time, they must have been tipped of by Porky, and he braced himself for a haggle.

The younger of the two men, muscular and dressed in a big T-shirt, shorts and trainers, opened the conversation. 'A lil' bird told us that you've got a few nice old pitchers.' Reggie took in the strong south-east London accent. 'Herrings, Stubbs, Reynolds..... Constables....' the man sniggered, '... if you'll excuse the dirty language.'

'Yeh,' Reggie nodded. 'Well, from their studios, like, of course.'

'Of course,' the old man growled as if he'd a sack load of scalp-ings in the back of his throat. 'Otherwise you'd be selling 'em in Suvverby's – not an effin' street market, wouldn't yer?'

Reggie was instinctively defensive. 'This isn't like a normal street market,' he protested.

'Nah, nah, but, know what I mean? Anyway that's not the point, if they're what we're after. What you got?'

Reggie turned and waved a hand at four of the Florence fakes he had hanging on a wire mesh at the back of the stand. 'These two Constables, a nice sort of early Turner, and this family portrait, thought to have been painted by in the studio of Sir Joshua Reynolds.'

'Yeh, more'n likely,' said the older man who was obviously in charge. He turned to the other. 'Vern, make him an offer for the two Constables. I like the idea of buying constables – won't be the first time, either, eh?'

'But one of them's crap,' Vern objected. 'It's got like little China-men all prancing about the village.'

The older man leaned into look. 'It don't matter. I think it's very charmin'.'

'Orright,' the younger one said. 'We'll give yer a grand apiece.'

Reggie laughed with as much heartiness as he could muster. 'Come on son, if you like thinking up jokes, you sell 'em to Jack Dee or someone who needs 'em. I'm getting around seven each for these.'

'No, you're not, you sold one last week for under five, and we wants two of 'em.'

Reggie realised then that these people must have had someone watching him, or maybe been in touch with the dealer who'd bought the 'Reynolds' and driven off in the Jaguar. So they weren't Porky's punters. 'If you want both pictures, I'll take ten grand.'

The older dealer had moved round to the side of Reggie's stand to get a closer look at the village painting. He peered hard at it as he ran his fingers around the deep contours of the elaborately moulded frame.

Vern responded with an offer of five thousand.

Reggie had just started shaking his head when Vern's boss looked at his watch, and turned to Reggie with an air of finality. 'Tell yer what, mate – seven grand, final offer, take it or leave it.'

Reggie wondered why they didn't seem ready to take their time haggling as most dealers would, upping their offers in small increments; they can't have been in much of a hurry; there weren't many places to go after this on a Sunday in Shropshire.

'Cash?' Reggie inquired.

'Wha' else.' Vern replied.

'Okay,' Reggie said. 'They're yours.'

As the two dealers carted the two pictures away, Reggie could hardly believe it had all happened so quickly. He turned to find Emmet, who had witnessed the whole transaction, grinning at him.

'D'you know who they were?' he asked. 'I've never seen 'em around the sales or anything. And I've never seen London dealers get reeled in so fast.'

Reggie shrugged a shoulder. 'I didn't have to do much reeling; it was like they'd made up their mind they could shift those pictures, and what they could give for 'em – and that was that.' From a stack leaning against the front of the stand, Reggie picked up two more paintings to fill the space left by his latest sale.

'I don't know how you've done it, but somehow, you've cracked this picture malarkey,' Emmet conceded, shaking his head in wonder.

'For one thing,' Reggie said, 'these pictures are quality'

'Apart from them frolicking Chinese tourists.'

'Maybe they looked like that in Essex where Constable worked.'

'What I seen on the telly on that *Only Way is Essex*, the women there are mostly orange with gigantic breasts,' Emmet chortled. 'Those weren't.'

'Whatever you say, these pictures are good for what they are, and at the prices I'm asking. And I didn't go all the way to Florence to bring them back so I could sit gawping at them in my drawing room at the Towers.'

Discreetly, Reggie faced away from his stall, under the cover of a tarpaulin draped across the back, and pulled from a pocket of his tweed jacket the bundle of notes he'd just been handed by his buyers. 'I hope these are all kosher,' he said, flicking his thumb over the end of the wedge of used fifties. 'I tell you what, Emmet, I'd a pretty good idea I could shift these Sextons, from when I first saw 'em, but to be honest, I never thought I'd get rid of 'em quite so fast or so easy.'

'You're right there.' The traveller shook his dark, handsome head in puzzlement. 'You've definitely pulled it off, though I can't see for the life of me what's so special about 'em.'

'Maybe, I just got the eye,' Reggie said, though privately he didn't think his was any better than Emmet's.

Reggie was standing behind his pitch, facing away from the public, when a gruff female voice reached him.

''Morning, Mr Finchley. I'd heard you got some lovely pictures.'

He turned to find standing on the far side of his stall Maggie Cadwallader, a thickset, no-nonsense sort of a woman, wearing a battered old olive Barbour. She was about sixty, and the wife of a prominent local farmer.

'Mrs Cadwallader, how are you?' he greeted her warily, conscious of her fearsome reputation for driving a hard bargain. 'Who did you hear that from?'

'Lady Wynyates told me, when she was tellin' me about that awful burglary they had. She was very unhappy they took the painting.'

Reggie had been struck by how un-sad Cecilia had been about it, but he let it go. 'It was a fine picture, that's for sure, though we can't say for certain that it came from the studio of the Senior Herring,' he added, sounding as learned as he could, and pleased not to have uttered an untruth.

'I like that one of the young fella in the high wheel gig.'

'Very handsome,' Reggie agreed. 'A vehicle like that was like the E-type of its day.'

Church-Pugh

Mrs Cadwallader nodded. 'Yes, I suppose it was really. They say the young bucks would drive along the turnpikes like maniacs, rather as they do today. How much are you asking for it?'

Reggie primed his response with an apologetic grimace and a lift of the shoulder. 'I'm afraid that one's got to be six thousand,' he said, as if he wished it didn't.

'Goodness – a lot more than Cecilia paid for hers.'

Inwardly, Reggie cursed Cecilia's big mouth. 'This is a bit superior to the one she had, and with a much better frame; look at the depth and figuring of the moulding – isn't it superb? In fact, the frame alone's probably worth a monkey. But Gwendoline, for you, I'll do it for five thousand.'

After a short pause, Mrs Cadwallader leaned across the table. 'Let me have a closer look,' she said, and squinted hard at the painting.

Reggie held his breath, hoping she wouldn't spot some anachronism or obvious flaws in the painting. After a good long look, intended, Reggie felt sure, to weaken his resistance, Mrs Cadwallader straightened herself and stood back.

'I tell you what, Reggie. If you can drop it round this evening – after you've packed everything up, like, I'll have a cheque for four thousand pounds waiting for you.'

Reggie didn't answer at once. He took a long, deep breath. The woman had just slashed his price by a third, and she was still looking him straight in the eye.

He sighed – not too heavily. 'You're a hard woman, Maggie, but all right; four thousand.'

Mrs Cadwallader beamed back at him and thrust a bony hand at him. 'And you promise you won't go and sell it anyone else if you're offered more?'

'You have the word of a Finchley ffinch-Leigh on it,' Reggie agreed, taking her hand and shaking it.

'Bloody 'ell!' Emmet muttered as Reggie's customer walked away. 'She's hard as nails, that one.'

'Would you have sold it to her?' Reggie asked.

'No.' Emmet shook his head. 'Well, that's to say, I'd have made her work harder for it, and maybe got her up a bit.'

'I suppose you're right. But I thought – what the hell, life's too short; I still double my money on it.'

'But Reggie, it only needed five minutes more pitching and you'd have got her back up to maybe four and a quarter. That's five minutes to earn an extra two hundred a fifty – and that works out at three grand an hour – and how often d'you get the chance to earn like that?'

'Gordon Bennet, Emmet! Have you turned into a chartered bleedin' accountant, or what?'

'It's what I says to m'self when I'm buying a big parcel of summat – ten more minutes spent on the haggle – and you might get another monkey off. There's not many proper jobs as pays three grand an hour, is there.'

'Yeh, but I know what she's like, and I didn't reckon she'd budge an inch – and when you've got a deal on the table that stacks up, grab it while it's there. I'm not surprised she wants some new pictures; I went to her place once and there were paintings everywhere, mostly ones she's painted herself.'

Reggie had become aware that he'd momentarily lost Emmet's attention. His friend had seen someone over his shoulder.

'The bloke what bought off you last week is coming over – and he looks in a hurry – and not too happy.'

Reggie turned around slowly, and found himself face to face with the greasy-haired individual who'd bought Tight-arsed Georgian Lady and Anorexic Whippet from him.

'Hello again,' Reggie greeted him affably.

'Listen mate,' the new arrival grunted and grasped Reggie's arm behind the elbow. 'Let's go round the back where no one's earwiggin'.' He led Reggie through the gap between two stands, and away from them. 'Did you just sell that picture of the geezer on the cart to that farmer's missus?'

Reggie shook his arm free of the man's grip. 'What's that to do with you?'

'I'll tell you what it's got to do with me, me and two of my mates who are on their way here right now, we're buying the rest of these paintings off you. How many have you got?'

Reggie made a quick mental calculation. 'Sixteen, in all.'

The man shook his head. 'Are you sure? Does that include matey on the cart?'Reggie drew himself up. He hated fisticuffs, but there came a time when you had to make a stand. 'Listen chum, that one's sold, so it's not for sale anymore. But if you like these pictures so much, believe me, I'll be getting more.'

'We want these ones, orright?'

As he hissed the words, another man appeared between the market stalls. The newcomer was in his late forties, tall, slender and dressed in a light beige double-breasted suit, a regimental tie and pristine Panama hat – a toff, Reggie thought, like a character from Wodehouse.

The man spoke as he approached. 'All right, Michael. There's no need to badger Mr ffinch-Leigh like that.'

A third individual, closer in form to the first lank-haired dealer, had followed the man in the Panama hat, who turned to him. 'You and Michael go and lose yourselves for ten minutes – all right?'

The man called Michael slunk away and walked off through the market with his colleague. Reggie looked at the tall man standing beside him.

'Listen, I'm really sorry about that,' the man said in almost music-hall upper-crust tones. 'These chaps mean well, of course, but let's face it, they lack polish.' He held out a well-scrubbed hand. 'My name's Rupert Church-Pugh.'

Reggie wondered if it was, and, inclined to think so, took the hand. 'Reginald ffinch-Leigh,' he said. 'But you seem to know that.'

Rupert nodded. 'I admit that I do. In my game, I have to make sure of whom I'm dealing with.'

'What is your game?' Reggie inquired.

The man seemed to put his shoulders back to announce his role. 'I am, in fact, Head of Procurement for the Trucial Kingdom of Al Hambra – specifically for the Royal Collection.'

Reggie took half a step back and waggled his head doubtfully. 'What? Are you having a laugh?'

Rupert drew himself up so sharply he almost fell over backwards. 'I never have a laugh.'

Reggie chuckled. 'I bet you don't, but I'm thinking the Royal Collection in Al Wossit has a few bob to spend. What are they doing sending people up from London to buy fake pictures in a Shropshire flea market?'

'I buy what I am instructed to buy. I can tell you, informally, that the royal family are constructing a small collection of English country houses, based on a number of classic English mansions of several periods which they intend to use as guest residences. And they want them furnished appropriately. At the same time, they do not consider it prudent to put pictures on the wall that might be worth millions of pounds. My royal clients may be fabulously rich, but they're not bloody idiots.'

An unexpected wave of relief swept gently through Reggie. It suddenly came home to him how agitated he'd been over the sale of his Sextons. Of course, he was chuffed that they'd been going so fast but, like Emmet, he couldn't understand why. Rupert's explanation made complete sense, especially when he thought of all the other bizarre Arab spending stories he'd heard over the years since the oil billionaires had arrived in London to make Mayfair their shopping mall.

'Ah,' he said. 'I can see why what I'm selling makes sense – good enough to fool 99.9% of the punters, but with – comparatively speaking – diddly squat downside if they get nicked.'

Church-Pugh allowed himself a tight-lipped grimace, which Reggie took as a smile of agreement. 'Precisely so. But the thing is Mr ffinch-Leigh, my employers do not like to be messed around. It's probably a little disloyal of me to say so, but people as rich as this are, frankly, somewhat spoilt and don't quite view obstacles as we do. I informed them of this batch of pictures, and they have demanded that I procure all of them. The one you sold earlier this morning – has it been paid for?'

'Not exactly.'

'You mean, 'No'?'

'No, that's right. Yes.'

'You mean you have been paid?'

'No, I mean I haven't.'

'Excellent,' Church-Pugh beamed this time. 'Then you're under no obligation to deliver; no contract exists.'

'Oh yes it does, even if it's only oral,' Reggie asserted. 'I know a bit about the Sale of Goods Act. Besides, I gave her my word I wouldn't sell it to anyone else, or take a better offer – and my word is worth something round here.'

'Nevertheless, I'm sure we can make you a better offer, and it's up to you to wriggle out of whatever commitment you think you've made as best you can.' Church-Pugh's cold grey eyes burned into Reggie's like a pair of lasers.

Reggie winced and looked away. 'There's no need get greedy about it,' he gulped. 'I'll be bringing in more of the same – well, similar – I told your sidekick. I've got a good reliable source, and I'll let you know as soon as they're here.'

'If they're as good as the ones you have now, we'll want them too. But right now, we want all that you've got – bar none!' He seemed to turn up the laser strength. 'Is that clear?' he asked frostily.

It was one of Reggie's more practical qualities that he knew when he was beaten. Bollocks to Mrs Cadwallader, he thought.

'Yeh, sure,' he said.

'Right, here's what we'll do,' Church-Pugh said, as if he was giving a military briefing. 'I don't wish to complete the transaction here in an open market. Nor do I want to be seen arriving at your private residence. My colleagues and I will meet you later, to give you time to finish your day's trading here in the normal way. I'll let you know when and where, and you bring all the paintings with you in your Bentley. Is that acceptable?'

Reggie tried to stop himself from shaking. A lot of thoughts were racing through his mind, and some of them were uncomfortable. They were talking about a deal worth about £70,000 and with deals that size, people were often prepared to take risks – like not paying the supplier. 'Listen, I'm not sure I'm happy about turning up with a pile of stock worth the thick end of seventy grand.'

'Sixty-five, Mr ffinch-Leigh; we'll pay you sixty-five. A very reasonable offer for a bulk purchase like this. I've no doubt that you expected to take months to shift them all.'

'I'm still not 'appy.....'Reggie started.

'Mr ffinch-Leigh, your unhappiness, temporary as it will be, is of no interest to us. Just keep your mobile on and we'll tell you where to bring the stuff. We'll give you plenty of time; we won't meet you before four o'clock, though God knows what I'm going to find to keep those two gorillas happy for a few hours.'

'There's a nice bit of fishing down on the Teme,' Reggie suggested.

Church-Pugh shook his head. 'I don't think so. Just be there, and we'll have your money for you. And make sure you have the Regency Buck in the High-Wheel Gig.'

He spun round on his heel and marched off as if he were changing the Guard at Buckingham Palace.

Reggie watched him go with a thumping heart before walking back to his pitch.

Emmet was watching him with a worried look. 'You all right, Reg? You look like you seen a ghost – and I don't mean Saucy Sue in a sheet, neither.'

'What's just happened is a bloody sight weirder than any ghost you could conjur up. I've just agreed with that geezer to let him have all the rest of my pictures – the Sextons, not the crap – for sixty-five grand.'

'Cor, bloody hell Reg. What's going on?'

'I'll tell you....' Reggie related the deal he'd been offered as verbatim as he could remember, including a good reproduction of Church-Pugh's guard's officer voice.

At the end of it, Emmet's main reaction, like Reggie's, was relief. 'D'you think that was really the bloke's name – Church-Pugh?'

'No one would make up such a dopey name, would they?

'You mean, like ffinch-Leigh?' Emmet grinned. 'But I agree with you – what he said explains it, mostly. But how did they know you had these pictures?'

'I reckon thay must have heard about them from one of Porky's mates in London. He said he told a lot of people, though as far as I know, none of them came up.'

'But what about the other ones you've sold – Cecilia, Miss

Wheeler-Smith, and Chatternerve.'

'He didn't mention them; he only seemed bothered about the one Mrs Cadwallader wanted.'

'What are you going to do about her then?'

'God knows – tell her your dog ate it, like your driving licence,' Reggie laughed. 'Anyway, I may as well pack up now. I'll take my stuff off and leave you on your own.'

'Just take your fakes. I may shift a few of these other ones for you. You should have it like business as usual; you don't want people asking questions.'

'I haven't got my car, have I? I'm not going to leave 'em in your pick-up. Will you be OK if we just tuck 'em out of sight under the table? I'm going off to Muffin Magee's; I think I've earned a drink.'

'Don't overdo it Reggie!'

No one paid much attention as Emmet and Reggie took down the sold Sextons and stacked them safely beneath the stall table. Emmet told Reggie he'd be fine on his own, and Reggie strolled away nonchalantly, although he felt like he was walking on the clouds. He pinched himself once or twice – feeling ridiculous, because he never knew people really did that – just to convince himself that the deal had happened.

There was the risk that it could yet go wrong if there were any shenanigans over payment, but Reggie was an optimist; Church-Pugh wouldn't have bothered to knock ten grand off the price if he wasn't planning on paying him, and it looked like he would want to buy from the next batch that Reggie was already planning to get from Florence. As he walked away from the Castle Square towards the Tippling Toad, he pulled his mobile phone from his pocket and rang Mortimer Towers.

'Rosi? Listen my rosebud, ring Tommy's Taxis and get him to bring you to the Toad; I'll have a bottle of Muffin's best pop open and ready for you.'

'Reggie,' his wife responded suspiciously. 'Why you are going drinking when you have the stall?'

'Emmet's minding the stall, 'cos I've...' Reggie took a quick look around the Sunday punters milling through the medieval lanes towards the market; he dropped his voice to a dramatic husk, '...I've sold all the Sextons, every single one of them!'

'O MY GOD,' Rosi shrieked over the phone. 'FanTAStic! Who to?'

'I'll tell you later; but it's all kosher. You get on the dog and bone to Tommy, and I'll see you in a while.'

Muffin Magee's tiny bar was crammed with some of the noisiest people in Ludlow – not raucous punters like the clientele of the Purple Pig around the corner where, on a Saturday night, men with large torsos, tight black suits and small bald heads stood guard on the door as the punters spilled into the quiet, elegant old street to smoke, shout, vomit and throw things through shop windows. In the Toad, the exuberance was less unruly and more erudite, but the crush greater. Reggie, using his charm and natural bulk, quickly squeezed his way to the bar.

'Mornin', Muffin,' he greeted the laconic, bearded proprietor.

'Reggie. How're you doing?'

'Give us half a dozen of your fattest oysters and a bottle of your best champagne.'

'What's going on Reggie? Did Millwall just win the FA Cup?'

'Muffin! You know I'm a Chelsea supporter. But it's nothing to do with footie. For a change, one of my deals has worked out even better than I thought, and you know what a flaming optimist I am.'

'I'm glad to hear it, if it means you're going to spend more money in here instead of at the Castle Inn.'

'Of course; you know you're my favourite landlord now, despite your miserable boat race and grumpy attitude. And my wife is your greatest fan – in fact she's on her way as we speak.'

'Your wife? I thought the lovely Rosita was your daughter.'

'Oh yeh? Listen, moostash, if you still look like this when you're my age...' Reggie passed a hand over his suntanned visage '...you'll be a lucky man.'

By the time his wife arrived at the Toad, Reggie had found a corner of a table where he could balance an ice-bucket containing a bottle of Pol Roger next to his plate of oysters. Rosi came in, to be greeted effusively by most of the customers in the bar, where she was always popular.

As quietly as he could, despite the effects of the Pol Roger, Reggie told her about the Royal Family of Al Hambra wanting all his Sextons, and why, and how they would probably take several more loads of them.

'That is *amazing*,' she cooed happily. She knew how much his lack of money and resulting dependence on her had been weighing on the man she loved, and now that he'd found a way out, she was happy for him. 'Are you sure you can trust this man – what his name?'

'Church-Pugh.'

'Like a chair in a church?'

'Spelled differently. I think I can trust him.' Reggie hefted a shoulder. 'It's such a weird story, I can't see why he would make it up.'

'What type of hombre is he?'

'Your standard English army officer – tidy, tight-arsed and organised. He's got hard, icy blue eyes – like those officers from the SAS in Hereford who come up shooting with Perry Rokesay – in fact I wouldn't be a bit surprised if he was one of them. The squaddies call them 'Ruperts' and that's just what he is.'

'But now he is buying pictures and stuff for Arabs' houses?'

'I should think the wonga's right – and I guess he does other, trickier jobs for them. Before he came, I sold a nice picture of a flash young bloke driving a yellow gig to Maggie Cadwallader – you know, Harry's missus – but she hadn't taken it yet, or paid for it. He said he wanted that one too; I told him I'd given my word I'd keep it for her, and he got pretty sharp.'

'Why he cares?' Rosi interrupted indignantly.

'Search me, my angel, but he said I'd just have to tell her she can't have it.'

'Did you do that?'

'Not yet, but I'll have to; he meant it, and I wouldn't want to get on his wrong side, that's for sure.'

'You be careful, Reggie.'

Tommy the Taxi was waiting in his rust-pocked Rover outside the Tippling Toad, with his right hand dangling from the driver's window, clutching a cigarette between nicotine-orange fingers, tapping ash onto the road.

'For gawd's sake, chuck that away!' Reggie moaned as he and Rosita clambered into the back of the vehicle. He was feeling noticeably queasy from a combination of too much champagne, twelve oysters gulped down in swift succesion, and the excitement of the deal he'd agreed, all blended in his guts with the fear that this deal could well foul up before it was completed. He had summoned Tommy to collect them both from the bar, call at the flea market pitch, which Emmet was still happily manning, pick up the five paintings he'd brought into Ludlow that morning, and take them back to Mortimer Towers.

At home, he and Rosita piled the rest of the Florence fakes into the Bentley and he set off, apprehensive and on his own, to tackle Mrs Cadwallader.

Maggie Cadwallader lived in a handsome Georgian farmhouse about five miles from Ludlow. Reggie swept through the gates and pulled up with a flourish outside the classically porticoed front door.

He'd barely touched the worn brass bell pull when the door was opened by Harry Cadwallader, Maggie's much-nagged husband. He seemed to have been expecting Reggie, and, judging from the haunted look in his eyes, he wasn't looking forward to it – which made two of them.

'Hello Reggie,' he said, warmly enough. 'I dare say you've come with the picture Maggie wanted?'

Something in his manner encouraged Reggie to hold back from admitting to his position straight away.

'That's right,'Arry,' he agreed cheerfully, 'and to collect payment,' he added, sensing that this might be the reason for Harry's discomfort.

'Yes... yes, of course. I'm afraid Maggie had to go out.' The man looked at him balefully. 'She asked me to give you this when you came.' He handed Reggie a small, folded piece of paper.

Reggie could see it was a cheque and took it with his heart pounding like an Ibiza disco.

He unfolded it, looked at it, and immediately wanted to warble with relief. It was made out for three and a half thousand pounds.

He tried to straighten his features before he lifted his head to look at Harry. He was sure there still must have been signs of the relief he felt. 'Oh dear,' he said. 'It must have slipped her mind, but we agreed on four thousand quid for it.'

Harry winced. He knew that. 'Will that be all right, though?' he asked in a quiet, sheepish voice.

'Unfortunately, I can't sell it for that.' Reggie tilted his head to one side and heaved a regretful shoulder. He refolded the cheque and handed it back. 'But tell Maggie I may have it up at the flea market next weekend, if I haven't sold it by then.'

Anxious to avoid any discussion about other options, he held out his hand to Harry, who took it unenthusiastically. 'Tootle pip, then,' Reggie said, and almost skipped back to the car.

He drove away feeling that Maggie Cadwallader's negotiating techniques were those of the lowest kind of horse-coper and must have become a habit over years of buying and selling horses – a trade, as he had discovered to his cost, with very little moral base to it. At least he hadn't been forced to go back on his own word, and his reputation, built up over five years of more or less straight dealing since he'd come to live in the Marches, was still in good shape.

As he drove away from the house between the high hedges of a narrow lane, his mobile phoned bleeped to tell him he had just received a text message. He picked up the phone from the passenger seat and, taking his eyes of the road for a few seconds, read what was on the screen: 16.00 hrs. old rail head. Titterstone Clee.

Reggie glanced at the handsome old Rolex which had so far escaped the fate of many of his other prized possessions. It was five to four. He cursed himself for his inherently useless time-keeping; he'd sat around in Muffin's with Rosi for far too long and wasted time chatting to Emmet when he'd been to pick up his stock from their market stall.

When he looked up again at the road in front of him, he thumped his right foot on the brake pedal almost before he realised he was just inches from ramming the Bentley's stately old radiator grill into a rusty old grass topper attached to the back of an old grey Fergie tractor.

When he was sure he hadn't made contact, he thumped the horn button set in the boss of the steering wheel.

The tractor's driver showed no sign of having heard. He was a rotund little man beneath a small green canopy, bouncing around on a well sprung seat like a ping-pong ball on a fountain, with a pair of heavyweight ear-phones rammed firmly over his ears.

Reggie gave another, longer blast on his horn. He guessed the driver must have been playing Ozzy Osborne full blast as he carried on bouncing with what looked like gleeful abandon.

Reggie was becoming apoplectic. He didn't have a chance of getting to the rendezvous with Church-Pugh in less than twenty minutes – at best.

The man was waiting up there, Reggie prayed, with £65k to give to him – £65k that would see him off the hook once and for all, after the penury, ducking and diving of the last twelve months, and be the start of what should be a steady series of lucrative deals – simple and, above all, straight.

But Reggie was well aware that his punter wasn't the kind of man who would tolerate it if he didn't show up on time; he might even get leery and think he wasn't coming and bugger off, just to show him who was in charge.

Fuming with frustration, Reggie followed the tractor and its bouncing driver for ten minutes, with his hand on the horn, and yelling until his tanned features had turned the colour of an Italian *pomodoro*.

Abruptly the old tractor and its antique attachment swung sharply into a field gate and were immediately out of sight. With relief, Reggie kicked the accelerator, to suddenly find himself heading at fifty miles an hour on a single track lane towards a female pedestrian heading straight for him.

For a second time, he jumped on the brake pedal, just in time to see that it was Maggie Cadwallader. Reggie looked in his driving mirror and gave her a wave over his shoulder. She was looking very peeved by now; he guessed she had thought he would have taken a lot longer before yielding up the painting at the heavily discounted price she was offering.

'Bollocks to you, Mrs Cadwallader,' he said to himself again and soon turned on to the main road that would take him up to his rendezvous on the Titterstone Clee Hill, while he tried to work out how to get to what Rupert had called the Rail Head.

Since Reggie had first seen the great basalt tor, like a monstrous wedge of cheddar lying on its side, he'd been struck by its iconic shape and mythical qualities as it towered over Ludlow from seventeen hundred and fifty feet. But he'd never driven up to the point near the summit which had been gouged out, as if by a cheese-loving giant, through centuries of mineral plunder and where a narrow gauge railway had once terminated.

When he saw a sign indicating 'Summit' pointing to a turning, he took a chance and swung into it, hammering up the narrow, rutted lane, past a few rows of old miners' cottages, as high as the road went, ending at plateau just below the summit.

He drove onto it and looked around at the immediate landscape – a harsh piece of rocky ground that looked like the setting for a shootout in a Spaghetti Western. Emmet had told him it was a popular spot for youths, stoned on cider or ganja, to drive up and watch the sun rise over the Worcestershire hills in the early hours of a summer dawn.

At four o'clock on a Sunday afternoon, it was empty apart from a highly polished black Mercedes G-Wagen.

Reggie nodded to himself; that was just the kind of vehicle Church-Pugh would drive. As he drove the Bentley slowly towards it, the passenger door of the G-Wagen swung open and Rupert Church-Pugh stepped down. He was still wearing his beige cotton suit, buttoned and somehow uncreased, with a square, soft brown leather bag dangling from his left shoulder. As he began to walk towards Reggie's car, his two henchmen jumped out and went round to open the back of the big boxy vehicle

Reggie brought his car to a halt, and turned off the engine. He lowered the driver's window as Rupert strode briskly towards him.

'Mr ffinch-Leigh, I'm so glad you're here. You have all your remaining paintings?'

'Like I said, I've got everything I had left from my last delivery.'

'From Italy?'

Reggie fielded the question without missing a beat. 'Italy?' He looked puzzled. 'No mate, Eastern Europe.'

Church-Pugh didn't react. 'What about the young buck driving the yellow gig?'

'Yes, yes; he's here.'

'I'm delighted to hear it; I know my employers will be pleased with that one. Arabs, as I'm sure you know, are very keen on equestrian content. Now shall we get them all out and check them?'

When they were all propped up against the side of the car, Reggie observed with some pride the display of pictures he was selling to Church-Pugh. He was getting a nice collection of what would easily pass for good 18th century English art, and was well worth the money.

'And that's all you had apart from seven others you've sold already?'

Reggie shook his head, wondering why these people were so adamant about having everything. 'Yes, of course – like I told you, and I've got a lot more coming.'

'Good. Make sure you give us first refusal.'

'As long as you pay the right money...'

'...with a discount for bulk, don't forget,' Church-Pugh added coldly. He turned and looked over his shoulder. 'OK, men, start loading them up.'

'Hang on.' Reggie kept any nervousness from his voice. 'I'll need the money before you load 'em.'

As he was speaking, a small group of walkers appeared from the other side of the hill. They were wearing turquoise and purple anoraks and each carried a pair of black Kevlar walking sticks.

Church-Pugh saw them too. 'Shit!' he snapped. 'What the hell are those people doing? And that kit of theirs is an affront to nature and

166

good taste!'

Reggie laughed; his punter was looking very irritated.

'I'm not going to be seen handing over a large amount of cash with half a dozen witnesses,' Church-Pugh said. 'We'll wait until they're gone. Have you got something you can cover this lot with before they see them?'

Reggie didn't mind if the transaction was witnessed, but he took a large blanket from the car-boot and dropped it over the stack of pictures. 'I thought you were going to pick a place where we wouldn't be seen' he said.

'I left someone down the road to stop any cars coming up; I wasn't expecting a horde of blasted ramblers!'

The walkers, a hundred yards away and unaware of the annoyance they were causing, were drinking from plastic water bottles and consulting the maps in clear plastic holders hanging round their necks.

'I don't mind waiting,' Reggie said with a nonchalant gesture. 'Just as long as I've checked the money before you take the pictures.'

'Mr ffinch-Leigh,' Church-Pugh drew back his shoulders and pursed his lips. 'Do I look like a man who'd try to duck out of paying, like a common criminal?'

'Not at all, but I learned a very long time ago never to trust appearances.'

Church-Pugh almost grinned. 'I intend to do a lot more business with you in the future.'

'Good,' Reggie said, refusing to sound impressed. 'Let's start off the way I mean us to carry on, then.'

The walkers started preparing to move off. Church-Pugh got twitchy when one of them put a camera to his eyes and appeared to be aiming it directly where they stood by Reggie's car.

'Relax,' Reggie said. 'He'll be photographing the view of the Black Mountains behind us.'

A few moments later, the walkers were strung out on the path leading up to the summit. When the last of them had disappeared over the top, without coming any closer to where Reggie and his customer stood, Church-Pugh unbuckled his leather bag. From it he pulled two well-stuffed A4 envelopes. 'Count it inside your car,' he said. 'When you're happy, we'll take the merchandise.'

A little more than five minutes later, Reggie watched the G-Wagen roll off the rocky plateau and head down the lane on the side of the hill.

Standing outside his car, he sighed with relief and looked down on Ludlow, seeing it differently from this vantage point. It seemed extraordinary to him that in the market place down there, in the middle of the ancient town, that morning he'd done the best bit of trade he'd done in years, despite the fact that only a few months before, he'd been completely boracic.

It just went to show, he thought, if you didn't give up looking for the deals, you were bound to find something sooner or later. But, he admitted to himself, this one had happened a whole lot quicker and better than he could have dreamed. He wondered how long he would be able to rely on that definitely dodgy dealer, Ficuzza, to go on supplying him – it would be strange if the Italian didn't know how easily his pictures sold in England. And what worried him was that there didn't seem to be anyone else importing these wonderful, high quality Sexton Blakes.

He walked forward and stood a little closer to the edge, where the ground dropped away to the west over sheep pasture and rocky outcrops. If anyone had told him ten years ago that he could come to live in this beautiful, sleepy back-of-nowhere place, and do deals like this, he'd have laughed at them. With a smile, he patted the bulges in his jacket pockets, and walked back to the Bentley.

Chapter Ten

Reggie let himself into Mortimer Towers and stood for moment in the dark Gothic hall, trying to work out what was going on in the kitchen towards the front of the house.

He could hear that his wife was angry and frustrated.

'You bloody idiot thing,' she was shouting. 'Why do you always do this to me? Why you say 'do this', and I do it, and then you say 'you must go back'.'

There was a pause. Reggie was intrigued. He waited for an answer from whoever was being so volubly harangued by his wife.

After a few moments a long anguished howl rent the air. 'Aaagh! Bloody bollocks! Why you do this to me?'

Reggie shook his head in bewilderment. It was his wife again.

He took a deep breath and walked into the kitchen, ready to make the peace between his wife and whoever she was rowing with.

Once in the big open space of gleaming white equipment and bat-tered old rustic artefacts, he stppped and looked around. The only person in the room was Rosita. She was sitting at the kitchen table, a vast scrub-top item of which she was very proud, staring at her lap-top.

'For gawd's sake,' Reggie sighed. 'I've told you before – it can't hear you; it's a machine.'

Rosita looked up. 'I know that,' she scathed. 'But it makes me feel better to yell at it, thassall.' As always, she forgot her problems the next moment and opened her eyes wider. 'How you get on?'

He could tell from the look in her dark expressive features that she'd been worrying about the deal – not about the money, but about him, because she knew what it meant to his own self-esteem.

He gave her a big slow smile.

She leaped to her feet and rushed around the table to put her arms round him and stood on tiptoes to cover his face with kisses. 'Oh Reggie!' she shrieked. 'You are a clever man, and a lovely man. I know you never give up, and though I think maybe these pictures, they stink a little, you have sold them all! So brilliant.'

Reggie wrapped his arms around his wife and hugged her back. 'I

169

have, and I've got all the sponduliks. It's a helluva deal, but...'

'But...? But what Reggie?' Rosita demanded to know what could be blighting this great moment. 'What are you think?'

Reggie sighed. 'I've been thinking as I drove back here, if I can pull off a deal like this, stuck out here in the sticks, why isn't anyone else doing it down in London?'

'Reggie, for Gossake! There just isn't – who cares? Why you so paranoy? You go to Florence, you find the studio, you choose the pictures and then bring them home, you tell Porky to put the word, you set up the market stall – this is what you done – is a lot! You done great! Stop being so misery-guts when you just pull on such fantastic deal. Anyhow, we are asked to dinner tonight by Ted and Belinda, so we can go celebrate.'

'Suits me,' Reggie said with genuine pleasure; he liked Ted Buckton and his wife, who had been the first people to welcome him and Rosita when they came to live at Mortimer Towers, and Ted had helped Reggie when he'd got into trouble on his very first, ham-fisted deal over a horse that wasn't all it was supposed to be.

The sun had dropped behind the wooded Welsh hills in the west, when they arrived at Ted and Belinda's farmhouse. In the small, warm red dining room they sat down to a vension casserole Belinda had made. Rosita rejected it on the grounds, she said, that it felt like eating Bambi, but as Reggie tucked in, Ted asked him how the pictures were doing.

Reggie found he was reluctant to boast. 'I sold a few to some locals – Cecilia Wynyates bought one off my pitch in the market last week. Unfortunately, she's already had it nicked.'

'She told me,' Belinda said. 'That seems a bit odd, so soon afterwards.'

Ted chuckled. 'I wouldn't be surprised if it was an insurance job.'

Rosita was shocked. 'Thass ridicoolous!' she gasped. 'Cecilia would never do that!'

'No, she wouldn't,' Reggie agreed. 'It must have been because it was such a beautiful picture and someone who saw her buying it from me decided they wanted it. Anyway, then Miss Whassaname-

Smith came and haggled me down to the bare bones for another one she wanted; strange thing is – she was burgled too, but whoever did her didn't fancy the picture and they never took it. Then last Sunday Chatternerve comes over to the Towers for a bit of a nosebag, and when he see Huffers trying to buy a couple, of course, he has to overbid him for them – just to show he could – that's the night he bought all that bloody wine off me.'

'I heard about that 1966 Burgundy – which you sold before you ever gave me a taste of it. Huffers said it was terrific.'

Reggie didn't have the energy to explain that what Huffers had drunk was only the moderately good stuff Reggie had bought to bait the trap.

'Sorry,' Reggie said with real regret. 'You'd have loved it. But, hey, don't worry! I should be getting some more.'

'If your French lady friend doesn't sell to someone else,' Rosita interjected cynically.

'Course she won't; she thought she was bloody lucky to find a mug who'd take it!' Reggie laughed, willingly sidetracked into describing how he and Porky had visited Chateau Harcort and Reggie had been sold a job lot of the chateau's wine, which its proprietor thought had gone well past its drink-by date.

By the time they left, Reggie still hadn't told Ted how he had shifted every single one of his remaining Florence fakes that afternoon, to be taken off to dress the walls of a series of bogus English country houses being built in a Middle East kingdom.

Somehow, he felt, it sounded so unbelievable, he didn't think Ted would be convinced.

Rosita had noticed Reggie's unusual reticence, and remarked on it on the way home.

'Reggie, is good that maybe you learning how to be discretion. Much better not to tell everyone your business.'

Reggie snorted a cynical laugh. 'It's such a bloody weird story, I found I didn't want to tell it, even with sixty-five grand in grubby notes to prove it.'

Reggie and Rosita awoke next morning to hear a strong wind hurling the rain wildly at the panes of their bedroom window. Reggie heaved himself out of bed to open the curtains, and found a sky the colour and texture of cold porridge obscuring the view of the hills he loved.

His mood, he found, seemed to match the weather. He didn't know why, but he, too, was enveloped in a gloom – and this despite the fact that his only chore that day was to think of somewhere to hide the big stash of cash that had recently come into his possession.

Later, in the kitchen with a large mug of caffe latte Rosita had made for him, he felt no improvement. Rosita saw, but was unsympathetic.

'What the hell is wrong with you?' she demanded. 'After all the crappolata you been through with your stoopid interweb inves'men' losing millions of quids, at las' you do great deal and now you like miserable old codger.'

'I'm sorry, my little Jersey Royal, I don't want to be a downer on you. Maybe it's a sort of reaction; maybe I'm feeling bad because I think I didn't deserve to recover so easily.'

'My God, Reggie you sound like my Catholic grandmother in Bogota! She so holy she think she always in mortal sin.'

'For Gawd's sake, Rosi, no more religious stuff or you'll really do my head in. I'll get over it.' He stood and walked to the window. 'Good, it's stopped raining, I can see the hills and there's a big chunk of blue sky winging in over the top of them. Where's Teresa? I could do with a walk.'

'I put her out to do her business.'

'Right.' Reggie picked up the dog's lead from the dresser and walked along the back corridor, into the stable yard and shut the door behind him.

Thirty seconds later, he was back in the kitchen, carrying Teresa, closely followed by another terrier.

'Reggie, what is that?'

'He was outside in the yard with Terry, at least I presume he must be a 'he', from the interest he was showing in her rear end. And he looks familiar.'

'Have a look the dog tag,' Rosita demanded

'It's okay, I remember whose it is, now; he was a contestant in the terrier race at the village shindig.'

Whe Reggie and Rosita had hosted what the village called a 'Pageant' in their grounds in the summer, a highlight had been the terrier racing, over which Reggie had presided as commentator. This had been followed by Lady Wynyates startling appearance as Queen Boadicea leading a mounted parade of Ancient British warriors across the lawn. This event had descended into spectacular chaos and carnage from a dispute which had started during the terrier races, leading to a war of attrition erupting under the nose of the horse being driven by Lady Wynyates in her 'chariot' – a rotten old dog-cart which Reggie had sold her. The fighting dogs were Foxy Warren's Rocket, and Dougy Swallow's Ginger.

Dougy was the owner of the village hardware stores. A mischievous old man now in his nineties, he still had a reputation for a wandering eye. His dog, a rust-coloured, wire-coated individual, also of some age, only left Dougy's side, it was said, when there was a bitch on heat anywhere within a mile radius of the village.

'Oh, Gawd! That's Dougy's Ginger. Teresa must be on heat.'

'OK,' Rosita announced sternly. 'I take him back to Dougy and I tell him to keep his dog home while Teresa is so hot. We do not want him to be father of her children.'

'Do you want to go now? Do you want to drive?'

'Yes. You bring the dog.'

Outside, Rosita climbed into the Bentley and moved the seat up close to the steering, wheel, so she was almost touching it with her chin.

Reggie got into the passenger seat, and pulled Ginger up to sit in his lap.

'OK, Rosi, off you go.'

Rosita was becoming more proficient as a driver, but she was still alarmingly haphazard in charting her course; they passed between the gates, missing the posts by a few millimetres.

'Rosi, angel, you must try not to get so close to the gatepost.'

'Reggie, for Gossake! How I learn to drive if always you are back-street driving?'

'What...?'Reggie murmured.

They made it unscathed for the rest of the way to the village, and Rosita pulled up the Bentley with a jolt, just beyond the entrance to a narrow alley that led to Dougy Swallow's cottage. Dougy lived there with his third, worn out wife whom he'd married thirty years before.

Reggie chuckled as Rosita checked her face in the driving mirror before leaving the car. 'Don't forget Rocket,' he said. 'And I've put him on Terry's lead, so make sure you bring it back.'

Rosita dragged the terrier across the front seat and strode off down the alley, tugging the resentful animal behind her.

Always curious, Reggie climbed down from the car and loitered where he couldn't be seen from the house.

When Rosita rattled the front door of the cottage, it was quickly opened by the third Mrs Swallow.

'Good morning,' Rosi said, using her best Belgravia English. 'I bring your dog, Ginger back from my house.'

'Do you? Why haven't you brought my husband back too, then? I wondered which of his fancy women he's been off to. And I've had my suspicions it was you. He's always talkin' about you – saying what a lovely arse you've got, and what smashing tits – self-sup-portin', like – he says, not like mine, hanging down to my waist.'

Reggie, hanging well back out of sight, stifled a guffaw.

The tirade had evidently taken Rosi by surprise; there was a slight pause before Reggie heard her voice again.

'What! What? You are loco!? What you say? You think your hus-ban' who is ol' enough to be my grandfather come to visit me at nine o'clock in the morning?'

'Who says anythin' about nine o'clock this morning? He's been gone since yesterday evenin' and that bloody dog don't never leave 'is side.'

'That bloody dog was at our house because our dog is on heat! Your husban' has been nowhere near our house. You think my hus-band sit by and watch if some dirty ol' man try to come sneakin' up on me?'

Mrs Swallow suddenly and dramatically burst into tears; her raucous, rasping sobs echoed through the stone alley.

Reggie sucked in a deep breath and started to walk down towards the cottage. He stopped outside the front door and Mrs Swallow lifted her damp, red eyes to him, accepting that she must have made a fool of herself.

'Mrs Swallow,' Reggie said kindly. 'I'm sorry about your ol' man going on a wander, but I can assure you he hasn't been to visit my wife. Don't get me wrong – I like your husband and I admire his spirit, but if he came round after Mrs ffinch-Leigh, I'd knock his wrinkled old bonce off. Ginger came; Dougy didn't. I suggest you get hold of PC Plank and tell him your husband's gone AWOL.'

Mrs Swallow started to howl again, much louder, and was beginning to attract the attention of passing villagers, when Library Linda appeared, running down the road from the Post Office, a hundred yards away.

'Miz Swaller, Miz Swaller,' she sobbed as she arrived. 'We found your Dougy in the path behind the hedge at the back of the Post Office.'

'What, has he been up at your Mum's again?'

Since Linda's father had walked out, soon after she was born, her mother had never been able to dispel her reputation as the scarlet woman of the village, unfounded though she always claimed it was.

'Course he hadn't. I just told you, we found him.'

'Well where is he now, then?'

'Like I said, he's on the path behind our place.'

'Well, why hasn't he come here hisself?'

Linda seemed to stagger and almost collapse with distress.

'Because he can't?'

'Why not, have she took him 'ostage?'

'No,' Linda wailed. 'He's dead.'

Reggie and Rosita gasped together as Mrs Swallow took a step back into the darkness of her cottage passage and sank to the ground, as flaccid as a punctured balloon.

They gaped, shaken by what they'd just heard.

They looked at Linda, who was also gazing in horror at old

Dougy's widow.

'Bloody hell!' she murmured. 'What we gonna do?'

'You'd better get Plank, I suppose,' Reggie suggested doubtfully, 'though I shouldn't think he can do much. And maybe phone an ambulance for her,' he nodded at the crumpled, silent heap that Mrs Swallow had become. 'I'll do that,' he added decisively, pulling his mobile phone from a pocket. 'Linda, you go and find PC Plank.'

Linda nodded dumbly and walked away towards the Post Office.

In a gallant gesture, Reggie suggested that he should take Ginger back to Mortimer Towers. Rosita didn't say anything about it until they were in the car, with her at the wheel and Ginger once again lodged on Reggie's lap.

'Reggie, you crazy to bring sex-mad dog home when Teresa is on heat.'

'Calm down, my scarlet geranium, I'll just lock him in one of the stables, and keep him there until we can find a new home for him – or maybe Mrs Swallow will want him back as a memento of Dougy.'

'Pooh' Rosita snorted. 'I don' think so!'

Reggie and Rosita were supposed to be going to a rehearsal of Diana Dove's show at the village hall.

'We should do something to help about Mrs Swallow, no?' Rosita said, her kinder instincts outweighing her indignation that his widow had thought the old man had come to see her.

'No,' Reggie shook his head. 'They don't want outsiders like us stickin' our noses in.'

'They are happy to come and use our place for their pageant.'

Reggie gave an indifferent shrug. 'That's the way it is. We may as well go to this rehearsal, for all the good it will do.'

Before it was time for them to leave, Emmet Rafferty appeared unexpectedly, having come in through the back door, as he always did.

'I 'eard you got Ginger,' he said 'He's a helluva ratter; d'you want me to take him off your hands?'

Reggie felt like a weight had been lifted off his chest; the friction between him and Rosita over Ginger's presence in the stables had been growing all day. 'Yes, please,' he agreed enthusiastically. 'Let's have a drink on it.'

Emmet settled down with Reggie in his study for a glass or two of the old Malmsey, for which he'd developed a strong liking.

'Did you hear what happened?' he asked.

'About what?' Reggie asked.

'Old Dougy – how he died?'

'Does it matter? By that age you just die of death, don't you?'

'Not Dougy; he went out with a bang; had a heart attack while he was what you called in *flagrante delicto*.'

Reggie sat up sharply. 'No! Good God, who with?'

'Doris Swift, of course; he's been visitin' her for years, on'n'off.'

'What? Were they doing it on the path?'

'Hell, no, but when Doris realised he was a gonner, she had to push him off the bed, and get Linda to help her dress him. Then they had to drag him down the stairs, to the back of the garden, and chuck him over the hedge. Lucky he was such a spindly old fellow.'

'Who the hell told you all that?'

'Mickey did; Linda told him. She was worried she and her mum would get done for murder.'

'Why, who knew?'

'Bloody PC Plank!' Emmet scoffed. 'When he come round, he has a look at where Dougy was found, and goes in to get a statement off Doris and Linda – who he's got the big hots for, as I showed you – and he sees a pair of men's underpants under a chair– like really old ones, which turned out to be Dougy's. Linda and Doris had dressed him in such a hurry they never put them back on him and they must've fell out of his trousers as they were dragging him through the kitchen. Plank, quick as a flash, gets onto the mort'ry and they confirms he's arrived there without any underclothes.'

'Bloody hell!' Reggie breathed. It wasn't often that that deaths like this took place in their village.

'What's going to happen to Doris and Linda, then?'

'Nothin',' Emmet said, satisfied that he'd told the story well. 'Plank isn't going to get Linda into trouble, 'specially as he knows there's those lovely romantic photos of him and Linda floatin' around somewhere.'

With a happy sparkle in his eyes, Emmet drained his glass of Malmsey and stood up. 'Orright,' he said. 'If you give us the dog, I'll be off.'

When Emmet had driven off with Ginger in the back of his pickup, Reggie and Rosita went to the village hall for the *Mamma Mia* rehearsal. There was a palpable tension there, which the death of such a prominent village character had inevitably caused. But although both Linda and PC Lank were both there, it seemed that most didn't know the truth about Dougy's sudden death.

Diana Dove, looking less than her best, had a resigned air. The rehearsal was a fiasco, and as each scene was played, she became gloomier, until she came to a decision.

'All right, you lot,' she announced. 'Everyone, whether you think you know your part or not, do it with the book. There's no way anyone will know it properly by Saturday.'

'I will,' Paul Lank declared indignantly from the back of the stage. He was playing a friend of Sky, the groom's. Reggie guessed he was anxious to show off to Library Linda.

Diana sighed. 'Well done, Plank,' she said. 'How many lines have you got?'

'Well, just the one.'

'And what is it?'

"Go for it, Sky!" the policeman proclaimed monosyllabically.

'Great,' Diana said flatly. 'You do your part without the book so it doesn't interfere with the powerful dramatic tension you give to the line. Everyone else – don't even try to remember, and even less, to sing, if you have a singing part – just try and lip-sync to the soundtrack – it'll be much easier on the audience. We are lucky enough to have a key magic ingredient in this show, which is that the audience will be on our side.'

'Excuse me, Diana,' Sir Compton Wynyates interjected. 'I know every note of my song.'

'All right, Compton, I suppose there's a chance you'll sing it better than poor old Pierce Brosnan did it in the film.'

Sir Compton smiled his satisfaction while Cecilia beamed proudly.

Reggie shook his head and asked himself why the hell he had ever agreed to be part of this show.

Rosita, on the other hand, was loving it. She and Belinda Buckton had even worked out an elaborate routine for doing *Dancing Queen* with Diana.

'OK everyone,' Diana was calling, with an edge of desolation in her voice. 'We may as well try the Wedding Scene again. Where are Sky and Sophie?'

Mickey Rafferty and Library Linda, who were playing the young lovers, emerged from the shadows at the back of the auditorium.

PC Lank watched them walk up to the stage with a look of fury on his face. Although only Emmet and Mickey had photographic evidence of the policeman's relationship with Linda, it was common knowledge in the village; so was her regular dalliance with the semi-criminal Mickey.

In contrast to how she had been that morning, Linda was looking bright and perky, as if the trauma of Dougy Swallow's death had passed, and she was relishing her role as Sophie, which required a lot of physical contact with Mickey.

They reached the point in the scene where the script demanded their first full-blown kiss.

Reggie nudged Rosita and grinned. 'Stone the crows!' he said, louder than he meant. 'He's giving it some welly, isn't he?'

Rosita laughed. 'And so is she!'

This was too much for PC Lank, who was standing close to them. He walked to the edge of the stage.

'Orright, you bloody little gyppo,' he uttered in strangled voice, and stepped up on to the platform, towering over Mickey. 'You bloody stop kissing her like that!'

'Like what, Plank? It's called acting; you don't think I like doin' it, do you?' He winked at Linda, who giggled.

'Mr Lank,' Diana called from her chair in the wings. 'Would you mind getting off the stage?'

The policeman ignored her. 'Look you little bastard...' he stabbed the air in front of Mickey with his forefinger '...don't let me see you do that ever again.'

'Or what?' Mickey taunted.

Plank stood in front of him, hyperventilating as the proto-human in him that wanted to thump Mickey battled with deeply embedded police training to control himself.

'You'll find out quick enough, don't you worry.'

'If you're around long enough after I've made a complaint against you for calling me a gyppo, which is dead racist, even if I'm not; I'm Irish descent, not gypsy.'

Plank drew himself up and backed off, but still with a vicious glint in his eye.

With an iron will, Diana Dove managed to get the rehearsal back on track, and for the next couple of hours things improved. Reading from the book and the lack of pausing for prompts let the action flow far more smoothly, and miming had vastly improved the musical content. Even Sir Compton's live singing did turn out to be no worse than the original soundtrack.

'Thank you all,' Diana announced. 'That was bloody awful, and the punters are going to love it. And please try to sort out your costumes before the dress rehearsal on Friday.'

Reggie caught Rosita's eye. 'D'you know what, in the end, I enjoyed that,' he said. 'And you were fantastic. You'll be glad to hear – what with doing this and the drama this morning over Dougy – I've completely got rid of the blues I was feeling! Let's go and have a drink with the others at the Fox & Ferret.'

'No; Lara has phoned. I go to see her in London tomorrow to get my costume, so I need to sleep.'

Reggie was feeling exhilarated and rebellious 'Well, I need a drink! Ask Belinda to take you home.'

Belinda said she would, and Rosita left in a huff.

There was still a good crowd in the Fox & Ferret when Reggie arrived there to join the Wynyates, Diana Dove and Terry Cotter. Compton and Terry the potter were were having an argument, with Cecilia acting as umpire, so Reggie bought a pint of Bishop's Riddle for himself and for Diana a large gin and tonic, which they took to a corner table.

'I enjoyed that rehearsal,' he said.

'Reggie, I'm glad. As it happens, you're OK – a bit of a natural – but I have to tell you, I think I'm barking mad to have taken this thing on. The trouble is when you come out to the deep sticks like this, you don't want to upset people by being too up yourself, do you?'

'No, I used to worry about everyone thinking I was just some flash London git with a bling'd up missus so I found myself agreeing to do anything anyone suggested and buying tickets for every bloody charity event you can think of. Before you know it, you're a soft touch, and every parasitical organisation in the county is trying to get inside your wallet.'

Diana laughed and nodded. 'I fear they think I'm a bit flash, too, after thirty years in the glitzy world of showbiz. Even though I'm really a local – I grew up here until I was eighteen – I've come back feeling a bit of an outsider. I'd hardly been here a week when the village busybodies were round saying, as I'd been in the business, I must take on the village show.' She raised her eyebrows. 'I thought it might be fun, and I'd get to know all the jolly locals so I said "Yes". But for God's sake! The people who think they can sing or act! What planet are they from?'

'It was a smart move to get us just to read our parts,' Reggie said. 'There was no way I was ever going to remember all my lines. And tonight I found, as long as I had the book, I did sort of remember them and I could give it a bit more oomph. And as long as the punters can sing along, they'll all love it. But I don't suppose old Huffers was happy about that. Is that why he chucked it?'

'Mainly,' Diana said, 'though there were other factors,' she added obscurely.

'Did he come onto you a bit strong?' Reggie couldn't help his curiosity.

'I wouldn't say that,' she smiled and changed the subject. 'Tell me, will your cousin Porky be coming to see it?'

'Maybe. He's coming up Wednesday to talk to me about something, but I don't know if he'll be staying. Why do you ask? You don't fancy him, do you?'

'As a matter of fact, I sort of do. The thing is, he's so direct. He does exactly what it says on the tin and says precisely what he thinks and, in my world, that's a bit of a rarity. '

'It's funny, isn't it – although he's built like a concrete khazi and has the worst taste in shirts I've ever seen, the women do seem to like him. The bird in France I bought the plonk from I sold to Chatternerve, she really likes him.'

'She sounds a bit of a bitch to me,' Diana said sourly.

Reggie chuckled. 'Never mind. She's in France; you're in England.'

Two pints later Reggie clambered into the Bentley which managed to find its way back to Mortimer Towers without hitting the banks of the lanes too often. When he got home and staggered upstairs to the bedroom, Rosita was pretending to be asleep.

At breakfast in the morning she was as snappy as an alligator, while Reggie nursed a mild hangover.

'I suppose you were drinking with that Diana Dove?'

'Obviously I had a few with her,' Reggie said, with nothing to hide. 'Just with her?'

'Yeh, Terry and Compton were working themselves up into a punch-up over human bloody rights, and I wasn't going to get involved in that.

'I s'pose you think Diana is sophisticated lady, eh?'

'Well, she is, isn't she,' Reggie said mildly.

'You fancy her?'

'Yeh, I think I would, if I wasn't spoken for.'

'You watch out for her, Reggie; she's after you.'

'No she isn't. It was Huffers she was after, but something's gone wrong there, and now it's Porky she's interested in.'

'Don't be ridicoolos. How can she fancy him – he is not at all couth.'

'Hhn?' Reggie grunted. 'You mean he's uncouth?'

'That's right.'

'So what? So am I.'

'Compared to him, you are very couth.'

Reggie laughed, 'I'm glad to hear it! Ah! ' he said, peering out of the window. 'Here's Postman Pete with some letters and a package.'

He walked through the hall and opened the door to take the bundle the postman handed to him. 'Thanks, Pete,' he muttered, intrigued by the scruffy parcel he'd just been handed. It was wrapped in a piece of battered corrugated paper with rough old strips of sellotape around it.

He carried it into the kitchen and started pulling off the wrapping. 'What is this?' Rosita asked.

'Dunno,' Reggie said. He gave it a final tug and it fell apart, allowing whatever it contained to fall on the stone kitchen floor with a ringing clatter.

He bent down and found a sausage-shaped piece of metal under a chair.He picked it up and held it out in front of him, so Rosita could see it too.

'What is that?' she asked.

'Gawd knows,' he said. 'Looks like a sort of bronze plonker.'

'For Gossake, Reggie! Don't be revolting.'

'No, it's not a plonker – it's a bloody finger! It's one of Joan's fingers!'

For a moment, Reggie and Rosita were stunned.

'Oh my GOD!' she gasped huskily. 'My poor Joan!'

'Rosi – it's a statue. Statues don't feel pain.'

Rosi dismissed that idea. 'To me she was alive. They do this to torment us.'

'You're sort of right there,' Reggie said drily, unfolding a sheet of paper he'd found in the package. 'Here's a ransom note. If we don't give 'em five grand, they're going to melt it down and sell the bronze.'

He handed Rosi the note which had been produced by cutting and pasting a series of individual handwritten letters on to the main sheet of paper.

'Oh no!' Rosita shrieked. 'They are going to burn Joan, like she is Joan of Arc.'

'Calm down, Rosi, for gawd's sake. I'll take this letter to the police, and let's see what they can do.'

'Plank?' Rosita almost spat. 'What is he going to do?'

'You never know. Maybe they'll find something. I'll ask around a bit, but I don't think we can do much.'

'But I want Joan back...' Rosita wailed.

'Orright, orright. Calm down. Aren't you supposed to be catching a train?'

Rosita looked at the clock on the kitchen wall. 'Aaagh!' she cried. 'Tommy Taxi will be here in ten minutes and I don't have packed.'

'Why? Are you staying the night in London?'

'Yes,' she answered defiantly. 'For two nights. On Thursday I go to have my hair done.'

'In London? What about the girl whose wedding you did in the summer; what's wrong with her?'

'Reggie! I tried her after that, and maybe you remember, I came back and my hair was looking like a pile of seaweed floating in a rock pond. I going to be on stage! With everyone from local, all looking at me. You want me have bad hair?'

Reggie loved Rosi's hair however it was.

'No, Rosi, of course I don't want you to have bad hair. You go up and have fun,' He felt inside his jacket pocket and pulled out a wedge of fifties. 'Look here's a grand for you. That'll get you a lovely hairdo.'

Rosiat waved the money away. 'Don't be ridicoolos. I have money.'

She swept from the room, and ten minutes later Reggie heard her clatter down the stairs, across the hall and through the front door. When he looked out of the window Tommy's rumpled Rover was already disappearing down the drive.

As Reggie drove to Ted Buckton's, he thought about Rosita, wondering what he'd done to upset her; he knew it was part of her nature to inflate her emotions more than, say, an Englishwoman. But she couldn't have been that stressed about him getting a bit plastered the night before at the Fox. He shrugged mentally, and pushed the problem to one side.

He was on his way to Ted's, to have a ride on a new horse Ted had bought with an eye to selling it to him – Reggie guessed – if he enjoyed himself on it.

When he arrived at Ted's handsome red brick Victorian stable buildings, he parked outside and walked into the yard. The big bay horse was already standing there, tied to a rail and tacked up, ready to go. Tethered beside him was a sharp-looking chestnut horse, also bridled and saddled. Reggie looked around but saw no sign of human beings until, after a minute or so, a girl in her late teens and a pair of jodhpurs walked shyly from the tack room in the corner.

'Good mornin',' Reggie boomed affably.

'Are you Mr Finchley?' she asked in a strong Shropshire accent, without making eye contact.

'I am.'

'I'm Kylie. My dad farms up there.' She inclined her head at a sheep-speckled hill to the west. 'I'm comin' along with you on the chestnut mare for Mrs Buckton.'

'Great,' Reggie said, politely. 'Where's Mr Buckton?'

'He's gone to look at a sale and says he'll be back when we are.' She untethered the bay and led him to stand alongside a solid stone mounting block. Reggie stepped up and swung his leg over; it was the first time he'd got on a horse since the previous spring. The animal jiggled under him in a friendly way.

'There you go,' Kylie said and swung herself up on the chestnut. 'A'right?' she asked, and together they walked out of the yard.

After an hour or so, which Reggie loved, and without any serious mishaps, they rode back into the yard where Ted was waiting for them. He held the horse's head while Reggie got down and Kylie took the horse off to his stable.

'Quick pint of Floppidik?' Ted asked. He was always ready for a drink, any time, day or night, and Reggie didn't want to disappoint him. 'Why not,' he agreed with a grin, while anticipating a bit of a session.

Floppidik was a notorious local cider of illicit origins and unknown strength, to which Ted had introduced Reggie a few years before. They sat as they often had on a hay bale in one of the barns.

Ted filled two pewter pint pots and Reggie felt the golden liquid enter his system and relax muscles in his thighs that he hadn't used since the last time he'd been on a horse.

'Hope you enjoyed your hack,' Ted said.

'I did. It was t'riffic to get back up the hills on a horse. I wish I'd done it years ago.'

'Well, you're doing it now, and you did well last season – especially for one who started so late in life.'

''Ere – not that late – I was a spring chicken of sixty.'

'You did well, Reggie – you won the hunt race, but are you going to try coming out with the hunt this year?'

'As long as I don't have to kill anything.'

'Don't worry about that. The punters at the back never see it when it happens, and anyway, our hounds hardly catch any foxes. Most of the foxes around here are shot by farmers on the hill with lambs to protect.'

'Like Kylie's dad?'

Ted chuckled. 'How did you get on with her?'

'Not much. She's a young woman of few words, isn't she? I tried to have a bit of a chat with her. I asked what she knew about sheep and she just says, "Allus I know about sheep is allus they ever want to do is get out – or die".'

Ted laughed. 'That's about right. And you could say that about some of the farmers' daughters. It's a lonely life for the women up in those hills.'

'I should think it is. Rosi wouldn't take it, that's for sure. She's gone off to London this morning for a couple of days and left in a right strop.' As soon as he'd said it, Reggie felt disloyal, describing his wife like that, and he became philosophical. 'But I can't complain. I mean, if you're married to a hot-blooded, fiery Latina woman, from time to time you're going to get fireworks, aren't you.'

'Don't ask me; Belinda's as unfiery and Anglo-Saxon as they come.'

Reggie sighed. 'I'm not sure what got into her this morning, though I should think a couple of days with Lara in London will sort her out. But anyway, Kylie said you've been off to have a look at a sale.'

'Yes, I did – the weekly one in the next village. I meant to tell you about it because they had a picture there that looked like how you described the one you sold to Cecilia Wynyates – a Herring type painting of grey horse, being held by a groom in livery. The one she had stolen'

Reggie sat up. 'What?' He shook his head. 'I don't think so, Ted. Why would anyone who nicked it put it in a crappy little sale like that? Have you got the catalogue?'

'No catalogues for this sale. People are bringing in stuff right up to the last minute. Maybe you're right, and it isn't Cecilia's, but in any case it might be a good one for you to buy; it's not going to go for much either – nothing ever does there.'

'What time do they start selling?'

'Midday.'

Reggie abandoned his pot of Floppidik and stood up. 'I'm going to get along there now and have a look, and I don't want to turn up with a few pints of this firewater in me. You know what happened last time.'

'Yes, you were so plastered, you bought a stuffed bull's head that you sold to Jones the Beef for ten times what you paid for it.'

'Yeh, that was a bit lucky. But I want to be sober to look at this picture.'

'OK,' Ted said, standing up too. 'I'll come with you.'

The WWII Nissen hut that was the venue for the sale was packed with stuff – mostly junk seeking reprieve from their final destination in landfill – grimy old sofas with no springs, chipped Formica kitchen cabinets from the '50s, baronial wall brackets made of plastic and, occasionally, a hidden gem of a piece of furniture or a painting. There were always a few optimists who would turn up to compete for these.

Ted led Reggie to where the equestrian picture, in a plain painted frame, was propped against the wall behind a hideous painting of a vase of gladioli. Reggie moved the gladioli to one side and peered at the picture behind it.

'Bollocks!' he gasped.

'Shhh,' Ted warned. 'You don't want to get anyone else excited about it.'

'No,' Reggie said more quietly. 'You're right, but it looks bloody like the one I sold Cecilia. But it can't be; it's in a much cheaper frame.' He stood back. 'It must have come from the same place, it's so similar. For all I know, it might be one old Bertie Cheney-Longville brought over from Italy years ago, and sold to someone local who's just kicked the bucket.'

'Bit of a coincidence, what?' Ted observed.

'I dunno,' Reggie said, bewildered, as he placed the gladioli back in front of the 'Herring'. 'But I'll buy it anyway and have a closer look at home.'

He and Ted carried on wandering around the hall, picking things up and finding a few more things to bid for, making sure that they didn't arouse any more interest by going back to look at the 'Spotty Dick' again.

When it was due to be sold, a porter with a hunchback and a wall eye held it up as high as he could. The auctioneer, whose regular job was selling cars on their way to the knacker's yard, started his spiel.

'Here's a lovely quality, high-class picture - eigtheenf cent'ry by the look of it. Oil on canvas, new frame. Is that a signature I see at the bottom there?' he asked the porter who was holding it.

The porter peered at it, and turned back to look at the corner of the hall beyond the auctioneer. 'No,' he said. 'S'bit o' birdshit.'

'Well, anyway, a t'rific picture – got to be worth a grand – a thousand pounds – who'll give me a thousand pounds for this?'

Instinctively Reggie checked his inside jacket pocket to make sure he had his wallet, which contained two thousand pounds from his stash at home for emergencies like this.

The auctioneer was gazing around at a sea of blank faces and knew he'd overegged it. 'OK, five hundred, then – just to get it going.'

Nobody made a visible move.

The auctioneer swept the room with his hawk's eyes, until he spotted a hand waving at the back, and heard a cry of 'Fifty quid,' which he ignored in favour of a bid from an invisible bidder on the wall.

'All right, I'll take a hundred.'

Reggie guessed the auctioneer was taking a punt with a starting bid off the wall. He waited while the man on the rostrum gazed around him with a hint of panic, then relief, as he took a real bid. 'One twenty,' then another, 'one forty,' bouncing around the room, until it reached six hundred. Reggie hadn't put his hand up yet, but he was comfortable; he knew exactly what Church-Pugh would pay for the picture.

It was sticking now. The punters in the room had taken it as far as they wanted. It was time to clinch it.

Reggie raised his hand. 'Six fifty!'

The auctioneer nodded. He recognised his bidder, and looked around jauntily for the next call.

'Seven hundred, who'll give me seven hundred,' he intoned as he examined every corner of the room for a sign. 'Come on, this is much too cheap for a quality English painting that'd look good in any fine mansion. Who'll give me seven hundred, seven hundred.'

He kept it up for another half minute before he banged his gavel down. 'Sold at six hundred and fifty pounds – Mr Finchley.'

Reggie carried out his purchase to stow in the back of his Bentley which was parked fifty yards down the road from the Nissen hut, where the sale was still going on. Ted was with him, having bought a Victorian mahogany saddle horse for fifty pounds.

'That was a result,' Reggie congratulated him.

'Are you happy with your buy?' Ted asked.

'Yes and no. I think it was the painting that was pinched, but I can't see why it's been reframed, unless it got broken or something. And it should have gone for a helluva lot more.'

'Not at this little sale,' Ted said.

'Then why didn't whoever entered it put it in a proper picture sale?'

'Reggie, for God's sake, stop worrying about it; you got it – cheap as chips as old marmalade features likes to say. Just relax.'

'Excuse me.'

Both men swung round to find a bearded man of medium height

in 'walking' trousers and a purple anorak. 'Didn't I see you up on Titterstone Clee on Sunday,' he said, 'delivering some pictures?'

Reggie froze while he tried to work out how he should react. 'What were you doing there?' he countered.

'Me? I was with the South Salop Rambling Club.'

'Yes,' Reggie said. 'I sold a few pictures to a gentleman at Ludlow flea market that morning, and he asked me to meet him there with them.'

'Why was that?' the bearded man asked.

'I have no idea,' Reggie answered truthfully, reminding himself that he hadn't done anything illegal.

On the other hand, what reason did Church-Pugh have for not making the exchange in public?

'I'm sorry. I'm in a bit of a hurry, if you don't mind?' he said, and turned round to lower the boot lid.

'Oh, that's all right; just curious,' the man said mildly and ambled off.

Ted was curious too. 'What was all that about?'

Reggie shrugged it off. 'Just a punter who wanted to meet me somewhere to hand over some pictures he'd bought. Gawd knows why he chose that spot. That geezer that just came up – he must have been with a bunch of ramblers who went past while we were there.'

'Oh?' Ted said. 'So you've been doing all right with the pictures you get in Italy, then?'

Reggie remembered he hadn't answered Ted's question fully when they had had dinner on Sunday night. 'Not bad,' he said. 'I should have 'em all shifted soon.'

On his own later, back at Mortimer Towers, Reggie propped his purchase on a chair in his study and had a closer look. After a while, he came to the conclusion that if it wasn't the painting he'd sold to Cecilia, it was pretty much identical and must have been produced in the same place.

It wouldn't be convenient – he thought – if any others as similar as this turned up, but at least the bulk of his stock had gone to Church-Pugh and would end up in the Middle East. Feeling wiped out after the day's dramas, Reggie poured himself a glass of Bertie Cheney-Longville's Malmsey and, from the table beside him, he picked up Joan's brass finger and looked at the rough edge where it had been sawn off.

He grimaced guiltily; he still hadn't reported the ransom note.

He reached out for the phone and picked it up; after a moment's thought, he put it down again. If he rang the police, he'd end up having a convoluted discussion with someone in a police call centre somewhere in the Black Country.

He decided he'd go and look for PC Lank in the morning.

The phone rang; he picked it up again.

It was Diana Dove.

'Hello, Reggie,' she said warmly. 'I hear you're a grass widow for a couple of days.'

'Yeh, Rosi's gone to get her barnet coiffed in Mayfair, and to find a rig out for your blasted show.'

'I did offer her a couple of outfits,' Diana said, 'but she turned them down flat.'

'Yeh, well she can be a bit finicky about that sort of thing. Anyway, what can I do for you?'

'I remember you saying you were keen to pick any mulberries that weren't wanted. Well mine are ripe and at their peak for harvesting. If you're not doing anything tomorrow, you'd be very welcome to come over and pick all you want. There's a large tree full of 'em – it could take you all day.'

'Do you know what the weather forecast's like for tomorrow?'

'Pretty mild, I just saw on the TV.'

'OK, thanks a lot, Diana. I'll be over some time in the morning.'

'Look forward to it,' Diana said with pronounced breathiness.

Reggie put the phone down, wondering if perhaps Rosi was right and Diana did have a bit of as crush on him. He liked Diana's company but he wasn't at all interested in having affairs with anyone, as long as he had Rosi; he'd have to be sure to keep his guard up while he was with her. These days with everyone, especially people like Mickey Rafferty taking snapshots of everything, you couldn't be too careful.

He thought of Diana and his cousin Porky Bacon, and if there really was something there, when the phone rang again. This time it was Porky.

''Ello, Reggie me ol' china plate.'

'Hello, cuz,' Reggie said. 'I was just thinking about you.'

'Oh yeh. What about me?'

'Nothing in particular,' Reggie said with unusual tact. 'What d'you want?'

'I want to talk to you. I won't say what about over the dog'n'bone in case the hacks at News of the World are listening in.'

'You're sounding a bit what Rosi would call 'paranoy'. The News of the World died a few years ago,' Reggie said, 'and why would they be listening in on my phone?' 'Not yours, Reggie – mine. They know I talk to a lot of interesting people. But listen, will you be at home tomorrow?'

'Not until the evening. I'm spending the day picking mulberries for my special vodka.'

'Bloody hell, Reggie you'll be making blackberry jam with the Women's Institute next.'

'Not likely! You should see our local lot; they're a terrifying gang; you wouldn't want to get caught up in unarmed combat with them.'

'I might give it a try some time. Anyway, I'll come up tomorrow. If I get there before you, will Rosi be in?'

'No,' Reggie said. 'She's left me.'

'What!!?' Porky exclaimed, horrified. 'Oh, Reg, I'm really choked to hear that.'

'It's all right, Porky; keep your syrup on; she's only gone to London for a couple of days to meet up with Lara and spend money. She's back Thursday, but if you get up here tomorrow before I'm home, I'll leave the keys in the usual place, and you can let yourself in, OK, and help yourself to anything you want?'

'Great, thanks Reggie. I'll see you tomorrow.'

Reggie always liked Porky coming up; but he knew it took a bit of stamina to keep up. He decided that he would go to bed early to be ready for a session the next evening. 'Cor blimey,' he thought. 'I must be getting old.'

Chapter Eleven

Reggie awoke bright-eyed and clear-headed to a warm, late September morning. He was looking forward to a day in the open air, followed by an evening with Porky.

He was in the kitchen, making his first cup coffee morning when Rosi rang.

'Ola, Reggie, querido!' she fluted.

Reggie breathed a sigh of relief; she sounded back to normal and full of her usual affection.

'Hello, my little Spanish Rose, how's it going?'

'I am out at shops all day today, so I just ring to say I love you.'

'I'm glad to hear it, and I love you.'

'Reggie, sorry if I so moody sometimes.'

'It's the way you are, and I wouldn't change it.'

'So, what you are doing today?'

'I'm off to pick mulberries.'

There was slight pause before Rosita answered. 'Where?'

'At Wicton Priory.'

'You mean Diana Dove's?'

Yes, of course. You remember, she invited me to, and this evening she rang to say they're absolutely ripe.'

There was another pause. When Rosita spoke again, her voice had an edge of menace to it. 'Just so long she is not absolutely ripe. You only pluck just her mulberries – nothing else, OK?'

'That's all I'm going there for,' Reggie said lightly, but conscious of the warm, honeyed tone Diana had used when they'd spoken the evening before.

'You better. Have you done something about Joan's finger?'

'No, but I'm going to see Plank this morning on my way to Wicton.'

Rosi sighed. 'Reggie, I want her back. I don't want insurance money.'

'I'll do what I can, and you have a great day of retail therapy. Ring me tonight.

Porky's coming up, by the way.'

'Hmm,' Rosi grunted. 'Be careful – he is bad influenza. I hope you don't get too drunk.'

'Don't you worry about me, Rosi,' Reggie said reassuringly. 'And look after yourself.' He put the phone down feeling a tad sorry for himself.

Reggie strapped a ladder onto the back of the rattling old Land Rover he was taking that day, and drove into the village where he found the policeman in the Post Office, talking earnestly to Library Linda. He apologised for interrupting and showed PC Lank the sawn-off bronze finger, the scruffy package and the ransom note composed of cut and pasted scrawl.

'Good 'eavens!' Plank said. 'I know that writing; that's Mickey Rafferty's; he sat next to me at school.' A big smile lit up his face. 'I'll nick him right away.'

'Hang on a minute, Plank – I mean – Constable Lank. Why would Mickey cut up his own writing and paste it if he wanted to disguise who'd sent the note? It doesn't make sense.'

'Nothing that little pike... ' PC Lank cut himself short before he could be accused of uttering another racist slur. 'Nothing he does makes sense, but it makes sense to me. Just you watch. We'll have this statue of yours back in no time, and Mickey Rafferty behind bars.'

Library Linda gasped with a look of horror. 'Oh Paul, please don't hurt 'im!'

Plank ignored her plea as he gave her a last passionate glance before marching out of the Post Office, climbing into his Police Corsa and skidding off in the direction of the Rafferty tribe's current encampment.

Frankly doubtful about Plank's line of inquiry, Reggie headed the old Land Rover through the rising mist and autumn sunshine towards Wicton Priory. In view of Rosi's frostiness and her suspicions that Diana was angling for him, he decided he'd have to be very careful how he dealt with Diana's natural flirtatiousness, which he thought was probably a simple by-product of working with theatrical luvvies all her professional life.

Other than that, he was looking forward to being outside all day and had equipped himself with a good fruit ladder, a pair of long-handled secateurs, large wicker baskets and appropriate clothing.

Reggie pulled up outside the venerable old stone pile with its Gothic windows and ecclesiastical trimmings; he had never visited the place before and looked around with fascination. Getting down from his vehicle, Reggie walked up to bang the heavy iron knocker on the great oak front door. When he reached it, he found an envelope wedged underneath the knocker. He slid it out and found it was addressed to him.

Inside was a sheet of writing paper, headed just Wicton Priory, with a note written in ink and a florid female hand.

Dear Reggie,

So glad you made it. Unfortunately, I am not here and will be out all day. I hope you will be all right. My Aunt Sylvia is staying in the house at the moment; I'm afraid she is rather unstable and can't be disturbed – especially by strangers, so you will not be able to go into the house. In case you need sustenance, I've left you some coffee and a lovely picnic in the orangery.

The tree is directly behind you.

Yours ever,

Love,

Diana

Reggie turned around and identified the target tree, which, as Diana had told him, was heavily laden with dark red fruit. It was probably a good thing, he thought, that he wasn't going to have to spend the day ducking Diana's advances; although, in any case, the letter also made Rosi's theories about her intentions less likely. He stuffed the letter in a pocket and went back to get his things from the Land Rover. He decided to base himself in the orangery which he saw attached to a gable end of the house, and took his equipment in there.

An insulated coffee pot with a mug, some milk and the picnic

Diana had promised stood on a tray, placed on a Victorian wrought iron table. He poured himself some coffee and started to undress.

Reggie hadn't forgotten Diana's story about picking mulberries in her bikini and, bearing that in mind, he removed all his clothes and put on only beige briefs and a pair of sandals. He saw himself partially reflected in the glass walls of the hothouse, and laughed. 'That'd scare the 'orses,' he murmured without vanity.

He went out and was glad to find that with the mist gone the day was turning out to be very warm. He propped the ladder against the upper branches of the tree, made sure it was steady and, toting one of the large wicker baskets he'd brought, climbed up to the top.

As he picked, enjoying the satisfaction of transferring the soft juicy fruit to his basket, he felt the sun on his back and started to sing his favourite Frank Sinatra songs. Every so often, he clambered down, transferred his haul to a bigger basket in the back of the Land Rover, and moved the ladder a couple of yards clockwise around the tree.

After an hour or so, he'd picked all he could see on the crown of the tree and decided, before tackling the inner branches further down, he would top up his coffee and have a smoke. He sat down with his back against the warm bark at the base of the tree, lit up a cheap Honduran cigar and took a satisfying pull.

After a short nap, he was thinking about getting on with his picking, when a grey Morris Minor 'Woody' Traveller futted up the drive and parked next to his Land Rover. Curious as always, Reggie waited to see who had come to see Diana and what they would do.

The person who emerged from the car was a small, wispy woman with pale, furrowed features and thick, uncared for grey hair.

Reggie recognised her right away as the wife of the vicar who looked after the church in the village and twelve other churches – a thankless task, Reggie guessed, given that the number of punters in his patch had dwindled to a few octogenarians per parish.

Rosita was a Roman Catholic, with whom Reggie had very occasionally been to extravagant, smoke-filled services in The Brompton Oratory in London, where most of the congregation, like Rosita, were foreign and exotic. Nominally, Reggie himself was a member of the Church of England. As a child, he'd been brought up by his mother to view God as a tidy, old-fashioned sort of a geezer, a little like Harold Macmillan, with a moustache, perched on a throne, somewhere up in the heavens, saying –'You never had it so Good!'

His commitment ran these days to a visit to the village church at Christmas and occasionally to coughing up a few quid for the church roof fund. Reggie had once met the vicar when he'd ventured into the bar at the Fox & Ferret in a vain search for new active members of his flock. The Fox regulars generally referred to him as Mogadon, for the soporific qualities of his sermons, although he would ask anyone who would listen to call him 'Vernon'. His wife, conveniently, was called Vera.

Now, with jaw clenched, Vera appeared to be on a mission. She hurried over to the front door with busy strides, hesitated a few seconds before tentatively lifting the knocker and allowing it to fall a few millimetres with a soft thud.

Reggie, enjoying his study of her body language, thought what hell it must be to be a vicar's wife.

After a while, and no sign of a response, Vera lifted the knocker again, a little higher and, this time, it came down with a good clunk.

Nothing happened for a while, and Reggie got to his feet. He was about to walk over to where Vera stood nervously in the stone porch, when the front door opened to reveal a wild-eyed woman with white hair, which was standing on end as if she'd just put a finger in an electrical socket.

Reggie assumed that this must be Aunt Sylvia and stepped forward to introduce himself. The quiet autumn air was abruptly rent by a long drawn out scream. Vera turned to see what the screaming was about; as soon as she caught sight of Reggie advancing, she joined in the screaming at a slightly higher and discordant pitch

Reggie was appalled that he should have been responsible for scaring them like this, and immediately tried to calm them. 'It's all right, ladies! Mrs Dove knows I'm here!'

He was met with a bout of reinvigorated screaming as he came closer. He was wondering what he should do to reassure them that he was there in bona fides when he caught a glimpse of his reflection in the windscreen of the Land Rover.

He didn't recognise the tall man clutching a pair of red stained secateurs, with wild white hair entwined, like the Clun Green King's, with leaves and twigs, whose apparently naked body was covered from head to foot with stains and blotches of livid red.

He stopped and tried again. 'It's all right, ladies. It's me, Reggie ffinch-Leigh.'

The two women emitted another terrified scream before they both turned and fled into the house, banging the great oak door shut behind them.

Reggie sighed and looked down at himself. His underpants, brief and flesh-coloured, along with the profusion of red mulberry juice close to the colour of blood, made him look more like the naked axe-man on the rampage in a Hammer Horror film, than the avuncular former London businessman he imagined others usually saw.

He walked up to the front door and put his ear to it. The screaming had ceased, but somewhere in the mediaeval bowels of the house he could hear faintly a panicked female voice with the sporadic bursts and intonations of a telephone conversation. When it seemed to have finished, he took a deep breath and knocked on the door, prompting an instantaneous resumption of the screaming.

Reggie had to bellow to be heard over the noise of it. 'Look, it's OK. It's only Reggie; I'm a friend of Diana's.'

This time he had a coherent response. 'Go away! We've called the police!'

Reggie returned to the orangery where he'd left his clothes. He thought about putting them back on, but there seemed no point, if they were only going to get stained by what was already on him. He looked around for a tap or source of water which he could use to remove some of the stains that had so alarmed the women.

While he was looking, he suddenly became aware of a police siren approaching fast, and recalled that the Rafferty pitch, which PC Lank had driven off to in such a hurry was only half a mile from where he was now.

A moment later, the Police Corsa shot down the drive of Wicton Priory and slithered to a halt on the loose gravel between the Morris Traveller and the Land Rover.

Plank tried to exit his undersized vehicle with such haste that he smacked his head on the door frame, and staggered out, weaving around partly concussed for a few moments before he saw Reggie walking round the back of the Land Rover.

'Stop!!' PC Lank bellowed, leaning down to grope inside the car for his truncheon. 'Stop right there!!'

'Plank! For Gawd's sake! It's Reggie; Reggie ffinch-Leigh. I was only talking to you in the Post Office this morning – a couple of hours ago.'

PC Lank executed a pantomime double-take. 'Bugger my bull!' he gasped a rustic oath Reggie had never heard. 'What the hell is going on? What's all that blood? Have you gone mad, or what?'

'No,' Reggie bellowed. 'I've been picking mulberries – off that tree.' He indicated it to Plank, who gaped blankly at it.

'Mulberries are very juicy!' Reggie went on. 'Look!' he leaned into the Land Rover and pulled out a basket of the fruit. He popped a berry into his mouth. 'As you can see the juice gets everywhere and stains anything it touches. So I took most of my clothes off to pick them, that's all.'

Plank shook his head. 'You've been up a tree, stark bollock naked to pick fruit?'

'I'm not stark naked – look!' Reggie waved a hand at the general area of his groin. 'I'm wearing underpants – aren't I?'

Plank stared straight ahead of him before gingerly lowering his eyes. 'Oh, yeh. You are, aren't you?'

'Yes, but I'm afraid when the ladies saw me they didn't take the time to look closely, and they banged themselves inside.'

Constable Lank knocked on the door and after taking a while to convince the women inside that he was who said he was, they let him in.

Reggie didn't try to follow him but continued his search for an outside water tap. When he found one at the back of the orangery, he tried to clean off some of the juice using cold water and an old dishcloth he'd found hanging off the tap, but this failed to make any impression on the mulberry juice that covered most of his body.

Reggie, always a pragmatist, was thinking about simply carrying on picking the mulberries when the policeman reappeared.

'I've managed to calm them down,' he said smugly. 'But they better not see you – not if you can't get all that juice cleaned off.'

'Maybe I could use some soap and hot water in the house?'

'No way, that'll just set 'em off again.'

Reggie shrugged. 'I might as well carry on picking, then.'

'No,' PC Lank pronounced firmly. 'If they look out and see you...'

'Orright, orright.' Reggie gave in. 'I'll go home then. There's no one there. I just hope I don't get waylaid on the way. I can't put any of my clothes back on until I've had a good soak.'

When he got back to Mortimer Towers, Reggie drove the Land Rover up the back drive and parked it outside the gates to the stable yard. He put his baskets of mulberries in an outhouse and draped muslin cloths over them to keep off the wasps and flies. Fishing his keys from the pocket of his trousers on the seat beside him, he went up the back steps and let himself in through the rear corridor entrance. Passing the door to his study, he glanced in, and took an apprehensive step in. There was a bottle of his Malmsey on the table which hadn't been there the night before. He was sure he'd put everything away after his last nightcap.

Thinking fast, Reggie tried to work out who could have been there. It looked like someone must have come into the house and helped themselves. And if they'd come in, they must have been there to rob him.

He went back out to the corridor, feeling a little chilly now he was out of the sun and wearing nothing but his underpants and a pair of sandals.

He shivered as he stood still and listened.

He heard nothing but the faint sounds of birds chirruping in the garden. He took a few stealthy paces towards the door that opened into the hall, when he thought he heard a noise inside the house. He stopped again, with his ears alert, but there was no sound, until he was about to move on, when he heard what he thought was a female giggle.

'Women burglars!?' he thought.

Or was it Saucy Sue Price?

No, she never came on Wednesdays.

Walking on silently toward the hall, he heard a creaking, and was sure it came from the drawing room on the far side of the hall.

He tiptoed across the hall as best as he could in a pair of floppy sandals, and stopped outside the door to the drawing room.

He held his breath. This time he heard a man's voice in a low murmur, followed by another female laugh.

Whoever these burglars were, they seemed pretty relaxed, and confident they weren't going to be disturbed. 'Right!' Reggie thought. 'I've got the element of surprise on my side.' He picked up an iron mace that belonged to one of his suits of armour and tried the door handle. When he was sure it was unlatched, he kicked it open and burst through.

He was met immediately by a cacophony – more shrill screaming, as a head sank below the line of a sofa that sat in front of the door, and the bellow of a familiar male voice.

Reggie stopped as if he'd run into a brick wall. 'Porky! What are you doing here?'

His cousin's face lit up at first, but quickly became horrified. 'Bleedin' 'eck, Reggie. What the hell have you been up to? You look like you've just murdered someone.'

'Of course I haven't. I've been picking her bloody mulberries!' Reggie exclaimed, pointing a quivering finger at Diana Dove, whose head had just reappeared over the back of the sofa.

'Oh my God, Reggie,' she gasped. 'Look at you! I thought you were some homicidal maniac escaped from the asylum or something.'

'Well, I'm not. Like I said – I've was picking fruit, but I was interrupted by a pair of mad, screaming women, so I've given up and come home to take a shower. '

'But, Reggie,' Porky asked, perplexed. 'Why were you picking fruit in the nood?'

'I'm not in the bloody nood.'

'You're certainly very bloody,' Porky chortled.'

'Yeh, but I am wearing underpants, because she told me about picking in her bikini.' As he'd been speaking, it dawned on Reggie that Diana and Porky were there for some kind of pre-arranged liaison. 'More to the point, just what are you two doing?'

'Nothing we're not allowed to,' Diana said haughtily. 'Neither of us is married.'

'And anyway,' Porky went on. 'You've come barging in before we've done anything at all.'

Reggie raised his eyebrows. 'Yeh, all right. But you both lied to me.'

'No, I didn't,' Diana said. 'I left you a note saying I'd be out all day.'

'And,' Porky went on. 'I said I might get up here early; when she rings me last night and says you're going to be over her place all day.... well – it was too good a chance to miss.'

'Especially,' Diana added, 'as we can't go to my place as long as batty Aunt Sylvia's around.'

Reggie's mind was whirling. He didn't know why he was annoyed; he guessed it was that he felt he'd been deceived and taken advantage of. But they hadn't done anything that he could complain of. He already knew that there was a bit of a vibe between the two of them – which was what he'd told Rosita.

It was possible, of course that Diana Dove had reached a stage in life where she knew what she wanted and was able to be indiscriminate about it. But, at least for the time being, with Porky keeping her busy, that would take any pressure off him.

'Tell you what, Reggie,' Porky said buttoning up his gold and purple shirt and tucking it back into his trousers. 'Just to make it up to you, I'll get you dinner at the Tippling Toad – as long as you've got all that blood off you and the greenery out of your hair.'

The moustachioed Muffin beamed with cynical pleasure at seeing this oddly assorted trio eating in his place. Watching the liaisons that went on was the fun part of running his business, and he always had a supply of exotic Mediterranean sausages and delicacies with which to encourage the players.

Here we go round the Mulberry Bush

All scrubbed up and fully clothed now, Reggie was in the mood to enjoy dinner with his cousin and Diana at his favourite eating place. It was also clear to him that Diana wouldn't be making any play for him now. Porky was on top form and had her completely captivated.

By the time Reggie was sticking his knife into a tender roast fillet of venison, he was completely relaxed. 'What was this deal you wanted to talk to me about?' he asked Porky.

'I'm not sure I can tell you in front of Diana.'

'Of course you can,' she said. 'We won't have any secrets between us.'

'All right, but neither of you can tell Lara, because she's part of the fashion press, and if she gets wind of it, she might let the cat out of the bag before we're ready.'

'Porky,' Reggie groaned. 'Just get on with it.'

'The thing is, then, we done pretty well with them mole trimmings last season, and the look's beginning to take a bit of a hold – it's like that with fashion sometimes, especially at our end of the game You never know if it will or not, then suddenly it does, and you've got to be ready. So we want to prepare a bigger range of it, just trimming the stuff with mole skin. But we want to do much bigger volume because we reckon most of the competition won't be able to get the volume they'd need to rip us off and take us on.'

Reggie's eyes rolled up. 'For Gawd's sake! How many bloody moleskins do you need?

'Maybe ten thousand.'

'Ten Thousand!!!' You must be bonkers. Nobody's going to get you ten thousand moleskins, especially if you've got some kind of delivery date in mind.'

'I want ten thousand. If you can do it, the contract's yours.'

Reggie shook his head and thanked the Harold Macmillan geezer up in the sky for producing Rupert Church-Pugh when he had. If he hadn't turned up, buying what he had and guaranteeing to take all Reggie could get from the same source, it might have tempted him. As it was – it was out of the question.

'I'm sorry, Porky; I've moved on. I've got a lot going on with my Spaghetti Sextons, and that's going to carry on. I haven't got time to sort out 10,000 bloody moles.'

Porky sighed. 'That's a real shame. Still – promise you'll think about it, won't you Reggie?' he entreated his cousin.

'No, Porky. No more bloody mole deals – and that's that.'

Diana, bored with the moleskin talk, also had something to ask Reggie. 'Do you think you could do me a favour, Reggie?'

'That obviously depends on what the favour is.'

'I've left it very late to get the props together for this blasted *Mamma Mia* show, just to add to the utter shambles of the acting and singing.'

'You want to borrow some stuff to dress the stage?'

'Correct. Bits and pieces, mostly, and I was thinking you have the most colossal amount of jun.... stuff hanging around here. Do you think Rosi would mind if I borrowed a few bits?'

'She'll be fine; she's very excited about it, as long as you don't try and borrow me,' Reggie laughed.

Diana sighed. 'Yes; I already guessed she thought I was after you; I could see it in her body language. Next time I see her, I'll tell her Porky's playing lead fiddle in my band.'

'You do that,' Reggie said, 'though she'll wonder why anybody would fancy Porky.'

'That's because she's never seen my secret weapon in action,' Porky explained.

'For Gawd's sake, Porky, we don't want to hear about that.'

'I was talkin' about my old-fashioned charm,' Porky said.

Reggie laughed with relief. 'Anyway, Di,' he turned back to her. 'We'll have a look around for some props when we get back from here, and you pick out what you want, OK?'

'Reggie, you're a poppet!' Diana gushed and leaned across the table to kiss him on the lips.

Back at the Towers for a nightcap, Reggie told Diana to wander around to see what she needed. 'Nothing too valuable, mind.

She sniffed. 'Not much chance of that, Reggie – not with your taste.'

Reggie laughed. He thought she only half meant it.

Here we go round the Mulberry Bush

He and Porky went to sit in his study and drink a glass or two from a bottle of applejack, distilled cider he'd bought from the maker, who claimed it had been aged for fifteen years.

'This is our local spirit, Porky, alleged to cure many embarrassing ailments,' Reggie announced.

Porky tried his. 'Cor!' he gasped with his customary bluntness. 'That's not 'alf bad, Reggie.'

By their third glass, Porky was raising his glass to the man who'd made the stuff when Diana Dove walked into the room.

Reggie fetched another glass from his baronial drinks cupboard. 'How did you get on prop hunting?' he asked as he filled a glass for her.

'Not great, I fear. I was being a bit optimistic; the set is meant to be a simple dwelling on a remote Greek island, occupied by a sophisticated New York lady. There was one thing, though. In the room where you've got all the pictures, there's an empty gilt frame, and I thought Donna might have a painting of her mother hanging on a wall. I can find someone to do that for me and drop it in. Would that be OK, then – if I took the frame?'

Reggie nodded, 'For sure. I sold a picture to a woman in Ludlow who said she had a better frame for it – I didn't think that was very likely, but she obviously had some other frame going spare and thought she could save a few quid – you know how it is with some rich folk – the more they've got the bigger the discount they want, so of course, she beat me down by a few hundred quid.'

'Don't worry – I'll bring it back safe and sound. '

'Yeh, that would be good because I just bought another picture – same sort of thing – that's got a nasty modern frame on it.'

'Great,' Diana said, taking a sip of the aged applejack. 'Gosh – that's good, Reggie. I've never had an applejack that good, and when I was a wild teenager growing up round here, we used to drink a lot of it. I don't think my liver's ever recovered, actually.'

Porky, who stood up, kissed the back of her neck and squeezed her waist with both hands. 'There's nuffin' wrong with your liver,' he murmured tenderly.'

'Yeh, well,' Reggie said. 'On that positive medical note I think I'll go to bed; I've had a very exciting day. Don't drink it all,' he added, placing the bottle on the table.

'Good night Reggie,' Diana said. 'Thanks for the prop, and if you want to come and finish off picking the mulberries tomorrow, do come. I'll keep Aunt Sylvia out of the way.'

'Thanks. I will,' Reggie said. 'And don't stop up all night.' With a nod and a wink, he left the room and walked slowly up the broad oak stairs to his bedroom.

As Reggie descended the stairs some eight hours later the next morning, he was met by the aroma of freshly made coffee and newly baked croissants.

He found Porky in the big kitchen, sitting at the breakfast table reading – Reggie noted with interest – the Financial Times.

'I see you've been into town, then,' Reggie remarked.

'Yeh. You know me – bit of an early bird.'

Reggie looked out of the window. 'And I see Mrs Dove's no longer with us.'

'Yeh, yeh. She went home a long time ago.'

Reggie didn't pursue that line. 'Did she take the frame?'

'She did, but she's not very happy about this show, though.'

'She'll learn; if you take anything on this place, you've got to commit yourself and give it plenty of welly – otherwise just say 'No'. As it happens, I think it'll be a laugh, at least for the locals. No one would pay money to see it unless they were just coming to laugh at their neighbours, or aunties and uncles.' Reggie chuckled. 'I wonder if she even knows that PC Plank has locked up her leading young man.'

'Oh dear,' Porky grinned. 'What happened?'

'Rosi and I got a ransom note for the return of Joan. It was made up of letters cut up from some hand written document. I showed Plank who said he knew it was Mickey Rafferty's writing. I told him even Mickey wasn't so stupid he'd cut up his own writing, but Plank's got his own agenda, because Mickey was coming on a bit strong with Library Linda in rehearsals, and Plank obviously saw it as a good wheeze for getting him out the way.'

'That's a bit strong – to get him banged up!'

'I don't suppose he can keep him there long – I'm sure he didn't do it, either. Still, I suppose Di will have to find someone else, though God knows who. Foxy Warren'll want the part because it's the only way he'll ever get in a clinch with Linda.'

'Maybe I could do it?' Porky suggested. 'Diana would like that.'

Reggie had to laugh. 'She's ended up playing opposite an octogenarian whose meant to be at least thirty years younger, and not by the wildest stretch of any bumpkin's imagination could you pass as a twenty-year-old, sylph-like youth.'

'Maybe not,' Porky said, gloomily accepting reality.

'Are you going to stick around to see the show this weekend.'

'Yeh. I think I will. Do you mind?'

'Course not, mate. Mi casa es su casa.'

'Who's Sue?' Porky asked.

'Are you havin' a laugh? Look, I'm off to Diana's to pluck her mulberries.'

'As long as it's only her mulberries you pluck,' Porky said, unconsciously imitating Reggie's wife.

After Reggie got back to Mortimer Towers that evening, with enough fruit to make a few gallons of his mulberry vodka, he found a message from Rosi waiting for him. She was coming back that evening on the train, and she wanted him to meet her.

He sent her a text to say he would, and went upstairs to lie in the bath which, by the time he'd finished, looked as if he'd just fished a couple of well-hacked corpses out of it.

There was no sign of Porky in the house, so he left him a note:

Gone to Muffin Magee's for a few jars before picking up the trouble & strife at eight. We'll go back there for a meal; see you then.

Chapter Twelve

The Tippling Toad was almost full to capacity with standing room only by the bar. Reggie had just bought a bottle of Pol Roger, when he was greeted by Perry Rokesay who'd come into the bar.

'Ah, the Berwick Street Barker. How's the trade in 18th century pictures of dubious provenance?'

'Not too bad, thank you, Perry. And I won't ask you how trade is because I know you don't do trade.'

'I'm sorry we missed that nice haughty woman with the skinny hound. I must say, she looked suspiciously like an ancestor of my Lydia's who was painted by Kneller.'

'I dare say I'll have others, similar, in due...' Reggie was inter-rupted by a jolt in the kidneys and turned to find the puce, harassed features of Archie Pemberton glowing like a beacon over his shoul-der. Archie hadn't seen him; he evidently needed to talk to Muffin.

Perry Rokesay took one look and swiftly moved on.

'I say, Muffin,' Archie said, 'the meat I ordered for my girlfriend is bloody well uncooked.' The words burst out as if they'd had been uncorked from a fizzy bottle.

Muffin roared with laughter. 'I'm so sorry; how do you like your carpaccio? In Italy it's always served raw. You should have told me you wanted a beef-burger and I'd have sent you along to the Purple Pig – and that would have cured you of the habit.'

Everyone else nearby was laughing now. Archie became pucer, looked around wildly, yammered his apologies and was about to sink back into the crowd when he realised he was standing on one of Reggie's well-polished brogues.

'Crikey, sorry Reggie – didn't see you there.'

'Don't take any notice of him,' Reggie said to him, nodding at Muffin. 'We all make mistakes. I once did just the same as you with steak tartare, only I was a lot more vociferous before I realised what I'd done.'

'Thanks Reggie. The trouble is, Camilla's a marginal veggie, and was pretty moody about eating meat in the first place – let alone raw! Still, I dare say it will do her good. But Reggie, I hear you're in this play thingy at the village hall.'

'Sort of,' Reggie agreed. 'Though I haven't learned a line yet and the performance is on Saturday, but Diana Lovely Dovely is pretty relaxed. She's told us we can read our parts off the page, and the ones that are supposed to sing can just mime to the soundtrack.'

Muffin was listening. 'She was in here and she told me that,' he said. 'Bloody brilliant wheeze if you ask me. Much easier on the audience and less embarrassing than having you lot all forgetting your lines and singing out of tune.'

'Well, that suits me,' Archie Pemberton declared.

'Why's that?'

'Because I've heard that Mickey Rafferty who was going to play Sky – the young chap who's getting hitched – has had his collar well and truly felt for stealing your statue.'

'Yeh, I know.'

'PC Plank's very upset about Mickey having it off with Library Linda at rehearsals, and they say he wants to get his own back.'

'How does this affect, you, though?' Reggie asked.

'Diana asked me to take on the part of Sky.'

Reggie used all his self-restraint to stop himself from exploding with laughter at this lanky, chinless, russet-faced, upper-crust Englishman playing a lissom young, nut-bronzed Greek islander – a notion almost as absurd as Porky playing the part

'That should be interesting,' he managed to say.

'Anyway, I expect I'll see you at rehearsals tomorrow.'

'Oh gawd,' Reggie groaned. 'What have I let myself in for?'

'See you,' Archie said, and dived into the crowd to give his guest the bad news.

'That bloke,' Muffin observed with a shake of his head, 'is as thick as a donkey's doodah.'

'Yes – like clotted cream – thick and rich,' Reggie suggested.

The next person to walk into the bar took Reggie by surprise. He hadn't expected to see Jason de Chateauneuf for at least a few more weeks. Before he'd left Mortimer Towers the last time he'd been there, Jason had said he was going to be at his house on the Cote d'Azur for a month or so.

'Chatternerve! What are you doing back so soon from the south of France? Did you miss us all too much?'

'A few things cropped up and needed my attention; you know how it is, Reggie – you can't delegate everything.'

'I was never any good at delegating anyway,' Reggie admitted. 'You'd better sit down and have a bevvy now you're here. I'll get another glass.'

He waved Jason into a seat at a table which had just become vacant while he shoved his way back to the bar to fetch another glass. Returning to the table with it, he filled it from his bottle.

Jason nodded at it. 'Got summat to celebrate or just feeling a bit flash, eh, Reggie?'

'Bit of both,' Reggie raised his glass and downed a mouthful.

'How are you gettin' on with those dodgy pictures of yours, then?'

Reggie held a hand, face down to the ground, and waggled it slightly. 'Not too bad,' he understated; he couldn't have said why, but all his instincts were warning him not to tell Jason that he'd now sold all his pictures to a single, highly fortuitous punter. 'Sold a couple on the Monday morning after you were up and bought those two Highland scenes. You happy with them, by the way?'

'Oh yeh, well happy. They're already up and hanging in my hall. You must come over and have a look some time.'

'And then I shifted a few more last Sunday at the flea market. That's the way I wanted to do it; keep it low profile, dribble 'em out slowly.'

'So, you've got a few left, then?'

Reggie felt as if he was walking into a one-way rat trap – the further he went in, the more trouble he'd have wriggling back out. 'Matter of fact, I may have a punter for the lot of them,' he said lightly.

Without realising it, he held his breath for a few seconds, praying that Jason wouldn't try to make some unassailable pre-emptive bid.

In the end, he said: 'Good for you, Reggie. I hope it all comes off.' He tilted his glass and drained the champagne from it. 'Right! Can I get you a bottl'a champagne now? I owe you one.'

'Go on then,' Reggie said

Chatternerve pushed his way to the bar and ignored all the other people waiting to be served. 'Can I get a bottle of Pol Roger?' he barked over the tops of their heads. A few moments later, he was back with a fresh bottle

'What's this for anyway?' Reggie asked as Jason filled his glass.

'That wine you sold me – bloody fantastic, it was!'

Reggie grinned. 'Glad you liked it, though I'm rather sorry I sold it all to you.'

'I would be too – especially at that price. Should'a been around £250.'

'Maybe,' Reggie shrugged a shoulder. 'But you know, I'm a bloke who likes to trade fairly; I made a good turn on the deal; I'm happy,' he said, not entirely truthfully. 'Besides, I've got another ten cases coming, and I'll hang on to them.'

A crease rippled across De Chateauneuf's tanned face. 'I'm sorry to say, you won't be getting those other cases.'

'What!' Reggie snapped. 'How the hell do you know?'

'Because I got on to Justine de Harcort, and offered her twice what you'd paid, and she said if I transferred the money toot sweet, I could have 'em.'

'But I've already paid her for them!'

'You'll have to sort that out with her,' Jason said dismissively.

'Have you got them yet?'

'Not yet. One of my people is picking them up next week on the way down to my French property.'

'What a little charmer you are,' Reggie said evenly.

De Chateauneuf, surprised by Reggie's quiet vehemence, winced and looked away. 'Sorry you feel like that, but I didn't do anything illegal. It's just that... when I see something I want, I'll do whatever it takes to get it – within the law, of course.'

Reggie picked up the bottle of Pol Roger and slowly filled his glass up to the rim. He put the bottle back on the table and got to his feet, still carrying his glass. 'D'you know what, Chatternerve, you can have your bloody champagne back!'

Before Jason saw what was going to happen, Reggie had tilted the whole glassful over Jason's head, and stood watching happily as the wine poured down his neck and into his silk, open-necked shirt.

A space had opened up around the two of them as everyone tried to see what was happening. There was a jubilant yell from the back of the bar. 'Go on, Reggie!'

Reggie turned towards the yeller. 'Thanks, mate,' he said, and turned to Muffin. 'My cousin Porky will be in later, and I'll be back with Rosita when I've picked her up from the train. Can you keep me a table for three, please?'

Muffin nodded and Reggie walked out of the Tippling Toad, feeling he'd made just the right exit.

Reggie was on the platform when the Welsh train, the last leg of the journey from London via Newport, pulled into Ludlow station. He was standing in the shadows of dusk, and stayed there to enjoy a spy's eye view of his wife getting off the train. He wasn't ashamed to admit that he still got a buzz out of seeing her as if she were a stranger, even after a short absence.

The first person to emerge from the train whom he recognised was Jolyon Prestbury, who stepped down with his handsome, white-maned head held high, as if there were an audience were waiting for him, and stood poised on the platform for a moment. Reggie was smiling at the sight of it, when his wife stepped down from the same door a few seconds later.

Reggie realised that Jolyon must have been waiting for her and, when she was on the platform beside him, they exchanged a few smiling words, before he leaned down to kiss her – if not on the lips, Reggie thought, then much too damn close to them. He was frozen for a moment, stunned by the thought that Rosista had spent the last few hours in close contact with this vain and predatory man.

Rosita and Jolyon walked out of the station, where Tommy's Taxi was waiting on the forecourt.

Tommy unwedged himself from his seat and lumbered round to open the rear door for Jolyon. The actor stepped in alone, but once he was seated, the window came down, Rosita leaned down to say something, and he kissed her again!

Reggie was burning with jealousy, but he'd lived long enough to keep these feelings in check, until the time was right to admit to them.

He waited until Jolyon's taxi had slowly moved off, leaving Rosita looking around for him or his car. She saw the Bentley first, where Reggie had parked it at the far end of the car park, and started walking towards it.

Reggie took a deep breath to calm himself, and walked out briskly to catch up with his wife. He had made up his mind that he wouldn't mention what he'd seen until he had an idea of what might, or might not have preceded it.

'Hello, my little pumpkin – lovely to see you back.'

She spun round on her heel, radiating warmth as she reached up and flung her arms around him.

Back at the Tippling Toad, Reggie wasn't surprised to hear that Jason de Chateauneuf had left straight after Reggie had, looking murderous and clutching to his dripping neck a towel Muffin had lent him.

Nor, to Reggie's disappointment, was there any sign of Porky. He was sure the evening would have been easier for him with a third party at the table. However, so far, Reggie hadn't given Rosi a hint of what he'd seen at the station and the suspicions that had aroused in him. For the time being at least, she seemed pleased to see him and hooted with noisy laughter when he told her how he'd dowsed Chatternerve with his own Pol Roger – a story which grew with the number of people who stopped to laugh about it as they passed their table.

Rosita responded with an inexhaustibly account of her London trip – the restaurants she'd eaten in, the shops she'd raided, the gossip at the hairdressers, and the nights out with Lara.

'Lara,' she said, 'is coming back tonight – to her father's, to stay there. He want to talk with her about what to do about Chatternerve's new plans for the willmills.'

'You should give her a ring and tell her Chatternerve's back already, in case she doesn't know. Maybe she could go up to Pant-y-

Hose first thing, and confront him with the memo from the planning geezer while he's still on his back foot after this evening's little episode.'

Rosita nodded her excitement and immediately pulled her smartphone from a Louis Vuitton bag Reggie had never seen before and rattled off a long text message at the speed it would have taken Reggie to speak it.

As the evening progressed, Reggie became less certain of what he thought he'd seen at the station earlier. Nevertheless, he didn't want to stir up anything by mentioning what Diana Dove and Porky might have been up to.

Later, when he and Rosita arrived back at Mortimer Towers, Porky's car wasn't there and, when Reggie checked discreetly, his luggage had gone too, along with any signs of his having been there.

He and Rosita went to have a last drink of the evening in the drawing room, where Reggie opened a bottle of Sauternes which Rosita loved, and put her favourite Brazilan Bossa Nova on the CD player.

Rosi, relaxed and happy to be back in her beloved Towers, stretched herself out on the sofa, where only the evening before, Porky and Diana Dove had been cavorting.

As she arranged the cushions her hand strayed beneath them, where her fingers made contact with a piece of flimsy silk, which, with her natural curiosity, she pulled out.

It was a stylish painted silk scarf, which Reggie recalled seeing adorning Diana's neck only the evening before.

Rosita's face had frozen – locked in a way that Reggie recognised as a danger sign.

'What is this?' she asked through tight, narrow lips.

'Looks like a scarf,' Reggie suggested nonchalantly from where he stood in the middle of the room.

'Is your scarf?'

'Course not,' Reggie said. 'It's a woman's.'

Rosita had scrunched it up in a tight fist, and scrutinising it closely, she held it up to her pert nose. She sniffed, pointedly. 'Oh? You're right! Shalimar – no men wear this. I tell you who wears it – Diana Dove.' She allowed her eyes to slide upwards until they were looking straight into Reggie's.

'Well it could be hers, I suppose – perhaps she left it the last time she came over.'

'She wasn't wearing this scarf last time I saw her here,' Rosita said icicly.

'Maybe from another time, then,' Reggie said airily, beginning to regret very strongly that he had omitted telling his wife about the Porky/Diana liaison; it was going to he hard to mention it now in a way that would convince.

'Diana – she like to throw herself at men; maybe when she know I am in London, she come here and throw herself at you, Reggie?'

Reggie, cornered, decided to lob his special weapon into the fray. 'Like you and Huffers?' he asked.

Rosita's eyes opened to the size of small chocolate brown saucers. 'Me and Huffers? You think that is likely?'

'I saw you both getting out of the train this evening.'

'So?'

'I saw you kissing.'

'For Gossake, Reggie! That wasn't kissing. That was just saying goo'bye to goo' fren'.'

'Did you meet him in London, then?'

'Lara and I, we bump into him at Chiltern Firehouse where he is with a lover.'

'Who was she, then?'

'No she. He.'

'Oh,' Reggie gasped, recognising at once that several delusions he'd been harbouring had been erased at a stroke.'

'When I see Huffer at Paddinton' we say to travel together, and have long talk, as very good fren's. It was him who tol' me about Diana Dove throwing herself...'

'Yeh,' Reggie interjected. 'That makes sense.'

He was thinking of Diana's caginess about the reason Huffers had dropped out of the show so abruptly. Diana must have had a shock when she found out that she'd been pushing hard at a closed door.

This was the moment to put Rosita right about him and Diana.

'Listen, my sweet-smelling Himalayan Balsam, Diana hasn't been throwing herself at me – not at all. It's Porky she's after, and she came to see him when he was staying here last night; now he's over at her place. So.... calm down; it looks like both of us were both being suspicious about nothing.'

Rosita allowed herself to relax a little; she gave Reggie a quizzical smile. 'Why you not tell me about Porky and her?'

'Frankly... because at his age, I suppose I find it all a bit...'

'A bit what? At their age? What about you age? Come here Reggie, mi hombre – I show you how old you are.'

Reggie had slept well, and woke next morning full of resolve to tie up some loose ends that were bothering him.

The fact that he'd disposed of his whole first consignment of pictures, for which he'd only paid half so far, was naturally very satisfying, and he was looking forward to driving back to Italy – with or without Porky – to settle the balance and come back with a fresh load of good quality, highly saleable Sexton Blakes.

One thing that was niggling at him was the painting he'd bought at the village sale with Ted Buckton. Without waking Rosita, he got out of bed and went downstairs to have another look at it.

He stood in front of it, perplexed. To him, it was more or less indistinguishable from the picture he'd sold Cecilia, which had then been stolen. But if this was the stolen picture, why had it turned up in such a potty little sale, and how had it lost its frame on the way? It made no sense.

He took out his phone and took a photo of it. From his wallet he extracted the business card which Rupert Church-Pugh had given him, and emailed the shot to him, asking him if he'd like first refusal on it.

Satisfied with this pre-emptive move, he went to the kitchen to start making breakfast for his wife.

He and Rosita were outside on the terrace with a second pot of coffee when Lara rang.

'I've just seen Jason,' she told Rosita. 'And it's not good news. I'm dreading telling my father.'

'Come over here first and tell us, then,' Rosita suggested.

'Cor' blimey, Lara!' Reggie oathed in self-parody. 'You scrubbed up well this mornin'.'

'I wasn't going on a mission like that unarmed, was I?'

'Some weaponry!'

'Never mind, Reggie!' Rosita hurried him. 'Let Lara say to us what happens.'

'I got there,' Lara said, 'feeling quite bullish – and more when I see he's looking very leery. He's sitting in his big white study, wearing a hideous purple shirt, with his feet up on his bloody great desk.

"What do you want?" he says.

"Can you confirm that you've resubmitted your application for a wind farm up here on the ridge?"

"I can confirm that," he says.

"And you're doing this, despite all the pledges you made to me and my father, and everyone else who lives around here, only a few months ago, that you wouldn't be re-applying?"

"Yeh, that's about it. I don't owe you, or your snotty father – who thinks I'm nothing, when I could buy him out a hundred times over – or that cockney tosser Finchley – I don't owe any of you a bloody thing – not after the way I've been treated. It's my land, I can apply for what I want; and if the planning authority can't find grounds for refusal – and there's no reason why they should – there's absolutely bugger all you can do about it. So get out and stop wasting your breath. Get back to your polo pitches and your Hooray Henrys."

"We'll see whether or not they have grounds," I tell him. "And I want to tell you that you're lucky....."

"It's got nothing to do with luck," he says.

But I'm going for it now. "You're in the fortunate position of owning a large piece of wonderful, mystical landscape that has survived, unchanged for tens of thousands of years, and if you think you can destroy it overnight by covering the hills with massive, hideous wind turbines, we won't let you. We have incontrovertible evidence of your attempts to pervert the planning process which will completely discredit your application, and lead to your facing criminal charges for attempting to bribe officials. And that will totally undermine any further applications you may make.'

Rosita clapped her hands, with her eyes shining. 'Fantastic, Lara! What does he do?'

'He puts his head back and laughs like a bloody hyena.'

Rosita's euphoria collapsed.

Lara went on. 'He takes his feet off the desk and stands up. He walks round towards me slowly. Suddenly, I'm scared, but I'm not going to let it show.

'Although you and my father thought that memo was enough to pull the rug from under him, I really wasn't so sure. But I thought if he didn't know exactly what I had, and he'd done similar deals with other councillors or officials, that might scare him off without my having to confront him with it.'

'He's standing right in front of me now, looking really nasty. "D'you think I'm a proper doylem, man?" he says, going all Geordie on me. "Whatever it is you've got, show it to me – right now– or yer can gan 'ome to yer pa."

Lara paused in her narrative, and shrugged her slender shoulders. 'I didn't have a choice. I got it out and showed it to him, the thing I'd photocopied right there in that very office – after he took me out to dinner that night – you remember?'

Reggie nodded vigorously. 'We remember. What'd he do?'

'He unfolds it, reads it and starts howling with laughter again.

"This bit of paper you took from me," he said, "is totally irrelevant, and it's got nothing whatever to do with my new application. For one thing – the bit of ground it refers to is the piece nearest to your pa's land, and I don't want to put my expensive, green-energy-cre-ating devices anywhere he might try and attack 'em. I haven't for-gotten all the horse shite he flung across my place in his pathetic replica mediaeval weapon. For a second thing, Gareth Owen has died, and he ain't in a position to confirm his part in any alleged arrangement, and for a third thing, I never signed it, and there is no copy of this document in the universe with my signature on it, so my complicity in any kind of arrangement can't be demonstrated in any way at all – let alone proved.'

He tears up the paper and chucks in a basket.

"Now you've had you little thrill for the day, d'you wanna stay for a bit of bait?"

"What?" I say, totally flummoxed.

"Stay for lunch," he says. "And I'll forget what a wazzock you made of y'self, and open a bottle of that amazin' claret your cockney mate let me steal from him."

'The little bastard!' Reggie growled. 'I poured half a pint of Pol Roger over him last night when he told me he'd nicked the rest of that wine from under my nose. I hope you gave him a bloody good kick in the Jacksons! '

Lara gave a flutey laugh. 'I did leave him doubled up,' she said. 'And confirmed I wouldn't be having lunch with him!'

Lara and Reggie drove together the seven miles to her father's house, Lydbury Manor, to break the news to him.

When they pulled up in front of the ancient back & white manorial dwelling, where Lara had grown up, Sir Lancelot Lydbury came out and greeted Reggie warmly.

'My dear chap, word has reached me that you nearly drowned Chatternerve in his own champagne! Pity you couldn't have held his head down a little longer!'

'Yeh, I shoulda done – specially as the news from the front isn't so great.'

Lara relayed to her father the tragic news that de Chateauneuf was definitely reapplying to have his wind farm built, and that the small piece of paper they'd put so much hope in had turned out to be valueless.

'It was a complete flop,' she said, 'I'm sorry.'

Sir Lancelot looked glum. He was deeply ecological in his outlook and detested the concept of inland wind farms, on the grounds that they didn't work, looked hideous and were just a bamboozling racket to make a few people a lot of money, while giving the government an apparent commitment to renewable energy.

'But, Pa,' Lara tried to cheer him. 'At least he's not building on the land nearest to us.'

'I don't give a damn about that. We don't want those bloody things anywhere in the Marches, or anywhere in Wales for that matter. But all is not lost,' he announced. 'I've been doing more research into Chatternerve's companies, and I have to tell you, the harder I look, the more convinced I am that there's something very suspect about the way he's made his money.'

'How d'you mean?' Reggie asked.

'I mean that his companies haven't been making anything like sufficient profits to pay for all the things we know he owns – his estate here, for a start, plus that bloody great place down near St Tropez that he's always boasting about. Pant-y-Groes belongs to a tiny company called Taunton Ltd, which in turn is owned by a Channel Islands company whose ownership is shrouded in smoke and mirrors. None of his official trading companies have ever paid dividends big enough to cover these purchases.'

'So, Pa, what are saying?'

'I'm saying that sooner or later, we'll find he's been robbing his shareholders in some way that could lead to his being banged up where he can't cause any trouble.'

'I don't think you can be right, Pa. He's always so full of how straight and ethical his businesses are, and I've read quite a few articles in the papers that back that up.'

'My dear girl, you work in what they call now the 'Meeja'; you should know a PR campaign when you see one.'

Reggie nodded. 'You carry on digging, Lancelot, and if you want a bit of serious nosy parkering, like the News of the World went belly-up for, my mate, Stan Frost, he could hack Her Majesty's mobile – if she had one – and her computer.

As Reggie was climbing in to his car to drive back to Mortimer Towers, Lara said she would stay at her father's.

'Aren't you coming to the dress rehearsal of *Mamma Mia*, then?' Reggie asked. 'Rosi'll be disappointed. And your car's at our place.'

'Pa can drop me over at yours tomorrow, can't you Pa? And I'll see the show tomorrow night.'

Reggie cruised in the Bentley through the narrow lanes, glancing up from time to time at the hills which he was so anxious to protect from Jason de Chateauneuf's vandalism. Now that their original plan for stopping it had finally been neutered, old Lydbury's certainty that there were big-scale financial shenanigans going on in Jaysoft, Jason's software company, might be their best hope. After his recent dealings with de Chateauneuf, Reggie would be happier than ever to see him go down, and the vague sense of guilt he'd felt about the way he'd sold the wine to him had been well and truly dispelled.

When he arrived back home, he was astonished to find Rosita sitting at the kitchen table, wet-eyed and in a state of serious distress.

'Rosi, little lily, what's the matter.'

'Bloody Chatternerve!'

'What! What's he done now?'

'He jus' lef'. Din't you see him drive his Ferrari down the lane like a loco?'

'Nope, missed him. What did he want?'

'He come here, all nice and sweet, and say is Lara here. I say 'no'. And he say he want to see you. One of the pictures he got – the Scotland scenes – the frame, it broke, he say, and he have heard we have a spare, from the picture Miz Wheeler-Smith bought.'

'How the hell did he know about that?'

'He say Emmet tell him.'

Reggie grunted. 'Maybe he did, though I'd be surprised.'

'He say to me to get it for him and he don't mind paying because it was his fault the other was broken. I say sure, we got it in the room where you kep' all the paintings and I go and look for it. But Reggie – it has gone! Some one nick it! I go back and tell Jason, and he don' believe me and grab my arms and lead me back to the room. He say, "I see all the others have gone, too." And he turn on me like a bloody savage animal and ask where the hell is it?

'I just have to say, I dunno, I dunno – he have to ask you. Or maybe some one steal it from us. He is mad – saying he has to have this bloody frame, and I think he is really going to hurt me.'

Rosita paused, eyes wide at the memory of what had undoubtedly been a traumatic experience for her. 'Then he say jus' tell your husban' to fine it, and let him know. Then he goes, roaring up the drive like a loonatick.'

Reggie had put an arm around his wife's shoulder, which he massaged gently to quell her tension. 'Calm down, my lovely one. The first thing is, it wasn't nicked; I lent it to Diana Dove for a prop for the show, and it's up at the village hall. And the second thing, I don't care how much he says he'll pay; he's not getting that frame – no way – not after what he's been doing. He must be crazy, coming round here and threatening my wife! Now, just settle down; he can't hurt you and if he tries again, I'll take Emmet's lot up with me to sort him out, I promise you that.'

'Reggie, OK. You be calm. We don' want you to get in trouble, too.'

As she spoke Reggie's mobile started bleeping with a new message.

He pulled it out and recognised Rupert Church-Pugh's number. 'Ah good,' he murmured. 'Church-Pugh's got back to me about this other painting I bought at the village hall auction.'

He opened the message:

Thanks for sending the picture, but absolutely no good to us. Not of the same quality as the others you sold us. Sorry about that. Keep me posted re next delivery. RCP.'

The blood had drained from Reggie's face. 'What!?' he barked at the phone. 'What's he talking about? This picture's exactly the same and just as good quality as the others he had from me.' He banged the phone on the table. 'If bloody Rupert tries to say that about the next lot I get from Florence, I'm going to be in a right mess!'

'No,' Rosita said. It was her turn to be the calming influence. 'No, you won't. Because you sell plenty to other people, don' you? Cecilia, the fellow from London, Chatternerve, Miz Wheeler-Smith, those men who come here – you got plenty other punters.'

'Yeah,' Reggie sighed. 'I s'pose I have. Just feeling a tad paranoid this morning.'

'Just wait for tonight, for the dress rehearsal – then you feel paranoy,' Rosita chuckled.

Reggie was standing at the edge of the stage, near Diana Dove, as the cast assembled on the low platform in the village hall that evening. She was looking unquestionably stylish in the designer dungarees that had made Rosita laugh when she'd first seen them, but there were clear signs of tension on her face. Reggie he had to admire Diana for her perseverance. He would have given up on this lot a long time ago, he thought, if he were trying to produce a show like this.

'Right you bunch of turnip-headed bumpkins,' she yelled. 'Let's have a look at you.'

The whole cast had decked themselves out in their idea of the excesses of glam rock, from which they imagined ABBA had risen: loon pants and tight tops in lurex, gold lamé, crushed velvet with stacked heels and thigh-length boots.

'My God!' Diana said. 'Well done, everyone! That is a truly hideous sight. That should have the punters rocking in the aisles before you've done a thing! Sir Compton, I'm afraid that blond wig of yours appears to have a life of its own, you might try anchoring it somehow. I also think the bandana and flower behind your ear are anachronisms – about ten years too late – but what the hell! Rosi, you look wonderful.'

Reggie's wife had squeezed her slender legs into sheaths of tight, white, shiny satin, flaring like the base of the Eiffel Tower from just below the knee. On her top she wore a flimsy blouse of purple Indian gauze with little covering power, beneath a Farah Fawcett wig of voluptuous shoulder length blonde waves.

'You're the spittin' image of the one who isn't Agnetha,' Reggie said encouragingly.

Reggie himself was dressed from a selection of stuff from a large holdall Porky had brought up for him, stuffed full of rumpled and musty '70s clothes. He was now clad in a green and blue tie-dyed Indian kurta and purple canvas flares which hung uncomfortably from halfway down his hips. Rosita's observation that he looked "as sexy Mick Jagger in *Performance*" had not convinced him. 'But what the hell!' he'd said, 'I can make an arse of myself as well as the next man.'

'Right everyone!' Diana boomed out over the excited noise of the nervous cast. 'A few things have changed since the last rehearsal, the most obvious of which you'll already know – unless you're a deaf hermit – that Mickey Rafferty has been arrested by the redoubtable Plank for removing Reggie and Rosita ffinch-Leigh's bronze statue, and is therefore unable to be present at this dress rehearsal, and possibly tomorrow's performance. His place will be taken by Archie Pemberton.'

The cast erupted with a gale of astonished laughter.

'Archie can't even read; how'll he learn his lines?' one of them called out.

'Never mind act!' yelled another.

'Nor sing!' hooted a third.

'Bloody hell, he's about thirty! And twice the height of Library Linda.'

The crowd looked around to find Archie, who hadn't been noticed until then and was now spotted lurking in a corner at the back of the hall, wearing a Hawaiian shirt and white shorts, with a puce face and his hair standing on end, as if he was about to face a firing squad.

'It's OK, Archie,' Diana bellowed over the noise of the rabble. 'You look magnificent, and I have every faith in you to carry off this demanding part. Now everyone, get your books out; stand by with the musical cues, and let's take it from the top.....'

Diana, as Donna, with the opening scene, took her place.

Reggie could only admire the fortitude with which she tried to extract a genuinely entertaining show from her ramshackle cast, which she was almost managing to do.

Things were going well when they reached the point where Sophie, the prospective bride, played by Library Linda, and Sky, played in the absence of Mickey Rafferty, by Archie Pemberton, undertook their first prenuptial embrace.

Diana, watching with lips stretched tight in order to stop herself cracking up, wanted to see a lot more passion in the scene.

'For God's sake, Archie, we know you're a nice old-fashioned sort of young gent, but this is acting, so please give it more welly!'

Archie, by nature an obliging sort of fellow, didn't argue. He wrapped both arms around Linda's small but voluptuous body, almost doubled himself up to bend down and plant his mouth on hers to begin some serious kissing.

Before he could get down to business in the way Diana would have liked, there was a massive crash as a small but chunky 3lb club hammer shot through the back of the canvas flat, depicting a wall of the main room in Donna's adobe house. As it passed through the wall beside the window opening, which was probably its intended trajectory, it hit the portrait of Donna's New York grandmother that hung beside the window, tearing through it and taking out a chunk of the heavy gilt frame which Diana had borrowed from Reggie.

The hammer struck Archie on his chin, and he fell to the ground like a redwood felled in a Californian forest, taking Linda with him and pinning her to the floor beneath him. As he fell, so did the flat on which the portrait hung and already ripped by the flying hammer, landed on top of the young lovers.

The collapse of the scenery panel revealed the hammer thrower at the back of the stage. PC Paul Lank stood there, looking deeply mortified at having been discovered.

Reggie and Rosita who had sat down in the auditorium for this scene, gazed at each other quickly and burst into spontaneous laughter, along with the rest of the cast, while Plank remained frozen to the spot .

'Oh my God!' Rosita spluttered. 'Plank throw that thing and hit Archie on the chin!'

'He must have helluva good aim, then; that's an almost invisible target,' Reggie observed.

'But look, Reggie, he has broken your good frame.'

'I knew anything Diana borrowed off me for this show would end up lost or broken.'

'And you can't sell it to Chatternereve now.'

'I told you, I wouldn't sell it to that wally for a million quid. Anyway, it shouldn't be too hard to repair.'

Chapter Thirteen

Sir Lancelot Lydbury arrived with his daughter at Mortimer Towers while Reggie and Rosita were still having breakfast. Lara bounced in full of beans, quite revived from the dejected creature she'd been the morning before. 'Pa's coming in too, is that OK?'

'Of course!' trilled Rosita, who considered Sir Lancelot a septuagenarian George Clooney and loved his old-fashioned charm. 'Come in, Sir Lydbury,' she tootled as the suave old baronet stuck his head around the kitchen door.

'Thank you,' he said, 'and good morning to you both.'

Reggie waved him to an empty chair, while Rosita put out coffee cups for him and Lara.

'How was the rehearsal?' Lara asked with a grin.

Rosita screeched with laughter. 'It was the mos' fantastic shamble!' What happened then?'

'The highlight,' Reggie said, 'was when Archie Pemberton had to snog Library Linda, with Diana egging him on, and PC Plank took offence – him bein' besotted with Linda – and hurled a mallet at Archie. He can't have actually been aiming at Archie's chin, 'cause he wouldn't have been able to see it from that distance, but that's where he hit him, and Archie crashed to the floor and was out cold for about five minutes – on top of poor little Linda. Plank looked like he'd been mummified; he must have known he'd just committed a serious act of GBH. Luckily for him, when Archie came round, he forgave him, said he'd have done just the same in Plank's position, and shook his hand.

'That's marvellous,' Sir Lancelot observed. 'But poor old Plank'll never be able to arrest anyone in his patch again, without them reminding him of it – I know I will if he ever tries to breathalyse me.'

'And me,' Reggie affirmed.

'And how did Compton Wynyates look?' Sir Lancelot asked. 'He was very proud of his costume when he was showing it to me the other day.'

'Oh dear!' Reggie grinned. 'He suffered from what you might call a serious syrup malfunction. He was wearing a long blond wig like that bloke they call Golden Syrup up in the town, but every time he turned his head, the syrup seemed to spin the other way. I think it may have had something to do with the bandana he was wearing.'

Rosita nodded. 'Maybe that why Diana Dove say is a knackerism.'

'A knackerism?' Sir Lancelot asked, puzzled.

Reggie smiled indulgently. 'She said "anachronism".'

'Yes,' Rosita agreed. 'That's what I say, a knackerism.'

'Anyway,' Reggie went on. 'Plank's mallet has ripped the scenery panel, which collapses and falls on Archie and Linda, and it's also taken a chunk out of that picture frame I'd lent Diana.' He nodded at the damaged frame, with the chunk that had fallen out beside it, propped against the cupboard beside him.

Lara crouched down in front of it to have a closer look. 'That's not too bad, especially as you've got the bit that was broken off. I can repair that for you. I used to do that sort of thing all the time when I was a student at the Institute.'

'That'd be great,' Reggie said. 'Apart from anything else, I'd like to sell it after. Which reminds me - when I got back here yesterday, I just missed bloody Chatternerve – Rosi said he'd turned up demanding to know where the missing frame was. He said Emmet had told him about Miz Wheeler-Smith not wanting hers, and he's broken the frame on one of the big Highland scenes he bought from me after we did the wine deal.

'Rosi didn't know where it was, and he got very heavy, didn't he, Rosi?'

'Yes, he did. He is so aggressive, threatening and swearing! Why he care so much?'

'Hang on a minute,' Lara said. 'I saw those big canvases; they're hanging in his front hall – they look great actually, but they weren't in gilt frame at all, just big plain wide dark oak ones.'

'That's a bit weird,' Reggie said. 'I suppose he wanted to put them up right away, and somebody dropped one and knackered the frame, so he had 'em put in a pair of frames he already had, planning to put them back into gilt frames as soon as he could. No wonder he was so anxious to get this one when he heard I had it.'

'Maybe,' Lara said. 'But you wouldn't think he'd have the gall to do that – not after the ways he chiselled you over the wine in France. On the other hand,' she went on slowly, 'he is sort of bizarrely house-proud.'

Sir Lancelot had brought Reggie a folder with all the data he had accumulated about Jaysoft Plc, its ownership, operation and profitability.

Before he left, they stood outside the house beside Sir Lancelot's car, talking.

'Jaysoft certainly exists,' Sir Lancelot was saying. 'It's a small public company, listed on the stock exchange. It's considered fairly cutting edge, but it's more of a research and development organisation than in the business of selling large volume software. It makes a small profit, but nothing, as I said, to tally with Chatternerve's extensive personal property. If only we could dig deeper, I'm sure we would come up with something that would allow us to put serious pressure on him.'

'You mean blackmail him?'

'That sort of thing,' Sir Lancelot nodded. 'You see, then it would fund our ongoing campaign, and lawyers these days are more or less highwaymen. I believe the motto of the firm I use in London is '*Stand & Deliver*'. Sometimes desperate causes call for desperate measures.'

Reggie watched him drive away, thinking that this quiet archaic countryman was a very canny man and might be just the one to halt the march of the wind farms across the Marches landscape.

Back in the house, Lara and Rosita had cleared the kitchen table so that Lara could put the frame on its back and work on tidying it up and putting back the broken chunk.

Rosita had found her a modelling knife and a small, soft badger hair brush to dust off the powdery white chalky stuff which the elaborate moulded frame was made of.

Reggie sat down in a chair opposite Lara and, always curious, watched what she was doing.

'It seem very crumbly,' Rosita observed.

'It's gesso; they put on layers of it on before they gild it. It's made of chalk and rabbit's skin glue and a few other things. Considering this is almost certainly a newly made frame – even if it has been distressed to the point of being near suicidal – it really shouldn't be so powdery.'

Lara was trying to prepare the surface so she could glue back the broken piece without any visible join, scraping it with the small-bladed knife and removing the surplus with the tips of her nimble fingers. She was picking away at a piece of it when she applied a little too much pressure; the blade slipped and the point of it dug deep into the thumb of her left hand which was holding the frame steady. It punctured a vein in the fleshy part of the thumb and produced a thick spurt of blood, which spattered the exposed gesso.

Rosita screeched at the sight of it. 'My God Lara! Are you OK?'

Lara sucked her teeth with the sharp pain of it. 'It's fine, it isn't much.'

She put her hand to her mouth and started to suck her thumb, in the way any mammal licks its wounds to staunch the flow of blood.

Abruptly, she stopped, with a puzzled look on her face.

'Lara what is it?' Rosita asked.

'Mmmm,' Lara mumbled and took the thumb from her mouth, looked at it, and started sucking the powdery fingers of her other, un-damaged hand.

'MMM!?' she grunted in astonishment, but carried on sucking for a few moments, and rubbing her gums.

'What is it' Rosita asked, panicking at this strange performance.

Lara took her fingers out of her mouth and gaped at them in amazement. 'Bloody hell, Rosi! It's a long time since I was naughty girl, but this powder doesn't act or taste like chalk. In fact unless my sensation memory is shot to bits, there's an awful lot of cocaine in this mix!'

'WHAT!!??' Reggie bellowed and leaped to his feet. 'You're joking! Please tell me you're joking!'

Lara rubbed her fingers once more on the exposed white chalky surface of the frame, sucked them again, and nodded vigorously. 'Here,' she dabbled her fingers until there was a good covering of the dust on them, and held up her hand to Reggie. 'You try!'

'Don't be daft! D'you think I've ever taken stuff like that? I learned a very long time ago round Soho in the sixties never to touch any substance that was white and powdery; you could never be sure what it was or what the hell it was going to do to you. That Mickey Rafferty gets into a bad enough state just smoking a bit of the wacky weed stuff he grows.'

'OK, Reggie, calm down. I wasn't planning to turn you into a raving junky. But I'm bloody sure that this frame consists of a great deal of cocaine, maybe mixed with a bit of chalk and water that can easily be separated out.'

'What! It's like a solid slab of cocaine?'

'Pretty much; that's what it looks like.'

The implications of this had taken a while to penetrate Rosita's thought processes. Suddenly, though, she too leaped to her feet and grabbed her husband by his upper arms.

'My God, Reggie!' she gasped with her eyes burning into his. 'You crazy man! You are being drug traffic!'

Reggie was dumbstruck for a moment. He was staring at the frame, trying mentally to assess how much of the white substance it contained.

'Oh Gawd. Oh Gawd! How much d'you think there is in that frame?' he asked Lara.

She shook he head. 'There's not a lot of wood in it, but it's a pretty hefty frame. I dunno – maybe ten pounds – say three kilos.'

'Three kilos!!? How the hell much is that worth?'

'I told you – I don't do that kind of thing any more, but from memory at about £50 a gramme, maybe £150,000.'

'Oh my God!' Reggie howled. 'Each frame's worth a hundred and fifty grand – and this Rupert geezer's paid me just under four.'

Rosita was rooted to the kitchen floor, staring at her husband, her eyes wide with horror. 'Reggie – what you got, the profee you make – thass like your wages for bringing the pictures from Italy to here – but not the pictures, millions of pounds of this drug. You have been used! You are just the donkey!'

Lara and Reggie both stared at her, wondering what she meant, until Lara laughed out loud. 'For God's sake, Rosi – you mean the 'mule'.'

Rosita quivered her shoulders with frustration. 'It dozen matter the word. These people have make Reggie a criminal. And all his life, whatever peoples he is doing business with, he never do criminal.'

Rosita was speaking as the sound of vehicles coming down the drive very fast reached them and two cars skidded to a halt on the gravelled area in front of the Towers' grandiose portico.

Reggie, Rosita and Lara rushed over together to the window that looked out on the area. The first car was an innocuous grey Ford; the second a big BMW SUV – a fully loaded police vehicle with all the trimmings.

From the Ford, two men in jeans and anoraks climbed out. Reggie recognised one of them at once – the bearded man whom he'd seen at the auction where he'd bought the frameless 'Herring' which he guessed had been stolen from Cecilia Wynyates.

Reggie quickly walked to the front door to open it before they started hammering on it in an undignified way.

He just made it. The bearded man was in the lead and had just reached the top of the stone steps.

'Hello again,' Reggie pre-empted him. 'You forgot to tell me you were a copper last time we met.'

Hello, Mr Finchley. Can we come in?'

'Of course you can. We've just discovered something that made me think you might turn up here at some stage,' Reggie extemporised. 'If you don't mind coming into our kitchen, I'll show you what we found.'

Reggie explained how the frame on their table had been damaged, as it happened, by a member of the local constabulary, which he enjoyed pointing out.

'Yeh,' the bearded man said, 'Plank told us.'

Lara laughed again. 'Do you call him that too?'

The detective looked blank. 'Isn't that his name?'

Reggie wanted to get to the nub of things as fast as possible, and make sure that he wasn't going to be implicated. 'Look, can you tell us who you are, exactly?'

'I'm Detective Inspector Ron Badger, Metropolitan Police Drug Squad. I didn't introduce myself when last time I saw you because we didn't know the extent of your involvement, and we didn't want other parties involved to know that we were there.'

'The first thing I want to tell you,' Reggie said, 'is that I didn't have a clue what these things really were until about twenty minutes ago. I've never had anything to do with drugs in my puff...'

'It's OK, Mr Finchley...'

'Reggie – call me Reggie.'

'OK, Reggie. We do know you were an unwitting party to what's been going on. We've been watching you since you arrived back in the UK with the paintings. We have video footage of you selling pictures to various parties last weekend, and the weekend before that. I was a witness to your passing over some 18 paintings to an in-dividual calling himself Church-Pugh.'

'You mean that's not his real name?' Reggie gave a short laugh. 'I thought it was too ridiculous to be phoney.'

'Like ffinch-Leigh?' DI Badger suggested.

'Not you, too,' Reggie groaned. 'Just tell me what you want to know.'

'I don't think there's much you can tell us we don't know already. You sold two of the loaded pictures to innocent parties, one of whom declined the purchase of the frame, which, I imagine, is the one on the table there?'

'That's right,' Reggie confirmed. 'Lara here... this is Miz Lara Lid-bury,' he added, making a late introduction.

'We know who she is, sir.'

'She is an expert in pictures and when Constable Lank broke this frame, she offered to repair it. While she was repairing it, she cut her thumb, licked it and discovered that the white powder wasn't gesso, it was cocaine.'

'I had already had already come to that conclusion, sir.'

'Listen, it makes me nervous if you call me 'sir'; please call me Reggie.'

Badger nodded and grinned. 'All right, Reggie. If I may go on. The other innocent purchaser, namely Lady Wynyates, subsequently had her picture stolen, precisely because of the contents of the frame. A third party must have come by it and bunged it, minus the frame, straight into that sale where you bought it back. Did you know it was the same painting, by the way?'

'I thought so,' Reggie said, 'but I wasn't sure. It didn't make much sense for someone to nick it, then chuck it in a little crapolatta sale like that. But listen, Mr Badger, I sold pictures to other people besides those two ladies and Church-Pugh. There was a greasy sort of fellow come up from London in the first Sunday, then another dodgy dealer came here and bought a couple. And I sold two more to a dinner guest, Sunday before last.'

'And?'

'Well they just bought them as pictures – in the case of the dealers, to sell down in London and, in the case of my guest, to hang on his walls at Pant-y-Groes, the big house up there on the hill.' Reggie waved a hand in the general direction of de Chateauneuf's place.

'That's very helpful, Mr Finchley – Reggie. We will require you to identify these paintings at some point. In the meantime, we'll need to take a full statement from you and, in view of the scale of this operation, we'll require you to come up to the station in Shrewsbury for full questioning.'

'Whaaaat?!' Rosita shrieked. It was the first time she'd opened her mouth since the policeman had come into the kitchen. 'You are takin' my husban' in to the p'leece station, like he is a criminal? When he was jus' innocent donkey? And you have police surrounding our house, like we are terrorism?'

The upper part of DI Ron Badger's beard twitched. Seeing it, Reggie thought he was going to lose control of it, but his many years of police training kicked in and he turned politely to address Rosita.

'I'm sorry, madam. You are Mrs Finchley?'

'I am Rosita Maria Solomayor ffinch-*Leigh*.'

'I can assure you, Mrs Finchley, that although we have found you here in possession of a very large quantity of cocaine, this will be a formality which has to be gone through because this is a very large investigation, and everything must be done by the book prior to charges being laid.'

'They are to be laid against my husban'?'

'I think that's very unlikely,' DI Badger said, as kindly as he could.

Rosita, more used to police methods in the country of her birth, was unconvinced and burst into tears.

Reggie caught Badger's eye, and winked. He put an arm around his wife and led her from the room.

'You will come back, sir, won't you?' the detective called after him, provoking another anguished howl from Rosita.

Reggie reappeared in the kitchen a few minutes later.

'Orright, Badger,' he said. 'Lead on. Lara would you mind following me up in my motor so I can get back here after.'

That's all right Mr Finchley, you can drive me up in your car if you like, and drive yourself back.'

Reggie nodded. 'Good idea. It'll be more comfortable than your little tin can out there. But I'll want my petrol money, which'll cost less than one of your boys driving me back.'

Rosita rushed back into the kitchen; she had clearly still been crying, although Reggie thought he had convinced her that he'd be back later.

'Reggie, Reggie,' she wailed. 'What we do about the show. What I say to Diana? That you are in prison – for something you haven't done?'

Ron Badger raised a hand to Reggie, and turned to Rosita. 'It's ok. Mrs Finchley, when is this show you're going to?'

'Not 'going to' – performing in. Tonight at the village hall. We have been practising for months, is a big event.'

'I can give you my word Mrs Finchley, your husband will be back to perform this evening.'

'Pssh!' Rosita uttered dismissively. 'You give you word! You are policeman; you have beard. What does that mean?'

'Rosi, my lovely flaming geranium, I give you my word that I'll be back for tonight's show. You won't have to tell Diana anything, and don't tell anyone else either. If anyone asks, tell then I'm off playing golf.'

'Pooh!' Rosita huffed. 'No one believe that. I tell them you are catching moles!'

'I must ask you,' Badger said, 'to make no contact with any of the parties you've dealt with over these pictures. And, of course, I shall have to take this frame with me.'

'Reggie! What we do for the picture for Diana for the show?'Rosita wept. 'We can't let her down.'

Lara came to the rescue. 'Rosi, don't worry, I'll find something for her. Now, the sooner Reggie gets off to the nick, the sooner he'll be back, eh, Badger?'

'That's it, miss.' The policeman nodded, picked up the heavy gilt frame and the chunk that had fallen from it, and ushered Reggie from the room. Outside, they both climbed into the Bentley, in which Reggie led a small procession down the drive.

After the Saturday night performance of Mamma Mia at the village hall, Diana Dove held a party at Wicton Manor. It was intended to be for the cast, but half the village turned up too, to celebrate what had been judged the funniest show the village had ever staged. The performance of Sir Compton Wynyates, in particular, as Donna's boyfriend, Sam, had the punters weeping with the kind of laughter a word-perfect rendition would never have done. Reggie's robust performance as the gay boyfriend, Harry, had evoked heartfelt approval from Huffers, who had snuck in to sit at the back. 'Marvellous, dear boy, to see a representation free of all the usual clichés. I wish I'd been part of it.'

Late the following morning, Reggie heaved his eyes open to find himself supine on a sofa in his drawing room, with his wife leaning over him, smiling tenderly.

'How you feel, Reggie?' she asked gently.

'I feel like a K-reg Cortina, just missed its hundred thousand service.'

'Do you want a cuppa tea?'

'No thanks, my lovely one, I think I'll go out and smoke a cigar.'

Outside, invigorated by the pungent smoke of black Honduran tobacco, Reggie tried to reflect on the previous day's events.

Above all, he was massively relieved not to have been detained beyond a couple of hours' questioning for his unconscious role in trafficking the huge quantity of cocaine. But he was nervous about where it would leave him financially. DI Badger had said no more than that he would hear in due course.

Reggie had been optimistically nurturing a suspicion that Jason de Chateauneuf was involved, at least on the fringes of the deal. Tantalisingly, Badger had refused to confirm or deny it, but he'd also firmly reiterated his warning that Reggie should have no contact with him, or the other 'picture dealers' who'd bought from him. Reggie had wondered before the party at Diana's place if Chatternerve would show up there, although he hadn't been seen in the audience at the show. But there was no sign of him, and when Reggie bumped into Foxy Warren, looking longingly at a locked glass cabinet containing Diana Dove's silver collection, he asked him if he knew where Jason was.

'No,' Foxy had said. 'Not a hair of 'im at Panty-Hose since he drove off in his Ferrari a couple of days ago.'

The late September sun they'd been enjoying was still performing and Reggie decided to extend his walk and headed towards the walled garden. He let himself in to feast his eyes on the autumn hues of the shrubs and bushes there, until, with a shock, he saw the plinth where first Joan, then *Bacchus* had stood was empty once again.

His heart plummeted. Rosita would be distraught; and he wasn't too happy about it himself.

He walked up to make sure it wasn't a trick of the light, or it hadn't just fallen over, but found only a few scuff marks around the base of the plinth, and trampled ground by the wall, where Joan had also made her exit. He walked back to the house in deep gloom, wondering how he was going to break the news to his wife.

Later, in an effort to take his mind off all the hassles besetting him, he drove to the Fox & Ferret to meet Ted Buckton for a pre-lunch Sunday drink, normally one of his favourite sessions of the week. After a couple of pints of Bishop's Riddle, Reggie was philosophical when he told Ted about *Bacchus* going AWOL so soon after Joan had.

'I had to tell Rosi if we didn't find it, I'd get her another one.' But as he was saying it, Reggie recalled with a jolt that he wouldn't be able to go back to Franco Ficuzza to get one; he still owed for half the pictures he'd taken. And besides, Ficuzza was obviously part of the whole massive cocaine scam, responsible for setting him up as the 'donkey'.

Ted broke into these ruminations. 'Didn't you say you were being asked to pay a ransom for Joan?'

Reggie nodded. 'Yeh, but they haven't been in touch again to tell us where or how to pay it. Not that we will, anyway. Emmet's going round every scrap yard in the county, marking their cards. Nobody'll take the statue if he's asked them not to, because he brings in so much stuff himself.

'The tinkers' mafia, eh,' Ted laughed. He was slightly envious of Reggie's ability to form close friendships with the diverse array of country folk he knew; from the lowest to the highest, they all seemed to trust him.

But Reggie had other things on his mind. 'Have you seen much of Chatternerve recently?'

'A few days ago. Actually, he told me something I suspect he wants me to pass on to you.'

'What's that?'

'He says once he's got the go ahead on his wind farm, which he's very cocky about, he's going to have his whole estate surveyed for fracking.'

Reggie felt his head explode in a haze of red mist. 'The little toe rag!' he bellowed, even turning the serious drinkers silent for a short while.

Reggie tried to get himself back into some kind of good humour as he drove back to the Towers. He'd promised Rosita, to cheer her up over the missing *Bacchus*, that he was taking her and Lara to lunch in Rosita's favourite restaurant in town, down by the weir where kingfishers flashed, herons fished and sometimes salmon could be seen leaping over the weir to head upstream to spawn.

After seven courses, and several bottles of fine claret, Reggie drove them home slowly. As they reached a hill which dropped down towards a dip where the road crossed the river, in a broad grass lay-by, they spotted a long low red car.

'Gosh,' Lara said. 'That looks like Chatternerve's beastly little Ferrari. What on earth would he be doing there? And who are those guys?'

There were a couple of men, youngish, darkish, more than likely part of the gang of Eastern European fruit pickers who laboured in the hideous, gleaming plastic tunnels which besmirched large swathes of the Herefordshire landscape.

Reggie slowed down, pulled the Bentley onto the broad verge, and stopped it so that they could watch from a distance. '

'It looks to me,' Lara said, 'as if they're siphoning the fuel from it.'

Rosita laughed. 'They are banditos sometimes, but goo' for them!'

'If it is Chatternerve's car,' Reggie added.

'It is,' Lara said. 'I recognise that strange little gold streak on the back. It's a nasty sort of metallic label, saying: "Hands off. Don't touch".'

'Hang on,' Reggie said, sitting up. 'There's a police car coming down the other way!'

As he spoke the police vehicle shuddered to a halt beside the lay-by and two uniformed man sprang out. Within seconds, the fruit pickers were disappearing behind the hedgerows, but the police paid no attention to them; they leaped over the gate into a water meadow, and sped away along the river bank.

'Well I never,' breathed Reggie. 'What do you think that was all about?'

'They are after him, of course,' Rosita said simply.

From behind them they heard a siren howling, especially strident in the quiet Marches air, and a second police car shot past them down the road and squealed to a stop beside the first one. Three more policemen piled out and set off in three directions from the gate.

Intrigued, Reggie, Rosi and Lara watched until the police posse had disappeared, when he restarted the car and they cruised slowly down the road to the abandoned Ferrari and two police cars.

'That looks like somebody parked in a hurry,' Reggie observed. 'Probably best if we get on home; I'm well over the limit and you know how they like to get blokes in big motors to blow in their bags.' Reggie clicked his gear lever back into 'D', and the Bentley surged off up the hill.

As they got closer to home, Reggie glanced at the clock in the burr walnut dashboard. 'They usually have news about now on Radio Salop,' he said. He turned on the wireless and tuned to the local BBC station.

A warning about a flock of sheep on the Welshpool road was followed by another item:

Police were involved in a high-speed road chase this afternoon after trying to stop a red sports car, believed to be a Ferrari which had been seen speeding on the A49 Ludlow bypass. The car turned off north of the town and headed west, where the chase continues.

'Chatternereve was just caught speeding then,' Reggie said, disappointed.

'Would they have two cars on him and start chasing him across fields, just for speeding?' Lara asked.

'They might,' Reggie shrugged, 'if he was going fast enough.'

'He's a ridiculous driver,' Lara snorted, 'and he told me he already had nine points; easily desperate enough not to get caught again.'

'Hmm,' Reggie grunted. 'Something tells me he could be in much deeper doo-doo than that.'

'Why for that?' Rosita asked.

'Because I'm remembering he was one of the few people I told about looking for good quality Sextons like the ones old Bertie Cheney-Longville left in our basement. And I told him we were going to Florence.'

'Yes,' Lara nodded. 'I remember you saying it at that dinner at Le Pelican. And he suggested somewhere, I seem to remember.'

'Yeh,'Reggie groaned. 'He did; he just slipped it in, but I suppose he knows what I'm like and took a punt on me taking it on board.'

Rosita was jumping up and down in the seat beside him. 'And, and Reggie, that little man who met us, Harold Hampton, I thought he was sort of expecting us.'

Reggie nodded. 'And there was that pair of Sloane Rangers in the bar who had met someone from the Marches in Florence – that was very likely Chatternerve – setting up his deal with Ficuzza.'

'And then you say you are coming, and you are perfect to be his burro!'

For the next twenty-four hours, Reggie felt like he was living in a state of suspension. He hardly dared to think what the ramifications of Chatternerve's crimes might be for himself. One thing he knew for sure, his days of dealing in high quality Sexton Blakes were over.

But not, as it turned out, quite yet.

Late on Monday afternoon, he had a brief call from DI Ron Badger. 'Thanks for your help, Mr Finchley. We apprehended Mr de Chateauneuf late last night, and we've been searching his place at Panty-Hose for the last twelve hours. We've been able to put our case together very satisfactorily. We already have the geezer calling himself Church-Pugh in custody, as well as the other two dealers who bought from you. We think the cocaine contained in the frame would have an ultimate street value of around two and a half million quid – and that's a good haul. I'm afraid, obviously, you'll be required to return the money you were paid by these individuals.'

Reggie gulped; he left like his guts had just fallen through his backside.

'W... W... What did you say?'

'You'll have to give back the money – Proceeds of Crime Act.'

'B..b..ut I didn't know what I was selling....'

'And that's why you won't be charged with any criminal offence – but you still have to hand over the money.'

Reggie was still yammering.

'What's the matter?' Badger asked.

'What the hell do you think's the matter? I made a sizable investment in that lot.'

Badger chuckled. 'Your an experienced businessman, aren't you Mr Finchley? I'm sure you know about the concept of caveat emptor – buyer beware?"

'All I know about is that I'm going to lose a packet, which I don't have.'

'Really? I find that hard to believe. I should say there will be an allowance for the frames valued as frames of their apparent style and age.'

'How much will that be?' Reggie asked gloomily, temporarily abandoned by his habitual optimism.

'Let's have a look,' Badger said, evidently consulting a screen in front of him. 'I should think it will be around £750 for each frame; we don't like to chisel people who have been substantively helpful in our enquiries. And of course, you'll get all your canvases back.'

Reggie was feeling slightly numb as Badger rabbited on for a little longer. When the policeman had finished Reggie put the phone down and let out a long breath, dispelling the last of the euphoric cloud he'd been floating on since exchanging most of the pictures on Titterstone Clee.

Gordon Bennett – he thought – I'm a bit old for see-saws.'

He knew that he'd have to hold his breath a little longer before he knew just where he was in this nightmare of a deal.

Reggie shook his head in a attempt to clear it and wandered through to the kitchen where Rosita was pragmatically – though interspersed with outbreaks of profanity – updating her wedding venue website. She could see that the great picture dealing era was at an end before it had really started. She didn't hold it against Reggie; she loved him and she knew he was trying hard to sort out the mess he'd got himself into.

'At least I didn't end up having my collar felt.'

'Why you want a felt collar? Is a bit ol' fashion, and make you look like ol' geezer,'

Reggie wondered what she was talking about and sighed.

'There is some goo' news,' Rosita said. 'While you were on the phone in your study, Emmet phone your mobile and say Joan was dumped in his place during the night. The boys who take her – and he won't say who they are – have give up trying to sell her to the scrap, because no one will take her. So,' she said with a lift of her shoulder, 'Emmet say they dump her rather than to be caught with her. He bring her back tomorrow.'

'But no sign of *Bacchus* yet,' Reggie added.

Chapter Fourteen

Later, Emmet brought Joan back to the Towers, where she was re-united with her severed finger. They put her in a stable until the Hugginses had time to place her back on the plinth so recently vacated by *Young Bacchus*.

As Emmet was leaving, another van arrived, bringing back twenty-two unframed canvases wrapped in police tape.

Ron Badger had the good manners to ring and check that they had arrived.

'Yes, Mr Badger...'

'Ron, to you Reggie.'

'Thanks, Ron; they've got here. And that hasn't made me feel much better, now I have to part with all that wonga to you.'

'Not all of it Reggie. You get to keep twelve and a half grand for the frames, and whatever you got for those other two. Anyway, with your sales skills, I'm sure you'll get a few bob for the canvases. After all you did sell those two without the benefit of their secret ingredient.'

'Yeh, but that's because I thought they were real.'

'Surely not, Reggie. You must have known they were fakes?'

'Yeh, but I mean I thought they were genuine, quality fakes.'

'Wouldn't know the difference, myself,' Badger admitted. 'I know you'll get what you can for 'em.'

Reggie felt no better when he'd finished the conversation and put the phone down, only to pick it up again to ring Lennons, the local fine art auctioneers.

'Good afternoon, Lennons,' fluted a self-confident young toff on the other end of the line.

''Allo, there. Can you tell me – when's your next Ant and Farts.'

'I'm sorry?' the young man fluted less confidently.

'When's your next *Antiques and Fine Arts* sale?'

'I see,' the man said censoriously. 'Our next *Fine Arts* sale is today week.'

'Is there still time to enter something for it?'

'The catalogue's about to go to press.'

'I've got twenty-two good quality English 18th and 19th Century oil paintings I'd like to enter.'

'No problem sir, as long as you bring them, in tomorrow. What name is it?'

'ffinch-Leigh – Reginald ffinch-Leigh.'

Before Reggie and Rosita set off the following Wednesday to see the pictures sell, Reggie had a call from the local police.

'Mr Finchley? You reported a statue missing last Monday.'

'Yes,' he replied cautiously.

'Could you describe it again for us?'

Reggie gave a succinct description of the *Young Bacchus*, his colour and dimensions. 'He looks like he's tripping along the street, half blotto,' he added.

'That sounds like it. He was found while searching the premises of Jason de Chateauneuf. A concealed panel had been removed from the back and there are traces of cocaine inside. We have concluded that this was used for the transportation of the drug. Were you aware of it?'

Reggie groaned. 'What do you think?'

'We have had a full report from the Metropolitan Police Drug Squad of how you were inveigled into buying these items without any knowledge of their contents.'

'Spot on mate. No change there.'

'We've finished with it, but unfortunately, at some point it seems to have been damaged while in our possession. We will therefore attempt to remedy that before it is sent back to you.'

Reggie was impressed. That's good of you. I look forward to seeing him again.

Reggie's pictures had been lotted more or less consecutively. As each sold, he sank lower and lower in his seat, in a state of dejection. In his haste to see the back of this deal which had turned so sour, he hadn't applied any reserves. Now he watched miserably, unable even to look at Rosita, as one by one they were knocked down for a hundred or two apiece – until the last one, the 'Constable' village wedding scene. This was the Florence fake that had come in for most criticism for the bizzarely oriental appearance of the dancing peasants it depicted in the Suffolk countryside.

The auctioneer, whose voice Reggie recognised as the young man he'd spoken to on the phone the week before, attempted to straighten his long, drooping back and impart a little vigour into the final lot of this disastrous batch.

'Lot number 401, English school, in the style of Constable, undated, unsigned, consigned by a private collector. A very charming village wedding scene, with dancing peasants, and cattle. Who'll start me at five hundred for this?' he asked, as a matter of form, and looked around the collection of punters – squiggle-eyed, shifty, broke, overweight, bored, part hostile, cynical – and was clearing his throat, preparatory to dropping back to a more realistic one hundred pounds when, suddenly, his eyes jerked up to the back of the room. 'Was that a bid, sir?' he asked, sounding incredulous. 'It was? Thank you, sir. Five hundred I'm bid for this very charming rustic scene. What?' he said, glancing down at the spotter beside him on the rostrum was pointing to the opposite corner. 'Right! Five fifty, six, six hundred pounds, six fifty, seven......'

Reggie, in midfield, slowly raised himself from his lethargy and carefully turned his head to look for a bidder. But although the auctioneer was brightly taking bids from each corner, whoever was bidding wasn't visible to Reggie.

The auctioneer stopped again, as his attention was demanded by another member of the staff manning the computer which took any incoming bids. 'Ah, we have a new bidder online, at two thousand pounds, two two, two five, two seven, three.' His head was waggling now like a spectator at a Wimbledon final. After another two minutes' of non-stop bidding, the computer dropped out, then, at £8,200 one of the bidders in the house.

The auctioneer knocked it down happily, thinking, no doubt, of the unexpected £1,200 commission he'd just made for his firm.

Reggie, weak with relief, reached for Rosita's hand beside him and squeezed it. If he had been on his own, he thought, he'd have had a good cry – the result of this sale did so much to vindicate his decision to go to Florence and do the deal he had. And it was ironic that this picture, which he personally had always liked, but which had been most criticised had turned out to be the top lot.

After the sale he saw the auctioneer and thanked him.

'Yes, that was good,' the tweed-jacketed young man agreed. 'We get quite a number of Chinese buyers coming up now, mainly, it has to be said, to buy old Chinese items, works of art, artefacts, ivory, amber, porcelain – anything of antique Chinese origin which they want to repatriate. Quite what they saw in this particular English picture, charming as it was, I can't imagine.'

Reggie chuckled. 'I can,' he said. And to himself – repatriation, that's about right!

Reggie wanted to push the boat out that evening. He asked Ted and Belinda to join him and Rosita at Le Pelican, the place where the Ficuzza gallery had first been obliquely drawn to his attention by Chatternerve.

He had worried for a while that Ficuzza might be coming after him for the rest of the dough, but somehow, in the light of Chatternerve's arrest and subsequent charging, it seemed unlikely the Italian would take the risk.

It might, of course, make it difficult for him to go to Florence again, but – what the hell – Rosi had seen it all now!

The jubilation continued into the morning, when *Young Bacchus* was returned by the police to Mortimer Towers, to vie with Joan for pride of place on the plinth in the walled garden. Reggie and Rosita were uncertain as to which of them should be given the star spot until they'd had a chance to see the repair the statue's police custodians had effected. Standing in the stable yard where it had been placed, impatiently they tore off the layers of bubble wrap in which it had arrived, until Bacchus was revealed once more in all his inebriated glory.

They took a step back, and gasped with horror, for onto his formerly curtailed manhood had been added a replacement of the piece that had been knocked off some four hundred years before. Whoever had repaired it quite obviously lacked Michelangelo's artistic skills and, Reggie observed, his sense of proportion.

Rosita stood for a moment, aghast, until she burst into long ripples of laughter like a gurgling mountain stream, which Reggie loved.

He turned to her to show his appreciation, but found her rushing off to the stables where Reggie kept a limited armoury of tools.

She reappeared moments later with an air of determination and a small club hammer not unlike the one which PC Lank had hurled at Archie Pemberton. She placed herself in front of *Young Bacchus*, with feet slightly apart, raised the hammer to shoulder height and brought it down with a firm clout on the recent clumsy extension to *Young Bacchus's* todger.

Rosita had struck it well. It snapped off neatly, exactly at the point where it had been appended, and fell to the ground with a rattle on the cobblestones beneath.

'Well done, my little rambling Rosita! But listen, don't you ever, ever, *ever* do that to me!'

With a last look back at the *Young Bacchus* they loved, they went inside, where Reggie happily opened a bottle of his very best Pol Roger and the celebrations started again. They hadn't been going long when the phone rang. Reggie picked it up from beside his chair and answered it.

'Mr Finchley?' a voice inquired.

Reggie recognised the voice of the gangly, toffee-nosed auctioneer from Lennon's salerooms.

'Speakin',' he admitted cagily.

'Bad news, I'm afraid; the buyer of your lot number 401 appears to have reneged. We seem to have no way of contacting the under-bidder, and we can't trace the online bidder who took it up to £7,500. We'll obviously do what we can, but I just wanted to warn you, we aren't very hopeful. Naturally, we can put it through the ring again at the next Fine Arts sale, and of course, all the twenty-one other lots sold.......... Mr Finchley?'

'Yeh, I'm still here. Send me the cheque for what you've sold, and bung the wedding scene through again – no reserve.'

He put the phone down and gazed forlornly at his wife.

Rosita, for once, couldn't think of any way to cheer him up.

Gloomily he picked up the phone again, and dialled Porky Bacon's mobile.

'Hello' he said, when Porky answered. 'It's Reg here. You know those ten thousand moleskins you wanted.........?'

The End